# The Loney

# The Loney

## ANDREW MICHAEL HURLEY

JOHN MURRAY

First published in Great Britain in 2014 by Tartarus Press

This edition first published in 2015 by by John Murray (Publishers)
An Hachette UK Company

1

A CIP catalogue record for this title is
available from the British Library

The publishers would like to thank Jim Rockhill and
Richard Dalby for their help in the preparation of the original edition of this book.

ISBN 978-1-47361-982-1
Trade paperback ISBN 978-1-47361-983-8
Ebook ISBN 978-1-47361-984-5

Typeset in Bembo by Palimpsest Book Production Limited,
Falkirk, Stirlingshire

Printed and bound by Clays Ltd, St Ives plc

John Murray policy is to use papers that are natural, renewable and recyclable products
and made from wood grown in sustainable forests. The logging and manufacturing
processes are expected to conform to the environmental regulations
of the country of origin.

John Murray (Publishers)
Carmelite House
50 Victoria Embankment
London EC4Y 0DZ

www.johnmurray.co.uk

For Ray and Rosalie

While they were going out, a man who was demon-possessed and could not talk was brought to Jesus. And when the demon was driven out, the man who had been mute spoke. The crowd was amazed and said, 'Nothing like this has ever been seen in Israel.' But the Pharisees said, 'It is by the prince of demons that he drives out demons.'

Matthew 9:32–34

And what rough beast, its hour come round at last, Slouches towards Bethlehem to be born?

W. B. Yeats, 'The Second Coming'

# I

IT HAD CERTAINLY been a wild end to the autumn. On
the Heath a gale stripped the glorious blaze of colour
from Kenwood to Parliament Hill in a matter of hours,
leaving several old oaks and beeches dead. Mist and silence
followed and then, after a few days, there was only the
smell of rotting and bonfires.

I spent so long there with my notebook one afternoon
noting down all that had fallen that I missed my session
with Doctor Baxter. He told me not to worry. About the
appointment or the trees. Both he and Nature would
recover. Things were never as bad as they seemed.

I suppose he was right in a way. We'd been let off lightly.
In the north, train lines had been submerged and whole
villages swamped by brown river water. There had been
pictures of folk bailing out their living rooms, dead cattle
floating down an A road. Then, latterly, the news about
the sudden landslide on Coldbarrow, and the baby they'd
found tumbled down with the old house at the foot of
the cliffs.

Coldbarrow. There was a name I hadn't heard for a
long time. Not for thirty years. No one I knew mentioned
it any more and I'd tried very hard to forget it myself.
But I suppose I always knew that what happened there

wouldn't stay hidden forever, no matter how much I wanted it to.

I lay down on my bed and thought about calling Hanny, wondering if he too had seen the news and whether it meant anything to him. I'd never really asked him what he remembered about the place. But what I would say, where I would begin, I didn't know. And in any case he was a difficult man to get hold of. The church kept him so busy that he was always out ministering to the old and infirm or fulfilling his duties to one committee or another. I could hardly leave a message, not about this.

His book was on the shelf with the old paperbacks I'd been meaning to donate to the charity shop for years. I took it down and ran my finger over the embossed lettering of the title and then looked at the back cover. Hanny and Caroline in matching white shirts and the two boys, Michael and Peter, grinning and freckled, enclosed in their parents' arms. The happy family of Pastor Andrew Smith.

The book had been published almost a decade ago now and the boys had grown up – Michael was starting in the upper sixth at Cardinal Hume and Peter was in his final year at Corpus Christi – but Hanny and Caroline looked much the same then as they did now. Youthful, settled, in love.

I went to put the book back on the shelf and noticed that there were some newspaper cuttings inside the dust jacket. Hanny visiting a hospice in Guildford. A review of his book in the *Evening Standard*. The *Guardian* interview that had really thrust him into the limelight. And the clipping from an American evangelical magazine when he'd gone over to do the Southern university circuit.

The success of *My Second Life with God* had taken

everyone by surprise, not least Hanny himself. It was one of those books that – how did they put it in the paper? – captured the imagination, summed up the zeitgeist. That kind of thing. I suppose there must have been something in it that people liked. It had bounced around the top twenty of the bestsellers list for months and made his publisher a small fortune.

Everyone had heard of Pastor Smith even if they hadn't read his book. And now, with the news from Coldbarrow, it seemed likely that they would be hearing of him again unless I got everything down on paper and struck the first blow, so to speak.

# 2

IF IT HAD another name, I never knew, but the locals called it the Loney – that strange nowhere between the Wyre and the Lune where Hanny and I went every Easter time with Mummer, Farther, Mr and Mrs Belderboss and Father Wilfred, the parish priest. It was our week of penitence and prayer in which we would make our confessions, visit Saint Anne's shrine, and look for God in the emerging springtime, that, when it came, was hardly a spring at all; nothing so vibrant and effusive. It was more the soggy afterbirth of winter.

Dull and featureless it may have looked, but the Loney was a dangerous place. A wild and useless length of English coastline. A dead mouth of a bay that filled and emptied twice a day and made Coldbarrow – a desolate spit of land a mile off the coast – into an island. The tides could come in quicker than a horse could run and every year a few people drowned. Unlucky fishermen were blown off course and ran aground. Opportunist cocklepickers, ignorant of what they were dealing with, drove their trucks onto the sands at low tide and washed up weeks later with green faces and skin like lint.

Sometimes these tragedies made the news, but there was such an inevitability about the Loney's cruelty that more often than not these souls went unremembered to join the countless others that had perished there over the centuries in trying to tame the place. The evidence of old industry was everywhere: breakwaters had been mashed to gravel by storms, jetties abandoned in the sludge and all that remained of the old causeway to Coldbarrow was a line of rotten black posts that gradually disappeared under the mud. And there were other, more mysterious structures – remnants of jerry-built shacks where they had once gutted mackerel for the markets inland, beacons with rusting fire-braces, the stump of a wooden lighthouse on the headland that had guided sailors and shepherds through the fickle shift of the sands.

But it was impossible to truly know the Loney. It changed with each influx and retreat of water and the neap tides would reveal the skeletons of those who thought they had read the place well enough to escape its insidious currents. There were animals, people sometimes, the remains of both once – a drover and his sheep cut off and drowned on the old crossing from Cumbria. And now, since their death, for a century or more, the Loney had been pushing their bones back inland, as if it were proving a point.

No one with any knowledge of the place ever went near the water. No one apart from us and Billy Tapper that is.

ॐ

Billy was a local drunk. Everyone knew him. His fall from grace to failure was fixed like the weather into the mythology of the place, and he was nothing short of a gift to people like Mummer and Father Wilfred who used him as shorthand for what drink could do to a man. Billy Tapper wasn't a person, but a punishment.

Legend had it that he had been a music teacher at a boys' grammar school, or the head of a girls' school in Scotland, or down south, or in Hull, somewhere, anywhere. His history varied from person to person, but that the drink had sent him mad was universally accepted and there were any number of stories about his eccentricities. He lived in a cave. He had killed someone in Whitehaven with a hammer. He had a daughter somewhere. He thought that collecting certain combinations of stones and shells made him invisible and would often stagger into the Bell and Anchor in Little Hagby, his pockets chinking with shingle, and try to drink from other people's glasses, thinking that they couldn't see him. Hence the dented nose.

I wasn't sure how much of it was true, but it didn't matter. Once you'd seen Billy Tapper, anything they said about him seemed possible.

We first met him in the pebble-dashed concrete bus stop on the one road that skirted the coastline from Morecambe down to Knott End. It would have been 1973, when I was twelve and Hanny sixteen. Farther wasn't with us. He had gone out early with Father Wilfred and Mr and Mrs Belderboss to look at the stained glass in a village church twenty miles away where there was apparently a magnificent Gothic Revival window of Jesus calming the waters. And so Mummer had decided to take Hanny and me to Lancaster to stock up on food and visit an exhibition of old Psalters at the library – for Mummer never missed an opportunity to instruct us on the history of our faith. It looked like Billy was going the same way from the piece of cardboard strung around his neck – one of the several dozen that made it easy for the bus drivers to know where he was supposed to be going.

The other places he'd either been to or might need to visit revealed themselves as he stirred in his sleep. Kendal. Preston. Manchester. Hull. The last being where his sister lived, according to the square of bright red card that was attached to a separate shoestring necklace and contained information that might prove invaluable in an emergency, with his name, his sister's telephone number and a note in block capitals that he was allergic to penicillin.

This particular fact intrigued me as a child, and I wondered what would happen if he *was* given penicillin, whether it could possibly damage him any more than he had damaged himself already. I'd never seen a man be so unkind to his own body. His fingers and his palms were shattered with filth. Every crease and line was brown. Either side of his broken nose his eyes were twisted deep down into his skull. His hair crawled past his ears and down his neck which had turned sea-coloured with dozens of tattoos. There was something faintly heroic about his refusal to wash, I thought, when Hanny and I were so regularly scrubbed and towelled by Mummer.

He slumped on the bench, with an empty bottle of something evil lying on its side on the floor and a small, mouldy-looking potato in his lap that comforted me in a strange way. It seemed right that he should only have a raw potato. It was the kind of thing I assumed down-and-outs ate, nibbling at it bit by bit over weeks as they roamed the highways and byways looking for the next. Hitching lifts. Stealing what they could. Stowing away on trains. As

I say, vagrancy wasn't entirely without its romance to me at that age.

He talked to himself in his sleep, scrunching his pockets – which, like everyone said, sounded as if they were full of stones – complaining bitterly about someone called O'Leary who owed him money and had never given it back to him, even though he owned a horse. When he woke up and noticed we were there he tried his best to be courteous and sober, offering a grin of three or four twisted black teeth and doffing his beret at Mummer, who smiled briefly but, as she managed to do with all strangers, got the measure of him instantly, and sat in a half-revolted, half-fearful silence, willing the bus to come by staring down the empty road.

Like most drunks, Billy bypassed the small talk and slapped his bleeding, broken heart into my palm like a lump of raw beef.

'Don't get taken in by the demon drink, lads. I've lost everything 'cause of this stuff,' he said as he held up the bottle and swilled the dregs. 'See that scar?'

He raised his hand and shook his sleeve down. A red seam ran from his wrist to his elbow, threading its way through tattoos of daggers and melon-chested girls.

'D'you know how I got that?'

I shook my head. Hanny stared.

'Fell off a roof. Bone ripped right through it,' he said and used his finger to demonstrate the angle at which his ulna had protruded.

'Have you got a spare fag?'

I shook my head again and he sighed.

'Bollocks. I knew I should have stayed at Catterick,' came another non-sequitur.

It was difficult to tell – and he looked nothing like the ruggedly handsome veterans that popped up in my *Commando* comics all the time – but I guessed that he must have been of an age to have fought in the war. And sure enough, when he doubled up in a coughing fit and took off his beret to wipe his mouth, it had some cockeyed metal, military insignia on the front.

I wondered if that was what had set him onto the booze, the war. It had done strange things to some people, so Farther said. Knocked their compasses out of whack, as it were.

Whatever the reason, Hanny and I couldn't take our eyes off him. We gorged ourselves on his dirtiness, on his brutal, alien smell. It was the same fearful excitement we felt when we happened to drive through what Mummer considered a *bad* part of London and found ourselves lost in a maze of terraces that sat shoulder to shoulder with industrial plants and scrapyards. We would turn in our seats and gawp out of the windows at the scruffy, staring children who had no toys but the bits of wood and metal torn off the broken furniture in their front yards where aproned women stood and screeched obscenities at the men stumbling out of corner pubs. It was a safari park of degradation. What a world without God looked like.

Billy glanced at Mummer and, keeping his eyes on her, he reached down into the plastic bag by his feet and brought out a few tatty bits of paper, which he pressed into my hand. They had been ripped out of a dirty magazine.

He winked at me and settled himself back against the wall. The bus appeared and Mummer stood up and held out her hand to stop it and I quickly stuffed the pictures away.

'What are you doing?' said Mummer.

9

'Nothing.'

'Well, stop messing about and get Andrew ready.'

I started trying to coax Hanny into standing so that we could get on the bus, but he wouldn't move. He was smiling and looking past me at Billy, who by this time had fallen asleep again.

'What is it, Hanny?'

He looked at me and then back at Billy. Then I understood what he was staring at: Billy wasn't holding a potato, but his penis.

The bus stopped and we got on. The driver looked past us and whistled at Billy but he didn't wake up. After another go, the driver shook his head and pressed the button which drew the door closed. We sat down and watched the front of Billy's trousers darken. Mummer tutted and peeled our faces away from the window to look at her instead.

'Be warned,' she said, as the bus pulled away. 'That man is already inside you. It won't take more than a few wrong choices to bring him out, believe me.'

She held her handbag on her lap and looked straight ahead. I clutched the dirty pictures tight in one hand and slipped the other inside my coat and pressed my stomach hard with my fingertips, trying to find the kernel of badness that only needed the right conditions of Godlessness and depravity for it to germinate and spread like a weed.

It happened so easily. Drink quickly possessed a man and made him its servant. Father Wilfred always said so.

When Mummer told him about Billy later that evening, he simply shook his head and sighed.

'What can one expect of a man like that, Mrs Smith? Someone so removed from God.'

'I said to the boys that they ought to take note,' said Mummer.

'And rightly so,' he said, taking off his glasses and looking at Hanny and me as he polished them on his sleeve. 'They should make it their business to know all the poisons that Satan peddles.'

'I feel rather sorry for him,' said Mrs Belderboss.

'So do I,' said Farther.

Father Wilfred put his glasses back on and raised a brief, condescending smile.

'Then you'll be adding to his already brimming store. Pity is the only thing a drunk has in abundance.'

'Still, he must have had an awfully hard life to have got himself into such a state,' Mrs Belderboss said.

Father Wilfred scoffed. 'I don't think he knows the meaning of a hard life. I'm sure my brother could tell you as many tales as I could about real poverty, real struggle, couldn't you, Reginald?'

Mr Belderboss nodded. 'Everyone had it tough in Whitechapel,' he said. 'No work. Kiddies starving.'

Mrs Belderboss touched her husband's arm in sympathy. Father Wilfred sat back and wiped his mouth with a napkin.

'No, a man like that is the worst kind of fool,' he said. 'He's thrown everything away. All his privileges and opportunities. He was a professional, I believe. A teacher. What a terrible waste.'

∽

It's odd, but when I was a child there were certain things that were so clear to me and their outcomes so inevitable that I thought I had a kind of sixth sense. A gift of foresight, like that of Elijah or Ezekiel, who had predicted drought and destruction with such unsettling accuracy.

I remember Hanny once swinging over a pond on the Heath and knowing, *knowing*, that the rope would break, which it did; like I knew that the stray cat he brought back from the park would end up minced on the tube line, and that he would drop the bowl of goldfish he'd won at the fair on the kitchen floor as soon as we got home.

In the same way, I knew after that conversation around the dinner table that Billy was going to die soon. The thought came to me as an established fact; as though it had already come to pass. No one could live like that for long. Being that filthy took so much effort that I was sure that the same merciful God who sent a whale to save Jonah and gave Noah a nod about the weather, would put him out of his misery.

# 3

THAT EASTER WAS the last time we went to the Loney for several years.

After the evening when he'd set us straight about Billy Tapper over supper, Father Wilfred changed in a way that no one could quite explain or understand. They put it down to him getting too old for the whole thing – after all it was a long journey up from London and the pressure of being shepherd to his flock during such an intense week of prayer and reflection was enough to wear out a man half his age. He was tired. That was all.

But as I had the uncanny knack of sensing the truth about things, I knew that it was something far more than that. There was something very wrong.

After the conversation about Billy had petered out and everyone had settled in the living room, he'd walked down to the beach and come back a different man. Distracted. Rattled by something. He complained rather unconvincingly of a stomach upset and went to lie down, locking his door with an emphatic swipe of the bolt. A little while later I heard noises coming from his room, and I realised he was crying. I'd never heard a man cry before, except for one of the mentally disadvantaged lot that came to do crafts at the parish hall once a fortnight with Mummer and some of the other ladies. It was a noise of fear and despair.

The next morning when he finally rose, dishevelled and still agitated, he muttered something about the sea and went out with his camera before anyone could ask him what was wrong. It wasn't like him to be so offhand. Nor for him to sleep in so late. He wasn't himself at all.

Everyone watched him walking down the lane and decided it was best to leave as soon as possible, convinced that once he was back at Saint Jude's he would quickly recover.

But when we returned home, his mood of fretfulness barely altered. In his sermons he seemed more worked up than ever about the ubiquitous evils of the world and any mention of the pilgrimage cast a shadow over his face and sent him into a kind of anxious daydream. After a while no one talked about going there any more. It was just something that we used to do.

Life pulled us along and we forgot about the Loney until 1976 when Father Wilfred died suddenly in the new year and Father Bernard McGill was relocated from some violent parish in New Cross to take on Saint Jude's in his stead.

After his inaugural Mass, at which the bishop presented him to the congregation, we had tea and cakes on the presbytery lawn so that Father Bernard could meet his parishioners in a less formal setting.

He ingratiated himself straight away and seemed at ease with everyone. He had that way about him. An easy charm that made the old boys laugh and the women unconsciously preen themselves.

As he went from group to group, the bishop wandered

over to Mummer and me, trying to eat a large piece of Dundee cake in as dignified a manner as possible. He had taken off his robes and his surplice but kept on his plum-coloured cassock, so that he stood out amongst the browns and greys of the civilians as a man of importance.

'He seems nice, your Grace,' said Mummer.

'Indeed,' the bishop replied in his Midlothian accent that for some reason always made me think of wet moss.

He watched Father Bernard send Mr Belderboss into fits of laughter.

'He performed wonders to behold in his last parish.'

'Oh, really?' said Mummer.

'Very good at encouraging the young folk to attend,' the bishop said, looking at me with the specious grin of a teacher who wishes to punish and befriend in equal measure and ends up doing neither.

'Oh my lad's an altar boy, your Grace,' Mummer replied.

'Is he?' said the bishop. 'Well, good show. Father Bernard's quite at home with the teens as well as the more mature members of the congregation.'

'Well, if he comes on your recommendation, your Grace, I'm sure he'll do well,' said Mummer.

'Oh, I don't doubt it,' the bishop replied, brushing crumbs off his stomach with the back of his hand. 'He'll be able to steer you all through safe waters, make good around the capes, as it were. In fact my sailing analogy is quite apt,' he said, looking into the middle distance and awarding himself a smile. 'You see, I'm rather keen on Father Bernard taking the congregation out into the wider world. I don't know about you but I'm of the opinion that if one is cosseted by the familiar, faith becomes stagnant.'

'Well, if you think so, your Grace,' said Mummer.

The bishop turned to Mummer and smiled in that self-satisfied way again.

'Do I detect that there may be some resistance to the idea, Mrs . . .?'

'Smith,' she said, then, seeing that the bishop was waiting for her to answer, she went on. 'Perhaps there might be, your Grace, among the older members. They're not keen on things changing.'

'Nor should they be, Mrs Smith. Nor should they be,' he said. 'Rest assured, I rather like to think of the appointment of a new incumbent as an organic process; a new shoot off the old vine, if you like; a continuum rather than a revolution. And in any case I wasn't suggesting that you went off to the far flung corners of the earth. I was thinking of Father Bernard taking a group away on a retreat at Easter time. It was a tradition that I know was very dear to Wilfred's heart, and one that I always thought worthwhile myself.

'It'd be a nice way to remember him,' he added. 'And a chance to look forward to the future. A continuum, Mrs Smith, as I say.'

The sound of someone knocking a knife against a glass started to rise over the babble in the garden.

'Ah, you'll have to excuse me, I'm afraid,' said the bishop, dabbing crumbs from his lips. 'Duty calls.'

He went off towards the trestle table that had been set up by the rose bushes, his cassock flapping around his ankles and getting wet.

When he had gone, Mrs Belderboss appeared at Mummer's side.

'You were having a long chat with the bishop,' she said,

nudging Mummer playfully in the arm. 'What were you talking about?'

Mummer smiled. 'I have some wonderful news,' she said.

∞

A few weeks later, Mummer organised a meeting of interested parties so as to get the ball rolling before the bishop could change his mind, as he was wont to do. She suggested that everyone come to our house to discuss where they might go, although Mummer had only one place in mind.

On the night she had set aside, they came in out of the rain, smelling of the damp and their dinners: Mr and Mrs Belderboss, and Miss Bunce, the presbytery housekeeper, and her fiancé, David Hobbs. They hung up their coats in the little porch with its cracked tiles and its intractable odour of feet and gathered in our front room anxiously watching the clock on the mantelpiece, with the tea things all set out, unable to relax until Father Bernard arrived.

Eventually, the bell went and everyone got to their feet as Mummer opened the door. Father Bernard stood there with his shoulders hunched in the rain.

'Come in, come in,' said Mummer.

'Thank you, Mrs Smith.'

'Are you well, Father?' she said. 'You're not too wet I hope.'

'No, no, Mrs Smith,' said Father Bernard, his feet squelching inside his shoes. 'I like the rain.'

Unsure if he was being sarcastic, Mummer's smile wavered a little. It wasn't a trait she knew in priests. Father Wilfred had never been anything other than deadly serious.

'Good for the flowers,' was all she could offer.

'Aye,' said Father Bernard.

He looked back at his car.

'I wonder, Mrs Smith, how you'd feel about me bringing in Monro. He doesn't like being on his own and the rain on the roof sends him a wee bit crackers, you know.'

'Monro?' said Mummer, peering past him.

'After Matt.'

'Matt?'

'Matt Monro,' said Father Bernard. 'My one and only vice, Mrs Smith, I can assure you. I've had long consult-ations with the Lord about it, but I think He's given me up as a lost cause.'

'I'm sorry,' said Mummer. 'Who are you talking about?'

'The daft feller mooning at the window there.'

'Your dog?'

'Aye.'

'Yes,' said Mummer. 'Well, I suppose that'll be all right. He won't, you know, will he?'

'Ah no, Mrs Smith, he's well house trained. He'll just doze off.'

'It'll be fine, Esther,' said Farther and Father Bernard went out to the car and came back with a black Labrador that sneezed on the doormat and shivered and stretched out in front of the fire as if he had always lived at our house.

Mummer offered Father Bernard the single armchair next to the television, a threadbare thing somewhere between olive and beige that Mummer had tried to pretty up with a lace-edged antimacassar, aligned using Farther's spirit level when she thought no one was looking.

He thanked her and wiped his brow with a handkerchief and sat down. Only when he was settled did everyone else do the same. Mummer clicked her fingers and shot me a look that was the equivalent of a kick up the backside. As with all social occasions at our house, it was my job to distribute the opening round of tea and biscuits, and so I knelt by the table and poured Father Bernard a cup, setting it down on top of the television which had been covered with a starched cloth – the way all the crucifixes and statues were at church now that it was Lent.

'Thank you, Tonto,' Father Bernard said, smiling at me conspiratorially.

It was the nickname he'd given to me when he arrived at Saint Jude's. He was the Lone Ranger and I was Tonto. It was childish, I know, but I suppose I liked the idea of the two of us fighting side by side, like the pals did in the *Commando* stories. Though fighting what, I wasn't sure. The Devil, maybe. Heathens. Gluttons. Prodigals. The kinds of people Father Wilfred had trained us to despise.

Listening to the armchair groaning under him as he tried to make himself comfortable, I was struck once again by how enormous Father Bernard was. A farmer's son from Antrim, he was no more than thirty or so, though he looked middle-aged from years of hard graft. He had a solid, heavy face, with a nose that had been bashed flat and a roll of flesh that bulged at the back of his collar. His hair was always well groomed and oiled over his head to form a solid helmet. But it was his hands that seemed so out of place with the chalice and the pyx. They were large and red and toughened to leather from an adolescence spent building drystone walls and pinning down bullocks to have their ears notched. If not for the dog collar and his wool-soft voice, he could easily have passed for a doorman or a bank robber.

But, as I say, everyone at Saint Jude's liked him straight away. He was that sort of person. Uncomplicated, honest, easy to be with. A man to other men, fatherly to women twice his age. But I could tell that Mummer was reserving judgement. She respected him because he was a priest, of course, but only as far as he more or less replicated Father Wilfred. When he slipped up, Mummer would smile sweetly and touch him lightly on the arm.

'Father Wilfred would normally have led the Creed in Latin, Father, but it doesn't matter,' she said after his first solo Mass at Saint Jude's. And, 'Father Wilfred would normally have said grace himself,' when he offered the slot to me over a Sunday lunch which it seemed Mummer had arranged merely to test him on such details.

We altar boys thought Father Bernard was fun – the way he gave us all nicknames and would invite us to the presbytery after Mass. We had, of course, never been asked there by Father Wilfred, and even to most of the adults in the parish it was a place of mystery almost as sacrosanct as the tabernacle. But Father Bernard seemed glad of the company, and once the silverware had been cleaned and put away and our vestments hung in the closet, he would take us across to his home and sit us around the dining table for tea and biscuits, and we'd swap stories and jokes to the sound of Matt Monro. Well, I didn't. I let the other boys do that. I preferred to listen. Or pretend to listen at least and let my eyes wander around the room and try to imagine Father Bernard's life, what he did when no one else was around, when no one was expecting him to be a priest. I didn't know if priests could ever knock off. I mean, Farther didn't spend his free time checking the mortar on the chimney stack or setting up a theodolite in the back garden, so it seemed unfair that a priest should have to be holy all the time. But perhaps it didn't work like that. Perhaps being a priest was like being a fish. Immersion for life.

℅

Now that Father Bernard had been served, everyone else could have their tea. I poured out a cup for each person – finishing one pot and starting on the next – until there was one mug left. Hanny's mug. The one with a London bus on the side. He always got a cup, even when he was away at Pinelands.

'How is Andrew?' Father Bernard asked, as he watched me.

'Fine, Father,' Mummer said.

Father Bernard nodded and pulled his face into a smile that acknowledged what she was really saying, beneath the words.

'He'll be back at Easter, won't he?' said Father Bernard.

'Yes,' said Mummer.

'You'll be glad to have him home, I'm sure.'

'Yes,' said Mummer. 'Very glad.'

There was an awkward pause. Father Bernard realised that he had strayed into private territory and changed the subject by raising his cup.

'That's a lovely brew, Mrs Smith,' he said and Mummer smiled.

It wasn't that Mummer didn't want Hanny at home – she loved him with an intensity that made Farther and I seem like we were merely her acquaintances sometimes – but he reminded her of the test that she still hadn't

21

passed. And while she delighted in any little advancement Hanny seemed to have made – he might be able to write the first letter of his name, or tie a bootlace, say – they were such small progressions that it still pained her to think of the long road ahead.

'And it will be a long road,' Father Wilfred had once told her. 'It will be full of disappointments and obstacles. But you should rejoice that God has chosen you to walk along it, that He has sent you Andrew as both a test and guide of your soul. He will remind you of your own muteness before God. And when at last he is able to speak, you will be able to speak, and ask of the Lord what you will. Not everyone receives such a chance, Mrs Smith. Be mindful of that.'

The cup of tea that we poured for Hanny that went cold and grew a wrinkled skin of milk was proof that she hadn't forgotten. It was, strangely, a kind of prayer.

'So,' Father Bernard said, putting down his half-empty tea cup and declining Mummer's offer of more. 'Does anyone have any suggestions about where we ought to go at Easter?'

'Well,' said Miss Bunce quickly, glancing at David who nodded encouragement. 'There's a place called Glasfynydd.'

'Where?' said Mummer, giving the others a sceptical look that Mr and Mrs Belderboss returned with a grin. They had never heard of the place either. It was just Miss Bunce trying to be different. She was young. It wasn't her fault.

'Glasfynydd. It's a retreat on the edge of the Brecon Beacons,' she said. 'It's beautiful. I've been lots of times. They have an outdoor church in the wood. Everyone sits on logs.'

No one responded apart from David, who said, 'That sounds nice,' and sipped his tea.

'All right,' said Father Bernard after a moment. 'That's one idea. Any others?'

'Well, it's obvious,' said Mummer. 'We should go back to Moorings and visit the shrine.' And buoyed on by Mr and Mrs Belderboss's murmurs of excitement in remembering the place, she added, 'We know how to get there and where everything is and it's quiet. We can go at Holy Week and take Andrew to the shrine and stay on until Rogationtide to watch the beating of the bounds, like we used to do. It'll be lovely. The old gang back together.'

'*I've* never been before,' said Miss Bunce. 'And neither has David.'

'Well, you know what I mean,' said Mummer.

Father Bernard looked round the room.

'Any other suggestions?' he said, and while he waited for a response he picked up a custard cream and bit it in half.

No one said anything.

'In that case,' he said. 'I think we ought to be democratic about it. All those who want to go to South Wales . . .'

Miss Bunce and her fiancé raised their hands.

'All those who want to go back to Moorings . . .'

Everyone else responded with much more vigour.

'That's that then,' said Father Bernard. 'Moorings it is.'

'But you didn't vote, Father,' said Miss Bunce.

Father Bernard smiled. 'I've given myself the right to abstain this time, Miss Bunce. I'm happy to go wherever I'm led.'

He grinned again and ate the remainder of his biscuit. Miss Bunce looked disappointed and shot glances at

David, wanting his sympathy. But he shrugged and went over to the table for another cup of tea, which Mummer poured with a flourish, as she relished the prospect of going back to the Loney.

Mr and Mrs Belderboss were already describing the place in minute detail to Father Bernard who nodded and picked another biscuit from his plate.

'And the shrine, Father,' said Mrs Belderboss. 'It's just beautiful, isn't it, Reg?'

'Oh, yes,' said Mr Belderboss. 'Quite a little paradise.'

'So many flowers,' Mrs Belderboss chipped in.

'And the water's so clean,' said Mr Belderboss. 'Isn't it, Esther?'

'Like crystal,' said Mummer, as she passed the sofa.

She smiled at Father Bernard and went to offer Miss Bunce a biscuit, which she took with a *thank you* that could have drawn blood. Mummer nodded and moved on. At Moorings, she knew she could beat Miss Bunce and her Glasfynydd hands down, being on home turf as it were.

She had grown up on the north-west coast, within spitting distance of the Loney and the place still buttered the edges of her accent even though she had long since left and had lived in London for twenty years or more. She still called sparrows spaddies, starlings sheppies, and when we were young she would sing us rhymes that no one outside her village had ever heard.

She made us eat hotpot and tripe salads and longed to find the same curd tarts she had eaten as a girl; artery-clogging fancies made from the first milk a cow gave after calving.

It seemed that where she grew up almost every other

day had been the feast of some saint or other. And even though hardly any of them were upheld any more, even by the most ardent at Saint Jude's, Mummer remembered every one and all the various accompanying rituals, which she insisted on performing at home.

On Saint John's day a metal cross was passed through a candle flame three times to symbolise the holy protection John had received when he went back into his burning house to rescue the lepers and the cripples staying there.

In October, on the feast of Saint Francis of Assisi, we would go to the park and collect autumn leaves and twigs and fashion them into crosses for the altar at Saint Jude's.

And on the first Sunday in May — as the people of Mummer's village had done since time immemorial — we would go out into the garden before Mass and wash our faces in the dew.

There was something special about the Loney. To Mummer, Saint Anne's shrine was second only to Lourdes; the two-mile walk across the fields from Moorings was her Camino de Santiago. She was convinced that there and only there would Hanny stand any chance of being cured.

# 4

HANNY CAME HOME from Pinelands at the start of the Easter holidays, bristling with excitement.

Even before Farther had turned off the car engine, he was running down the drive to show me the new watch Mummer had given him. I had seen it in the window of the shop where she worked. A heavy, golden-coloured thing with a picture of Golgotha on the face and an inscription from Matthew on the back: *Therefore, be aware. Because you do not know the day or the hour.*

'That's nice, Hanny,' I said and gave it back to him.

He snatched it off me and slipped it on his wrist before handing over a term's worth of drawings and paintings. They were all for me. They always were. Never for Mummer or Farther.

'He's very glad to be home, aren't you, Andrew?' said Mummer, holding the door open for Farther to bundle Hanny's suitcase through the porch.

She tidied Hanny's hair with her fingers and held him by the shoulders.

'We've told him that we're going back to Moorings,' she said. 'He's looking forward to it already, aren't you?'

But Hanny was more interested in measuring me. He

put his palm on the top of my head and slid his hand back towards his Adam's apple. He had grown again.

Satisfied that he was still the bigger of the two of us, he went up the stairs as noisily as he always did, the banister creaking as he hauled himself from step to step.

I went into the kitchen to make him a cup of tea in his London bus mug and when I found him in his room he still had on the old raincoat of Farther's that he had taken a shine to years before and insisted on wearing whatever the weather. He was standing by the window with his back to me looking at the houses on the other side of the street and the traffic going by.

'Are you all right, Hanny?'

He didn't move.

'Give me your coat,' I said. 'I'll hang it up for you.'

He turned and looked at me.

'Your coat, Hanny,' I said, shaking his sleeve.

He watched me as I undid the buttons for him and hung it on the peg on the back of the door. It weighed a ton with all the things he kept in the pockets to communicate with me. A rabbit's tooth meant he was hungry. A jar of nails was one of his headaches. He apologised with a plastic dinosaur and put on a rubber gorilla mask when he was frightened. He used combinations of these things sometimes and although Mummer and Farther pretended they knew what it all meant, only I really understood him. We had our world and Mummer and Farther had theirs. It wasn't their fault. Nor was it ours. That's just the way it was. And still is. We're closer than people can imagine. No one, not even Doctor Baxter, really understands that.

Hanny patted the bed and I sat down while he went

through his paintings of animals and flowers and houses. His teachers. Other residents.

The last painting was different, though. It was of two stick figures standing on a beach littered with starfish and shells. The sea behind them was a bright blue wall that rose like a tsunami. To the left were yellow mountains topped with mohicans of green grass.

'This is the Loney, isn't it?' I said, surprised that he remembered it at all. It had been years since we'd been there and Hanny rarely drew anything that he couldn't see right in front of him.

He touched the water and then moved his finger to the camel-hump dunes, over which hung a great flock of birds. Hanny loved the birds. I taught him all about them. How you could tell if a gull was in its first, second or third winter by the mottle of its plumage and the differences between the calls of the hawks and terns and warblers. How, if you were very still, you could sit by the water and the knots would move around you in a swarm so close that you could feel the breeze from their wings on your skin.

I'd copy the cries of the curlews and the redshanks and the herring gulls for him, and we'd lie on our backs and watch the geese high up in a chevron and wonder what it would be like to part the air a mile above the earth with a beak as hard as bone.

Hanny smiled and tapped the figures on the painting.

'That's you,' I said. 'That's Hanny.'

Hanny nodded and touched himself on the chest.

'That's me?' I said, pointing to the smaller of the two and Hanny gripped my shoulder.

'I'm glad you're home,' I said, and I meant it.

Pinelands didn't do him much good. They didn't know

him. They didn't care for him like I did. They never asked him what he needed. He was just the big lad in the TV lounge with his paints and crayons.

He held me close to his chest and stroked my hair. He was getting stronger. Every time I saw him he looked different. The puppy fat that had been there at Christmas had slipped from his face and he had no need to fake a moustache with a piece of burnt cork any more like we used to do as children. It seemed unimaginable, but Hanny was becoming an adult.

I think he sensed the strangeness of it too, albeit dimly. The way one might feel there was something different about a room but not be able to say what. Was there a missing picture, say, or a book shelved in a different place?

Sometimes I caught him looking at the span of his hands, the nest of black hairs on his breastbone, his hard, oval biceps, as though he couldn't quite understand what he was doing inside this man's body.

⁊

As we had always done in the past, we left for Moorings at first light on the Tuesday of Holy Week.

Once everyone had gathered at Saint Jude's and stowed their bags on the minibus, Father Bernard went to get into the driver's seat. But before he could start the engine, Mummer touched him on the arm.

'Father Wilfred usually led us in prayer before we left,' she said.

'Yes, of course,' said Father Bernard and he got down and started on the sign of the cross.

'We tended to go around the corner, Father,' said Mummer. 'And pray with Our Lady.'

'Oh, right,' said Father Bernard. 'Yes, of course.'

We gathered at the foot of the little Alpine rockery on which the Virgin stood and bowed our heads as Father Bernard made an impromptu prayer of intercession, asking her for a safe journey and a successful pilgrimage. After the Amen, we took it in turns to go to the railings, lean forward and kiss Mary's feet.

Father Bernard made way for Mrs Belderboss, who lowered herself slowly to her knees and had Mr Belderboss hold her by the shoulders as she leant over. Once she had kissed the Holy Mother's toes, she closed her eyes and began a whispered prayer that went on so long that Father Bernard began to look at his watch.

I was to be the last to go up, but Father Bernard said, 'Leave it, Tonto. Otherwise we'll be sitting on the North Circular all day.'

He looked up at Mary with her expression of vacancy and grief. 'I'm sure She won't mind.'

'If you say so, Father.'

'I do,' he said and jogged back to the minibus, making everyone laugh with a quip that I didn't catch as he climbed up the steps to the driver's seat.

I hadn't seen them all so happy for months. I knew what they were thinking. That this time it would be different. That Hanny would be cured. That they were on the cusp of a wonderful victory.

℘

We drove out of London, heading north through the East Midlands and across Yorkshire to Lancashire. I sat in the back with Monro wedged under my seat and slept on and off as a dozen counties went by. Every so often I woke up with the feeling that I was repeating parts of the journey. But then England is much the same all over, I suppose. A duplication of old farms, new estates, church spires, cooling towers, sewage works, railway lines, bridges, canals, and towns that are identical but for a few small differences in architecture and stone.

The sunlight that, as we left, had begun to creep over the London suburbs, disappeared the further north we went, returning only momentarily on the shoulder of a yellow hill miles away or picking out a distant reservoir in a second or two of magnesium brilliance.

The temperature dropped and the clouds darkened. The road steamed in driving rain. Shreds of mist hung over the cold lakes and woods. Moorland turned the colour of mould and becks coursed in spate down the peaty slopes, white and solid-looking from a distance, like seams of quartz.

No one had mentioned it – hoping presumably that it would go away of its own accord – but for the last few miles the minibus had been making an awful racket, as though something was loose in the engine. Every time Father Bernard changed gear there was a loud shuddering and grinding and eventually it refused to shift at all and he pulled in to the side of the road.

'What is it, Father?' said Mr Belderboss.

'The clutch, I think,' Father Bernard replied.

'Oh, it'll be the damp, it gets into everything up here,' said Mr Belderboss and sat back satisfied with his assessment.

'Can you fix it, Father?' Mrs Belderboss said.

'I certainly hope so, Mrs Belderboss,' Father Bernard

replied. 'I get the impression that you have to rely on your own ingenuity out here.'

He smiled and got out. He was right, of course. In every direction there was nothing but deserted, muddy fields where seabirds were blown like old rags.

The rain battered onto the windscreen and ran down in waves as Father Bernard lifted the bonnet and propped it open.

'Go and help him,' Mummer said to Farther.

'What do I know about cars?' he replied, glancing up from the map he was studying.

'You could still give him a hand.'

'He knows what he's doing, Esther. Too many cooks and all that.'

'Well, I hope he does manage to get us going again,' said Mummer, looking out of the window. 'It's only going to get colder.'

'I'm sure we'll survive,' said Farther.

'I was thinking of Mr and Mrs Belderboss,' Mummer replied.

'Oh, don't worry about us,' said Mr Belderboss. 'We've known cold, haven't we, Mary?'

'I should say so.'

They started to harp on about the war and having heard it all before I turned to Hanny who had been tugging at my sleeve for the last five minutes, desperate for me to share his View-Master.

Hanny grinned and handed me the red binoculars that he'd had stuck to his face for most of the journey, clicking through the various reels he took out of his school satchel. It had been *Mountains of the World* until we stopped at Kettering for a toilet break, then *Strange Creatures of the*

*Ocean*, and *Space Exploration* until Mummer had finally persuaded him onto *Scenes from The Old Testament*, which he now urged me to look through again. Eve with her private parts delicately blotted with foliage, Abraham's knife poised over Isaac's heart, Pharaoh's charioteers tumbling in the Red Sea.

When I had finished I noticed that he had his hands jammed between his legs.

'Do you need to go?' I said.

Hanny rocked back and forth, kicking the side of his boot against the door.

'Come on then.'

While Father Bernard was poking about in the engine, I took him outside and walked down the lane a little so no one else would see. He went over to a fence and unzipped his jeans while I waited in the rain and listened to it tapping on the hood of the parka Mummer had insisted I bring.

I looked back at the minibus and thought I could hear raised voices. Mummer. Farther. They had tried their best to hold onto the cheerfulness that had been there when we left Saint Jude's, but it had been difficult not to feel despondent once the rain began pounding the roads and everything had been obscured by mist.

A stiff wind blew in across the fields bringing the smell of brine and rot as strong as an onion. It seemed that all our past pilgrimages were contained in that smell and I felt a tension start to grow in my stomach. We had been coming here for as long as I could remember, yet I'd never felt completely comfortable in this place. It was rather like my grandfather's house. Glum, lifeless, mildly threatening. Not somewhere you wanted to linger for very long. I was always glad to see the back of it once our Easter pilgrimage was over, and I'd breathed a private sigh of relief when we stopped going altogether.

The rest of them kept up their spirits with hymns and prayers but at times it seemed as though they were, without knowing it, warding things off, rather than inviting God in.

Hanny finished and waved me over to where he was standing.

'What is it?' I said.

He pointed at the fence in front of him. A hare had been shot and skinned and its hide splayed on the barbed wire, along with several dozen rats. Trophies or deterrents, I suppose they were both.

'Leave it alone, Hanny,' I said. 'Don't touch it.'

He looked at me pleadingly.

'We can't save it now,' I said.

He went to stroke it but withdrew his hand when I shook my head. The hare stared at us through a glassy brown eye.

We were starting to cross the road back to the minibus when I heard the sound of a car approaching. I grabbed Hanny's sleeve and held him tightly as an expensive-looking Daimler went past us, throwing water into the ditches on either side. There was a young girl asleep in the back, her face against the window. The driver slowed at the corner where we were standing and turned his head briefly to look at me before he rounded the bend and was gone. I had never seen a car like that here before. There was little in the way of traffic at all around the Loney. Mostly hay trucks and farm wagons and not always motorised either.

When Hanny and I got back to the minibus Father

Bernard still had his hands deep in amongst the pipes and wires.

'What's wrong with it, Father?' I asked.

'I don't know, Tonto,' he said and wiped the rain out of his eyes with his sleeve. 'It might be the fly wheel, but I'd have to take the whole thing apart to be sure.'

He closed the bonnet with some reluctance and followed me back on board.

'Any luck?' said Mr Belderboss.

'Not so far,' Father Bernard replied, smoothing his sopping hair back over his head. 'I think it'll be a garage job to be honest.'

'Oh dear,' said Mrs Belderboss. 'What a start.'

'Well at least it got us this far,' said Farther.

'Aye, there's that,' said Father Bernard.

Monro was whining. Father Bernard shushed him and he shrank into a white-eyed nervousness.

'I think the best thing to do,' he said, 'will be for me to walk on to the village and see if there's anyone there who can help us.'

'In this weather, Father?' said Mrs Belderboss. 'You'll catch your death.'

'To be honest, the walk will do me good, Mrs Belderboss,' he said. 'I don't do well sitting for so long.'

'It's a fair way, Father,' said Mr Belderboss. 'It must be a good three or four miles.'

Father Bernard smiled dismissively and started to wind his scarf around his neck.

'You'll go with him, won't you?' Mummer said to me.

'Ah, don't worry yourself, Mrs Smith,' said Father Bernard. 'There's no sense in two of us getting soaked.'

'It's no trouble, is it?' Mummer nudged me.

'No,' I said.

The wind buffed around the minibus. Monro piped up again and Father Bernard leant down and scrubbed his neck to comfort him.

'What's the matter with him, Father?' said Mr Belderboss.

'I don't know,' said Father Bernard. 'Maybe it was that car going past.'

'Perhaps you're right,' said Mr Belderboss. 'He was going at a fair gallop. I didn't think he was going to slow down for the bend.'

'The girl was a pretty little thing, though, wasn't she?' said Mrs Belderboss.

Mr Belderboss frowned. 'What girl?'

'The girl in the back.'

'I didn't see a girl.'

'Well then you missed out, Reg.'

'Oh come on now, Mary,' he said. 'You know I only have eyes for you.'

Mrs Belderboss leant over to Miss Bunce.

'Make the most of David's sincerity while it lasts,' she said, but Miss Bunce was looking past her at Monro, who had crawled back under my seat and was shaking.

'Come on, old feller,' said Father Bernard. 'You're showing me up. What's the matter?'

ॐ

Three men were coming across the field towards us. They were dressed in filthy green wax jackets and rubber boots. None of them wore hats or had umbrellas. They were local men, either hardened to the weather or possessed of the knowledge that it would pass over in a few moments.

One of them carried a shotgun over his arm. Another had a white terrier on a chain. One of those ones with a long face and wide-set eyes. A dog drawn by a child. The third man was older than the other two and walked several yards behind, coughing into his fist. They stopped and looked at us for a few moments before carrying on towards the road.

'Should we ask them for some help, Father?' said Mr Belderboss.

'I'd rather we didn't,' said Miss Bunce, looking at David, who reassured her by taking her hand.

'Well, it's either that or we spend the rest of the week sitting here,' said Mummer.

Father Bernard got out and looked along the road before crossing. The men climbed over the stile and waited when Father Bernard called to them. The tallest of them, who was bald and had the build of a Charolais bull, held his shotgun over the crook of his arm and looked at Father Bernard while he explained about the clutch. The one with the dog held its snout tightly closed and alternated his interest between what Father Bernard was saying and the strangers on the minibus. His left arm seemed to hang more loosely and on that hand he wore a black mitten tied at the wrist with some string. The elder man coughed again and sat down on a broken bit of wall. He was a strange colour. The colour of nicotine or dried daffodils. The same colour my grandfather went when his liver packed in.

'Oh dear,' said Mrs Belderboss. 'He doesn't look at all well, does he, Reg?'

'Toxoplasmosis, most likely,' said Mr Belderboss.

'Toxo what?'

'They get it from cats,' he said. 'It's very common with farmers. Their cats pick up all sorts of things.'

'What are you on about?'

'I read it in the paper,' he said. 'You have a look at their hands. They don't wash them properly. All they have to do is swallow a bit of cat's doings and that's that. I'm right, aren't I?'

'I think so,' said Farther.

Mrs Belderboss shook her head.

'I'm telling you, it's toxoplasmosis,' said Mr Belderboss. 'Look at him. Poor bugger.'

Outside, Father Bernard patted the bull man on the shoulder and brought him over to the minibus. The bull man handed the shotgun to his friend with the dog and leant over the engine when Father Bernard lifted the bonnet.

I could hear them talking, or rather Father Bernard talking and the other man listening or giving the occasional *aye*. After a few moments the man with the dog came over and put in his two penn'orth, and, eventually, Father Bernard dropped the bonnet and got back into the driver's seat.

'I think Mr Parkinson may well have saved the day,' he said, responding to the bull man's gesture that he should start the engine.

'Mr who?' said Miss Bunce.

'Parkinson,' said Father Bernard. 'And the feller with the dog is called Collier.'

'How do you know that?' said Miss Bunce.

'I asked them,' he replied. 'It's a wee habit I picked up in the Ardoyne. Ask a feller's name and shake his hand and more often than not he'll help you out whoever he is.'

38

'I thought you'd come from New Cross,' said Farther.

'Aye I did, but I was two years in the Ardoyne after I left seminary.'

'No one told us that,' said Mummer.

'Ah, you see, Mrs Smith, there's more to me than meets the eye.'

The minibus slid smoothly into gear and Father Bernard gave a thumbs up which Parkinson returned with a slight nod of the head. We edged forward, the wheels spinning momentarily in the sludge by the side of the road and set off towards Moorings.

The men stood and watched us all the way down the lane, the dog straining on its leash, desperate to tear something to pieces.

∾

A while later, familiar landmarks appeared – a pub with an unusual name, a monument on a very green hill, a crown of standing stones in a field. It only remained for the road to bore through a thickness of overhanging oak trees and then the coastline of the Loney was suddenly flung out to our left.

I remember how my eye used to leap instinctively to the horizon, how looking suddenly across that immense distance of grey seemed to produce the same feeling as looking down from the spire of Saint Jude's or the top floor of Farther's office block. A kind of vertigo.

'Lovely view, isn't it, Joan?' said Mrs Belderboss.

Miss Bunce looked past me at the grim plain of the sea and the gulls turning on the wind, frowned uncertainly and went back to the half sleep she'd been in since we'd set off again after the breakdown.

'Lovely view,' Mrs Belderboss said again, verifying it to herself this time as fact.

Over the water, the cloud thinned and fingers of sunlight touched the bare bulge of Coldbarrow, lighting up its brown tundra and catching the windows of Thessaly, the old house sitting at its northern tip. They flared and then faded again, as if the place had been woken for a moment out of a long sleep.

I'd never liked the look of Thessaly and even though in the past we had always been under strict instructions never to cross the sands to Coldbarrow, we wouldn't have gone there anyway.

There were stories, naturally, of it being haunted. A witch had once lived there, they said; a beautiful woman called Elizabeth Percy who lured sailors onto the rocks, and who remained there in some form or other even though they'd hanged her in the old bell tower next to the house. In fact, all around the Loney people still clung to old superstitions out of conviction, it seemed, rather than nostalgia, and it wasn't unusual to come across farms where the occupants hadn't quite the courage to take down the horseshoes nailed to barn doors to keep boggarts from spoiling the hay, or for people to leave an acorn in their window to turn lightning away from the house.

It's easy to scoff, I suppose, but there was so little of the modern world there that it was difficult not to think of the place being at a sort of standstill and – how shall I put it? – *primed* in some way.

A sudden mist, a mumble of thunder over the sea, the wind scurrying along the beach with its crop of old bones and litter, was sometimes all it took to make you feel as though something was about to happen. Though quite what, I didn't know.

I often thought there was too much time there. That the place was sick with it. Haunted by it. Time didn't leak away as it should. There was nowhere for it to go and no modernity to hurry it along. It collected as the black water did on the marshes and remained and stagnated in the same way.

ॐ

Father Bernard drove at a snail's pace, hunched over the steering wheel, looking through the gaps he had rubbed out of the condensation with his sleeve. The track was strewn with potholes and everyone hung on as the minibus bounced in and out of the ruts.

It went on this way for half a mile or more, the suspension groaning, until we rounded a sharp bend at the top of the lane.

'Look,' said Mummer suddenly, pointing up the hillside to our right. 'There it is.'

Moorings stood alone in a field of iron-coloured weeds and limestone boulders on the gentle rise of land that began at the seashore a mile away and continued to the foot of the steeper hills behind the house, where a spread of ashes, yews and oaks called Brownslack Wood marched over the top of the hill and down into the moorland of the next valley.

With its bowed roof, the house looked like a ship that had been washed far inland on a storm tide. A huge wisteria vine was its rigging. A crumbling chimney its crow's nest.

It had been the home of a taxidermist who retired there with his third wife in the late 1950s. She died within a year of them moving in and he didn't stick around for much longer than that himself, leaving the property to his son, a banker who lived in Hong Kong. Unable to sell the place, the son rented it out, and as far as I knew we were the only people who ever stayed there.

∾

Going up the lane, I turned Hanny's face towards the large limestone boulder over to the left. We'd christened it the Panzer. Or at least I had. And when Mummer hadn't been watching us we'd thrown pebble grenades at it. Launched stick rockets at its tracks. Crawled on our bellies through the grass to do in the scar-faced Kapitän like the Tommies did in *Commando*.

I wondered if Hanny remembered any of that. He had remembered the beach, after all, and we were always very good at picking up our games where we left off, no matter how long it had been since we'd played them. Perhaps he would want to play soldiers again when we got to the shore. He never seemed to tire of it. Though what it meant to him, I don't know. I mean, he can't have had any conception of war or of the bravery and sacrifice we pretended to experience. It was the excitement of it all, I suppose. Charging down the dunes with driftwood machine guns and winning, always winning.

As we approached Moorings, there was a Land Rover parked up on a grass verge. It was dented and filthy and had crude white crosses painted on the doors like something that might have ferried men out of the Somme.

'Oh, there he is,' said Mrs Belderboss, pointing out of the window. 'Still the same as ever.'

'Who?' said Miss Bunce, craning around her seat to see.

'Clement,' said Mrs Belderboss.

Miss Bunce peered at the large man standing by the front door with a woman half his size. Mrs Belderboss caught the look of concern on her face.

'Oh, he'll not bother you,' she said. 'He's just a bit, you know. Smile at him. That seems to do the trick.'

'Who's the lady?'

Mrs Belderboss turned to her. 'That's his mother,' she said. 'She's blind as a bat, poor thing.'

'But she's wearing glasses,' said Miss Bunce.

Mrs Belderboss laughed. 'I know. She's a funny old bird.'

Clement watched us as we pulled up in front of the house. Father Bernard waved to him, but he just stared like his mother.

There were unkind whispers about him, as there always are in such places about quiet, lonely men, but the general consensus was that he was harmless. And although the pig farm he kept with his mother was a desolate and ramshackle place thrown way out on the windswept fields south of Moorings, I got the impression that it wasn't in such poor repair from wilful neglect. By all accounts his mother took as much looking after as the swine.

Poor Clement. I always thought of him as something akin to a shire horse; in build and temperament. Clumping. Plodding. Head down in deference. Dependable to a fault.

The taxidermist's son could hardly have checked up on him all the way from Kowloon but he paid him to look after Moorings all the same, safe in the knowledge that Clement didn't have the brains to rip him off.

Everyone got out of the minibus and stretched. Miss Bunce buttoned up her coat and wrapped her arms around herself, pacing back and forth to keep warm, while David fetched her bags. Mr Belderboss struggled down the metal step with Farther taking his weight and Mrs Belderboss fussing around him like a moth.

Father Bernard put on his jacket, zipped it up to the neck and went over to Clement, bidding us to follow him.

As we got closer, Clement started to look confused.

'Where's t'other feller?' he said.

'Sorry?'

'The priest.'

'Father Wilfred? Didn't anyone tell you? He passed away.'

'Died, did he?'

'I'm afraid so.'

'How?'

Father Bernard looked at us and then said, 'I'm Father McGill, if that's any good.'

'You're a priest an all?' said Clement.

'For my sins, aye.' Father Bernard smiled and Clement shook his hand with relief.

Father Bernard paused and looked at Clement's mother, waiting to be introduced.

'Mother,' said Clement, and the old lady jerked into life and held out her hand.

Father Bernard took it and said, 'Good to meet you.'

The old lady said nothing.

'Go and wait in the van,' said Clement.

She remained expressionless.

'I said wait in the van.' Clement nudged her and she set off with her stick, driving a wedge through the crowd of us standing there.

As she went past, she lifted up her glasses and looked at me with her grey milky eyes that were slick and glossy like the underside of a slug.

'Do you want to come inside?' said Clement.

'Aye, 'tis a bit raw,' said Father Bernard.

'Rooks say we'll have a good summer, though.'

'How's that?'

Clement pointed past the house to the woods where several dozen of the birds were going in and out of their nests.

'Building them right high up this year,' he said.

'That's good,' said Father Bernard.

'Aye, but it's not normal,' Clement mumbled.

He turned up the path to the front door along the miniature boulevard of apple trees that were still winter-naked, their branches speckled with blight like the putrefying windfallen fruit that lay underneath them. There was always something rather sad about those trees, I thought. The way they dutifully grew their produce every summer only for it to blacken and fall off uncollected.

Every movement of Clement's was slow and heavy and it took an age for him to find the right key. Once the house was open, Mummer muscled her way through to the front and led everyone along the hall that, as it had always done in the past, smelled of cigars and spent matches and the air had a hard, porcelain coldness to it.

'Sitting room, drawing room, lavatory,' she said as she turned the handle of each door.

Mr and Mrs Belderboss followed her down the hall and back, delighted at finding things in exactly the same place as they had always been and having new people to show around, although Miss Bunce seemed reluctant to go much

45

further than the dead grandfather clock by the front door. She looked up anxiously as the bare bulb that illuminated the hallway faded and then came back on, brighter than it had been before.

'It's only the wind,' said Mummer.

'It catches on the wires,' said Clement, who was still lingering at the threshold.

I noticed for the first time that he was wearing a wooden crucifix around his neck. One he had made himself by the look of it. Two chunks of split wood bound with string.

'There you are,' said Mummer. 'It catches on the wires.'

Clement adjusted his cap and turned to go.

'I'll bring thee some more firewood in a day or two,' he said, nodding to the bags lined up in the hallway.

'Are you sure you need to, Clement? It looks like there's enough there for a month,' said Father Bernard.

Clement frowned and looked very serious. 'Quite sure, Father. When the wind gets down the chimney it draws the heart out of the fire in no time,' he said.

'Is there bad weather on the way?' asked Father Bernard.

'There usually is,' Clement replied.

Miss Bunce smiled thinly as he looked at us all one last time and closed the door.

'Now, come on, Joan,' said Mr Belderboss, once Clement had left. 'There's nothing to worry about.'

And he took her arm and led her past the peeling wallpaper and the oil paintings of wild seascapes into the sitting room to show her the amount of expensive objects that had been left by the taxidermist. Something that charmed him and bewildered him in equal measure.

At his bidding, everyone else followed and listened as

he pointed out the delicate knick-knacks worth hundreds apiece.

'Ah, now then,' he said, plucking out a small clay pipe from a wooden box lying on the window ledge. 'This is interesting. You can still see the teeth marks on the stem. Look.'

He offered it to Mummer but she frowned and he put it back where he found it, making a beeline for Miss Bunce, whose attention had been taken by the books on the rosewood Davenport by the window.

Among them was a first edition of *The Island of Doctor Moreau*, one bound in leather that looked to have been signed by Longfellow, and a children's pop-up book of *Goldilocks and the Three Bears*, which Miss Bunce began to read, turning the fragile pages slowly. Late Victorian, Mr Belderboss reckoned, about the same time Moorings was finished.

'Chap called Gregson built it,' said Mr Belderboss. 'Cotton mill owner. That's what they were round here, wasn't it, Esther? Cotton men?'

'Yes,' said Mummer. 'Cotton or linen.'

'There's a photograph of him and his missus somewhere,' said Mr Belderboss, looking around the room. 'Was it seven children they had, Mary? It might have been more. I don't think many of them saw their fifth birthday, mind you. TB and all that. That's why they built these sorts of places. To keep their little 'uns alive. They thought the sea air would do them good.'

'They built them to last, as well,' said Farther, smoothing his hand over the plaster. 'They must be a yard thick these walls.'

Miss Bunce looked around her and then out of the

window, clearly unconvinced that anyone who stayed here would leave the place healthier than when they came in.

It came as no surprise to her when Mr Belderboss explained how the house had changed hands many times since it had been built and carefully renamed by each successive occupant in an attempt to make it deliver what it seemed to promise sometimes, sitting there quietly under the gentle ruffling of the wood and the flour-soft clouds.

Gregson had christened it Sunny Vale; then it was Rose Cottage, Softsands, Sea Breezes, and lastly Moorings by the taxidermist.

'It must have been lovely, though, in its heyday,' said Mrs Belderboss, pushing aside the curtains a little more. 'What with that view and everything.'

'Clever landscapers, the Victorians,' said Farther.

'Oh, yes,' said Mr Belderboss. 'The view was all part of the prophylactic, wasn't it?'

'There's something timeless about it,' said Mrs Belderboss, looking out at the sea. 'Don't you think?'

'Well, it's a very old part of the country,' said Mr Belderboss.

Mrs Belderboss rolled her eyes. 'It must be the same age as everywhere else, you fool.'

'Oh, you know what I mean,' he replied. 'Untrodden, then. Some of the yew trees up in the woods must have been ancient in the time of Bede. And they do say there are places around here that haven't been set foot in since the Vikings came.'

Mrs Belderboss scoffed again.

'It's true,' Mr Belderboss replied. 'A century in this place is nothing. I mean, it's quite easy to imagine that that book', he said, nodding to Miss Bunce's hands, 'could have been read by some poor little consumptive only yesterday.'

Miss Bunce put the book down and wiped her hands on her duffle coat, as Mr Belderboss went over to the other side of the room, enthusing over the seascapes of tiny ships under colossal stormclouds that the taxidermist had spent his last years painting. His brushes were still there in a jam jar. His palette had a dry crust of dark oils. And under the dust a rag, a chewed pencil, some loose, pre-decimal change all contributed to the uneasy feeling I always had when I stayed at Moorings, that the taxidermist had merely stepped out to smoke one of his expensive cigars and that he might return at any moment and pop through a door like one of the three bears in the old book, to find a Goldilocks sleeping in every room.

# 5

THE ROOM HANNY and I shared was at the top of the house where the rooks scrabbled across the slates for the insects in the moss. Every so often, one of the more daring would come to the window ledge, quite unperturbed that we were watching it, and rake its pencil-sharp beak down the glass with a horrible squeal to nibble out the things living in the decaying woodwork of the frame.

Only when I banged on the window did it finally disappear, flapping away in a peal of grating laughter and sailing in a smooth scoop back up to the others in the woods. Hanny was sad to see it go, but I couldn't let it stay there. Mummer didn't care much for those kinds of birds. Crows, ravens, jackdaws and the like. She would even shoo the jays and magpies out of the back garden in London. There was an old saying in her village that they prevented the sick from getting better, and that when they gathered in numbers a death was imminent.

'Sorry, Hanny,' I said. 'We can go and look at them later if you like.'

He took his face away from the window, leaving a little oval of condensation.

'We ought to unpack,' I said and nodded to the dufflebag at his feet. He bent down and handed it to me, looking over my shoulder, his face suddenly brightening at the abundance of interesting junk in the room.

I suppose it was like looking at it anew for him, but to my eyes nothing much had changed. Only the water stains on the ceiling had grown. The dark patches had assumed the shapes of foreign countries, and a succession of tide lines showed how the empire of dampness had expanded year on year since we'd last been.

I put Hanny's clothes away for him, hung up his coat on the back of the door and set his *Lives of the Saints* book down on the bedside table. At Pinelands they encouraged them to do these sorts of things for themselves, but Hanny was too excited by what was in the room to care about anything else and took the various objects down one by one to look at them: all the colourful stones and shells, the splints of driftwood, the bottles, cuttlebone, hornwrack, dried twists of coral, mermaids' purses. There was a whole shelf of scrimshaw: whale teeth polished to the delicacy of bone china and engraved with intricately detailed pictures of schooners and battleships. Against one wall was a chest of drawers that contained specimens of birds' eggs, each one labelled with common and Latin name and the date it had been found. Some were decades old.

On the floor and on top of the long wardrobes were Victorian curios under dusty glass domes that had always frightened me to death when I was a child. Exotic butterflies, horribly bright, impaled to a stump of silver birch, two squirrels playing cricket in caps and pads, a spider monkey wearing a fez and smoking a pipe.

There were music boxes and broken wind-up toys, grinning marionettes and tin humming tops, and between our beds sat a clock on which the hours were indicated by little paintings of the apostles. Mummer thought it wonderful, of course, and when we were children she told us the story of each of them: how Andrew had elected to be crucified on a saltire; how James was chosen to be with Jesus during the transfiguration and how he was beheaded by Herod Agrippa on his return to Judea; how Matthias had replaced the treacherous Judas and converted the cannibals of Ethiopia.

They had all suffered and toiled so that we could do the same. For God's work should never be easy.

I touched Hanny lightly on the shoulder and he turned around.

'Mummer says I've to give you a bath,' I said.

I mimed washing under my armpits and Hanny smiled and went over to a shelf where there was a stuffed mallard.

'You can't take that in the bath,' I said.

He frowned and held onto it tightly.

'You'll ruin it, Hanny.'

I fetched some towels and he followed me down the landing to the bathroom. He insisted on bringing the duck with him and sat it on the rim of the bath while he lay there in the foam listening to the wind playing in the pipework and the drains. He nodded and listened and then nodded again.

'It's just the wind, Hanny,' I said. 'It's not talking to you.'

He smiled at me and slipped under the water, sending a mushroom of bubbles to the surface. He stayed there for a moment longer than I was comfortable with, and then, just as I was about to reach in and pull him out, he resurfaced open-mouthed and blinking, his mop slapped down over his ears.

I got him out after half an hour. The water was cold and the suds had all dissolved. I dried him slowly in a ritual drummed into me by Mummer. One of the many she insisted Hanny and I follow for the sake of our health, like cleaning our teeth with hot water and cutting our fingernails every other day.

Once he was completely dry, I helped him on with his pyjamas. But he had stopped smiling. His whole body was stiff and uncooperative, making it difficult to get his arms down the sleeves and the buttons done up. I noticed that he was staring past me at the darkening sky outside and then I understood what was wrong. He had realised that we were staying here and he didn't like it. He wanted to go home.

I settled him into bed and let him pet a stuffed hare that he'd taken a fancy to, hoping it might send him off to sleep. He held it close to him and stroked its ears as I went and sat by the window and tried to look beyond my reflection to the sea, which was rapidly fading in the dusk.

The room went suddenly silent. The rooks had stopped croaking. A stillness settled around the house and over the fields, and everything seemed watchful and timorous.

The night crept in at the Loney, in a way that I've never known anywhere else. At home in London, it kept its distance from us, skulking behind the streetlights and the office blocks and could be easily knocked aside in a second by the rush of light and metal from the Metropolitan Line trains that flashed past the end of our garden. But here it was different. There was nothing to keep it away. The moon was cold and distant and the stars were as feeble as the tiny specks of light from the fishing boats way out at sea.

Like the shadow of a huge predatory bird, darkness moved slowly down the hillside, past Moorings, across the marshes, across the beach, across the sea, until all that was left was a muddy orange on the horizon as the last of England's light ebbed away.

∽

I was about to draw the curtains when I saw someone cross the lane that led up to the house and make their way through the fields where the Panzer lay. A moment later someone else followed carrying a large haversack and once he had caught up with the first, I saw them both head over to the hedgerow on the far side. Farmers, I thought, taking a short cut home. I looked to see where they were going, but it was too dark and the rain was teeming down again.

Behind me, I heard Hanny getting out of bed and scratting about on the floor, rubbing his hands over the bare wood and knocking here and there with his knuckles.

'What are you doing?' I said. 'You should be in bed. Mummer will be cross if you don't go to sleep.'

He pointed to the floor.

'What?'

He pointed again.

'No, you can't go downstairs, Hanny.'

He smiled and pulled me by the sleeve so that I knelt like him next to the grubby pink rug in the centre of the room. He turned it back and underneath there was a floorboard with a knothole pushed through. It was where we used to hide things we didn't want Mummer to see. I'd forgotten all about it.

'Can you open it?' I said and Hanny jammed his finger into the hole and lifted up the board. It creaked against the others but came out easily enough and Hanny shuffled forward and peered into the darkness.

'Reach in, Hanny,' I said and mimed with my hand and Hanny stuck his arm into the cavity and felt around. A penknife came out, mottled with rust and blunt as a brick. The pornographic photographs Billy Tapper had pressed into my hand that day we saw him in the bus shelter. One, two, three, half a dozen stuffed rats that Hanny took out and threw into a pile without so much as flinching.

Reaching further than he'd been able to do the last time we came, he brought out a leather strap. He pulled it and something large banged against the underside of the floorboards.

℘

It was an M1 Garand. I remembered from *Commando* that all the Yanks had them in the war. Bullets came in a metal clip that slotted into the top and jumped out with a loud ping when all the rounds had been used up – an unfortunate signal to the enemy that you were out of ammunition, but the rifle's only fault. It could put a bullet through an oak tree.

Protected by the bedsheet in which it had been wrapped, its wooden stock was still polished to a chestnut gloss and made of solid, sural curves like a muscle extracted from the leg of a racehorse. The sight mounted on top looked as if it would pull in a thousand yards or more.

God knows where the taxidermist had got it from.

I dusted down the barrel with my sleeve and we took

it in turns to hold it. Then, uncertain what else there was to do, we laid it on the bed and looked at it.

'This is ours now,' I said. 'It belongs to you and me. But you mustn't touch it without me. All right?'

Hanny looked at me and smiled.

There was a knock at the door. I quickly covered the rifle with a blanket and sat down on top of it.

It was Father Bernard.

'How are you boys?' he said, looking around the door. 'Have you settled in all right?'

'Yes, Father.'

'Do you mind if I come in?'

'No, Father.'

He stepped into the room and closed the door behind him. He wasn't wearing his dog collar and had his shirt sleeves rolled up over his ham-hock forearms that were surprisingly bare.

'Can I tempt you to half an hour of gin rummy?' he said.

I shifted uncomfortably, feeling the rifle digging into my backside. I realised that I had no idea if it was loaded or not, or if it was possible that by sitting on it I might inadvertently pull the trigger and blow Father Bernard's kneecaps off.

'I don't know about you boys,' he said, fetching a stool from the side of the washbasin. 'But I'm not tired at all.'

He sat down and produced a pack of cards from his shirt pocket and handed them to me, moving the *Lives of the Saints* book off the bedside table to make room.

'You deal, Tonto,' he said.

'Yes, Father.'

He rubbed his hand over his mouth and we started

playing, silently at first, though it didn't take long before he was on to the stories about the farm where he grew up, and then I could relax a little.

It was by all accounts a fairly miserable hovel on Rathlin Island, some barren speck of rock I'd never heard of between the Antrim coast and the Mull of Kintyre full of guillemots and storm petrels and razorbills. Mist and bog. Endless grey sea. It's easy to imagine the sort of place.

The only thing of note about it was that it was where the spider supposedly egged on Robert the Bruce to clobber the English, and there that the English replied by massacring the McDonnells. Even the children. Apparently you could still find bloodstains on the rocks that the sea refused to wash away.

So little happened on the island that memories were as long as the savage winters that were the starting point of most of Father Bernard's stories.

'Would you listen to that rain?' he said, looking towards the window. 'It reminds me of the winter our stores were flooded out.'

'When was that, Father?'

'Oh, I was only a wee boy. I can't have been any more than eight or nine.'

'What happened, Father?'

'My daddy, God love him, was a good farmer but he was a lousy roofer. He'd patched up the storehouse with old bits of wood, you see, and they just rotted away like everything else on the island. One night the whole thing went in and nigh on every scrap of food we had was ruined. I remember my mammy chasing a whole load of carrots and turnips that were floating out of the yard.

'I shouldn't laugh,' he said. 'It wasn't funny. We weren't that far from starving.'

'Didn't you have animals, Father?'

'Aye.'

'Couldn't you eat them?'

'If we'd done that we'd have been poor as well as hungry come the New Year market in Ballycastle. The animals were why we nearly starved. We had to feed them first, you know?'

'Couldn't you have got some food from somewhere else?'

'Oh aye,' he said. 'The O'Connells from the farm over the way came around with potatoes and meat, but my daddy was too proud to take anything off them. He'd rather we all wasted away than rely on charity.

'When my mammy found out, she was furious. It was the only time she ever raised her voice to him, and when the O'Connells came around again she took everything they'd brought.

'You know, Tonto, it sounds daft, but I don't think my daddy was quite the same from then on. I think it half killed him, sacrificing his pride like that.'

I stopped dealing and put the pack of cards in the middle of the table.

'Anyway,' he said. 'I'm going on. How's school at the moment? Almost done now, aren't you?'

'Yes, Father.'

'Exams soon, is it?'

'Yes.'

'Well make sure you work hard. Otherwise you might end up with a career in the priesthood.'

He smiled and pulled his cards together, tapping them on the table.

'Are you a good lad at school?'

'Yes, Father.'

'I was a wee terror,' he said. 'When they could get me to go, that is.'

He fanned the cards in his hand and laid one down.

'Mind you, if you'd seen the place, Tonto, you wouldn't have gone either.'

'Why's that, Father?'

'There were fifty of us in one room. Half of us hadn't any boots to wear. And it was so cold in the winter that the ink iced over in the wells. Can you imagine?'

'No, Father.'

He frowned at my expression and then laughed.

'Ah, I'm just pulling your leg,' he said. 'It wasn't that bad. Apart from O'Flannery.'

He threw a card down onto the pile, before picking up another.

'You'll not have anyone like O'Flannery where you are, I'm sure. He was a very old fashioned sort of teacher. You know what I mean? A real hardliner.'

'Yes, Father.'

'Some of the other lads said he wore a cilice. And I wouldn't have put it past him, the face he had on him sometimes. You know what a cilice is, right, Tonto?'

'Yes, Father.'

He tapped his fingers on his cards and took his turn and then smiled to himself.

'I laugh hearty at it now,' he said. 'But O'Flannery was an out and out bullyman. Even the mammies and daddies were frightened of him. He made sure he put the fear of God into you from day one.'

'How?'

'Well, whenever anyone new joined the class, he'd always ask them the same question.'

'What was that?'

'It was to translate *dura lex, sed lex.*'

He looked at me.

'Aye, that was the face they pulled too. Right before he'd give them a whack on the arse with his cane.'

He pursed his lips and shook his head.

'You know, I can still feel it now. He'd hit you so hard with the old birch that all he had to do after that to stop us silly wee cubs in our tracks was to go to the desk and touch it. We shut up pretty quickly then, I can tell you.'

'Didn't you have other teachers though, Father?' I said.

'Aye, we did in the end.'

'How do you mean?'

He laughed drily to himself.

'Mr O'Flannery's career was cut short let's say.'

'Why, what happened?'

'The silly sod fell off the cliffs at Rue Point, photographing the puffins. When they told us on the Monday morning, all the lads cheered, and to my eternal shame so did I.

'We were still cheering when the headmaster came in. I thought we were done for, you know. But he didn't scold us at all. He knew what O'Flannery was like. What people thought of him. He just sat on the edge of the desk asking us questions about geography and science and mathematics. And do you know what? Between us we answered every single one. He must have been there for an hour and then he said something that I've never forgotten to this day.'

'What was that, Father?'

'He said, "In time to come, each of you will thank the man who gave you your mind." Then he got up and left. And he was right. I mean he was hard as nails, O'Flannery, and I hated him at the time, but I feel kind of grateful to him now, you know? There aren't many lessons of his that I don't remember.'

'What did it mean, Father?'

'What did what mean?'

'The Latin.'

He laughed. 'The law is harsh, but it is the law. Then there was, let's see, *Ex fructu arbor agnoscitur* and *Veritas vos liberabit.*'

'What does that one mean, Father?'

'The truth will set you free,' he said and played his card.

'John,' I said, automatically.

Father Bernard raised his eyebrows and then looked at me thoughtfully.

'Father Wilfred taught you a lot, didn't he?'

I nodded and was about to show Hanny which card to lay down when I realised that he had won.

'Show,' I said and bent the cards towards Father Bernard.

Hanny pulled them back to his chest.

'It's all right, Hanny,' I said. 'You've won. You're the winner.'

'Aye, he is that,' said Father Bernard looking at Hanny's hand, and then throwing in his own cards.

He sat back and looked at me as I scooped the cards into a pile to deal them again.

'There was something I wanted to ask you actually, Tonto,' he said.

'Yes, Father?'

'On behalf of Mr Belderboss.'

'Yes, Father?'

'When Father Wilfred passed away,' he said. 'There was something of his that went missing. A book. You've not seen it knocking about have you?'

'A book?'

'Aye, you know, a diary, a notebook, that kind of thing. It was quite important. To the family. Mr Belderboss is pretty keen on getting it back.'

'No, Father.'

'Not in the vestry? Or the presbytery?'

'No, Father.'

'Do you think any of the other lads might know?'

'I don't know, Father.'

'Would it be worth me asking them?'

'I'm not sure, Father. Maybe.'

He looked at me and I started dealing.

'You know, Tonto, confession is bound by a seal of secrecy. I can't tell a soul what you say to me,' he said, pausing for a moment. 'Even with a gun to my head.'

I looked up at him sharply, thinking that he had somehow seen the rifle, but he was gathering his cards together and spreading them in his hands.

'But I'm not in confession, Father,' I said.

He laughed and then outside on the landing I heard Mummer calling for him.

'You have a think about it, Tonto,' he said and got up to open the door. 'If anything comes to you, let me know.'

Mummer came in. 'Oh, there you are,' she said. 'I hope these two weren't keeping you up, Father.'

'No, no, not at all, Mrs Smith,' he said. 'I just wanted to see if they'd got any better at cards.'

'Oh,' said Mummer, confused as to whether Father

Bernard had set up some elaborate test to see if we were secret gamblers. 'Have they?'

'No,' he said, winking at me. 'They're still terrible cheats.'

'Oh,' said Mummer. 'Well, if I could borrow you for a moment, Father, there are a few things I wanted to speak to you about.'

'By all means, Mrs Smith,' he said.

He got up and went past Mummer who held the door open for him. When he had gone down the landing Mummer snapped at me.

'Why isn't Andrew asleep? You know he'll be no good if he's tired.'

'I know.'

'Well if you know, stop messing around up here and get him settled.'

'Yes, Mother.'

She looked at us both and then walked away. I waited for a moment and then went to the door and onto the landing.

'I don't know if you realised, Father,' said Mummer as they went down the stairs. 'But Father Wilfred made himself available for confession when we came here.'

They had stopped in the hallway outside Father Bernard's room. Mummer had her arms folded in the way she had started doing since he had arrived at Saint Jude's.

'I see,' said Father Bernard. He nodded at the door of the under-stairs cupboard. 'Not in here, surely?'

Mummer gave him an indulgent smile.

'No, we used Father Wilfred's room. The room you're in. It has the little curtain around the wash stand you see.'

'Ah.'

'He was very accommodating.'

'I'm sure.'

Mummer moved closer to him. 'I don't ask for myself particularly, Father,' she said. 'It's the others. Mr and Mrs Belderboss really. They find this place, this time of year, well it encourages an openness with God. A chance to cleanse the soul.'

He held Mummer lightly by the shoulders. 'Mrs Smith,' he said, 'rest assured that I will listen to whatever you wish to tell me.'

'Thank you, Father,' said Mummer. 'Now about Andrew.'

'Aye?'

'It's very important that he fasts like the rest of us over the weekend. I'm sure you'll agree that he must be properly prepared.'

'Aye, of course.'

'Then I'll need your help, Father.'

'Naturally, Mrs Smith.'

'Now, when we get to the shrine itself . . .'

They moved off into the kitchen but I knew what Mummer was saying to him. What she wanted him to do. How they would get Hanny to drink the water. How the power of Jesus would cleanse his body and drive out the sickness that had kept him silent since the day he was born.

When they had closed the door, I went back to the bedroom. Hanny was standing by the window. He had taken the rifle out from under the blanket. He saluted me, fiddled with the firing pin, twisted the sight and before I could tell him to put it down, he pointed the rifle at me and pulled the trigger.

# 6

FOR A MOMENT I thought I was dead. I was dead and it was all right. I was strangely relieved that it was all over and that it had been as quick and painless as I'd always hoped it would be. But Hanny was still there, I was still in the room, we were still at Moorings. I realised that I'd been holding my breath and now I let it out and went over to him.

'Give,' I said.

Hanny refused and turned away from me, clutching the rifle to his chest. They were forever taking his stuff off him at Pinelands and the bugger had learnt to fight his corner. I was proud of him for that but I couldn't have him thinking that he could parade around Moorings with a rifle. Mummer would have had a fit, I would have got the blame, and that would have been the end of that.

'I said give it to me.'

I held out my hands and sensing that I was serious Hanny passed me the rifle. I wound the strap around the stock, slotted it under the floorboards and laid the rug back over the top.

Hanny sat down on his bed and then folded up his legs the way a child might do, grasping his ankles and shuffling his feet under his backside. He picked up the book Father

Bernard had removed from the bedside table and opened it. He wanted me to read to him.

'You need to go to sleep, Hanny,' I said. 'You heard Mummer. She'll only get cross.'

He flipped through a few pages until he found the story that he wanted.

'All right, Hanny. But afterwards you've got to go to sleep or I'll get it in the neck.'

⁊

We had barely got halfway through the story before Hanny was snoring. I turned off the lamp but I couldn't sleep at all and lay there in the darkness for a while before I fetched a torch out of my bag, took up the loose floorboard and brought out the rifle to look at it again. I felt around the metalwork and found the bolt that opened the receiver. It was empty of course. I closed it up again with a quiet click and then slipped it back under the floorboards.

I lay down on my bed once more and tried to sleep but I was too restless, and rather than staring at the dark, I went out to look at the photographs of the taxidermist and his wife that had been placed at intervals up the stairs.

He had been a diminutive man and looked to have owned only one shirt in the whole of his time at Moorings. He wore bottle-end glasses and slicked his hair back over his head. He looked a little like Charles Hawtrey, I thought. Or Himmler.

In each shot, he and his wife posed with a stuffed animal between them. A lioness. A beaver up on its back legs. A kangaroo wearing boxing gloves. The date neatly written in the corner.

The poor sod. Apparently he lost it when his wife died. Ended up sectioned in some hospital near Preston, where I always imagined him painting those seascapes over and over again. The boats getting a little smaller and the clouds a little bigger each time, until there was nothing but tempest.

As I was looking at the photographs, someone came out of the sitting room and knocked softly at Father Bernard's door. From the sniffing I knew it was Mrs Belderboss.

'Hello, Father,' she said, when the door opened.

'Mrs Belderboss.'

'Did Esther mention confession to you?'

'She did.'

'Could I come in, Father?'

'Aye, of course,' said Father Bernard. 'But are you sure you want to? It's getting late.'

Mrs Belderboss's voice went down to a whisper. 'I know, but Reg is asleep on the sofa,' she said. 'And I thought while I've the opportunity. There's been something I've been wanting to get off my chest for a while now.'

She went into Father Bernard's room and closed the door. I stayed very still to try and hear what was going on but there were only mumbles. Even at the foot of the stairs, their voices were muffled. I checked that no one else was around and slipped into the broom cupboard. Settling in next to the brushes and mops I could hear them both clearly. The wall between the cupboard and Father Bernard's room was only made out of plywood and where the damp had warped the wood there were gaps that let in little skewers of light.

I didn't mean to stay. As an ethical crime, it fell off the

end of the scale. Listening to Mrs Belderboss's confession was like watching her take off her clothes. But now that I was ensconced, it would have been difficult to get out again without making a racket, and I reasoned that it was better to stay put and wait until they had finished. I couldn't imagine that Mrs Belderboss had very much to confess anyway.

I heard the chinking of the metal rings as Father Bernard yanked the curtain around the washbasin.

Mrs Belderboss rhymed off the Act of Contrition and Father Bernard said, 'What is it you want to tell me?'

'It's Reg, Father,' said Mrs Belderboss.

'Aye?'

'I'm worried about him.'

'Why's that?'

'He won't sleep, Father. At home, I mean. He just lies there, staring at the ceiling until he gets up and goes out.'

'Where does he go?'

'Well, this is it. I've asked him but he won't answer me, not properly. He just says he can't sleep and walks around to take his mind off things. Off what things? I ask him, but he just changes the subject, or gets cross with me.'

'Is it his brother, do you think?'

'Father Wilfred? No. I don't think so. Reg would have said if that was bothering him. If anything, he's been remarkably philosophical since he passed away.'

'You know, Mrs Belderboss,' said Father Bernard. 'It's often hard to explain how we feel when someone close to us dies. Even to those we love. People can put on a bit of a brave front. Wilfred did pass away very unexpectedly. Maybe Mr Belderboss hasn't quite come to terms with it yet. Grief is a peculiar business anyway and when it's compounded with shock, it can take a wee while longer to get over it.'

'A month he's been at it now. Lord alone knows what the neighbours must think.'

There was a pause and then Father Bernard said, 'What is it you want to confess exactly, Mrs Belderboss?'

'Well,' she said. 'I was so worried about him, Father, wandering around at all hours, what with his heart and his hip. You hear such dreadful things, don't you? There are all sorts of odd folk about at night who wouldn't think twice about taking advantage of someone vulnerable like Reg.'

'Aye, go on.'

'Well, I went to the chemist to see if there was anything they could give me.'

'I'm not sure I'm following you, Mrs Belderboss.'

'For Reg. To take. To help him sleep.'

'And did they?'

'Yes. Only he wouldn't take them, would he? You know what he's like.'

'Aye.'

'So I crushed up one of the pills and put it into his Horlicks.'

Father Bernard cleared his throat.

'I feel awful, Father, but I couldn't stand it any more. I'm frightened he's going, you know. It happens, doesn't it? It always starts with little things like this. They say you've got to watch out for the warning signs, don't they?'

'And did it work?' Father Bernard asked. 'The medicine?'

'It was the first decent night he'd had for weeks, but

the guilt of it's been playing on my mind and now *I* can't sleep. It was wicked, wasn't it, Father?'

'I wouldn't call it that, Mrs Belderboss.'

'But drugging my own husband.'

'Mrs Belderboss,' said Father Bernard. 'When I look at you and your husband I see the love that God would wish us all to have if it were possible. There is no malice in your heart. The worst you're guilty of is a little desperation and that puts you in the company of a good many others, believe me. Go and say your rosary and pray for God's help to be patient with Reg. He'll tell you what's wrong in his own time.'

'Are you sure that's all I need to do, Father?'

'Quite sure.'

There was a pause and then Father Bernard spoke again.

'You seem a little disappointed, Mrs Belderboss.'

'No, Father.'

'Were you expecting me to say something else?'

'No.'

There was a moment of silence and then Mrs Belderboss sighed.

'Oh, I don't know. Perhaps you're right about Wilfred, Father. It's only been a few months after all. And the way he went was, well, sudden, as you say.'

'Aye.'

'He'll get tired of all this gadding about, won't he, Father? Once he's stopped feeling so upset.'

'I'm sure that'll be the case, Mrs Belderboss,' said Father Bernard. 'It's still raw in his mind. It's going to take time. I don't think you ever stop feeling for people that have died, but the feelings themselves do change if you give them time. I missed my mammy and daddy terrible when they went, so much that I didn't even want to think about them. It took a while but when I talk about them now it's a joy; it's when I feel closest to them and I know that they haven't really gone anywhere. It's not unlike our relationship with God, Mrs Belderboss. How's your Joshua?'

'Sorry, Father?'

'Joshua, verse one. "Be strong and courageous. Do not be afraid; do not be discouraged, for the Lord, your God, will be with you wherever you go."'

Father Bernard laughed quietly.

'Sorry,' he said. 'I can be an awful show-off with that one. They made me learn it by heart at school.'

'And you're right, of course, Father,' Mrs Belderboss said. 'I know in my heart of hearts that Wilfred's looking down on us and keeping us safe, it's just he seems so – absent.'

'And I think grief comes from that very contradiction,' Father Bernard replied.

'Yes, perhaps it does, Father.'

'Try and have a good night's sleep, Mrs Belderboss, and I'm sure in the morning things won't seem quite so bad.'

'I'll try, Father. Goodnight.'

I listened to her going past me and up the stairs. When it was quiet, I crept out and went back to my own room and held the rifle once more before I went to sleep.

# 7

L ATE IN THE night, I heard far-off voices. Shouting.
Whooping. Like a war dance. It only lasted for a few
seconds and I wasn't sure if I was dreaming, but in the
morning everyone was talking about it around the breakfast
table where the smell of toast mingled with the stew
Mummer had been making since first light.

'I didn't sleep a wink afterwards,' said Mrs Belderboss.

'I wouldn't worry about it,' said Father Bernard. 'It
was probably just farmers calling in their dogs, eh
Monro?'

He reached down and rubbed at Monro's neck.

'At three in the morning?' Mrs Belderboss said.

'Farmers do keep odd hours, Mary,' said Mummer.

'Well I wish they wouldn't.'

'I thought it sounded as if it was coming up from the
sea,' said Mr Belderboss. 'Didn't you?'

Everyone shrugged and finished drinking their tea. Only
Miss Bunce passed any more comment.

'At Glasfynydd, it's totally silent at night,' she said.

Mummer looked at her and took the dirty plates and
bowls out to wash.

I didn't say anything, and I couldn't be certain that
the wind blustering around the house in the early hours

hadn't tricked my ears, but as I'd lain there in the dark, I had been convinced that the voices were coming from the woods.

I wondered if I ought to catch Father Bernard as everyone was leaving the dining room and tell him, but there was a crash from the kitchen and we could hear Mummer shouting.

When I went to see what had happened, she had Hanny tipped back over the sink, her fingers inside his mouth. Hanny was gripping the edge of the basin. The dish of stew that was to be eaten later that evening lay in pieces on the floor in a slick of beef and gravy.

'Spit it out,' Mummer said. 'Get rid of it.'

Hanny swallowed whatever was in his mouth and Mummer gave a sigh of exasperation and let go of him.

Father Bernard appeared behind me. Then Farther.

'What's the matter, Mrs Smith?' said Father Bernard.

'Andrew's been at the stew,' she said.

'Sure, he's not had all that much,' he laughed.

'I told you, Father. He's got to fast, like the rest of us,' said Mummer. 'It's very important. He's got to be properly prepared.'

'I don't think a mouthful of casserole will do much damage, Esther,' said Farther.

'He's had half the lot,' said Mummer, pointing to the brown puddle that Monro was sniffing with interest.

Father Bernard called him away but Mummer flicked her hand dismissively.

'No, let him eat it, Father. It's all it's good for now.'

Hanny started to lick his fingers, and Mummer gasped and grabbed him by the arm and marched him over to the back door. She opened it to the hiss of rain and pushed

Hanny's fingers further into his mouth until he emptied his stomach on the steps.

I cleaned him up at the kitchen sink and then took him to the bedroom to lie down.

∞

I tried to get him to go back to sleep but he was still wound up and kept on wandering to the toilet. Each time he came back he looked paler than the last, his eyes red and sore. In the end he came and sat on the edge of my bed and rattled his jam jar of nails.

'Where does it hurt, Hanny?' I said, touching him on the temples, the forehead, the crown.

He put his hands over his head like a helmet. It hurt everywhere.

'Try and sleep, Hanny,' I said. 'You'll feel better.'

He looked at me and then touched the mattress.

'Yes, all right,' I said. 'But only for a little while.'

I lay next to him and after a few minutes he began snoring. I extracted myself as quietly as possible and went outside.

It had stopped raining and the last of the water was trickling down the old gutters that ran through the cobbles to a large iron drain in the middle of the yard.

Outside, as well as in, Moorings felt like a place that had been repeatedly abandoned. A place that had failed. The drystone walls that formed the yard were broken down to a puzzle of odd-sized rocks that no one had ever had the skill to rebuild, and so the gaps had been merely strung with wire. There was a small, tin-roofed outhouse in one corner, locked and chained, and plastered with bird muck. And beyond the yard stretched wide, empty fields that had been left fallow for so long that the rusting farm machinery that had been there since we'd first started coming here was now almost buried under the nettles and brambles.

The wind came rushing in off the sea, sweeping its comb through the scrubby grass and sending a shiver through the vast pools of standing water. I felt the wire moving forward and Father Bernard was standing next to me.

'Andrew all right now?'

'Yes, Father. He's sleeping.'

'Good.'

He smiled and then nodded towards the sea. 'You used to come here every year, Tonto?'

'Yes.'

He made a quick sound of disbelief with his lips.

'Can't have been much fun for a wee lad,' he said.

'It was all right.'

'It reminds me of the place I grew up,' he said. 'I couldn't wait to get away. I tell you, when they sent me to the Ardoyne, the place they gave me in the Bone was a paradise compared with Rathlin Island. It had an indoor toilet, for a start.'

'What's it like? Belfast?' I said.

I'd seen it night after night on the news. Barricades and petrol bombs.

He looked at me, understood what I was getting at, and gazed across the field again. 'You don't want to know, Tonto,' he said. 'Believe me.'

'Please, Father.'

'Why the sudden interest?'

I shrugged.

'Another time, eh? Suffice to say the Crumlin Road in July isn't much fun.'

He nodded across the field.

'I was going to take a walk,' he said. 'Do you want to come?'

He parted the wire and I climbed through and did the same for him. Once through, he brushed down his jacket and we walked towards the Panzer, disturbing a pair of curlews that burst out of the grass and clapped away.

'She means well,' Father Bernard said. 'Your mother. She only wants to help Andrew.'

'I know.'

'She may not seem it, but she's frightened more than anything else.'

'Yes.'

'And fear can make people do funny things.'

'Yes, Father. I know.'

He patted me on the shoulder and then put his hands in his pockets.

'Will he get better?' I said. It slipped out before I could help it.

Father Bernard stopped walking and looked back at the house.

'What do you mean by better, Tonto?'

I hesitated and Father Bernard thought for a second before he rephrased the question.

'I mean, what would you change in him?' he said.

I hadn't thought about it before.

'I don't know, Father. That he could talk.'

'Is that something you'd like? For him to talk?'

'Yes.'

76

'You don't sound all that sure.'

'I am sure, Father.'

'Do you think it makes Andrew unhappy? Not being able to talk?'

'I don't know. It doesn't seem to.'

He considered this with a deep breath and then spoke.

'Look,' he said. 'I don't know if Andrew will get better in the way you want him to. That's up to God to decide. All you can do is pray and put your trust in Him to make the right decisions about Andrew's happiness. You do still pray, don't you, Tonto?'

'Yes.'

He gave me a wry smile. Even as he asked the question I think he knew that I didn't and hadn't for some time. Priests are like doctors. They know that people lie about the things they think will disappoint them.

We came to the Panzer and Father Bernard laid his hand against the rock and felt its texture. He ran his finger up a long crack and picked at a clod of moss, teasing the fibres of it between his fingers.

'God understands it's not all plain sailing, you know. He allows you to question your faith now and again,' he said, looking closely at the fossils, the tiny bivalves and ammonites. 'Come on now, mastermind, what does it say in Luke fifteen?'

'Something about lost sheep?'

'Aye. See, if you can remember that, sure you're not damned for all eternity just yet.'

He moved around the rock, feeling for hand holds and pulled himself up onto the top. He put his hands on his hips as he surveyed the view, then something under his feet caught his attention.

'Hey, Tonto,' he called down. 'Come up here.'

He was on his knees, paddling his fingers in a hole full of water. He looked at my puzzled expression.

'It's a bullaun,' he said. 'We had one on the farm when I was a wee boy.'

He looked at me again and took hold of my hand, pressing my fingers to the edges of the hole.

'Feel that?' How smooth it is? That's not been made by water. It was cut by a man.'

'What's it for, Father?'

'They made them hundreds of years ago to collect rain. They thought the water was magical if it didn't touch the ground, you see.'

He stood up and dried his hands on his coat.

'My granny used to make the cows drink out of the one in our field,' he said. 'And if I ever had a fever, she'd take me down there and wash me in it to make me better.'

'Did it work?'

He looked at me and frowned and gave a little laugh. 'No, Tonto, it didn't,' he said.

He climbed down and I was about to do the same when I noticed the Land Rover parked on the road down below. I could tell it was Clement's by the cross painted on the door, though Clement wasn't inside.

The two men in the front had their faces turned towards me, though it was hard to tell whether they were staring at me or Moorings or the woods behind. Whatever they were looking at, it was clear even from this distance that it was the two men Father Bernard had asked for help the day before. The one built like a bull and the one with the dog. Parkinson and Collier.

'What do you think those noises were last night, Father?'
I asked.

'Between you and me,' he replied, 'I didn't hear a thing.'

'But you said it was farmers.'

'It was a wee fib.'

'You lied to them?'

'Ah come on, Tonto, I was just trying to reassure them
that they weren't going to get murdered in their beds. Are
you coming?'

'Yes, Father.'

I looked back at the Land Rover and after a moment
the driver set off in a plume of steel-coloured smoke.

ဢ

Hanny was still asleep when I got back. Mummer hadn't
yet forgiven him and the effort of rousing him and getting
him dressed and nursing his headache was too much for her
to cope with. So she allowed him to stay in bed while they
went off to church for the Blessing of the Oils and the
Washing of the Feet. It wasn't an integral part of his preparation for the shrine and he would only spoil it if he came.

'But don't let him lounge around all day,' said Mummer,
looking up the stairs as they were all leaving.

'Keep out of mischief,' Farther added as he plucked his
flat cap from the peg and helped Mr and Mrs Belderboss
out.

I watched them go and when I closed the front door
and turned around, Hanny was standing at the top of the
stairs. He had been waiting for them to leave too. Now
we could go down to the beach at last. We could leave
their world and find ours.

# 8

SINCE WE HAD decided to come back to Moorings, I had rehearsed the journey down to the beach many times, trying to re-imagine the road and what I used to be able to see on either side. Now that I was here and walking across the marshes with Hanny it all seemed to unfold as it should. I remembered the single, twisted hawthorn tree overhanging the road, like the sole survivor of a shipwreck that had staggered inland, torn and cowed by the sea. I remembered the way the wind rasped through the reeds and shuddered across the black water. The way the sea hung between the valleys of the dunes.

This was the real world, the world as it should be, the one that was buried in London by concrete plazas and shopping parades of florists, chip shops and bookmakers; hidden under offices and schools and pubs and bingo halls.

Things lived at the Loney as they ought to live. The wind, the rain, the sea were all in their raw states, always freshly born and feral. Nature got on with itself. Its processes of death and replenishment happened without anyone noticing apart from Hanny and me.

When we came to the base of the dunes, we veered from the road and took off our boots to feel the cold sand under our feet.

I slung the rifle around so that it sat against my back and helped Hanny up. He had insisted on bringing the stuffed rats with him in his school satchel and kept slipping down, gouging deep scars into the sand with his feet.

At the top we could see the grey sea spreading out towards the horizon that was pressed flat by the huge block of sky. The tide was coming in quickly, washing over the mudflats.

Everything here was as it always had been, apart from the botched swastika someone had spraypainted on the side of the pillbox as a companion to the letters *NF*.

'How are you feeling now, Hanny?' I said and put my hand on his brow, the way Mummer did to check his temperature.

He smiled and shook his head. The headache had gone.

'Mummer means well,' I said. 'She's just worried that you won't get better. Fear can make people do funny things, you know.'

We walked down onto the beach, following a ragged trail of debris. Seagulls had been strangled by the sea into sodden, twisted things of bones and feathers. Huge grey tree stumps, smoothed to a metallic finish had been washed up like abandoned war-time ordnance. All along the beach, in fact, the sea had left its offerings like a cat trying to curry favour with its owner. The Loney had always been a dumping ground for the North's detritus, and tangled with the seaweed were shoes and bottles, milk crates and tyres. Yet all of it would be gone at the next high tide, raked back into the jumble of the sea.

With a difficulty that I didn't remember from the last time we'd come here, we climbed up onto the roof of the pillbox and stood either side of the hole. Inside it was deeply carpeted with sand. Pools of seawater sat in the gloom.

Hanny jumped down first and held me round the waist as I came down through the hole. Someone had been in here: the same person who had sprayed the outside wall, no doubt. It smelled of urine and spent matches. There was litter thrown up against one corner. Beer cans and chip wrappers. But despite all that, it remained more or less as sturdy as when it had first been built. There was never any bombing here and until we had claimed it for our own, I doubted that it had ever been manned at all. The Loney was just a place the Luftwaffe passed on their way to the Clyde. And the Third Reich never did come marauding up the Irish Sea in the end, of course.

We'd had to smash a hole in the roof to get inside – as the dunes had swallowed the back end where the door was – and the side facing the sea had begun to reveal its rusty skeleton, but it still felt as though it would last forever.

Using our hands we picked up and dumped the sand against the walls. Hanny worked like a machine, raking great clods of the stuff between his legs, checking his watch to see how long it was taking him.

Once there was space, Hanny opened the satchel and carefully arranged the rats on the floor and then his toy soldiers to face them. I took the rifle off my shoulder and positioned it through one of the gun slits, fitting my eye to the rubber cup at the end of the sight. It took time to get it right – for a few seconds there was only the magnification of my own eyelashes – but once I had the sea contained in the circle, it was brought to me sharp and silent.

The horizon I had seen with the naked eye from the

top of the dunes was dragged closer and replaced by another much further out. A boat with a white sail that had been too far away to see before tracked slowly from one edge of my vision to the other, rising and falling, outrun by the terns and gulls scudding over the waves. There was another world out there that no one else but I could see.

I fancied myself as a naval captain on the lookout for U-boats, or a lone gunner charged with the defence of the coastline.

Those sorts of games only ever seemed real at the Loney. London was hard to convert into the kinds of places the men in *Commando* seemed to find themselves.

Although I had assassinated the park keeper – who morphed from one important Gestapo officer to another – several times from a hideout in the huge oak tree by the tennis courts and blown Mummer to pieces when she stepped on the land mine I'd buried in the vegetable patch, the parks, our garden, they were too prim and clean.

The cemetery up in Golders Green with its flat, white graves that looked as though they had been levelled by a bomb blast made for a half-decent blitzed town, but the groundsman had a dog that was supposed to be rabid. And anyway I could only play there on Saturdays, when the Jews weren't allowed to do anything, even visit the dead.

At the Loney, on the other hand, one could be at Sword Beach, Iwo Jima, Arnhem, El Alamein without much strain on the imagination. The pillbox was easily transformed into a cell in a German prisoner of war camp, which we'd fight our way out of with our bare hands, thwacking *Achtung!*-ing Nazis in freeze frames. Or it was a jungle hideout from which we watched a line of buck-toothed

Japs come stalking through the marram and the sea holly and then we'd unzipper them with a burst of machine-gun fire before they had time to draw breath. The Japs were cruel and devious but screeched like girls when they died. They were always weaker than the Krauts and the Krauts were always more arrogant than the Brits, who naturally won every time.

'Here,' I said and Hanny, half crouching, took over, adjusting his grip, squinting into the sight. I moved to the slit next to Hanny's and watched the hordes of birds come in with the rushing tide, ransacking the foaming bore for the things dragged along in its thrust, or heading inland to the marshes with food for their young.

A flock of gulls came to land, squabbling over some dead thing from which they tore bits of fur and skin, the craftier ones making off with larger portions – a cluster of innards, or bones still jointed in the middle.

The sudden boom of the sea against the rocks close by scared them and they took off together, screeching and honking. All but one. A large gull thrashed about on the sand, trying to lift itself out of the incoming water. It beat one wing against the air, while the other stuck out from its body at an angle. It had been broken in the scrum.

It cawed, nuzzled at its leg and then resumed its strange dance, hopping one, two, three steps, lifting off and tumbling back onto the sand.

Hanny looked at me.

'We'll have to kill it,' I said. 'It's cruel to leave it in pain.'

Hanny frowned. He didn't understand. I took the rifle off him and mimed stoving the bird in with the butt. He nodded and we climbed out of the pillbox and watched the seagull floundering on the sand. It stared back, wide-eyed.

'It's the right thing to do,' I said, and gave Hanny the rifle.

He looked at me and smiled and then he turned his head sharply the other way, when he heard the sound of a car. I took the rifle back and ushered Hanny up onto the dunes, making for a natural trough in the grass, from where we could lie flat and observe the road across the marshes.

Once the car had passed the hawthorn tree, I could see through the crosshairs of the sight that it was the one that had passed us when we'd broken down on our way to Moorings.

This time there were three people in the car. Two in the front – a man and a woman – and one in the back, presumably the sleeping girl. The car slowed and as it came closer the tyres threw out waves of spray before passing through the gap in the dunes and coming to a halt on the fringes of the beach. Seeing that the sandflats were rapidly disappearing, the driver reversed. The engine idled for a moment, then shrivelled away to a rapid ticking as the mechanisms cooled under the bonnet. The birds that had been frightened away returned to what they were doing – the gulls coming down again to fight over the carcass on the beach, the curlews chunnering in the grass.

We moved carefully along the ridge and at the end where it sloped down to the road, we pressed ourselves into the sand. Parting the grass with the muzzle, I could see the front passenger more clearly now. Mummer would have thought her common for the way she was applying lipstick in the mirror of the sun visor, rolling her lips in and out. She was the kind of woman Mummer would have pointed out to Farther. The kind of woman she would have commented on.

Lifting her chin and turning her head, she began clearing up some imperfection in the corner of her open mouth with a folded arrowhead of tissue and then ran the tip of her little finger down her philtrum, giving it a flick at the end.

The driver distracted her for a moment and she turned to face him. There was evidently some kind of disagreement and the woman went back to her preening, impatiently dabbing powder across her cheeks and nose and pausing to shout something halfway through the process.

Inching to the right, I could see the girl sitting in the back. She leant forward and tried to intervene, but the adults in the front ignored her and she stared out of the window instead.

She looked straight at me, but didn't see me. I was careful to stay well hidden. I always was. When I played my games in London, I could be as silent as the dead in the Jewish cemetery. Deader than the dead.

Watching the girl, I didn't even hear my own breath, only sensed its warmth coming and going on my trigger finger.

Hanny was shaking my arm.

'What's the matter?'

He showed me his empty wrist, marked red from his watch strap.

'Did you drop it?' I said.

Hanny looked at his wrist again.

The driver finally got out and stood with the door open. He adjusted his tweed trilby, looked up at the seagulls and at the marshes through which they had just driven. I heard the clank of a lighter opening; a moment later the wind blew copper-blue smoke towards me, bringing the sweet dung smell of the man's cigar and the woman's voice.

'What are we going to do, Leonard?' she said, and the man ducked down to speak to her.

'The tide will be going out soon,' he said.

'Before dark?'

'Of course.'

'We can't have her sitting here in the cold for hours in her condition. We need to get her back across to the house.'

'I know. Don't worry about it.'

They argued quietly and I caught her name as he lifted his head again and tacked it contemptuously onto the end of his sentence. Laura.

Hanny was scuffling about in the sand looking for his watch. I nudged him to be quiet. Leonard slammed the car door, sending little birds flapping away, and stepped down off the road onto the sand. He walked away and stood watching the injured gull with an amused curiosity. He took off his hat, brushed it with the back of his hand and put it back on.

In his toffee-coloured jacket and his expensive shoes, he looked as out of place here as his Daimler. He was a lounge lizard, a spiv, a bent bookie with fingers full of sovereign rings and his blue shirt open two buttons at the collar. A smell of aftershave drifted up from him – a coniferous sap stirred with a fumigant like the stuff Farther sprayed over his roses to kill off the aphids.

Laura got out and fiddled with the boot of the car, eventually unlocking it and calling to Leonard. He sloped back up onto the tarmac and went over to her. They had a conversation that I couldn't hear properly, then Laura went to open the girl's door. Leonard grappled with something in the boot, heaved, twisted and finally dragged out a wheelchair that by pressing some lever with his foot sprang open.

Laura held the door and Leonard parked the chair with its seat facing the girl. She inched slowly out, puffing and wincing as she held onto her belly. She was as pregnant as it was possible to be.

Leonard held her hand as she shuffled towards the open door and when she was close enough half fell into the chair, making it creak with her weight. She ran her fingers through her coppery hair and tucked it behind her ears and grimaced again. She was younger than me; thirteen or fourteen, I guessed. One of those girls that every school had. Even the Catholic comps. Girls that Mummer and the other ladies at Saint Jude's pretended they didn't like to talk about. They had probably brought her here to have the baby in this deserted place out of shame.

Leonard wheeled her to the edge of the road and carefully down onto the beach, where he headed towards the pillbox, leaving thin tyre tracks and scattering gulls from a pile of weed fizzing with flies. In her heels, Laura followed more slowly, coming to a standstill now and then as she decided how best to negotiate the swathes of wrack and litter.

She was dressed out of her time, somehow, like I imagined fashionable women might have dressed in the 1930s – a bottle-green coat with a stole made from an entire fox, a short haircut parted at the side.

Leonard set the wheelchair so that it faced the sea. Laura stayed with the girl and Leonard went off to investigate the pillbox. I put him in the sights and tracked him as he crossed the beach slowly and awkwardly with a gait that suggested a gammy knee. He came to the pillbox, looked at it, removed his shoes and took his hands out of his pockets so that he could swing his arms and get up the drift of sand. Rather satisfyingly, he slipped a few times on his bad leg before he managed to put his fingers into one of the gun slits and pull himself up.

Making a visor with his hands, he peered inside and then suddenly jerked backwards, losing his footing and sliding ridiculously, one leg outstretched and the other crooked in such a way that it rolled him slowly but unavoidably onto his back. His shoes came out of his hand and tumbled away.

He got up, looked to see if anyone had witnessed his fall, and twisted to wipe the sand off his backside, before limping along the foot of the dunes in search of his brogues. He found one nestled in a pile of bladderwrack and stopped right underneath us to put it back on.

Having heard his involuntary cry, Laura made her way towards him.

'Are you all right?' she asked.

'Full of bloody rats.' Leonard nodded to the pillbox.

Laura smiled to herself and took out a packet of cigarettes.

'Well, you will come to these sorts of places,' she said, lighting up.

Leonard gave her a look. She walked away and picked up his other shoe, tipped it over, let a stream of sand come out and gave it back. Leonard slipped it on and then bent down to pick up something else – it was Hanny's watch. He thumbed away the sand, shook it, put it to his ear and then stuck it in his pocket.

I turned to tell Hanny, but he was staring past me over to where the girl was sitting in the wheelchair. The injured gull had stopped shrieking and was hopping tentatively over to her outstretched hand. When it was close to her, it angled its head and nipped at the weed she was holding, its damaged wing open like a fan. It came again for another feed and stayed this time. The girl stroked its neck and touched its feathers. The bird regarded her for a moment and then lifted off silently, rising, joining the others turning in a wheel under the clouds.

# 9

SPRING DROWNED THE Loney.

Day after day, the rain swept in off the sea in huge, vaporous curtains that licked Coldbarrow from view and then moved inland to drench the cattle fields. The beach turned to brown sludge and the dunes ruptured and sometimes crumbled altogether, so that the sea and the marsh water united in vast lakes, undulating with the carcasses of uprooted trees and bright red carrageen ripped from the sea bed.

Those were the worst days; the days of mist and driving rain, when Moorings dripped and leaked and the air was permanently damp. There was nowhere to go and nothing to do but wait for the weather to change. And sitting by the bay window of the front room watching the water flowing down the fields and the lanes, listening to the rooks barking in the cold woods, filled me with a sense of futility that I can remember even now.

I've not said anything to Doctor Baxter about Moorings or the Loney but he says he can tell that I'm harbouring a lot of negativity from the past – his words – and that I ought to try and let it go.

I told him that with me working in a museum the past was something of an occupational hazard and he laughed and wrote something down on his notepad. I can't seem to do or say anything without him making a note of it. I feel like a damn specimen.

∽

With everyone stuck indoors, Moorings began to feel more and more cramped, and as we waited for a break in the weather people drifted away from the sitting room to find their own space. Mummer and Mr and Mrs Belderboss split off to different parts of the house to see if they could root out some decent cutlery to use instead of the huge, tarnished implements we'd made do with so far. Farther went to look at the rosemaling on the old furniture in the study. Miss Bunce and David sat at opposite ends of an ottoman reading. Hanny was upstairs drawing pictures of the girl he had seen at the Loney. The girl and the gull with the broken wing.

Only Father Bernard ventured out, taking Monro on a long walk that brought him back late in the afternoon.

I was in the kitchen, making Hanny some tea, when he came through the door saturated and dripping. He took off his cap and wrung it out on the doorstep. Monro sat beside him, blinking away rainwater and panting.

'And there's me thinking that the good Lord promised not to flood the world again,' he said, hanging his coat on the back of the door. 'I hope you've started work on the ark, Tonto.'

He ruffled his hair with his fingertips and sent Monro off to the corner where there was an old blanket on the floor.

'Your mother's been hard at work, I see,' he said, dusting his hands and going over to the stove where Mummer had something simmering. He lifted the lid and his face was swathed in vapours.

'God preserve us,' he said. 'It's a good job I have a will of iron. Otherwise I'd have a spoon in this before you could say jack rabbit.'

Mummer appeared and closed the door behind her. Father Bernard put the lid back on the pot and smiled.

'God bless you, Mrs Smith,' he said. 'My old teacher in seminary always said that there was no better way to praise the Lord than feeding a priest. Mind you, I'm not sure whose side you're on, tempting me like this.'

Mummer folded her arms.

'We were wondering, Father, if you knew about the arrangements for wet days,' she said.

Father Bernard's smile wavered a little. 'No, I don't think so.'

'When it was too wet to go out anywhere,' said Mummer, 'Father Wilfred liked to gather everyone together for prayers at ten, noon and four. To give a structure to the day. Otherwise it's all too easy for people to get distracted. Hunger can do funny things to the mind. Pledges get broken. Father Wilfred always made sure that we stayed focused on our sacrifice so that we would remember the greater one.'

'I see,' said Father Bernard.

Mummer looked at her watch.

'It's almost four, Father,' she said. 'There's still time. As long as it won't keep you from whatever else you need to do.'

He looked at her. 'No, that's quite all right,' he said and he went off to dry himself and to change his trousers, while Mummer gathered everyone in the sitting room to wait for him.

'Give him time,' Mrs Belderboss was saying as I came in. 'He's doing his best.'

'I'm sure he didn't need to be out for quite so long,' Mummer retorted.

'They need a lot of exercise those sorts of dogs,' said Mrs Belderboss.

'Well, perhaps he ought not to have brought his dog with him,' said Mummer.

'He couldn't very well have left it behind now could he? And anyway, I'm sure the boys are enjoying having a dog around, aren't you?'

She looked at me and smiled.

'Father Wilfred would never have kept a dog,' said Mummer.

'Everyone's different, Esther.'

'That's as may be,' she replied. 'But it's not the dog I'm concerned about.'

'Oh?'

'I'm sure I smelled drink on him when he came in just now.'

'On Father Bernard?'

'Yes.'

'I don't think so.'

'My father was a drunk, Mary,' said Mummer. 'I think I know the stench of ale well enough.'

'But even so.'

'I know what I smelled.'

'All right, Esther,' said Mrs Belderboss. 'Don't get upset.'

Mummer turned on me and frowned.

'Instead of earwigging,' she said, 'why don't you make yourself useful and see to the fire.'

I got up and looked in the wicker basket for a chunk

of wood that might last the rest of the afternoon. Mummer sat with her legs crossed, red-faced, her eyes fixed on the door the same way she had watched the road the day we'd met Billy Tapper in the bus shelter. Father Bernard couldn't come back quickly enough.

I'd learnt by now that my grandfather was a disgrace Mummer liked to keep under the carpet along with my uncle Ian who lived with another man in Hastings and a second cousin who had been twice divorced.

I'd asked her about him a number of times in the past, of course – as all boys are interested in their grandfathers – but I still knew little about him other than that he was an alcoholic and a layabout and had spent his short adult life carting his withering liver from one public house to the next until he died one Saturday afternoon in the tap room of the Red Lion, his head on a table of empties.

Eventually, Father Bernard came in, his face red from scrubbing and his hair slicked back over his head. He had his thumb stuck inside his Bible, marking a particular passage that he perhaps thought might redeem him.

'You must be freezing, Father,' said Mrs Belderboss, getting up. 'You have my chair.'

'No no, Mrs Belderboss, don't worry about me, I'm like rhubarb.'

'Come again?'

'I don't mind the cold,' he said.

'Well, if you're sure you're all right,' Mrs Belderboss said and sat back down.

Mr Belderboss stared out of the window.

'Will you look at the weather?' he said.

The rain blustered about the yard and the fields, where mist lingered in stretches over the grass.

'Do you think we might be able to get out tomorrow, Father?' said Miss Bunce.

'I don't know,' Father Bernard replied. 'Perhaps we could listen to the forecast later.'

Mr Belderboss chuckled as he looked at the ancient radio sitting on the sideboard – the sort of dark, wooden thing that would still be broadcasting Churchill's speeches if we were to turn it on.

'Oh, you'll not get a station here, Father,' he said. 'It's the hill, you see. Blocks the signal.'

'Well,' said Father Bernard. 'We'll just have to take it as the Lord gives it. Is that everyone here?'

'No,' said Mummer. 'My husband seems to be dragging his heels somewhere.' She looked at me and gestured at the door. 'Go and see where he is.'

I went to get up when Farther appeared, sorting through the huge bunch of keys Clement had left us.

'Oh, there you are,' said Mummer. 'We were about to send out the search party.'

'Mm?' Farther said, distracted by a small brass key he had twisted off the ring.

'Where have you been?' said Mummer.

'In the study,' he replied.

'All this time? What have you been doing?'

'I've found another room,' he said.

'What are you talking about?' said Mummer.

'At the back of the study,' Farther said. 'There's a little room. I've never seen it before.'

'Are you sure?' Mr Belderboss said.

'You know the old tapestry?' said Farther. 'Between the paintings?'

'Yes?' replied Mr Belderboss.

'I knocked it aside by accident and there was a door behind it.'

'Good Lord,' said Mr Belderboss.

'I thought if I could find a key for it, we might be able to get inside and have a look.'

'Well, it'll have to wait,' said Mummer, gaining Farther's attention for the first time and indicating with her eyes that Father Bernard was poised to lead the prayers.

'Oh, sorry, Father,' he said and sat down.

'We're still missing someone,' said Mrs Belderboss. 'Where's Andrew?'

'He's upstairs resting,' I said.

'Well go and fetch him,' said Mummer.

'Oh, leave him,' said Mrs Belderboss.

'Leave him?' said Mummer. 'He ought to be here if we're praying for him.'

'He's tired,' I said.

'What's that got to do with anything?' said Mummer. 'We're all tired.'

'I know,' said Mrs Belderboss. 'But with all that noise last night, I should think he slept less than any of us. If he's settled, it's probably best to leave him where he is.'

'I agree with Mary,' said Mr Belderboss.

Father Bernard cleared his throat. 'Perhaps we should make a start, Mrs Smith?'

'Esther?' said Farther.

'Yes, all right,' said Mummer sharply and she leant forward to light the candles set out on the table.

Mrs Belderboss sighed and looked out of the window.

'I do hope it improves for when we go to the shrine on Monday,' she said. 'It won't be the same if it's raining, will it, Reg?'

'No,' said Mr Belderboss. 'Not like last time, do you remember?'

Mrs Belderboss turned to Father Bernard. 'It was a glorious day,' she said. 'The sun came out just as we arrived. And the flowers were just beautiful. All the magnolias and the azaleas.'

Father Bernard smiled.

'Everyone was so happy, weren't they, Reg?' she went on. 'Wilfred, especially.'

'It must be nice to have that memory of your brother, Mr Belderboss,' said Father Bernard.

Mr Belderboss nodded. 'I suppose so. They do say that you ought to remember people at their happiest, don't they?'

'Aye,' said Father Bernard. 'I can't see that there's much to be gained by doing anything else.'

Mr Belderboss looked at his hands. 'It's the last time I remember him being so – certain – about everything. After that, I don't know. He just sort of seemed to . . .'

'Seemed to what?' Father Bernard asked.

Mr Belderboss looked around the room at everyone. Mummer narrowed her eyes at him, very slightly, but enough for him to notice and stop talking. There was a moment of silence. Mrs Belderboss touched her husband on the arm and he put his hand over hers. Mummer blew out the match she was holding.

'I thought we were going to begin?' she said.

Father Bernard looked at her and then at Mr Belderboss.

'Sorry, Reg,' he said. 'I didn't mean to upset you.'

'Oh, don't worry about me,' said Mr Belderboss, wiping his eyes with a handkerchief. 'I'm all right. You carry on, Father.'

Father Bernard opened his Bible and handed it to me. 'Would you read for us, Tonto?' he said.

I set the Bible on my knees and read Jesus' instructions to his disciples to prepare for the persecution that would most certainly be coming their way.

'"Brother will betray brother to death, and a father his child; children will rebel against their parents and have them put to death. You will be hated by everyone because of me, but the one who stands firm to the end will be saved."'

Mummer looked at Father Bernard and nodded her approval. The passage was her manifesto. Back at home, it was up in a frame in the kitchen, scribed in ornate calligraphy like the page of an illuminated Bible. Duty, or rather the active show of duty, was everything and to ignore the call to service was, in Mummer's eyes, possibly the most heinous sin of all. She was of the opinion that men should at least consider the priesthood and that all boys should serve on the altar. In some ways, she said, she was envious of me because I had the opportunity to be closer to God, to assist in the miracle of the transubstantiation, whereas she had to make do with organising fêtes and jumble sales.

It had been mooted a number of times since my Confirmation, but when we returned from Moorings the last time, it became Mummer's mission to get me into a cassock. It was time, she said, and it was obvious that Father Wilfred needed help.

'You ought to do it for your brother's sake, if anything,' she said. 'He'll never get the chance.'

I think it came as something of a surprise to her when I agreed so readily. I wanted to be an altar boy. I wanted to be a servant to the Lord. I wanted, more than anything, to see the parts of the church that no one else did.

And so I see myself aged thirteen walking up the path to the presbytery one wet Saturday morning in an ill-fitting beige suit with Mummer's instructions on the etiquette of speaking to a priest fixed firmly in my head. Yes, Father Wilfred. No, Father Wilfred. Speak when you're spoken to. But look interested. Answer his questions like a boy who's been going to church since the day he was born. Don't drop your aitches.

Miss Bunce answered the door and I told her what I'd come for. She let me in and pointed at the row of chairs in the hallway. There was another boy there, suffering from the first fierce assault of acne and breathing loudly. He had been stuffed into an even worse suit than I had, the lapels of which were sprinkled with dandruff and stray hairs. He looked at me and smiled nervously as he put out his hand.

'Did your mother send you too?'

Plump, freckled, a little older than me, poor Henry McCullough with egg breath and spots was to become my opposite number on the altar, performing the parts that required little or no wit. He was a towel holder and a candle straightener. He opened the lid of the organ before Mass and brought out the stool for Miss Bunce to sit on.

'Yes,' I said, to make him feel better. 'She did.'

Father Wilfred came out of the dining room, wiping away the remains of his breakfast from his lips with the corner of a handkerchief. He looked at us both sitting there and weighed us up from our polished shoes to our parted hair.

'Miss Bunce,' he said, nodding to the door. 'Would you be so kind?'

'Yes, Father.'

Miss Bunce withdrew a black umbrella from the stand and handed it to Father Wilfred once he had buttoned his long raincoat. He gave her a rare smile and then clicked his fingers at us to follow him down the gravel path to the church, keeping the umbrella to himself.

**ஐ**

It's gone now, demolished to make way for flats, and much lamented by those who remember it, but I always thought Saint Jude's was a monstrosity.

It was a large brown brick place, built towards the end of the nineteenth century when Catholicism became fashionable again with a people that didn't do things by halves. From the outside it was imposing and gloomy and the thick, hexagonal spire gave it the look of a mill or factory. Indeed, it seemed purpose-built in the same sort of way, with each architectural component carefully designed to churn out obedience, faith or hope in units per week according to demand. Even the way Miss Bunce played the organ made it seem as though she was operating a complicated loom.

As a token bit of mysticism, the mason had fixed an Eye of God way up on the steeple, above the clock – an oval shape carved into a block of stone that I'd noticed on the old country churches Farther dragged us round at weekends. Yet at Saint Jude's, it seemed more like a sharp-eyed overseer of the factory floor, looking out for the workshy and the seditious.

Inside, a bigger than life-sized crucified Christ was carefully suspended in front of a vast window so that when the sun shone his shadow fell among the congregation and touched them all. The pulpit was high up like a watchtower. Even the air felt as though it had been specially commissioned to be church-like; to be soup-thick with sound when Miss Bunce touched the organ keys, and when the nave was empty to be thin enough to let the slightest whisper flutter round the stonework.

'So,' said Father Wilfred, indicating for us to sit on the front pew. 'Let's start at the beginning. McCullough, tell me something about the Penitential Rite.'

Father Wilfred put his hands behind his back and began a slow pacing alongside the altar rail, looking up into the vault like a teacher awaiting the answer to an impenetrable maths question.

Actually, I often thought he had missed his calling on that score. Mummer had cut a photograph of him out of the paper when he'd protested about a new horror film they were showing at the Curzon, and in it he looked every inch the Edwardian schoolmaster – thin and pale behind the round-rimmed glasses, the hair raked into a severe parting.

Henry looked down at his sweaty hands and shifted uncomfortably as though something unpleasant was passing through his gut. Father Wilfred suddenly stopped and turned to face him.

'Problem?'

'I don't know,' said Henry.

'I don't know, Father.'

'Eh?'

'You'll address me as Father.'

'Yes, Father.'

'Well?'

'I still don't know, Father.'

'You don't know if there's a problem or you don't know what the Penitential Rite is?'

'Eh?' said Henry.

'Well at least tell me when it comes in the Introductory Rites, McCullough.'

'I don't know, Father.'

'You wish to be a servant of God and you can't even tell me the order of the Mass?'

Father Wilfred's raised voice echoed briefly around the church. Henry looked at his fingers again.

'You do want to become an altar boy, don't you, McCullough?' Father Wilfred said, more quietly this time.

'Yes, Father.'

He looked at him and then resumed his pacing.

'The Penitential Rite comes at the start of the Mass, McCullough, once the priest has come to the altar. It enables us to confess our sins before God and to cleanse our souls ready for the reception of His holy word.

'Now, Smith,' he said, stopping to buff the golden eagle lectern where Mr Belderboss struggled with the Old Testament names when it was his turn to read, 'what comes after the Penitential Rite?'

'The Kyrie, Father.'

'And then?'

'The Gloria, Father.'

'And then?'

'The Liturgy, Father.'

Suspecting I was being facetious, his eyes narrowed for a second, but he turned and walked back the way he had come.

'Right, McCullough,' he said. 'Let's see if you've been listening. Tell me the order of the Introductory Rites.'

And so it went on until Henry could recite the structure of the Mass down to where people stood, sat or knelt.

While they spoke, I stared at the altar, wondering when we would be allowed up there, if it would *feel* holier beyond the invisible screen where only the privileged directors of the Mass were allowed to penetrate. If the air was different. Sweeter. If I might be allowed to open the tabernacle in the reredos, and look upon the very resting place of God. Whether there was some evidence of Him inside that golden box.

Having passed one test, I was sent away to complete another. I was to go into the office next to the vestry and bring back a pyx, a censer and a chaplet of the Divine Mercy. Father Wilfred handed me a key and then looked at me sternly.

'You are to go to the vestry office and nowhere else,' he said. 'Do you understand?'

'Yes, Father.'

'You are to touch nothing other than the things I have asked for.'

'Yes, Father.'

'Good. On you go.'

The office was cramped and smelled of old books and snuffed wicks. There was a desk and several bookshelves and locked cupboards. In the corner was a sink with a grimy mirror above it. A candle in a red jar guttered in the draught coming through the window frame. But the things which interested me the most, as they would any boy of thirteen, I suppose, were the two crossed swords fastened to the wall – long and slender and curving gently towards their tips – the kind Hanny's Napoleonic soldiers wore. I longed more than anything to hold one of them. To feel my chest tighten like it always did when we sang 'O God of Earth and Altar'.

I searched for the things Father Wilfred had asked me to fetch and found them easily, setting them down on the desk where a few books had been left open.

One had a painting of Jesus standing on the edge of a mountain in the desert being tempted by Satan, who flitted about him like a giant red bat. I didn't like that one at all. It was the Devil of my nightmares, all cloven hooves and horns, with a snake for a tail.

I turned the page and found Simeon Stylites standing on his tower. He was a popular figure in Father Wilfred's sermons. Along with the Rich Fool and the Prodigal Son, he was an example to us all of how we could change, how we could rid ourselves of temporal desire.

Surviving only on the Eucharist, he had lived on top of a stone pillar in the desert so that he could meditate on the Word untouched by the world of sin below him. His devotion was absolute. He had stripped his life to the quick for God. And his reward was that he needed to look no further than heaven for all the things that the sinners beneath him pursued through selfish, lustful means and suffered for in the chase. Food, love, fulfilment, peace. They were all his.

In the painting he had his face turned to the sky and his arms outstretched as though he was letting something go or waiting for something to fall.

Next to it was a photograph album full of pictures of

a place that I recognised. It was the Loney. Shots of the beach, our pillbox, the dunes, the marshes. Dozens of them. These were the photographs he had taken that last morning of the pilgrimage.

He had left a magnifying glass on top of a photograph of the mudflats at low tide, the sea far out, the way over to Coldbarrow clear and Coldbarrow itself a grey mound in the distance. I picked it up and moved it back and forth but couldn't find that there was anything much to see apart from the black sludge and the sea and the low sky. What he had been looking for, I couldn't tell.

'Smith.' Father Wilfred was at the door, with Henry behind him.

'Yes, Father?'

'What are you doing?'

'Nothing, Father,' I said and stood up.

'I trust that you've found what I asked you to find?'

'Yes, Father,' I said and showed him the stuff on the table. He looked at me and came over and picked up each object, turning them in his hands as though he'd never seen them before. After a moment or two he realised that we were waiting for him to dismiss us and he turned sharply.

'On Sunday morning,' he said. 'I shall expect to see you both standing outside the vestry door at nine o'clock on the dot.'

'Yes, Father Wilfred.'

'Let me be absolutely clear,' he said. 'Lateness is not only a discourtesy to me, it is a discourtesy to God, and I will not tolerate it.'

'Yes, Father Wilfred.'

He said no more but drew back the chair I'd been

sitting on and wedged himself under the desk to look at the books. He licked his finger and turned the page in the photograph album and squinted into the magnifying glass.

# 10

EARLY ON GOOD Friday, just before the clock chimed for Saint Matthew, Mummer came into our room and drew back the curtains. Hanny rolled over and snuffled into his pillow.

'Ten minutes,' she said. 'Don't keep us waiting.'

I watched her go and then got out of bed. Outside the sky was obscured by a low swirling cloud of moisture that was somewhere between fog and drizzle. Down in the front garden where the fruit trees dripped and bent in the wind, I saw Father Bernard setting a wooden crucifix against the gate – the last of the fourteen Mummer would have had him distributing round the outside of the house since the first washes of dawn.

Once this was done, he put his hands on the drystone wall and let his head tip forward before coming back inside. He was as tired as I was.

I rolled back the rug, took up the floorboard and checked the rifle. It was still there, of course. I touched the cold metal of the trigger, flicked the little safety catch on and off and tried to imagine what it would be like to fire it. To feel it punch my shoulder. The noise it would make.

The small hand of the clock found Matthew the tax collector and rang five times in soft dabs that seemed to come from deep inside the mechanisms. I put the rifle back and then shook Hanny until he was awake.

He immediately touched his wrist and looked at me expectantly.

'Yes, Hanny,' I said. 'I know. We'll get your watch back today.'

∞

When we got downstairs, everyone was already sitting around the kitchen table in their coats.

'Morning, lads,' said Father Bernard. He had his hand inside a shoe and was scuffing off the dirt in quick movements. 'Sleep well?'

'Yes, Father.'

'Thank you for asking,' Mummer said, looking at me and then to Father Bernard.

'Thank you for asking, Father,' I said and he slowed his brushing for a moment, glancing up at Mummer and then me.

Hanny went over to one of the cupboards and started looking for cereal. Mummer snapped at him and then, remembering herself, she smiled at him instead and touched him gently on the arm.

'No, Andrew,' she said. 'We don't eat until it goes dark. And when we do, it will be fish, not cornflakes.'

Hanny didn't understand. Mummer took the box off him and put it back in the cupboard.

Farther came in coughing and sat down, laying a single key on the table.

'I've got that door open,' he said. 'The one in the study.'

Mummer rolled her eyes, but Mr Belderboss leant forward.

'What was inside?' he said.

'A bed,' Farther replied.

Mr Belderboss frowned.

'And some toys,' said Farther.

'Was it a playroom, do you think?' Mr Belderboss said.

'No,' said Farther, barking into his fist again. 'I've a feeling it was a quarantine.'

'For the children with TB?'

Farther nodded. 'There's a little barred window that's been bricked up from the outside. That's probably why we've never noticed it before.'

He launched into a rasping cough.

'Oh, will you stop,' said Mummer. 'What is the matter with you?'

'I think it's that room,' said Farther. 'Full of dust.'

'Funny place to keep the children, right next to the study,' said Mr Belderboss.

'Perhaps it wasn't a study then,' said Farther. 'Or perhaps it was so Gregson could keep an eye on them while he worked. I don't know.'

'It's a constant surprise this place,' said Mr Belderboss. 'I shall look forward to seeing it.'

'Not now, Reg,' said Mrs Belderboss. 'Father's waiting to begin.'

Father Bernard was standing by the back door in his coat and shoes.

'Only if everyone's ready,' he said.

∽

The rain came down harder as soon as we went outside and the back yard became a delta of little streams gushing through the cobbles. Father Bernard walked across to the middle and stopped.

'Here?' he said to Mummer.

'That's where Father Wilfred started, yes,' said Mummer.

Father Bernard nodded and then began.

'In the name of the Father and of the Son and of the Holy Spirit. As it was in the beginning, is now, and ever shall be, world without end. Amen.'

Everyone responded and then went to their knees, apart from Mr and Mrs Belderboss who wouldn't have got up again if they had. Hanny was looking around, more interested in the way the rain was pattering out of the broken gutter, until I pulled him down next to me.

Father Bernard closed his eyes and lifted up his hands.

'We ask our Lord Jesus Christ to forgive us our sins. And we pray especially for Andrew that he be filled with the Holy Spirit and find peace this Eastertide. Hail Mary, full of grace . . .'

Hanny watched as we all spoke the words together.

Once the prayer was over, everyone stood up and moved across the yard to the first station. There we got on our knees again and Father Bernard said, 'We adore thee, O Christ, and we praise thee.'

Everyone replied: 'Because by Thy holy cross, Thou hast redeemed the world.'

Father Bernard opened a small prayer book, shielding it from the rain with his hand.

Pilate condemned Jesus to death and he took up the cross that was given to him. He fell. His mother came to wipe away the blood and Simon picked him and his crucifix up off the floor. He fell again. And again.

And so it went on, until we had circled Moorings and Jesus was dead.

ဢ

Once it was over, I was allowed to take Hanny out for a few hours before the Tenebrae service at Little Hagby.

We went down to the beach, chancing that the crossing to Coldbarrow would be clear and we could get his watch back. I didn't want to go at all. I'd have quite happily let Leonard keep the damn thing – Hanny would have forgotten about it in a day – but Mummer would notice it was missing and make me pay for a new one. It would be my fault that he had lost it.

We had no idea of the tides any more. We hadn't been here for so long that that kind of knowledge had been lost. But when we got there the sea was well out – a line of foam at the edge of the mud flats. A huge stillness had settled now that waters had retreated but the clouds on the horizon had the look of something building to attack. Darkening and darkening, turning the silent gulls that swooped before them an unnatural white.

Had it been like this for the farmers that had once grazed their cattle here? Had they always looked out to sea, wondering when it would come sweeping in again and with what ferocity? I suppose they must have done.

For half a mile, we followed the marker posts of the old causeway and then, when they gave out, the wandering tracks the Daimler had left in the sand were the only thing to guide us around the patches of sinking mud and the deep cuttings still eroding from the withdrawal of the tide. It was out here in the maw of the bay that one felt most exposed. The flatness of the sands made everything seem a long way away. There was nothing but the wind and the coming and going of light; and the gulls were bigger and unafraid. This was their territory, and we were nothing.

When we finally came to Coldbarrow itself there was a cobbled slipway leading onto a dirt road that ran around the perimeter. Rutted and claggy with sludge and sand it looked impassable, yet there were footprints and tyre grooves criss-crossing the lane all the way towards Thessaly, the house which sat away on the edge of the cliffs at the north end. Nevertheless, it was better to cut across the heather moor and save our boots. Mummer would only start asking questions if we came back up to our knees in mud.

I held open a barbed wire fence for Hanny to climb through and then showed him where to hold it so that I could do the same. The land rose a little and then we were on the peat moor where the heather had been ravaged to stubble by the wind.

It was easy to see why no one ever came here. What was there to come for? No livestock could survive for long on the stony ground and anything one tried to build would be knocked flat by the first storm to come barrelling across the Irish Sea. For there was nothing beyond Coldbarrow, only a yawning openness of grey water until one hit the coast of County Louth a hundred and fifty miles away.

Perhaps that was what made me stop and look across the sands at our footprints. To know that there was a place we could go back to.

The mainland was a thin strand of grey, the pillbox barely distinguishable in the range of dunes. Only Moorings stood out, white against the trees of Brownslack Wood that moved in the wind like the pelt of a huge, dozing animal.

Seeing it like that, so thickly heaped over the fell, I reckoned Mr Belderboss was right. Maybe no one had set foot in there for centuries. There must still have been places like that, even in England. Wild woods left to themselves.

Hanny tugged at my hand and we carried on through the heather. As we walked, I became aware of a faint ringing sound, like someone running a finger around the rim of a wine glass.

'Can you hear that?'

He stopped and I touched my ear.

'That sound,' I said.

He shook his head.

The grass rustled and then a flash of white fur made us both turn at the same time. A slender, staring cat emerged and mewed with a tiny voice. Hanny put out his hand and it came to him. It had no collar and no name tag, but it wasn't feral. The fur had been well looked after.

It was an albino, with eyes that looked as if they had been marinated in blood. It mewed again and sprayed its musk onto a rock, its tail erect and shivering. Again came that faint, high-pitched smoothing of the air. It seemed to be calling the cat. It licked its paw and then sprang off through the grass towards Thessaly.

∽

Hanny got there before me and was standing at the end of a cutting that led to the house through the black stems of heather and the ferns that had yet to unfurl their little crosiers.

The ringing sound was stronger here and I realised that I had been hearing the wind moving the bell in the small brick tower that they said the Devil had built for Elizabeth Percy to entice poor foreign sailors onto the rocks.

The wind wasn't strong enough to swing it against the clapper and it shimmered over its surface instead, producing a delicate, liquid sound that floated on the damp air.

The girl we had seen at the Loney was sitting under the lopsided portico of the house in her wheelchair. After a moment she held up her hand and Hanny started to walk towards the house, following the albino cat.

Standing close to it for the first time, Thessaly was an ugly place. Built low and long to withstand the weather, it seemed to have emerged from the earth like a stunted fungus. Every window was black and stains ran from the sills down the grimy plasterwork as though the place was permanently weeping. The portico was an attempt at elegance that had failed in the most spectacular way and reminded me of the gateways to the vaults in the graveyard at Saint Jude's with their life-sized angels and broken gates.

Hanny stopped a few feet from the girl and was staring at her as she smoothed her hands over her swollen stomach. Perhaps it was the dry, russet hair and its attendant dribble of freckles across the bridge of her nose; perhaps it was pregnancy that had given her a fleshiness about the face, but she seemed even younger than I'd first thought. The prettiness that Mrs Belderboss had noticed came and went too quickly for it to be a constant quality and it disappeared altogether when she grimaced as the baby moved.

The door behind her was open and Laura's voice came from inside the house.

'Is that him back?' she said, and then looked disappointed as she came out and saw Hanny and me standing there.

She was smoking a cigarette and was dressed in a matching liver-coloured skirt and jacket. She had pearls around her neck and, like her husband, smelled strongly of fragrance.

'Can I help you?' she said, touching the edges of her painted mouth with her little finger.

I told her that we'd come for the watch.

'Watch?' she said.

'Your husband found a watch yesterday at the Loney. It belongs to us.'

'The where?'

'The beach,' I said. 'He found it in the sand.'

'I don't recall seeing you there,' she said.

'Well, we were.'

Laura took another drag and tapped the ash from the end with her forefinger.

'What's the matter with him?' she asked, gesturing towards Hanny.

'Nothing,' I said.

'Why is he staring at me? Is he a bit slow?'

I nudged Hanny to stop and he looked at his feet instead.

'Do you live around here?' Laura said.

'No.'

'On holiday?'

'Yes.'

'Poor you,' she said, as the rain started again.

She looked at us both and then turned back into the house.

'Come in,' she said. 'I'll see if he's left it lying around. Give Else a hand over the step.'

The girl smiled at Hanny again, hoping that he would do the honours.

'He doesn't understand,' I said.

But Hanny took hold of the handles and wheeled her backwards through the doorway and into a long corridor lined with empty coat hooks on which a smell of old, damp gabardine hung. There was room for little else other than a pair of wellingtons and an umbrella.

There were no stairs, only doors either side and one at the end, next to which there was an upturned plant pot for a telephone to sit on.

The rain came down hard outside and the hallway darkened. I had been right to think of the place as a tomb. The plaster had been left unpainted, the woodwork without varnish, as though it had been built and immediately abandoned. Its walls had never contained a family. No one had ever laughed there. It had a kind of airlessness, a heavy silence, that made it immediately unsettling. I've never felt it anywhere else since, but there was definitely something that I picked up with a different sense. Not a ghost or anything ridiculous like that, but something nevertheless.

'Wait here,' Laura said and went along the hallway to the door at the end where she paused to sort through the bunch of keys. She unlocked the door, there was a brief glimpse of a bare kitchen, and then she closed it behind her, locking it from the inside.

'What's his name?' Else said to me.

'Andrew,' I said.

'That's a nice name,' she said and smiled at Hanny.

Hanny smiled back and touched her hair.

'Don't do that,' I said.

'No, it's all right,' said Else, rearranging it back behind her ears.

She shifted in her chair and winced a little and breathed out.

'The baby's moving,' she said to Hanny. 'Do you want to feel it?'

She took Hanny's hand and placed it on her belly. He hesitated but Else put her hands over his and a grin spread across his face as he felt the baby kicking against his palm.

Laura came back out of the kitchen and then went to a different door, moving the keys around the ring until she came to the one she needed. She was about to go into the room when the telephone rang.

'Let them in here,' said Laura.

Else looked at her.

'Don't worry,' she said. 'This room is all right for them to be in.' And she went to pick up the phone.

Like the hallway, the room was bare and cold. There were no curtains, only yellow nets covering the windows that were thick with cold condensation. The fireplace was boarded up and there were footprints in the dust where someone had walked in and out of the room carrying the boxes that were stacked against the wall. A porcelain doll in a bonnet and pinafore sat on top of one of the boxes staring at us. Hanny went over and picked it up. He smiled and showed me how its eyes closed and opened when he tipped it back and forth.

'He might have put it there,' said Else, pointing to the battered desk in the alcove of the chimney breast. 'That's where he keeps the things he finds.'

I went over and looked through the various shells and bits of glass and bone. There was a sheep's skull resting as a paperweight on a pile of brown envelopes and next to it was an old toothbrush in a mug. Leonard had evidently got halfway through cleaning off the green mould stuck between the sutures. I picked up the skull and looked into one of the eye sockets. The white worm of the optic nerve was still attached, though the eye and brain had long since been eaten or rotted away.

Hanny was sitting on a chair with the doll on his knee. The box next to him was open and he reached inside and took out an old encyclopaedia. I told him to leave it alone.

'It's all right,' said Else.

Hanny flipped through the pages, stopping now and then to show Else a picture that he liked. A matador. A mandarin duck. A magician.

The albino cat wandered in and jumped up onto Hanny's lap. He stroked it gently and then picked it up and pressed it to his cheek. The cat licked his face and then hopped down to Else.

'Thank you for bringing her back,' she said. 'She goes off for days sometimes, don't you?'

She scolded the cat and then kissed Hanny, leaving a smudged half-moon of red on his lips.

It took me more by surprise than it did Hanny. He smiled and looked back at the book.

'Do you want to keep it?' she said to him.

'No, he doesn't,' I said.

'It's all right,' said Else. 'They're just old books. He's got hundreds of them. He never looks at them, but he won't throw them out.'

'Do you want the book?' I said to Hanny.

He looked at me and I went over and put it in his satchel.

'Take some more, if you like,' said Else.

'One's enough.'

'Please, she said. 'I want him to have them.'

'He'd rather just have his watch back.'

'Well, it'll be here somewhere, if you're sure it was picked up.'

'It was.'

She frowned and cocked her head to one side.

'Are you really here on holiday?' she said.

'Yes,' I replied.

'Why?'

'What do you mean?'

'I mean why come here? What is there to do?'

'There's the beach,' I said.

'Is that it?'

I shrugged.

'It didn't look much fun to me,' she said.

'Well it is.'

'What do you do there, apart from hide in the grass?'

'You wouldn't understand.'

'Wouldn't I?'

'No.'

'Boys' stuff is it?'

I said nothing. Her smile suddenly faded again and she gave a sudden sharp intake of breath and put her hands on her stomach. Exhaling slowly, she caught the expression of concern on Hanny's face.

'Oh, don't worry, Andrew,' she said, holding his hand. 'It's nothing. I've done this before. It gets easier the more you have.'

Hanny smiled and she touched his face and kissed him again. I reached into the box and took out a pile of other books and gave them to Hanny. He put them in his bag and went over to the desk to look at the sheep's skull.

I heard Laura put down the phone and then she came into the room.

'Well?' she said.

'It's not here.'

'Then I'm afraid you've had a bit of a wasted journey.'

'Is there nowhere else it might be?'

Laura lit another cigarette and shook her head. 'If it's not in here, I wouldn't like to say.'

'But it's my brother's. He wants it back.'

'I'm sorry,' she said, and then holding the cigarette in her lips, she dipped into her pocket and brought out a purse. She thumbed open the catches and took out a five pound note.

'Here. Buy him a new one,' she said, holding the note out to me.

'He doesn't want a new one,' I said.

Laura looked at me and then took out another note.

'Buy one for yourself as well,' she said, folding the two notes together and pressing them into my hand. 'All right?'

I held the notes back to her.

'Isn't your husband in?'

'No.'

'When will he be back?'

'I'm afraid I don't know.'

'Will he be here tomorrow?'

'Possibly. It's hard to say. He's very busy.'

'We'll come back tomorrow.'

'I wouldn't want you to waste your time again.'

'It won't be a waste if Hanny gets his watch.'

'It's all right,' said Else, pulling aside the net curtains. 'He's here.'

∽

The rain was coming down in needles now and battering the roof of Leonard's Daimler. Water washed under its tyres and seeped away into the bracken. He looked at us standing on the porch.

Laura flapped open an umbrella and went down the steps to the car. Leonard got out and said something to her that I couldn't hear for the rain. She spoke back to him and then they both looked at us. Leonard hitched up the collar of his jacket and came stiffly up the steps to the house while Laura took a wicker basket from the back seat.

'I'm told you've lost a watch,' he said.

'Yes.'

'And that you think I've got it.'

'You found it at the beach yesterday.'

'Did I now?'

He lit up a stump of a cigar in his cupped hands.

'What did it look like, this watch?' he said, blowing smoke out of the side of his mouth.

'Just give it back, Leonard,' Laura said quietly as she passed him. 'Before the tide comes in,' she added.

He clamped the cigar in his teeth and withdrew a handkerchief from his breast pocket. He looked at us as he shook it loose and then refolded it into a square pad. Another long suck on the cigar and then he tossed it away and held the hankie to Hanny's face. Hanny drew back, but Leonard held him firmly by the shoulder.

'She's right, boys,' he said, wiping the lipstick off Hanny's mouth. 'The thing you have to remember about the tides here, is that no one can say they know them. Not really.'

He took hold of Hanny's chin and moved his head left and right, inspecting it for any more traces of make-up.

'I mean,' he said, spitting on the hankie and moving over to Else, 'someone could tell you to set off now and before you know it you might be swimming home, or not swimming home, if you know what I mean.'

Leonard dabbed at Else's lips, taking off the redness there, and then shoved the hankie into his pocket.

'They say it's the biggest graveyard in the north of England,' he said, looking behind him at the sea and the sludge.

He took out a paper bag of mints and ate one. He noticed Hanny staring at them, and he smiled to himself and put them away. Laura banged on the window at him and after waving her away, Leonard looked at Hanny and me in turn and then pulled up his sleeve.

'Is this it?' he said, showing us the watch he was wearing.

'Yes.'

He looked at us again and undid the buckle and handed it to me.

'I should stay well away from here if I were you,' he said. 'Dangerous place. It's very easy to misjudge things. You could get well out of your depth and end up in all sorts of trouble.'

Hanny put the watch back on his wrist.

'Listen,' said Leonard. 'Hear that?'

A steady hiss was coming as the sea began to wash up against the rocks at the bottom of the cliff behind the house.

'I should get a move on if I were you,' he said. 'I wouldn't want you to be stuck here all night.'

He looked at us again and went behind Else, turned her chair around and pushed her into the house.

# 11

WE LEFT COLDBARROW at the right time.

Looking back once we reached the pillbox, the sea was pounding the rocks by Thessaly, sending up spikes of foam that hung in the air before disintegrating back into the swell. The sands were gone.

Hanny was pleased to have his watch back and kept on showing it to me, wanting me to tell him the time.

'We're late, Hanny,' I said. 'That's all that matters.'

When we got back to Moorings, Father Bernard was standing at the top of the lane, looking out for us.

'Come on, you two,' he said as we passed him. 'You'd better get a move on before your mother has an aneurysm.'

Everyone was waiting on the bus with firm-set faces. Mummer pulled up her sleeve to reveal her watch and looked at me. That was all she needed to say.

I sat next to Hanny and he smiled at me and put his fingers on his lips where Else had kissed him. I took hold of his hand and moved it away.

'Leave it, Hanny,' I said and gave him a look that made him lower his head. I didn't mean to scold him like that. It wasn't his fault after all. It was just that I didn't want Mummer to see.

That was what I told myself anyway. There was another feeling that I didn't want to recognise at the time but seems rather obvious now. I was jealous. But only in the way that I was jealous of the boys at school whose sexual exploits had elevated them above the playground proles.

It wasn't that I particularly wanted their experiences – my God, I would have been terrified – only to be in their club, where membership guaranteed that you didn't have your gym shoes rammed down a toilet pan full of muck and urine or your ribs blackened by discerning elbows in the corridors. The sex stuff didn't really matter. I didn't care about that.

I suppose I was jealous because that kiss had been wasted on Hanny. It didn't matter to him or to his peers at Pinelands. What I could have done with that experience back at school. To have had the ears of the changing room as I described it all in lurid detail, to have been thought of in another way, if only for the final term, might have made all the difference. I don't know.

Hanny touched his face again. There were still faint traces of lipstick on his chin that Leonard hadn't managed to get rid of. I wondered if Mummer might notice, as she noticed every small difference in Hanny's appearance, but she had her back to me and was watching silently out of the window like everyone else.

No one spoke at all, in fact, until a few miles further on when Mrs Belderboss patted the back of Father Bernard's seat.

'Stop, Father,' she said and he pulled into the side of the road. 'Look.'

Everyone peered out of the windows as a swarm of

bright red butterflies spun over the field in a flexuous shape, twisting and spiralling as one entity.

'Have you ever seen anything so beautiful?' said Mrs Belderboss.

'What are they doing out? It's too early in the year for them,' said Mr Belderboss. 'They'll die before the day's done.'

''Tis God's world, Mr Belderboss,' said Father Bernard, smiling. 'I'm sure He knows what He's doing.'

'I think it's a sign,' said Mrs Belderboss to Mummer and put her hand on hers. 'That God will be with us when we go to the shrine.'

'Yes,' said Mummer. 'Perhaps it is.'

'I'm sure of it,' Mrs Belderboss replied.

After all, signs and wonders were everywhere.

Father Wilfred had told us time and time again that it was our duty as Christians to see what our faith had taught us to see. And consequently Mummer used to come home from the shop with all kinds of stories about how God had seen fit to reward the good and justly punish the wicked.

The lady who worked at the bookmakers had developed warts on her fingers from handling dirty money all day long. The Wilkinson girl, who had visited the clinic on the Finchley Road that the women at Saint Jude's talked about in hushed tones, had been knocked down by a car not a week later and had her pelvis snapped beyond repair. Conversely, an elderly lady who came into the shop every week for prayer cards and had spent much of the previous decade raising money for Cafod, won a trip to Fatima.

Mummer would tell us these tales over the dinner table without a flicker of doubt that God's hand was at work in the world, as it had been in the time of the saints and martyrs, the violent deaths of whom were regularly inflicted upon us as exempla of not only the unconditional oath we had to make to the service of the Lord, but of the necessity of suffering.

The worse the torment, the more God was able to make Himself known, Mummer said, invoking the same branch of esoteric mathematics Father Wilfred used in his sermons to explain why the world was full of war and murder – a formula by which cruelty could be shown to be inversely proportionate to mercy. The more inhumane the misery we could inflict upon one another, the more compassionate God seemed as a counterpoint to us. It was through pain that we would know how far we still had to go to be perfect in His eyes. And so, unless one suffered, Father Wilfred was wont to remind us, one could not be a true Christian.

In the vestry after Mass, if it wasn't chastisement over one thing or another, it was a lesson on a particular saint that he considered to be an encouragement for young boys to seek the opportunity of hardship, though it was hard to tell the difference between the two sometimes when he used the saints like a birch rod.

When Henry turned up late for Mass one Sunday, Father Wilfred thrashed him with the Blessed Alexandrina De Costa – the Portuguese mystic who had leapt from a window to escape being raped, had crippled herself in the fall, but still managed to come to Mass every Sunday on time. Even when she decided to devote her life to God, and ate nothing but the Eucharist, and each Friday had the blessed joy of experiencing the agony of Our Lord on the cross, she was still there at church before everyone else. It was the least

Henry could do, even if his bicycle had developed a puncture on the Edgware Road.

'I'm sorry, Father,' Henry said. 'I'll pray to Saint Christopher,' he added in a moment of inspiration.

'Idiot boy,' Father Wilfred said. 'We pray *with* the saints, not *to* them. The saints intercede on our behalf and petition God to help us.'

'Oh, yes, Father.'

'Will you remember that, McCullough?'

'Yes, Father.'

'But how will you remember it, McCullough?'

'I don't know, Father.'

Father Wilfred looked on the desk and picked up a metal ruler. He grabbed Henry by the wrist and before Henry could flinch he brought the edge of the ruler down on his knuckles, splitting them open.

'Will that help you to remember, McCullough?'

Henry gripped his bleeding hand tightly and moved backwards and sat down on a chair.

'Well?' said Father Wilfred.

'Yes, Father,' said Henry. 'I won't forget.'

Father Wilfred looked at him and after a moment he went to the sink and handed Henry a paper towel with a look of contempt.

I suppose I took it for granted that Henry was one of those children that adults dislike – there are children like that – but quite why Father Wilfred despised Henry so much I didn't know. Perhaps it was because Henry was rich when he had been so poor. The Poor, after all, were Father Wilfred's favourite yardstick. They were the caste by which all things had to be measured and in doing so he made every small enjoyment an affront to their dignity.

We were to think of the Poor when we reached for a second helping of cake. We were to think of the Poor when we wished for presents at Christmas, or when we coveted the new bicycle in the shop window. Father Wilfred had never had enough to eat. Never enough clothing to keep him warm in the Whitechapel slums. He had never possessed anything other than an old tyre which he used to knock along the road with a stick, trying to keep it from falling into the gutter.

It wasn't simply out of some obligatory moral stance demanded by scripture that he felt for the Poor so much, it was the core of his calling. Everyone was disappointed, but perhaps not surprised, that he chose in the end to give up his plot in Saint Jude's churchyard and requested that he be interred with his mother and father and his dead brothers and sisters in the Great Northern Cemetery instead.

But it seemed that there was more to it than that. We Smiths were better off than the McCulloughs by a long way and Father Wilfred never berated me the way he did Henry. Henry just seemed to rile him for some reason.

Father Wilfred had turned to me suddenly, aware that I was staring at them both.

'Carry on, Smith,' he said.

I went back to winding the handle of the spirit bander that was copying the parish newsletters. It was something I did on the first Sunday of the month and always tried to hold my breath as much as possible to stop the methylated spirits from raking out the back of my throat.

'Why were you late, McCullough?' said Father Wilfred, folding his arms.

'I told you, Father,' he said. 'I got a puncture.'

Father Wilfred nodded. 'Yes, I know that's what you *said*.'

He went to a bookshelf, pulled out a Bible and dropped it into Henry's lap.

'But I'm not convinced that it is necessarily the truth. Psalm one hundred and one, verse seven,' he said.

'Sorry, Father?'

'Find it, McCullough.'

'But I'll get blood on it, Father.'

'You won't.'

Henry carefully flipped through the book, trying not to bleed onto the pages.

'Well?' said Father Wilfred.

'I can't find it, Father.'

'Psalms, McCullough. Between Job and Proverbs. It's not difficult.'

At last Henry found the right place and started reading.

'"He that worketh deceit shall not dwell in my house; he that telleth lies shall not tarry in my sight."'

Father Wilfred repeated what Henry had said in a slow, measured way, pacing up and down the office.

'God hates liars, McCullough,' he said, nodding to the Bible on Henry's knee. 'It's in there a thousand times over. Proverbs, Romans, Jeremiah. When you lie, McCullough, you are brethren with the serpent in the garden. You forfeit your place in heaven. God has no time for deceivers. I'll ask you again. Why were you so late?'

Henry looked down at his bleeding knuckles.

'You were too lazy to get out of bed, weren't you?'

'Yes, Father.'

'And too overweight to make up the lost time.'

'Yes, Father.'

'Yes, Father,' he repeated. 'Psalm fifty-five, verse twenty-three. Quicker this time, McCullough.'

Henry sped through the pages and traced his finger along the line.

'"But thou, O God, shalt bring them down into the pit of destruction; bloody and deceitful men shall not live out half their days."'

Father Wilfred held out his hand for the Bible.

'Do you know what the most terrible torment of Hell is?' he said.

Henry passed it to him. 'No, Father.'

'The worst torment, McCullough,' he said, 'is not being able to repent of the sins you have committed.'

'Yes, Father.'

'In Hell, it is far too late.'

'Yes, Father.'

'You must come and see me in confession, McCullough.'

'Yes, Father. I will.'

'And then at least we may stand a chance of saving your soul.'

# 12

THE BUTTERFLIES DISPERSED as the rain returned and began the next washing of the land. Stone walls shone like iron. The trees bowed and dripped. The sullen countryside disappeared behind condensation and for a long time we could have been going anywhere until a low spire appeared on the other side of a cattle field, barely rising above the trees that surrounded it.

The Church of the Sacred Heart was an ancient place – dark and squat and glistening amphibiously in the rain. The large front door was green with moss and over the years long sinews of ivy had wormed their way around the tower.

We crowded under the lych-gate to wait for a particularly heavy burst of rain to pass. Water leaked through the canopy onto the stone seats that had been worn into scoops over the years by the backsides of countless pall-bearers or by people like us simply sheltering from the rain.

The churchyard itself was small but well stocked with the village dead – a second, more populous settlement bordering the first – all of them lying east–west as though the wind had combed them that way over the centuries. Gravestones listed against one another under the shade of several huge, dripping yew trees, one of which had been blasted by lightning at some point and had a new stem growing out of the blackened split.

'What do you think, Father?' said Mummer, nodding towards the church itself.

'Very atmospheric, Mrs Smith.'

'Fifteenth-century,' said Farther.

'Is that right?' Father Bernard replied.

'Some of it anyway. The stonework inside's all Saxon. They managed to escape the Reformation.'

'How's that?'

'I don't think they could find it, Father.'

The rain shower ended as suddenly as it had come. Water poured off the slate roof and along the lead flumes to spew from the mouths of gargoyles that had been weathered to lumps of stone. Father Bernard held open the gate and everyone went quickly up the path to the church before the rain came back, but Hanny stood looking up at the mangled grey demons, trying to pull his face to match theirs.

Inside, we took up a pew towards the back, shuffling along as quietly as possible so as not to disturb the silence. All around the church, the statues of saints had been covered up for Lent, like ghosts half hidden in the shadows of the alcoves. Now and then their drapes shivered in a draught. The wind was getting in somewhere and whistled like a seabird around the rafters.

Hanny held my hand.

'It's all right,' I said as he glanced nervously at the nearest shrouded saint. 'Just don't look at them.'

Once everyone was settled, Farther inclined his head to Father Bernard.

'See the windows in the clerestory,' he said, pointing at the tiny arches high up on the wall, each of them letting in a trickle of red light. 'Look at the thickness of the mullions. And the glass, that's Romanesque.'

'Is that good?' said Father Bernard.

'It's about seven hundred years old.'

Father Bernard looked impressed.

'They should open this place for a museum,' he whispered to Farther. 'They must have kept everything they've ever owned.'

It was true. Nothing, it seemed, had ever escaped the oak doors or the castle-thick walls. Any light that had entered through the windows had been held captive and absorbed into the wood. Over the centuries the pews, pulpit and misericords had blackened to ebony like the beams which supported the roof – each one made from the fork of a huge oak tree, giving the congregation the sense of being inside an upturned boat.

The smells of benedictions and snuffed candles remained as steadfast as the gravestones that floored the central aisle. The doors to the aumbry opened on hinges that had been forged at a time when they still dunked witches and died of plague. It was a place where wafer ovens, alms boxes and rush-holders remained as working tools; where there was a sanctuary knocker, a parish chest carved out of a single trunk of walnut, and a Table of Consanguinity attached to the wall above the font as a ready-reckoner to prevent interbreeding amongst the ignorant poor. Though I suppose by the time the child was being dipped into the water, it was rather too late.

At the end of pews were effigies of the Seven Deadly Sins, smoothed almost to anonymity by the countless hands that had gripped them during genuflection. But one could just make out Sloth curled up like a dormouse, and Gluttony vomiting on his own beard and Wrath beating his brother-man with the jawbone of an ass.

Between the nave and the chancel, the church still had its rood screen with its painted melange of saints at the bottom and the crucifixion at the top. Above it was part of a Doom painting, and though much of it had flaked off it was still a considerable size and sprawled like dark rot across the stone.

'It's the only one I've ever seen north of Gloucester,' said Farther, leaning close to Father Bernard again and pointing up to it. 'I mean, it's got nothing on the ones at Patcham or Wenhaston, but still.'

'I wouldn't have it on my wall,' Father Bernard said.

'I don't know,' said Farther. 'It has a certain charm.'

'Rather you than me.'

When I was a child and I believed all that Father Wilfred said about Hell and damnation, the Doom gave me no end of sleepless nights at Moorings. I suppose because, in a sense, I already knew the place it depicted and that meant it might just be real.

It reminded me of the school playground with its casual despotism and the constant anxiety of never knowing which traits in a boy might be punishable with instant violence. Too tall, too small. No father, no mother. Wet trousers. Broken shoes. Wrong estate. Sluttish sister. Nits.

Hell was a place ruled by the logic of children. *Schadenfreude* that lasted for eternity.

In the painting, the damned were forced down through a narrow crack in the earth, crushed against one another, swimming headfirst through the soil, before they tumbled in a naked landslide towards the clutches of lascivious black-skinned demons who grasped their hair and drove red-hot knives into their flesh. Yet, this was only the initial punishment. They had merely fallen on the welcome mat, where some of the old lags of Hades had gathered to pray for the souls of these newcomers in the vain hope of their own redemption, their faces upturned, their mouths wide open and desperate, like blackbird chicks.

From here, the wicked were collected in enormous cauldrons to be cooked for Satan, who squatted like a sort of horned toad and dipped into the pots with a fondue fork, impaling the squirming human worms and swallowing them down whole, presumably to slither through his bowels and out the other end to begin the whole process once more.

In other parts of Hell were tortures so vile they bordered on being funny, which in turn worried me even more. The mockery of Hell, I thought, would result in an even worse punishment if I ever ended up there.

In one dark corner a demon had its arm down a man's throat so far that it came out of his backside to throttle the woman cowering beneath him. People had their limbs torn off and were hung upside down by hooks through their privates. Some had their tongues nailed to trees and their bellies slit to feed the slavering dogs that obediently attended the devils. Eyeballs were pecked out by things that looked like oversized starlings. Boiling lead was funnelled down throats. Severed heads were emptied of blood to irrigate the paddy fields of black weeds that grew up the sheer rock walls of Hell and broke through into the lush green pastures of the living to ensnare the sunflowers and the lilies growing there. It was all Father Wilfred had promised us it would be.

As we had always done when we'd come to the Tenebrae service in the past we doubled the congregation in one fell swoop. The few people kneeling with their faces in their hands were the same people that had always been there. And when they broke out of their prayers, they looked at us not as strangers but as people they half-recognised even though it had been years since we'd last come.

'Isn't that Clement?' said Mr Belderboss, pointing to someone sitting alone in one of the side pews.

'Yes, I think it is,' Mrs Belderboss replied and she tried to attract his attention.

'His mother's not with him, though,' said Mr Belderboss. 'I wonder why?'

'Well, she's perhaps not up to church any more,' Mrs Belderboss replied. 'She is getting on, I suppose.'

Mummer shushed them as the organist struck up a dirge and a miserable-looking altar boy, acned and gangly, brought out the hearse, placed it on a low table and lit the fifteen candles with a taper. He went away again and came back with a small, fat candle that he lit and placed down under the altar out of sight.

The priest came in and we all stood up. He gave a brief introduction – his voice thudding around the stone walls and gathering into a boom – and then the two-hour cycle of Matins and Lauds began – all in Latin of course – and after each a candle was extinguished by the altar boy until little by little the church darkened to match the encroaching gloom outside.

The wind continued to rise and fall. Whining and shrilling. It was as insistent as the priest, louder sometimes, preaching an older sermon, about the sand and the sea. Warning the faithful to stay away from the Loney.

Hanny fell asleep but no one bothered him, as Mr Belderboss had done the same, leaning his fluffy white head against my shoulder. In any case, Mummer was too engrossed in a contest with Miss Bunce as to who could be the most moved by the ceremony. At each increment of darkness, Mummer held her rosary tighter and prayed harder. Miss Bunce had tears in her eyes when Jesus called out to God and the candles on the hearse were snuffed out in quick succession. She even managed a small, anguished wail of her own when in the darkness the altar boy went down the aisle and slammed the heavy church doors shut to symbolise the earthquake that had buckled Golgotha at the moment Jesus' human heart stopped beating.

Mr Belderboss woke with a start and clutched at his chest.

഍

Once the service was over and the single candle that had been secreted under the altar had been brought out to symbolise the promise of resurrection, we filed out into the rain. The altar boy held an umbrella over the priest as he quickly clamped each cold hand in his and passed on God's blessing. The regulars disappeared quickly, back to the sombre little houses hunkered down in the rain

139

around the village green and as soon as the last person was out of the church, which was Mr Belderboss, rolling up and down on the cam of his bad hip, the priest went back inside and closed the door.

'Well,' said Mummer, as we walked back to the minibus. 'I thought that was a lovely service.'

She was talking to Farther but he had stopped several paces behind and was running his hand over the carvings worked into the stone around a side door.

'I say it was a lovely service,' she called over to him, but he either didn't hear her or he ignored her and moved his glasses to the end of his nose to better inspect the men and demons locked in mortal combat.

'It was,' said Mr Belderboss. 'It was.'

'What do you know, you great lug,' said Mrs Belderboss, batting his shoulder with the back of her hand. 'You missed most of it.'

'I did not,' he said, rubbing his arm and smiling. 'I was deep in prayer.'

'Cobblers,' said Mrs Belderboss.

'I think moving is probably the right word,' said Miss Bunce. 'It's meant to be quite a sombre service.'

David nodded in solemn agreement.

'Oh, I didn't enjoy it, as such,' said Mummer.

'I didn't say I didn't enjoy it,' Miss Bunce said.

'So where's this fish feller?' Father Bernard said, leading Mummer back to the minibus.

⛬

Mummer sat in the front with Father Bernard and directed him to a wooden shack in the middle of nowhere where a man with a face full of scars sat behind plastic trays of skate and mackerel and vicious-looking eels freshly pulled out of the Irish Sea. It had been a tradition in the time of Father Wilfred to stop here on Good Friday and Mummer was delighted to see that the shop was still there and the same man was still taking the money, using an old chum bucket for a till. The change came out greasy but Mummer didn't seem to mind.

We all waited in the minibus as Mummer and Farther chatted to the man while he wrapped up their fish in newspaper. A Land Rover went past us and pulled up next to the stall. It was Clement's. The same one that I had seen parked on the road down from Moorings. Parkinson, the bull man, got out first and looked at us, nodded at Father Bernard specifically, and then wandered over to the stall, followed by Collier and his dog. Freed from the cab but still on its chain, it went off sniffing and barking and then squatted in the middle of the road.

'Aren't those the men we saw on the way here, Father?' said Miss Bunce.

'Aye,' he said, with a look of irritation that Parkinson had singled him out.

'Where's Clement, I wonder?' said Mrs Belderboss.

'I don't know,' Mr Belderboss replied. 'Why?'

'That is his Land Rover, isn't it?'

'So?'

'Well, why have they got it?'

'How should I know?'

'Do you think he's lent it to them?'

'Don't be silly, Mary.'

'I'm not being silly, I should think they all muck in together round here, don't they?'

'Hardly,' said Mr Belderboss. 'If they've got his Land Rover, then it's because he's sold it to them. Or it's an exchange for something. I mean they don't always deal in money out here, but they don't give things away either. It's a tough life being a farmer. You can't afford charity.'

The elderly man got out last and, coughing violently into his sleeve, he leant against the side of the Land Rover watching us.

'Toxoplasmosis,' said Mr Belderboss, nodding to him.

'Oh, give it a rest, Reg,' Mrs Belderboss sighed.

Parkinson and Collier went and stood by the side of the fish stall smoking cigarettes. Mummer said hello to them, these were her people, after all. The men listened as she tried to start up a conversation, but they didn't talk back. Rather, they grinned, Collier winding the chain around his forearm to keep the dog obedient.

'Who *are* they?' said Miss Bunce as Mummer and Farther got back onto the bus.

'Who?' said Mummer.

'Them,' said Miss Bunce, pointing out of the window. 'They don't seem very friendly.'

Mummer looked back at the men who were now selecting fish and laughing with the fishmonger, as the one with jaundice spluttered into his fist.

'Oh, Joan, you really have lived in London too long,' she said. 'They just have different ways. Here, hold this.'

She handed the newspaper packet to Miss Bunce while she settled herself into her seat and we pulled away.

The men watched us leave, Parkinson nodding to Father Bernard and Collier saluting with his black mitten.

ဆ

The smell of fish filled the bus and steadily bloomed as we ran along the lanes back to the house.

Miss Bunce held her hand over her nose. 'I think I'm going to be sick,' she said. David reached across and held her hand.

'Oh for goodness' sake, Joan,' said Mummer. 'Don't be so dramatic.'

Miss Bunce wafted the smell away with her hand. 'I thought that fish shouldn't smell at all if it was fresh.'

'No, that's beef, isn't it?' said Mr Belderboss.

'Chicken,' Mrs Belderboss replied. 'Is it beef or chicken?'

'Look,' said Mummer. 'We've bought fish from that stall for years and it's never done us any harm, has it?'

She looked at Farther.

'No,' he said. 'It's always been very nice.'

'Well, I'm not having any of it,' Miss Bunce said.

'Well then you'll be hungry,' said Mummer.

'And I'll be glad,' said Miss Bunce. 'We ought not to be eating at all today.'

Mummer rolled her eyes. 'That rule only applies to meat, Joan,' she said. 'Fish is fine, isn't it, Father?'

'I think we might risk it, aye,' said Father Bernard as he changed gear and slowed down to take a hairpin bend in the road.

'That's just as well. I'm not sure I'd last until tomorrow with nothing inside me,' Mr Belderboss laughed from the back seat.

Around the corner we came across someone walking on the edge of the ditch.

'That's Clement,' said Mrs Belderboss. 'Slow down, Father.'

Father Bernard pulled in a few yards ahead and wound the window down. Clement stopped.

'Can I give you a lift?' Father Bernard called.

Clement looked around him and then came to the window, peering at us all and then at Father Bernard.

'Nay, you're all right,' he said.

'It's no bother to take you home.'

'I've not far to go,' Clement said.

'Well how about I at least take you as far as Moorings?'

Clement looked up into the rain. 'Aye, all right,' he said. 'Take me to Moorings and I'll see me sen right from there.'

Clement wedged himself between Hanny and me on the back seat. His wax jacket smelled of dried-up bodily excretions and damp straw. An astonishing, curdled smell that had subtle layers of foulness for the nose to explore.

He didn't say a word all the way back, but stared straight ahead and I got to know his profile intimately: a mangled ear stuck on the side of his head like a lump of bubble gum; a nose that had, like his cheeks, turned purulent with end-stage rosacea; a few stray wiry hairs around his lips that the razor had missed several times. When he went to scratch his nose, his sleeve slipped down and revealed a swallow tattooed on his forearm. He saw me staring at it and covered it up.

There was a rumour that he had done time at Haverigg, though whether it was true or what he was supposed to have done, I didn't know.

When we arrived back at Moorings, Clement waited until everyone had gone into the house and there was only Father Bernard and I coaxing Monro out from under the seat where he had been sleeping. Monro yawned and ambled down the steps and into the house. Father Bernard watched him go and then turned to Clement.

'Are you sure you won't let me take you back to the farm?'

Clement shook his head. 'I'd rather walk from here.'

'All right, well you take care of yourself.'

Clement walked away and then stopped and came back.

'I don't know if I should say anything, Father,' he said. 'But I'd not forgive me sen if I didn't give thee a word of warning.'

'Oh? About what?'

'Stay indoors as much as you can.'

'With the weather, you mean?'

'No, I mean keep thaselves to thaselves.'

'What makes you think we were going to do otherwise?' said Father Bernard with a small laugh.

'There are folk around here who aren't that happy that you've come.'

'Like who?'

'I'd rather not say.'

Father Bernard smiled faintly to himself. He knew who Clement was talking about.

'Well, I'm sure we won't do anything to upset them, Clement. And in any case, it didn't seem like that to me.'

Clement frowned. 'How do you mean, Father?'

Father Bernard glanced at me.

'Well, I stopped in the Bell and Anchor the other day to get out of the rain and someone very kindly bought me a drink.'

Clement looked as though he had swallowed something nasty.

'Who was it?'

'Mr Parkinson, the butcher. Why?'

'And did you return the favour?'

Father Bernard shook his head. 'I hadn't time to stay.'

'I don't mean a drink, Father.'

'I don't follow you, Clement.'

'I mean, did you invite him up to Moorings?'

'I don't recall—'

'He has a way of making folk feel obliged to him, you see,' Clement cut in.

'Well, I didn't feel like that,' said Father Bernard. 'Like I say, it was just a drink.'

But Clement wasn't listening. He clutched Father Bernard's arm.

'Because if you were to invite him, he wouldn't just take it as a pleasantry. He'd come and bring them all with him.'

'Who's all?'

'It's just better if tha keeps away from him.'

'But there must be a reason, Clement.'

'Aye, plenty.'

'Such as what?'

'I can't say.'

'Clement?'

'I'm sorry, Father. I must get back to Mother.'

Clement looked at Father Bernard and then down at his feet, as though he had failed in some way. Then he walked to the lane, paused while he looked around him again, and then went off through a gate and over the fields.

# 13

CLEMENT'S ODD BEHAVIOUR was all everyone talked about once he had gone.

'He's always been a little eccentric,' said Mrs Belderboss.

'It's not surprising living out here,' Mr Belderboss added. 'Stuck with his mother day in, day out. It's enough to make anyone go a bit strange.'

'I'm sure he doesn't think of her as a burden, Reg.'

'Oh, I didn't mean that. I meant he focuses so much of his time on her that the rest of the world, the real world, sort of gets pushed to the sidelines.'

Everyone seemed to agree, and perhaps it was this consent that made Father Bernard dismiss Clement's warnings as easily as he had obviously wanted to.

Perhaps they were right. Maybe Clement was just paranoid, but he had seemed so serious, so genuinely concerned.

Mummer and Mrs Belderboss went into the kitchen to prepare the fish while the rest of us waited. Miss Bunce and her fiancé sat together on the sofa. She was back with her Bible and he was reading a battered Dickens novel that had pages like tissue paper. Mr Belderboss snored in an armchair, Father Bernard went to his room to pray, and Farther sat at a table, looking at the nativity set he had found in the little room next to the study.

A new wave of rain swept in off the sea and made its fingertaps on the windows. Mummer came in from the kitchen and handed me a box of matches.

'Here, make yourself useful and light the candles,' she said and shooed me off around the room, distracted by Farther's coughing.

It had got worse and there was a soft wheeze every time he breathed.

'You ought to stay out of that room,' said Mummer. 'It's not doing your chest any good.'

'I'm fine,' said Farther.

Mummer looked at the figures on the table. 'I hope you've cleaned those,' she said. 'TB can live on for years.'

'Of course I have,' he said, setting a shepherd down next to a lamb.

'I really think you ought to have left them alone.'

'Why?'

'I don't know,' said Mummer. 'It just doesn't seem right going through people's things.'

Farther ignored her and rooted amongst the tissue paper that the little figurines had been wrapped in.

'Funny,' he said. 'There's no Jesus.'

ဢ

The meal was brought out and placed in the centre of the table among the tea lights Mummer had brought from the shop. On each jar was a portrait of a blond-haired Jesus blood-streaked from the crown of thorns and pointing to his huge blazing heart. We ate quietly, the rain hitting the windows and slithering down. Miss Bunce would only eat the vegetables. There was no dessert. Only water to drink.

148

Afterwards, Hanny was excused from the table and he went off to play in our bedroom, while the rest of us prayed again, thanking God for the meal.

'I thought I'd go for a walk up the field to the woods and back,' said Miss Bunce, dabbing at her mouth with a napkin. 'If anyone wishes to join me.'

Mummer looked out at the dusk. The rain had stopped but the wind shuddered against the window.

'I'll give it a miss,' she said. 'It'll be bitter out there by now.'

'I know,' said Miss Bunce. 'It's a penance.'

Mummer looked at the window again. The wind got in through a gap in the frame and made a sound like cattle. She looked back at the table full of dirty plates and dishes.

'You go,' she said. 'I'll devote the washing up to God.'

'Are you sure you don't want to come?' said Miss Bunce.

'It's not that I don't want to come, Joan,' Mummer replied. 'It's just that there's a more pressing need to clear the table. You go for your walk and I'll scrape the plates. I'm sure God is capable of receiving two offerings at once.'

There was a pause and everyone looked at the table.

'I'll come with you,' said David.

'Thank you,' said Miss Bunce.

'Would you take Monro?' said Father Bernard. 'The poor wee man hasn't been out for hours.'

'Yes, all right, of course, Father,' said Miss Bunce, looking at David who smiled to reassure her.

அ

Hanny was in the bedroom, pitting his toy soldiers against the stuffed rats again. So far the soldiers were winning. One of the rats lay on its side surrounded by tanks.

He smiled at me as I came in and he showed me his watch for the millionth time.

'Yes, Hanny,' I said. 'I know. It's good that we got it back.'

He ought to have been tired, but he seemed agitated and excited. I thought it was because he had found his watch or he had been so involved in the game he'd been playing, but he took me by the hand and led me to where his satchel was hanging on the back of the door. He opened the flap and took out the encyclopaedia he'd been looking at with Else.

He closed his eyes and touched his lips with his fingers.

'What does that mean, Hanny?'

He touched his lips again.

'You mean the girl at the house? I know, she gave you the book, didn't she?'

He sat on the bed and opened the book near the back. Inside was a brown envelope. One of the ones on which the sheep's skull had been sitting. He must have put it into his bag while I was talking to Laura. He took it out and opened it so that I could see. It was full of money.

'Give it to me, Hanny.'

Seeing my outstretched hand, he gave his head a little shake, frowned and hid the book behind his folded arms.

'I said give it to me.'

He shook his head more slowly this time, uncertain about what he should do. I held my foot over his soldiers.

'Give, Hanny,' I said and he looked at me and then slowly brought it over, nudging me aside and kneeling down to resume his game.

I sat on the bed and looked inside the envelope. There were dozens and dozens of ten pound notes, and in amongst the money was a list of names

Hale. Parry. Parkinson. Collier.

'You shouldn't have taken this, Hanny,' I said. 'You got your watch back, didn't you? Why did you have to take this as well?'

He didn't respond.

'Christ, Hanny,' I said, grasping him by the arm and showing him. 'There must be thousands of pounds here.'

He caught the tone of my voice and sat against the bed and put his head in his hands.

'Tomorrow,' I said. 'You're going to take this back. I'm not getting the blame. Whatever they want to do to you, I'll let them.'

It was a cruel thing to say, I know, but Hanny deserved to feel as worried as I was, especially after what Clement had said. He went to put on his gorilla mask and I let him. It would do him good to be frightened. He had to learn to deal with the consequences of the things he did. I wasn't going to be around to look after him forever. I mean, it was inevitable we would drift apart. University, career, marriage, mortgage, children. Even though they seemed unimaginable then, I was certain that, even without necessarily desiring them, I would receive these sacraments of adulthood sooner or later. They were as predictable as ageing. It was just what happened in life. Wasn't that so?

Hanny lay down and after glancing at me once or twice for some sympathy he went still and didn't wake even when the door banged open downstairs a while later.

தி

Going out onto the landing, I heard someone sobbing and Monro's claws skittering on the tiles. People went rushing out to see what was going on. I quickly stuffed the money back into the book and shoved it under my pillow.

Miss Bunce was sitting on the bottom step, crying and gasping, several hands rubbing her back, trying to coax out of her what was wrong. Mummer stood with her arms folded. David was nowhere to be seen.

'It was horrible,' Miss Bunce said.

'What was?' Mrs Belderboss asked.

Miss Bunce waved her hand towards the darkness and blubbed again.

'Where's David?' Mr Belderboss said, moving to the open door.

'I don't know,' she said. 'I just ran. I thought he was behind me.'

'Did you get lost or something, dear?' Mrs Belderboss said.

'No.'

'Did you and David fall out?'

'No, no,' Miss Bunce snapped. 'It wasn't that at all.'

'Well, where is he then?'

'I told you, I don't know.'

'I'm sure he won't be far away,' said Father Bernard, gesturing for Farther and I to put on our coats. 'We'll go and look for him.'

We left the commotion in the house and walked up the lane to the field gate, where a smaller path cut through the grass to the wood. Monro charged off ahead and as we got further Father Bernard whistled for him and we heard him come bungling out of the darkness to appear on top of a pile of stones to our right, daft with the run, his tongue hanging over his teeth, sending out little puffs of breath.

'Good lad, Monro,' said Father Bernard, ruffling his ears.

We stopped for a moment and then Father Bernard called David's name.

Nothing. Only the wind through the wood and a blackbird twittering in the darkness.

We climbed a little further and then stopped again at the tree line, our torch beams shaking and crossing, catching the eyes of animals just before they bolted. Father Bernard called out again and Monro went off, lumbering into the gloom. When we caught up with him, he was sniffing around David, who had heard Father Bernard and come to meet us.

'David?' said Father Bernard. 'Is everything all right? Joan's in a terrible state.'

'It's this way,' he said. 'In the trees over there.'

'What is?' said Father Bernard.

'A man's hanged himself, I think.'

'Jesus,' said Farther, then apologised to Father Bernard.

'Show me where,' said Father Bernard.

'I'm sorry, Father,' said David. 'Monro just slipped his lead and he was off before we could catch him. He obviously got the smell of it.'

'Show me where, David,' said Father Bernard again.

But David shook his head.

'I'd rather not,' he said.

'All right,' said Father Bernard. 'You go back to the house and make sure Joan's all right.'

'Should I call the police?' he asked.

'You can't. There's no phone,' said Farther.

David looked distressed.

'Look,' said Father Bernard. 'I'll see what's what and if we need to fetch the police, I'll drive to Little Hagby, all right? There's a pay phone in the pub.'

David nodded and took the torch Farther offered him and went back down the field to Moorings.

Father Bernard watched him go, and then turned to look at the trees. 'Come on, then,' he said quietly. 'And Tonto, you shut your eyes if I tell you to, is that clear?'

'Yes, Father.'

The dark of the wood was absolute. Even with the torches we tripped over roots and caught our feet on brambles. Farther slipped and fell into a mire of foetid leaves and mud. We helped him out and went on, with one beam trained on the floor and the other scanning the trees, which moved to and fro in the wind and made a noise like rain. Some had been beaten down by storms and lay like the spines of dinosaurs, rotting into the ground or leaning heavily against the living. Others had fallen but not died and, searching for the daylight again, had grown serpently along the ground.

There was no easy way through. Every turn took us to a fresh tangle of branches that were impossible to part without being scratched and snagged.

In the dark, the place seemed boundless and every sound carried a long way, from our boots breaking down the branches that had fallen between the trees to the noise of something thrashing through the undergrowth deep in the wood.

'Deer,' said Father Bernard when we stopped to listen.

'I hope so,' said Farther.

The crashing came again, sending a wood pigeon blundering through the trees nearest to us.

'It must be,' said Father Bernard. 'They can be noisy buggers sometimes.'

'Won't they bother about Monro?' said Farther.

'No,' said Father Bernard.

'I thought deer didn't get on with dogs.'

'They'd be long gone before that lummox got anywhere near them,' Father Bernard replied.

'Where is he, anyway?' said Farther, roving his torch beam across the trees.

Monro's barks echoed around the wood and it was impossible to tell which way he had gone. Father Bernard whistled for him and there was a great deal of rustling and when Monro barked again it sounded as if he was much closer and directly over to our left. He, of course, could slip under the branches and nose through the bracken, but for us the way was blocked and we skirted around the limbs and briars until Farther spotted a gap where the undergrowth had been trodden down by David and Miss Bunce as they chased Monro earlier.

Yet they hadn't been the only ones to have come this way. There were beer cans in the undergrowth and the damp smell of an old fire hung about the place, stirred with the dungy odour of cooked meat.

We came to a clearing and there was indeed a pile of burnt logs, white with ash and heaped with the remains of some animal. At first I thought it might still be alive, as its skin seemed to be moving, but as I stepped closer I could see that it merely crawled with flies and beetles foraging in its belly.

Farther swallowed. 'Where's that dog got to?' he said quietly.

'There,' said Father Bernard and pointed to where

Monro was jumping up at a long dark shape suspended from the bough of an oak tree, surely one of the oldest in the wood, swollen and contorted by its own weight.

We stopped short and Father Bernard called Monro to heel, which he complied with at the third, more irritable command.

'What have you found, old man?' he said and put the light on what Monro had been sniffing.

The beam illuminated a leering, bone face for a second before Father Bernard dropped the torch.

'Jesus,' Farther said again, his breath shivering out of him. 'What is it?'

'Well,' said Father Bernard, with a little relieved laugh and knocking the torch back into life on the palm of his hand. 'It's not a man, thank God.'

He put the light back onto the face again and held it there. From inside a dark cowl, a sheep's skull rubbed with boot polish lolled against the pull of the rope by which it had been strung to the bough, its snooker ball eyes knocking against the bone. The rest of the body, as we discovered when Father Bernard poked at it with a branch, was made of sandbags and wood covered in a rough woollen blanket.

'Then what is it?' said Farther. 'A scarecrow?'

'No, I think you were right first time, Mr Smith.'

'Sorry?'

'I think 'tis meant to be Himself,' said Father Bernard. 'See the crown of thorns there.'

He put the beam back on the head and lifted the cowl with the stick. Farther winced at the twisted band of barbed wire that had been hammered into the skull.

'Who'd do something like that?' Farther said.

'I couldn't say, Mr Smith,' he said, moving closer and moving the folds of the cloak covering the torso. 'But they've obviously spent some time on it.'

Father Bernard glanced at me and I knew that he suspected, like me, that the effigy had been strung up here by the men Clement had warned us about. Parkinson and Collier. But, he kept it to himself and showed us how the chest had been made from what looked like an old rabbit hutch.

'There's something inside,' said Father Bernard and he poked it with the stick.

'What is it?' asked Farther.

Monro was jumping up again, sniffing the air. Father Bernard popped the latch on the wire mesh door and it swung open and something landed at his feet. Monro leapt upon it immediately and took a chunk out of it before it slithered out of his jaws.

'Bloody hell,' Farther said and backed away, taking me with him.

Father Bernard grabbed Monro's collar and hauled him off.

'Let's go,' he said and we made our way quickly back through the trees, almost running by the time we got to the field above Moorings.

Back on the lane, we walked three abreast, Farther's boots squelching with mud. Monro padded along just ahead. No one spoke. Each of us was thinking how we might explain what we'd seen in the wood. We'd tell them that there was no man hanging there. It was a joke. There was nothing to worry about.

There was nothing else we could say. At the moment it had fallen from Jesus' chest and onto the ground we had agreed instantly and silently that we would tell no one about the pig's heart stuck through with nails.

# 14

Everyone was waiting in the hallway, and as soon as we got through the door, they all broke off from their conversations and moved towards Father Bernard. What had happened? Had someone really hanged themselves? Should they fetch the police? Father Bernard sent Monro off to the kitchen, closed the door behind him and waved his hands to quieten everyone down.

'It was nothing,' he said. 'Someone's strung up an old blanket for a joke, that's all.'

Farther nodded in assent and took off his coat.

'There, Joan, you see. It'll just be kids from the village messing about,' said Mrs Belderboss, patting Miss Bunce on the shoulder.

She was still sitting at the foot of the stairs, biting the edges of her fingernails, puffy-eyed and cross with herself for being hysterical in front of everyone.

Mr Belderboss clicked his fingers. 'That's probably what we heard the other night,' he said. 'The noises.'

'Aye, well, there you go,' Father Bernard replied.

'Honestly, some people have got nothing better to do,' said Mrs Belderboss.

'Not round here, they haven't,' said Miss Bunce, directing her resentment at Mummer.

Mummer's face began to open with indignation and before anything could flare up Father Bernard took her by the shoulders and steered her away.

'In my room there is a bottle of brandy on the dresser. Would you be so kind as to go and fetch it for me?' he said.

'Brandy, Father? It's Lent,' said Mummer.

'I brought it for Monro. The cold plays havoc with his chest. I thought a drop of it might do Miss Bunce some good,' he said. 'For the shock.'

Mummer folded her arms and rolled her eyes.

'She's been sat there for half an hour, Father. I should think the shock will have subsided by now.'

Father Bernard gave her a straight look. 'Even so.'

'Will you need to call the police, Father?' said Mr Belderboss.

Father Bernard looked at Mummer for a moment and then shook his head.

'To be honest, I can't see them taking it too seriously.'

'Well, I'm not staying here, Father,' said Miss Bunce.

'Oh, will you talk some sense into her,' said Mrs Belderboss to Father Bernard. 'She's sent poor David upstairs to pack her bags for her.'

'I don't care,' said Miss Bunce. 'This is an awful place. I said we ought to have gone to Glasfynydd.'

'But how will you get home, dear?' Mrs Belderboss said, sitting down next to her and taking her hand.

Miss Bunce looked up at Father Bernard.

'I was going to ask Father if he'd drive us to Little Hagby,' she said. 'We'll be able to phone for a taxi to take us to the station in Lancaster.'

'Oh, for pity's sake, Joan. You can't expect Father to go

out now,' said Mummer. 'It's gone nine. You'll have missed any trains to London.'

Miss Bunce squared her face.

'There are rooms at the pub,' she said. 'We can stay there overnight and get a train in the morning.'

'Don't be ridiculous,' said Mummer.

'Mrs Smith,' Father Bernard said abruptly. Then, calming his voice, 'Would you please go and have a look for that brandy?'

'Go on, Esther,' said Farther.

Mummer looked at Miss Bunce a second longer and then went off along the hallway. Everyone turned to Father Bernard. He regarded Miss Bunce and then took off his coat and hung it up on the rack by the door. He rubbed his eyes, kneading them with the heels of his palms.

'Miss Bunce,' he said, sitting down on the chair next to the grandfather clock. 'I know you've had a fright, but I should try and forget about what you've seen in the woods and make the most of the time we have here.'

Mummer came back with a glass tumbler of brandy and handed it to Father Bernard, who in turn passed it to Miss Bunce.

'I don't want it, Father.'

'Just take a sip and you'll feel better.'

Miss Bunce wetted her lips with the brandy and screwed up her face.

'You may not agree at the moment,' said Father Bernard, taking the glass from her as she held it out. 'But, given what I know of your commitment to your faith, I think that in the cold light of day you would regret it very much if you went home so soon.'

'Father's right,' said Mrs Belderboss. 'We haven't been to the shrine yet. You wouldn't want to miss that.'

Miss Bunce nodded and wiped her eyes. David came down the stairs, alternately banging Miss Bunce's suitcase against the wall and the banisters.

'Are you ready, Joan?' he said.

'False alarm,' said Mrs Belderboss and David hesitated for a moment, looked at Miss Bunce and then went back upstairs.

℘

When everyone had dispersed, I went up to check on Hanny. He was sound asleep, an arm lolling out of the bed towards his soldiers, the stuffed rats and the envelope of money. He'd taken it out from under my pillow and rifled through the contents. There were bank notes all over the floor. I collected everything together and hid the money under the mattress so that Hanny wouldn't find it again before we had to take it back.

In his other hand were the pornographic pictures Billy Tapper had given me. I took them off him and screwed them into a ball. They needed to go on the fire whenever the opportunity arose. Why we'd kept them, I didn't know, and what Mummer would have done had she found him with them, I couldn't imagine. Though I'd have naturally got the blame and been branded a deviant like poor Henry McCullough who had been caught in mid strike as he lay on his bed with his mother's underwear catalogues.

It had been around that time that a boy called Paul Peavey joined us as an altar server. He was younger than Henry and I, thin and pale, small for his age and keen as mustard to please Father Wilfred. He was the type that, given a different time and place, would have joined the Hitler Youth like a shot or been on the front row at a public hanging. His father was a regular fixture at the bar of the church social centre, where I helped collect the glasses on a Friday night. One of those loud individuals whose thinking is done for them by the tabloids. With him it was usually something about immigrants, or the unemployed or the Labour Party, or the nefarious connection between all three.

One Sunday after our cassocks had been inspected for dirt and creases and stowed in the vestry wardrobe, Father Wilfred went into his little office next door and came back with two pairs of gardening gloves. One for me and one for Paul. Henry held out his hands for his pair of gloves but Father Wilfred told him to sit down and guided Paul and I to the vestry door with instructions to go to the end of the graveyard and pick as many nettles as we could carry.

Not daring to question Father Wilfred, we duly hurried out, found a clump of nettles by the large Victorian vaults and came back with fistfuls of the things, which, despite the gloves, had still managed to sting our arms.

Henry looked up at us, his eyes widening when he saw what we'd brought back, knowing that they were destined for him in some way, his mind racing with terrible possibilities.

'Sit down,' Father Wilfred said to us and we did so, trying not to let the nettles sting us any more.

Henry started to ask us what was going on, but then jumped back into a rigid shape when Father Wilfred slammed the door to the vestry. For a few moments,

Father Wilfred stood against the wall looking at us, prolonging Henry's unease.

'I have a question for you, boys,' he said at last, setting off on his routine of pacing back and forth across the stone flags, patting his Bible. 'Come the Day of Judgement, who is to be cast down the deepest?'

Paul immediately raised his hand.

'Heathens?' he said.

'No,' said Father Wilfred. 'Even lower than the heathens.'

'Protestants?' said Paul.

Father Wilfred stopped abruptly and stood in front of Henry.

'What do you think, McCullough?'

Henry looked up at him nervously.

'Murderers, Father?'

Father Wilfred shook his head.

'No, McCullough,' he said. 'The people I am talking about will look on with envy at the punishments of murderers.'

'Fornicators,' Paul said suddenly.

'Close, Peavey. Onanists,' said Father Wilfred.

Henry looked down at his feet.

'Wicked little fellows who have too much time on their hands,' he said. 'McCullough, your mother tells me that you are an onanist.'

'No, Father.'

'She tells me that you keep vile magazines in your room.'

'I don't, Father. They're hers.'

'Are you calling your mother a liar?'

Henry said nothing.

'Fifth Commandment, Peavey.'

'Honour thy father and thy mother,' said Paul, watching Henry expectantly.

Father Wilfred put down his Bible on the table. 'I'll ask you again, McCullough. Is your mother a liar?'

'No, Father.'

'Then what she tells me is true?'

Henry put his head in his hands and Father Wilfred curled his top lip as though he had smelled something unpleasant.

'Sinful boy,' he said. 'I didn't have time for that kind of behaviour when I was your age. I was too busy begging for the scraps the butcher's dog wouldn't even eat, to feed my family and the family next door. Think of the Poor next time you're tempted; they don't have idle hands, lad. They're either working or praying for work.'

'I'm sorry, Father,' Henry sobbed.

Father Wilfred continued to glare at Henry, but held out his hands towards me and Paul, and after a moment where we looked at one another uncertainly, we passed him the nettles, which he took from us without flinching.

'Hands,' he said to Henry.

'What?'

'Give me your hands.'

Henry held out his hands and Father Wilfred put the nettles into his open palms.

'Squeeze them,' he said.

'Please, Father,' Henry said. 'I won't do it again.'

'Squeeze them, McCullough.'

Henry gently closed his hands and Father Wilfred suddenly clamped them tight. Henry cried out, but Father Wilfred only crushed them harder until green juice seeped out from between his fingers and ran down his arms.

'Believe me, McCullough, this is nothing to the pain onanists receive in Hell.'

After another minute of sobbing, Father Wilfred told Henry to put the nettles in the wastebin and sent him out into the church to pray for forgiveness.

'Not a word, boys,' said Father Wilfred to me and Paul as we put on our coats. Paul had gone a shade of pink with the excitement of it all. 'These lessons are for you and nobody else.'

'Yes, Father Wilfred,' we said in monotone chorus.

'Good,' he said. 'Kneel down now.'

We knelt down before him on the stone flags of the vestry, and in turn he placed a cold hand on our heads, reciting one of his favourite passages from Proverbs.

'"Trust in the Lord with all your heart and do not lean on your own understanding. In all your ways acknowledge Him, and He will make your paths straight."'

'Amen,' we said and he smiled and went into his office and closed the door.

We were like that old bike tyre he used to roll down the streets of Whitechapel as a boy, giving it little corrective taps to stop it tumbling into the filth, something which poor Henry frequently seemed to do.

We found him in the lady chapel, kneeling in front of the Virgin, looking up into her doe-eyes, whispering and crying, his swollen hands shaking as he desperately tried to keep them together. Paul laughed and zipped up his coat and went outside.

# 15

E VEN THOUGH MOORINGS had been built fortress-
solid to withstand the weather, and Mummer, out of
London habit, made a point of checking every door and
window before she went to bed, I still had the rifle next
to me that night.

I couldn't stop thinking about what we'd seen in the
woods. It seemed clear that Monro had been lured up
there on purpose by the smell of the meat. We were supposed
to find the thing hanging from the oak bough. It was
meant to frighten us into leaving. And if we didn't, what
then?

I thought about the animal roasted on the fire; the flies
crawling in and out of its face.

Every knock and creak of the house brought me back
from the edge of sleep and I felt my hands tense around
the rifle. Quite what I would do if anyone broke in, I
didn't know. The sight of the rifle might be enough to
make most people turn heel and run, but Parkinson and
Collier were used to guns and they'd know immediately
that it wasn't loaded.

⁊

It must have been around eleven o'clock when I heard someone knocking on Father Bernard's door. It was Mr Belderboss. I stood at the head of the stairs and waited until he had gone in and then went down one step at a time, sticking to the edges where they didn't creak quite so much, and slotted myself into the darkness of the understairs cupboard.

I could hear the clink of glasses and Father Bernard said, 'Do you want a drink, Reg?'

'Do you think we ought to, Father? Esther was right. It is Lent.'

'I'm sure the Lord would permit us a small one, Reg. After all that's gone on this evening.'

'Well, I will, Father, thank you,' Mr Belderboss said. 'Just don't tell Mary. You know what she's like. Anything stronger than Typhoo and she thinks I'm going to drop down dead.'

Father Bernard laughed. 'Is everyone all right now?'

'Oh, yes,' said Mr Belderboss dismissively. 'They don't half get into a two-and-eight about nothing sometimes. Like I say, it'll just have been kids from the village messing about.'

'Aye,' said Father Bernard.

They knocked their glasses together and there was a moment of silence while they presumably took back whatever it was they were drinking.

'Father,' said Mr Belderboss.

'Yes?'

'I'd like you to hear confession.'

'Of course, Reg,' said Father Bernard. 'If you're sure you want me to.'

'I am, Father,' he said.

'Well, finish your drink first,' said Father Bernard. 'Then we'll talk.'

'All right.'

Edging back a little, I found a box that would take my weight. Lower down there was a crack between the wooden boards and I could see a narrow slice of the room. Mr Belderboss was sitting on a chair in front of the grubby curtain that curved around the washbasin.

He crossed himself and said the Act of Contrition.

'What's on your mind?' Father Bernard asked.

'It's Wilfred,' said Mr Belderboss.

'Ah look, Reg, I'm sorry if it seemed as though I was prying the other day.'

'Oh, no no, Father,' said Mr Belderboss. 'That isn't why I came to speak to you. I'm not cross with you.'

He hesitated and rubbed the back of his neck.

'Father, Mary doesn't know, but the police brought me home from the cemetery one night the other week,' he said.

'Why, what happened?' Father Bernard asked.

'Nothing happened, as such,' said Mr Belderboss, shaking his head. 'I think they were going to take me in, but I got the impression they thought I was a bit doolally, being out at that time of night, so I let them think it and they brought me home instead.'

'What time was this?'

'Oh, I don't know. After midnight sometime. One. Two. Perhaps. I can't remember.'

'What made you go and see Wilfred at that time of night?'

'I just wanted to make sure no one had pinched the flowers,' said Mr Belderboss. 'They were quite expensive, you see, but it wasn't the money really. I just couldn't sleep for worrying that he was lying there all alone and thinking no one cared.'

'Wilfred's with God,' said Father Bernard. 'He knows how much you miss him. I'm not sure you need flowers to convince him of that.'

'But someone had taken them,' said Mr Belderboss.

'Oh,' said Father Bernard. 'So what did you do?'

'Well this is it, Father. I wandered around for a bit, trying to see if they'd been put on someone else's grave. People do that, don't they? If they forget to bring some or they can't afford them. Then I saw this woman. She was sitting in one of the little shelters they have there, you know the ones, Father?'

'Aye.'

'She looked quite normal at first,' said Mr Belderboss. 'She was dressed up in a fancy hat and she had a fur round her neck and new shoes, like she was on her way home from a party or something. I was going to ask her if she'd seen anyone acting suspiciously, but when I got closer I could tell she was a drunk. You know how they smell of the stuff? And when she moved, her coat opened and she wasn't wearing anything on her lower half, if you know what I mean, apart from her shoes. She went on and on about someone called Nathaniel. I thought, who on earth is she talking to? But then I realised she thought I was him. She kept on thanking me for sending her these flowers. So I said – what flowers? – and she had Wilfred's next to her on the bench. Even the little card was still there with them.'

'Go on.'

'Well I tried to take them off her and she started

screaming and next thing I knew there were two bobbies coming along the path with torches. She'd disappeared and I was there holding this bunch of hyacinths. I felt such a fool, Father. I mean, getting into trouble with the law at my time of life, can you imagine?'

'It's perfectly all right, Reg. To miss people that have died, I mean.'

'But not normal to go to their graves in the middle of the night?'

'I'm not sure normal comes into it when you're grieving,' said Father Bernard. 'But it might be better to go and see your brother during the day. I'm not sure I'd want to be wandering round Great Northern in the dark.'

Mr Belderboss looked up at the ceiling and sighed.

'I just feel ashamed that I've kept it from Mary,' he said. 'I ought to tell her what happened, just in case she gets to hear about it secondhand. They're a nosy bunch down our street. One flash of a blue light and the curtains are going.'

'I'm sure she'd understand if you did tell her.'

'So you think I ought to, Father?'

'I can't answer that. It's up to you. You know her best.'

'So it wouldn't be a sin to keep something important from someone?'

Father Bernard paused.

'Reg,' he said. 'I'm struggling to see what sin you've committed exactly. I'm not just going to send you off like a child to say three Hail Marys for mouthing off to your mammy. I think you need time to think about what to do for the best.'

'But what does God want me to do?'

'Whatever decision you make will be the right one, if you trust in Him.'

Mr Belderboss rubbed the back of his neck and breathed out heavily.

'Look,' said Father Bernard. 'It seems to me that you need to be in a dialogue with God, not putting out your hands for a caning. Take some time, talk to Him, pray for guidance, not punishment. God will answer you, Reg.'

'Yes, of course, I know.'

'You need to think about what there is to be gained from telling Mary,' Father Bernard went on. 'Are you going to be happier for telling her, but make her worried in return? Or would it punish you too much to keep it to yourself?'

Mr Belderboss shook his head.

'I don't know,' he said. 'It all just seems wrong.'

'Well, grief can often make you feel like that.'

'No, I don't mean that, Father. I mean where Wilfred's buried seems wrong.'

There was silence for a moment and then Father Bernard spoke.

'Why did he choose to be buried away from Saint Jude's, Reg?'

'So that he could be with the family.'

'You don't sound so sure.'

Mr Belderboss said nothing but stared at the floor in front of his feet.

'Tell me if I'm prying again,' said Father Bernard. 'But the other day you said that Wilfred seemed to change after you came here the last time.'

'Yes, Father, he did.'

'How?'

'I don't know. He just wasn't himself any more. He just seemed to give up.'

'Give up what?'

'Honestly, Father?' said Mr Belderboss. 'I think it was his faith.'

'Why would that have happened?'

'I don't know, Father, but for all he said every Sunday at Mass, I wasn't convinced he believed any of it any more. It just seemed like lip service. Like he was trying too hard. You know how if you say something often enough you can get yourself to believe it? And then in the end, well, he just seemed to shut himself away from everyone. Wouldn't speak to me or Mary.'

Mr Belderboss closed his eyes.

'Poor Wilfred,' he said, shaking his head. 'It's bad enough for anyone to stop believing, but it must be a terrible thing for a priest. It must have driven him out of his mind.'

⁏

Father Bernard pulled back the curtain and poured Mr Belderboss another drink, but he didn't touch it. They sat for a while and didn't really talk other than to eventually bid one another goodnight. They shook hands and Father Bernard patted Mr Belderboss on the shoulder.

'Peace be with you,' he said.

'And also with you, Father,' said Mr Belderboss.

When he had gone, Father Bernard stared at the door, deep in thought, then downed Mr Belderboss's brandy as well as his own and got up, disappearing from the splinter of the room I could see. I heard him talking to Monro, scolding him affectionately, then he returned with a book.

I made no sound, but he suddenly turned as though he had seen my eye in the crack. He looked directly at me, but then went back to reading, shivering a little as the wind lowed against the window and dimmed the bulb in the room.

# 16

A GALE BATTERED MOORINGS all night long and I woke several times and clutched the rifle. Sometime in the small hours there was an almighty bang and in the morning I woke to find that the doors to one of the outhouses had been taken clean off and lay several feet away, scattered like playing cards.

Hanny was up and dressed already, standing at the window, stroking the stuffed hare. He set the hare down on the windowsill and put his fingers to his lips. He wanted to see Else.

'Yes, Hanny, we'll go back today,' I said. 'But you might not be able to see the girl. They might not let you.'

He kissed his fingers again. And rubbed his belly slowly like Else had done to soothe the ache of the baby inside.

'I said, we'll go back.'

This seemed to satisfy him and he picked up the hare again and looked out of the window at the outhouse.

'Do you want to go and see?' I said.

There was no one else around. Monro lifted his head when we came into the kitchen and I gave him some of the biscuits Father Bernard had left on the table to quieten him down. I wanted to have the outhouse to ourselves first, before it became everyone's discovery.

We walked across the yard, trampling over the heavy wooden doors, and stood at the gap where they had once been.

Inside was an ark of stuffed animals — a hundred or more. These were the unsold, uncollected, unfinished works. Botched jobs. Seconds. The cold and damp had taken its toll and there were rows and rows of shrunken squirrels and rabbits. A poodle's head had sunk in on itself like an old balloon. In the far corner we found a tandem being ridden by two mangy chimps. Neither of us wanted to touch them, so we fetched a broom and pushed them off. They fell stiffly to the floor, still grinning, their hands like claws, as though they had been frozen solid.

Hanging from the ceiling were dozens of bird skeletons, hawks of some kind, trussed up by the feet and left to decompose. Why he hadn't stuffed them too, I didn't know. Perhaps he had died before he'd had time, but there were so many of them and the way they were hung they seemed more like the hare and the rats Hanny had found stretched out on the fence. Proof of a victory of some kind.

Although the floor was littered with their bones and feathers, the smell of rotting was strangely absent, as the air had been allowed to move freely through the gaps around the wooden doors and out of the barred window set just above head height on the far wall. There was a chest of drawers underneath it with bootprints on the top where the taxidermist had stood to look out of the window. On the floor, almost obscured by dust and spiderwebs were spent bullet casings. This must have been a firing step, though what he was trying to shoot, I didn't know. The hawks, perhaps, as they came out of the woods.

'Look in the drawers, Hanny,' I said and rattled the handles to show him.

He took hold of the top drawer and yanked it open. Spiders darted away, following the dark into the corners. Inside were dozens of old spanners wet with rust.

'Try the next one,' I said.

And here we found what I'd hoped was there. Under a thin cotton sheet were boxes and boxes of bullets. Hanny went to touch them, but I held his sleeve.

'Let me get them,' I said, and took out the nearest box and opened it. The bullets were set in a metal clip and were sharp and cold.

'You mustn't let anyone know that they're here, Hanny,' I said. 'This is a secret now. We'll take them down to the pillbox on our way to Coldbarrow.'

He stared at the bullets and I closed the drawer tightly.

∞

Eventually, everyone came to look and wandered between the animals with curiosity or revulsion.

Miss Bunce stood in the doorway and refused to come in.

'It's awful,' she said. 'Poor things.'

David put his hands on her shoulders and steered her away.

'That's a decent-looking machine, mind you,' said Father Bernard, nodding at the tandem that the chimps had been riding.

Hanny and I managed to haul it out and pushed it around the yard. The tyres had perished and the gears were clotted with rust but it didn't seem as though it would take much to be able to ride it again and Father Bernard only put up a mild protest about his clothes getting dirty before he fetched his tool box from the minibus.

Before long he had the tandem upside down in the kitchen on sheets of old newspaper and was taking apart the cogs and gears, his usually well-slicked hair flopping in front of his eyes. He seemed to be in his element as he knelt down with a spanner in his hand. More at home with nuts and screws and other pieces of greasy metal than giving out communion.

Mummer tutted and fussed until she finally stood over us with her arms folded.

'Boys,' she said. 'Will you please let Father have his breakfast now? There's too much to do to be spending the day messing about with that bit of junk.'

'It's quite all right, Mrs Smith,' said Father Bernard. 'It's nice revisiting one of the few genuine pleasures of my youth.'

She looked irritably at his black hands and the smudges on his face, as though she was, at any moment, going to spit on a handkerchief and start wiping.

'Well, everything's on the table, Father,' she said. 'We'll wait for you to say grace.'

'Oh, don't let me stop you, Mrs Smith,' he said. 'I might be a wee while getting all this oil off my hands.'

'All the same. I think we'd rather do things properly, Father, even if it means eating things cold.'

'As you wish, Mrs Smith,' he said, looking at her with a curious expression.

I've thought about that look quite often as I've been getting all this down. What it meant. What Father Bernard had let slip just at that moment. What he really thought of Mummer.

A line of dominos, spinning plates, a house of cards. Pick a cliché. He had realised what I'd known about Mummer for a long time – that if one thing gave way, if one ritual was missed or a method abridged for convenience, then her faith would collapse and shatter.

I think it was then that he began to pity her.

&#8477;

Father Bernard went off to clean himself and Hanny and I went into the dining room to wait for him. Everyone was sitting around the table watching Mr Belderboss. He seemed in a brighter mood than he'd been in the previous night with Father Bernard, though I got the impression he was deliberately distracting himself from thoughts of his brother with the object he was examining. It was a small, brown earthenware bottle with a cork stopper in the end and a gargoyle face crudely scratched on one side.

'It was on the window ledge, you say?' said Mr Belderboss.

'Yes,' said Farther. 'Stuck between the bars.'

'Oh, put it down, Reg, it's absolutely hideous,' said Mrs Belderboss. 'No one wants to see that at the breakfast table.'

He looked around at the others and then went back to studying the face on the jar.

'I don't see anyone complaining, Mary.'

Mrs Belderboss made a noise of exasperation that Father Bernard caught as he came in through the door.

'My, my, Mrs Belderboss,' he said. 'That sounded like a soul in distress.'

179

'Oh, you tell him, Father,' she said. 'He won't listen to me.'

'About what?'

She gestured to the bottle Mr Belderboss was looking at.

'He's obsessing again.'

'It was in the quarantine room, Father,' said Mr Belderboss. 'Between the bars on the window. There's definitely something inside it.'

He shook the jar and handed it to Father Bernard.

'Sounds like liquid of some sort. What do you think?'

Father Bernard put it close to his ear and listened as he moved it from side to side.

'Aye,' he said. 'There's definitely something in there.'

'Ugly thing, isn't it?' said Mr Belderboss.

'Aye, it is that.'

'What do you think it is?' asked Farther.

Father Bernard passed it back to Mr Belderboss and laughed and shook his head.

'I'm afraid I've no idea.'

'Father Wilfred would have known,' said Mrs Belderboss. 'Wouldn't he, Esther?'

Mummer handed Father Bernard a plate but didn't look at him.

'I'm sure he would,' she said.

'He'd a doctorate from Oxford,' said Mrs Belderboss, leaning towards Father Bernard, as he began buttering a slice of toast.

'Cambridge,' said Mr Belderboss, without taking his eyes off the jar that he was now turning round and round in his hands.

'One of those places, anyway,' said Mrs Belderboss. 'He was a very clever man.'

'And so well travelled,' said Mr Belderboss, shaking the jar gently next to his ear.

'Oh, yes,' said Mrs Belderboss. 'I'd have given my eye-teeth to have gone to some of the places he did. You were very lucky, Joan.'

Father Bernard looked confused. Mrs Belderboss leant towards him again and smiled at Miss Bunce across the table as she explained.

'Miss Bunce was lucky enough to accompany Father Wilfred on his trip to the Holy Land last summer. As his personal secretary no less.'

'Really?' said Father Bernard, looking at Miss Bunce. 'Well, well.'

Miss Bunce flushed slightly and scraped off a clod of butter from the block in the middle of the table.

'Mrs Belderboss makes it sound grander than it was, Father, but it was a wonderful experience,' she said.

Mummer suddenly remembered there was something she had to do and went out of the room.

It was still a bone of contention with her that Miss Bunce had been picked to go to Jerusalem with Father Wilfred. It wasn't because she hadn't been asked herself – she could hardly have accepted anyway, what with the shop to run – but because it was Miss Bunce who *had*.

She put on a front but had soon become utterly sick of the endless talk about the trip and had sat sour-faced through the slide show that had done the rounds of people's houses during the autumn of 1975: Father Wilfred coming out of the tomb of Lazarus. Father Wilfred standing outside the Church of the Holy Sepulchre. Father Wilfred walking along the Via Dolorosa. Father Wilfred in Al Bustan, waist deep in a crowd of poor, grinning Palestinian children wanting sweets as he tried to find the garden where King David set down the Psalms.

After a while, she came back in with a tray of tea cups, and during the silence as she set them out on the table, there was a knock at the front door. Everyone looked up. Father Bernard wiped his mouth and went to see who it was. We heard him speaking to someone in a tone of surprise and then the door to the dining room opened and Clement's mother appeared, dressed in a long coat – the hem of which met the tops of her wellingtons – and carrying a sack of firewood. Everyone watched as she moved backwards across the room, dragging the sack towards the nook beside the fireplace.

'Don't you want some help, Mrs Parry?' said Mr Belderboss, looking towards Father Bernard, who shrugged in a way that suggested he had already asked her and she had declined.

'Nay,' she said and looked up at us. She wasn't wearing her glasses any more and her eyes were a bright blue.

'Where's Clement?' asked Mrs Belderboss.

'He's out,' she said, dusting off her hands.

'Oh,' said Mrs Belderboss. 'Well how did you get here?'

She lifted her wellingtons in turn. 'Shanks' Pony,' she said.

'On your own?'

'Aye,' she said.

'Oh.'

Clement's mother put her hands in the pockets of her coat and looked at the wood she had brought in.

'That should be enough for now,' she said. 'As long as it dunt get any colder.'

She went to the door and Father Bernard opened it for her.

'It's all right,' she said. 'I'll see me sen out.'

Father Bernard watched her as she went down the hallway and out through the front door.

'I thought she was blind,' Mrs Belderboss said quietly to her husband.

'Well, perhaps she had an operation,' he replied. 'They can sort out cataracts nowadays, can't they?'

'Is that what you think it was? Cataracts?'

'I don't know. Probably.'

'That's astonishing,' said Mrs Belderboss. 'It was so quick. We only saw her the other day.'

'You see what I mean about this place,' said Mr Belderboss, looking around the table. 'A constant surprise.'

෨

After breakfast, I went upstairs and fetched the envelope of money from under the mattress. Mummer was still annoyed about Mrs Belderboss bringing up the Jerusalem trip, and was so distracted by all the preparations she needed to make for the visit to the shrine that she agreed Hanny and I could go out for a few hours.

Hanny wanted to take the tandem. I told him it was broken and pinched the tyres until my fingers met, but he still didn't understand.

'Father Bernard said he would mend them,' I said.

Hanny grasped the handlebars and rocked the bike back and forth, looking at me expectantly.

'No, Hanny. We can't ride it yet.'

As a compromise, I let him push it from the kitchen out into the yard, but he was soon distracted by a hare running off down the lane and he left the bike against a stone wall and chased after it. I went into the outbuilding and took a box of bullets out of the drawer. The box was too big, so I took out one of the clips and pushed it deep down into an inside pocket. I would stow it away in the pillbox when I got a chance. And then I could fire the rifle. Send a bullet out over the sea. Practise my aim in case Parkinson and Collier came.

The mist had thinned a little and looking over the fields there was something different that I couldn't quite place until I got further down the lane.

Hanny had stopped running and held on to the wall, breathing hard and looking across the field at the hare. I stood next to him and watched as it cut a furrow through swathes of fresh green grass that seemed to have appeared overnight.

&#8474;

Down at the beach and over the sea, the fog had lingered in the cold air and was so thick that we couldn't see more than a few yards. We waited and tried to listen for the sound of the sea to gauge whether the tide was in or out. Hanny went and sat on a rock and picked off the dried seaweed. I moved a little further towards the water, but was reluctant to go too far in case I lost Hanny in the mist. I looked over at him and he stared back and kissed his fingers.

'I know, Hanny, I know,' I said, and picked up a stone and pitched it into the fog. It landed with a single thud, and walking a little further I could see that there was only a thin wash of water. The tide was receding. The weed on the rocks was still wet.

'Come on, Hanny,' I said. 'We need to go now.'

Hanny walked off quickly and I had to jog at times to keep up with him. When I finally called to him to wait, he stopped in the mist up ahead.

'Hold my hand tight,' I said.

We had come to the last of the timber posts and there was half a mile of open sand that couldn't be crossed as quickly. The tide had scrubbed away any tracks Leonard's car might have made and even if I could have roughly remembered the route they had marked, a safe path yesterday could be quite the opposite now.

'Hold my hand,' I said again, but Hanny was too distracted and so I took hold of his arm and led him around the standing water.

'You mustn't let her kiss you again,' I said. 'The man will be cross with you.'

He smiled.

'I'll be cross with you too.'

He touched his lips again.

'No, Hanny.'

He stuck out his tongue and turned away.

'Listen,' I said, holding him by the shoulders and nudging his chin with my knuckle so that he faced me. 'There are men who don't want us to be here. Men who might hurt you. So we've got to be careful about what we do. We just need to give the money back and leave them alone.'

He looked down at his feet.

'Hanny, I'm serious,' I said, hitting him a little harder this time. 'I won't be able to stop them if they want to hurt you.'

He rubbed his chin and felt around in his coat pockets until he found the plastic dinosaur and handed it to me.

'You don't need to say sorry,' I said. 'Just don't do anything stupid.'

He held my hand and we carried on. Not for the first time, I wished that I'd brought the rifle. The mist had turned the sands an ashen colour, and was so thick that all sense of space was lost. Oystercatchers and gulls would sound far off one moment and then suddenly loud as they flew by. And from time to time there was a steady rumble that I thought at first was thunder or an aeroplane but realised that it was the sea churning its way over the sands, drawing out to its limit, like a bowstring.

✂

Leonard's car was parked outside Thessaly when we got there. The place was Sabbath quiet. I knocked on the door, waited, and then when no one had come after a minute, I knocked again.

Hanny had wandered away to look at the bell tower.

I called him back, but he ignored me. I shouted a little louder, but he was too intent on opening the door and so I went over to try and lead him back to the house.

It was impossible to tell from the mainland, and even from Thessaly one could miss it, but it seemed that there had once been another building there – a chapel, perhaps, by the fragments of stone archways half hidden in the bracken. What had happened to it, I didn't know. I'd never heard of any place of worship on Coldbarrow. Perhaps they had got it wrong, or the old stories had succumbed to Chinese whispers as old stories do. Perhaps the Devil hadn't built the tower at all, but knocked down the church around it. Perhaps he had built Thessaly from the remains. They were of the same stone after all.

Before I could stop him, Hanny put his shoulder to the door and it grated open enough for us to look inside. Water dripped and something fluttered up to the belfry where the wind murmured around the wooden scaffold that held the bell in place. I wondered if, long ago, they had crept in here to satisfy themselves that Elizabeth Percy was really dead and had stood as quietly as we did now, looking up, watching her turning on the end of the rope, her bare soles curled in rigor mortis.

A stronger gust came in off the sea and swung the bell into a soft tolling. Hanny looked suddenly frightened and started to back away, almost running into Leonard, who had come out of the house and was standing in the door watching us.

'I didn't expect to see you two here again so soon,' he said.

He was dressed down from the last time we'd been here. No jacket or aftershave, just shirt sleeves and corduroys. The kind of thing Farther put on when he was creosoting the fence or touching up the gloss work on the skirting boards.

But Leonard's arms were spattered with dried blood.

He saw me looking and rolled down his sleeves.

'What do you want?' he said.

I opened my coat and took out the envelope.

'I've brought this back,' I said.

Leonard took it from me and frowned.

'Where did you get this?' he said, opening the envelope and looking inside.

'It was in the book your daughter gave Hanny to keep. I don't think she knew it was in there.'

It was the lie that I thought the least damaging.

'Daughter?'

'Else.'

'Oh,' he said. 'No, I dare say she didn't know.'

'It's all there,' I said.

'How do you know that?' Leonard smiled and looked inside the envelope again. 'Had a quick count of it, did you?'

Hanny was tugging at my sleeve and stroking his stomach.

'What's the matter with him?' said Leonard.

'He wants to see Else.'

'Does he now?'

'Yes.'

'Well, I'm afraid that isn't possible.'

From somewhere inside Thessaly there came the sound of a baby crying. Hanny stopped what he was doing and looked at the window at the far end of the house. He smiled. Leonard followed Hanny's gaze and then looked at me, considered something, and took out several notes from the envelope. He came closer to me, hobbling on his bad leg, and slipped them into the breast pocket of my parka. I went to remove the money but Leonard kept his hand on my chest.

'Please, it's the least I can do,' he said. 'Since you came all this way to bring it back.'

'But I don't want it.'

'That's us settled,' he said. 'I don't expect there's anything else you'll need to come back for now, is there?'

'No.'

'Good lad,' he said. 'And those names on that list.'

'What about them?'

'Can you remember any of them?'

'No.'

'That's the way,' he said.

The baby cried again and Leonard nodded towards the lane.

'On you go then.'

I pulled Hanny away and Leonard watched us go before he went back inside the house. Hanny insisted on walking backwards so that he could keep looking for Else. He kept on stumbling and fell over more than once, on the last occasion refusing point-blank to get up. I went to pull him to his feet, but he wrestled out of my grip and kept his eyes fixed on the house.

'You can't see her, Hanny,' I said. 'Didn't you hear what the man said?'

Suddenly he stood up and stared. A figure had appeared at the end window. It was Else. She waved at Hanny and after a moment Hanny raised his hand and waved back. They stood staring at each other until Else turned sharply as if called by someone and disappeared.

## 17

'FORGIVE ME, FATHER, for I have sinned,' said Miss Bunce. 'It has been three months since my last confession.'

'I see.'

'It was with Father Wilfred, just before he passed away.'

Father Bernard sounded genuinely surprised. 'Not that you have a multitude of sins to confess to, I'm sure, but it doesn't seem like you to distance yourself from God for so long, Miss Bunce. It's not me putting you off, I hope.'

Miss Bunce sniffed.

'No, Father. It's not you. I did try to come and speak to you, several times. I even made it to the door of the confessional once, but I went home again.'

'Well, confession isn't always easy.'

'I thought that I might be able to forget about it, but I can't. The more you try and forget the more you remember. Sin's like that, isn't it? It haunts you. That's what Father Wilfred used to say.'

Father Bernard paused. 'Well, you're here now, Miss Bunce,' he said. 'That's all that matters. You take your time. I'm quite happy to sit here and wait until you're ready. I'm not on the tight schedule of absolutions I usually am at Saint Jude's.'

Miss Bunce laughed joylessly, sniffed again, mumbled a bunged-up thank you and emptied her nose.

'I don't know how to begin, really,' she said. 'It was listening to Mrs Belderboss talking about that trip to Jerusalem that set me off again. I just feel so upset about Father Wilfred. It was me who found him, you know.'

'So I believe,' said Father Bernard. 'It must have been a terrible shock.'

'It was, Father. And we parted on such bad terms.'

'Bad terms? Why, what happened?'

'Well, the last time I saw him at the presbytery before he died he was acting so strangely.'

'In what way?'

'He was worried about something.'

'About what?'

'I don't know. I didn't like to ask.'

'But you could tell he was worried?'

'He was just so distracted, Father. Like there was something behind him all the time, you know?'

'Aye, go on.'

'Well, he asked me to go back to Jerusalem with him. For a longer trip. He said that was where he felt safe.'

'Safe?'

'That was the word he used, Father.'

'All right.'

'Well, I told him I couldn't. I didn't want to be away from David for so long, not with the wedding to organise and everything.'

'And what happened?'

'Well, we had a row.'

'I can't imagine you having a row with anybody,' said Father Bernard. 'Let alone Father Wilfred.'

'Well, it wasn't a row so much as, well, it felt more like he was lecturing me. He didn't approve of David, he said. He said that I had to stop seeing him. I had to call off the engagement. I couldn't understand why. He's got a good job. He goes to church every Sunday. He's kind and considerate. What is there not to approve of?'

Father Bernard laughed quietly.

'I'm sure Father Wilfred had his reasons, but I must confess I can't for the life of me think of one. David's a fine feller.'

'He said there was something about him that he didn't like. I asked him what, but he wouldn't tell me. I thought that perhaps he knew something about David that I didn't, but it seemed to be more the fact that I would be moving away after we got married that he wasn't happy with. David has this job lined up in Saint Albans, as you know.'

'Aye, well, maybe that's it. He had a good cook and he didn't want to let you go. I know I'm reluctant myself.'

Miss Bunce managed a little laugh but quickly went back to her concerns.

'Why do you think he was so angry with me, Father?'

'I think what you have to remember, Miss Bunce,' he replied, 'is that Father Wilfred was an old man. I'm not saying you have to excuse his bad temper, but a lifetime's service to the Church and you get stuck in your ways and it's hard to change. I'm sure that he didn't mean to upset you and he probably spent as much time kicking himself for it as you did worrying about it.'

He paused and when Miss Bunce didn't say anything but sniffle into her handkerchief, he went on.

'You know,' he said, 'my daddy used to say that death has the timing of the world's worst comedian and I think he was right. When people die, it's natural to regret how we treated them when they were alive. Heaven knows, there are dozens of things I wished I'd asked my mammy and daddy when they were around; times I'd like to wipe clean away. Things I wish I had or hadn't said. It's the worst kind of guilt, because it's completely irreparable.'

'Oh, I know,' said Miss Bunce. 'I'd just hate to think of him still angry with me.'

'The blessed souls in heaven don't take anything like that with them. Father Wilfred is at peace now. He doesn't bear you any grudges. I'm sure that he only wishes you to be happy. And being unable to grant him that wish is the only sin you've committed, Miss Bunce.'

Miss Bunce began to sob again. 'No,' she said. 'There's more I haven't told you, Father. I don't think you'll be so kind to me when you hear it.'

'Ah, I see. And this is what made you hesitate outside the confessional?'

'Yes, Father.' Miss Bunce snivelled again.

'Well, it sounds to me like it's been bothering you, whatever it is, so it might be best just to tell me and have it out in the open.'

'Yes,' said Miss Bunce, sounding as though she was steeling herself. 'You're right.'

She took a deep breath and sighed.

'I got drunk, Father,' she said. 'There. That's it. I went home and I drank half a bottle of Mum's sherry.'

'All right.'

'I did it to spite Father Wilfred.'

'I see. And there's me forcing brandy down your neck the other night.'

'I don't know what came over me. I wasn't like me at

all. I mean, Mum has a drink to calm herself down some-times, so I suppose that was why I had a glass. But I just couldn't stop. It was so deliberate. I was so angry.'

'With Father Wilfred?'

'With myself. I said nothing to defend David. Father Wilfred was so determined about it that for a moment I thought he was right and that I ought to call it all off.'

'You didn't, did you?'

'No, of course not.'

'Did you tell David?'

'I phoned him when I got home, but by the time he came round I was so drunk that I could hardly speak. I don't know what I said to him. I must have looked a complete idiot. It's a wonder that he still wants to marry me at all. But he was so kind. I don't remember getting there, but he put me to bed and stayed with me until Mum came home.'

'See. He's a good man.'

'Yes, he is.' Miss Bunce blew her nose. 'Father,' she said. 'Drunkenness is a terrible sin, isn't it? Father Wilfred always said so.'

'I think,' said Father Bernard, 'that it depends on the person. I think it depends on what the drunkenness leads to. It's a venial sin at most perhaps but in your case I wouldn't call it a sin at all.'

'But I knew what I was doing was wrong and I still went ahead and did it, Father. Doesn't that mean I'll end up in Purgatory? I mean, the drunkenness aside, wrath is one of the Seven Deadly Sins.'

Father Bernard coughed and hesitated for a moment before he answered.

'There is a school of thought in the Catholic Church,

Miss Bunce, that says it's possible to experience Purgatory here on earth, that guilt is a kind of purification in itself. It sounds to me like that's exactly what you've been through already and that being the case I can't see God wanting to make you go through it again. You've tormented yourself over what happened with Father Wilfred, you've burdened yourself with guilt and I should think the hangover alone was punishment enough.'

'I've never been so sick in all my life.'

'So I can assume that you won't be hitting the bottle anytime soon?'

'Oh, never again, Father.'

'Well then, listen. God forgives you your anger and your moment of weakness. Don't dwell on it any more. Put Father Wilfred's feelings down to those of an old man afraid of being lonely, and marry David. You have my blessing, if you want it.'

'Thank you, Father.'

'All right now?'

'Yes, Father.'

I heard Father Bernard draw back the curtain, then saw him stand next to Miss Bunce. He put his hand on her head and she crossed herself.

❧

It made sense now why, after the carol service, Miss Bunce had come into the vestry from the presbytery, crying and agitated, looking for her umbrella.

'Have you seen it anywhere?' she asked.

All three of us, Henry, Paul and I, shook our heads and watched with interest as she upended the room and then went out into the rain without it, running down the path and out of the church grounds.

'She's very odd,' said Paul. 'Don't you think?'

Henry and I said nothing and continued stacking the hymn books on the shelf as we had been instructed to do by Father Wilfred.

Paul sat down on a bench and crossed his legs. Father Wilfred had asked him to supervise us and he thought himself quite the foreman.

'She's not a bad-looking woman, though,' he said.

It was a phrase I'd often heard his father use in the social centre.

'Quite pretty in a certain light,' he added. 'Bet you like her, don't you, Henry?'

Henry said nothing, only looked up at me briefly as he straightened the books.

'I bet you've thought about what she looks like naked, haven't you?'

Paul got up and went to the door to check that Father Wilfred wasn't coming. He wasn't. The lights were still on in the presbytery and he always switched them off when he left the place, even for a minute.

'Go on,' he said. 'You can tell me. Do you think about her when you're at it?'

Henry turned and looked at him.

'You do, don't you?' said Paul.

He looked across to the presbytery.

'I suppose Father ought to know,' he said.

'Don't,' said Henry.

'Why not?'

'Don't,' Henry said, though this time it wasn't a plea.

'He's coming now,' said Paul.

We heard the presbytery door slam and then Father Wilfred's footsteps on the gravel path.

'Don't you say anything, you sod,' Henry said.

'Oh dear, oh dear,' said Paul shaking his head. 'Foul language as well.'

'I mean it,' said Henry.

Paul smiled at him as Father Wilfred appeared at the open door.

'Are you still putting the books away?' he said. 'I thought you were supervising, Peavey?'

'I am, Father, but they won't listen.'

'Won't they?'

'No, Father. They're being impertinent,' said Paul and waited eagerly to see Father Wilfred's reaction.

'I'm not interested in your excuses, Peavey,' he said. 'Did Miss Bunce happen to come here?'

'Yes, Father,' said Paul, his smile fading.

'Where did she go?'

'I don't know, Father. She seemed a bit upset.'

'Did she?'

'Yes, Father.'

'Did she say anything to you?'

'No, Father. She just wanted her brolly.'

Father Wilfred looked on the back of the door where a red umbrella was hanging. He took it down and then went out, looked for her on the street and then hurried back to the presbytery.

# 18

ON EASTER MORNING, it was still dark as we walked about the yard looking for stones. Ones about the size of a fist were the best, the shape as close to an egg as possible.

Mummer and Farther had already found some for Mr and Mrs Belderboss and were back at the foot of the dry-stone wall looking for more. Miss Bunce and David, who couldn't see the point in any of it, had satisfied themselves with the first pebbles they had laid their hands on and returned to the warmth of the kitchen, where Father Bernard, who had overslept, was hurriedly putting on his boots.

'Morning, Tonto,' he said, coming out with his hair wild at one side and his face black with stubble. 'Happy Easter.'

'Happy Easter, Father.'

Mummer came over. 'I'd try over by the wall if I were you, Father.'

'Right,' he said.

He went off and kicked about in the rubble, eventually selecting a flat block of slate. He held it up to me for approval and I shrugged and he tossed it back and moved on.

∾

With pockets weighed down with stones, we made our way up the lane to the woods. What we'd seen the other night still troubled me and it was obvious that Miss Bunce and David were reluctant to go back as well, but the sky was lightening moment by moment and the trees were coming out of the shadows. It seemed a different place altogether.

Mummer led the way through the field and up behind Moorings, bearing right and heading for Nick's Lane – the treeless stripe that cut through Brownslack Wood as cleanly as if someone had taken a razor and drawn it up the hill. No trees had ever grown there and Mr Belderboss thought that the land must have been poisoned in some way. Hadn't they used lime on their fields around here? Too much of it might have killed off the trees. Farther suggested that by some freak of nature the wind blasted that particular part of the ridge and knocked the trees flat, but neither of their theories seemed any more plausible than the old story about the Devil burning a path through the woods as he left the Loney in a fit of rage the night they strung up Elizabeth Percy.

Mr and Mrs Belderboss were left far behind and by the time they caught up with us on the ridge, the sky had started to lift in the east – the distant Pennines becoming noticeable moment by moment, pale and lavender-coloured in the dawn.

Mummer let her stone drop from her hand and it tumbled down the fellside as she whispered a prayer. Farther did the same and then everyone followed so that there were several rocks bouncing through the ferns and knocking against the limestone shelves, rousing pheasants and curlews from their sleep.

Hanny was tugging at my sleeve and pointing.

'What is it?' I whispered.

He went down the hillside a little and beckoned me to follow him.

'What's the matter, Hanny?'

'What has he seen?' said Mummer.

Hanny went off, wading through the ferns. Mummer called him back but he didn't respond.

'Stay here,' said Farther. 'I'll fetch him.'

Farther went after Hanny, following the trail he had cut through the undergrowth, calling to him. Hanny turned around once or twice, but was determined to get to whatever he had seen from the ridge.

Way down the hill, he stopped. Farther caught up with him a minute later and he looked at what Hanny had found. He waved and called for Father Bernard and me to come.

⁛

Before we got within twenty yards of Farther, he raised his hand to keep us quiet, never taking his eyes off the thing by his feet.

'What is it?' Father Bernard said.

'Look,' said Farther.

A pregnant ewe was there in the ferns, her eyes yellow and wild, possessed by the ancient hormones that had driven her to hoof out a nest in the soil and lie down.

'Is she all right, Father?'

'Aye, I think so.'

Father Bernard knelt down and put his hand on the ewe's belly, hushing her when she jerked suddenly and scuffled in the mud.

'There now,' he said softly.

'Did you keep sheep, Father? On your farm?'

'We'd a few, aye.'

The ewe raised her head a few times and then laid it down on the ground. In the cold of the early morning, her hot breath hung around her nose and mouth.

'She's breathing hard, isn't she?' said Farther.

'Aye, well look,' said Father Bernard. 'She's at her time.'

He moved around to her rear end, where a hoof protruded, then another, before the lamb's nose appeared, opening and closing behind the water sac. He edged a little closer and put his hand on the ewe's side, stroking her fleece with his thumb.

'It won't be long now,' he said.

The ewe looked at us with her black keyhole eyes and stiffened her legs as her stomach bulged. She gave a loud bray as her body shuddered in the final contractions that squeezed out the lamb in a steaming discharge.

It lay there, tarred and feathered by its mother's gunk and the dead ferns, shivering and convulsing as it tried to breathe.

Father Bernard ripped up a few leaves and scrubbed the lamb with them, breaking the caul that had been covering its face. It opened its mouth to cry and tried to stand and then lay down again, bleating feebly. Father Bernard took hold of the lamb and pulled it around so that it lay in front of its mother's face. The ewe lifted her head and began to lick.

Mummer and the rest of them had appeared by this time, having taken the path that wound down the hillside, and stood around watching. Miss Bunce held her nose and David's hand. Mr Belderboss crossed himself.

'God be praised,' he said. 'Is she all right?'

Father Bernard nodded.

The ewe had got up and wandered away from us into the bracken. After a few attempts, the lamb followed on its crumpled legs and began its first tottering steps, crying out with a little red spike of a tongue. The ewe called and the lamb went to her, ramming at her udders.

'Father Bernard saved its life,' said Farther.

'I did nothing so heroic, Mr Smith. His mammy would have got rid of the caul herself right enough. I just didn't want to see the poor lad struggling.'

'First those butterflies,' said Mrs Belderboss. 'And now this. God couldn't have sent us a more obvious sign. And Andrew finding it as well. Wonderful things are going to happen at the shrine, Esther.'

'If only Wilfred were here,' said Mr Belderboss. 'He'd have had quite a take on all this, wouldn't he? He had that way about him, didn't he? Of knowing just what to say.'

'He did,' said Mrs Belderboss. 'It's a rare gift, isn't it, Father?'

'Aye it is that,' Father Bernard replied.

'Do you remember the outing we had to the Fens that weekend?' said Mr Belderboss.

Everyone nodded and exchanged knowing smiles. Mrs Belderboss touched her husband on the arm.

'There was that terrific thunderstorm, wasn't there, Reg?'

'Oh, Lord yes. Almost apocalyptic it was, Father,' Mr Belderboss laughed.

'We were all stuck in that bird hide,' said Mrs Belderboss. 'Do you remember?'

'Golden Orioles,' said Mr Belderboss.

'Sorry?' said Father Bernard.

'We were looking at the Golden Orioles.'

'They have the most beautiful song,' said Mrs Belderboss.

'Like someone playing a flute,' Mr Belderboss added.

'Well,' said Mrs Belderboss. 'We hadn't seen one all day, had we? And then when the storm came, one started singing its heart out, didn't it? It never stopped, right through all the thunder and lightning. And Father Wilfred got us all to kneel down and pray. What was that bit from Saint John he read, Reg?'

'Oh, don't ask me,' he said. 'I've got no memory for that sort of thing.'

'A voice of one calling in the wilderness?' Father Bernard suggested.

'Yes, that was it, Father,' said Mrs Belderboss. 'He said that we had to keep on singing like that little bird no matter what befell us in life.'

&#8367;

The Christmas of 1975 came and went and Father Wilfred performed his duties at Mass but, as Mr Belderboss had said, he seemed to have retreated from the world. When the service was over he didn't lecture us any more. He barely spoke a word before he was off to the presbytery where he shut himself away until he was next required. Miss Bunce came and made him his meals but left immediately afterwards. He no longer went to visit the sick, or took communion to the housebound. If anyone called he wouldn't answer. People began to worry about him again as they had done at the Loney.

It was only when his diary went missing that we saw something of his former self.

The Sunday after Christmas Day was the Feast of the Holy Innocents. Mr Belderboss had read the lesson from Matthew and Father Wilfred had given a long sermon about the reasons why the children slaughtered by Herod had been martyred, though it drifted off into incoherent mumbles from time to time, and it sounded as if he was talking to himself rather than the congregation.

Afterwards, we were getting changed in the vestry, when Father Wilfred came out of the office in a foul temper.

'Where is it?' he said, looking from me to Henry to Paul.

'Where's what, Father?' said Paul.

'My book.'

'Your book?' said Paul.

'You're starting to sound like a parrot, Peavey. Yes, my book. I left it in the office by mistake. Where has it gone?'

'What did it look like, Father?'

'Black,' he said. 'A black diary.'

'I don't know, Father,' said Paul. 'Henry was the last one in the office.'

'McCullough,' said Father Wilfred.

'I haven't got it,' Henry said, looking at Paul who smiled and hung up his cassock.

'But Peavey says you were in the office.'

'I was cleaning the sink, like you told me to.'

Father Wilfred grasped his elbow. 'Do you know what a syllogism is, McCullough?'

'No, Father.'

'It's a form of deductive analysis. A method of coming to a logical conclusion about something.'

'Eh?'

'My book has gone missing from the office. You were the last person in the office. Therefore you have the book.'

'But I don't, Father. I've never seen it before.'

'I should check his coat pockets, Father,' said Paul.

'Be quiet, Peavey,' said Father Wilfred. 'Of course I'll check his pockets. Where is your coat, McCullough?'

Henry pointed to the back of the door, but his coat was gone.

'I left it there,' he said, his mouth quivering a little now, knowing that Paul had set him up.

'Well it isn't there now, is it, McCullough?'

'No, Father.'

'So where is it?' he said, shaking Henry's arm.

'I don't know. It wasn't me, Father,' Henry said, pointing at Paul. 'It's him. He's trying to get me into trouble.'

Father Wilfred suddenly gripped Henry by the collar and turned him to face me.

'Proverbs, Smith,' said Father Wilfred.

'Sorry, Father?'

'Tell McCullough the things set out in Proverbs. The things that Our Lord hates above all others.'

'Pride?'

'Yes.'

'People that kill the innocent.'

'Yes, yes. What else?'

'The devious, troublemakers.'

'And?'

'Liars, Father.'

'Yes,' said Father Wilfred. 'Slanderers, McCullough. Those who bear false witness. Those who blame others for their own failings. God orders us to cast them down with Satan.'

Henry was twisting under Father Wilfred's grip, his puffy face bright red.

'Tell me where it is, McCullough,' Father Wilfred said, trying to grasp Henry's flailing hands.

Henry got hold of Father Wilfred's wrist suddenly and pulled him to one side, making him stumble into the wall and fall to the floor.

'I'm sorry, Father,' he said, immediately reaching out to see if he was all right.

Father Wilfred was breathing hard, the skin under his eye already swelling and reddening. He put his hands on his knees.

'Get out,' he said quietly. 'All of you get out.'

'I'm sorry,' said Henry again, looking to Paul and me for help.

'I said, out, McCullough.'

'But are you hurt, Father?'

Father Wilfred looked up at Henry with a face like that of a child knocked flat by the school bully. Frightened, angry, but bewildered more than anything.

'Why must you torment me?' he said and went into the vestry office and closed the door.

The three of us stood there in silence for a moment, not sure whether we ought to wait for him to dismiss us. Then Paul made a noise of contempt and shook his head and went outside. Henry and I looked at one another.

'Do you think he'll be all right?' said Henry.

'Yes.'

'I didn't mean to hurt him.'

'I know.'

Henry made a move towards the office door.

'Perhaps I should make sure,' he said.

'Leave him,' I said and Henry looked down at his feet and then followed me outside.

'I thought he was going to kill you, McCullough,' said Paul, glancing over his shoulder as he unchained his bike from the drainpipe.

'Where is it?' said Henry.

Paul slung his leg over the saddle.

'Where's what?'

'You know what.'

'Your coat?'

'Yes.'

Paul looked over Henry's shoulder and nodded. His coat was wrapped around a branch of one of the beech trees next to the presbytery.

'And what about the book?' said Henry.

'I don't know,' replied Paul. 'Who cares?'

Paul tried to set off, but Henry held onto the handlebars.

'Where is it?' Henry asked him again.

'Let go, McCullough. Do you want me to call Father Wilfred?'

'Depends. Do you want me to smash your teeth in?'

'You wouldn't dare.'

'Wouldn't I?'

'No, fatty, you wouldn't.'

Henry looked down. 'Just tell me if you took it,' he said.

'You'd love that, wouldn't you?' said Paul. 'Going off to grass me up.'

Henry suddenly raised his voice. 'Do you think I'm going to come back? I never want to set foot in this place ever again, so it doesn't really matter what you tell me.'

This wrong-footed Paul, but he pretended to be bored with the whole thing.

'It's in the belfry,' he said, then scowled at Henry. 'You need to lighten up, McCullough. It was only a bloody joke.'

Henry let go of the handlebars and Paul went off slowly so that he could give Henry a grin. We watched him go and then Henry sat down on the steps outside the vestry.

'It's all right,' I said. 'I'll tell Father Wilfred.'

'Will you?'

'Yes.'

'Thanks.'

I looked at him.

'What will your mother say when you tell her you want to leave?'

'Make me come back.'

'Can't you tell her what Father Wilfred's like?'

'No,' he said. 'She wouldn't believe me. She thinks the sun shines out of his arse. Help me get my coat down, will you?'

'All right.'

We walked around the base of the tree trying to find a stick long enough to reach it. In the end, with some effort, I gave him a leg up and he managed to get his fingertips to the sleeve that was hanging down.

It was, I remember, an expensive-looking leather thing with wide lapels and a belt with a circular buckle. He turned it over to inspect the damage and then spat on his hand and rubbed away the moss stains with his fingertips.

'Do you believe in Hell?' he said.

'About as much as Father Christmas,' I replied.

'Seriously, though. What if it does exist?' he said.

'It doesn't.'

'Yeah, but what if it does?'

'It's just an idea,' I said. 'That's all.'

'But where did the idea come from?'

'Someone's imagination.'

'You can't imagine something like that,' he said. 'No one can have invented Hell. It's like saying someone invented air. It's just always been there.'

'Look, don't worry about Father Wilfred,' I said. 'I'll make something up.'

He smiled weakly and put on his coat and did up the belt as he went to fetch his bike from the holly bush where Paul had evidently thrown it.

'Thanks, Smith,' he said.

He stood with one foot on the pedal, pushed himself along and once he was moving lifted his leg over and went out through the gate, the front wheel wobbling. The bike was much too big for him. Or he was much too big for the bike. One or the other.

I waited for a moment, wondering if I ought to go home too and just let the whole thing blow over. But if I knew Father Wilfred he wouldn't let up and in any case I felt sorry for Henry. If his mother did force him back, as he was convinced she would, then it wouldn't be fair for him to face Father Wilfred's fury when he'd done nothing wrong.

I make it sound so noble, but in truth I just didn't want Paul to have the satisfaction of making Henry the whipping boy any more.

I climbed back up the steps to the vestry and Father Wilfred was still turning the office upside down.

'Yes? What is it, Smith?'

'I know where your diary is, Father.'

'Ah, McCullough owned up to stealing it, did he?'

'No, Father. Henry didn't take it.'

'Then who did? Peavey?'

'No, Father.'

'You?'

'Of course not, Father.'

'Surely not Miss Bunce,' he said.

'It wasn't Miss Bunce.'

'She has been acting rather rashly these last few weeks. Talking about leaving Saint Jude's. Moving away.'

'Father, it wasn't her.'

He stopped and sat down on the wooden chair. He had one of his antique swords laid across the table.

'All that I do seems to go amiss,' he said, picking it up and inspecting the blade. 'Why won't McCullough change?'

'I don't know, Father.'

'I punish him and still he sins. When will he see that I'm trying to save him?'

'I don't know, Father.'

'I fear for his soul as I fear for my own.'

'Yes, Father. I know you do.'

He turned his attention to the portrait of Jesus hanging over the sink.

'When will he realise that I give these lessons out of love? Because I do love him. If I could only save one, it would be him.'

'Father, your diary.'

'What about it?'

'I told you, I know where it is.'

'Who took it? McCullough?'

210

'No, Father.'

'Where is it then?'

'In the belfry.'

'The belfry? How did it get up there?'

'I don't know, Father. Perhaps you left it there by mistake.'

'Yes, perhaps I did. I don't remember,' he said, staring into space.

'Would you like me to get it for you, Father?'

He snapped out of his gaze and looked at me.

'I don't know what I would do if I lost my diary, Smith,' he said. 'It has everything in there, you see. Everything. It's how I keep control of my thoughts. It's how I can understand where a thought has come from. I can trace it back to its origin. I can pinpoint where things went wrong. It's a map. Do you see?'

'Where things went wrong, Father?'

'With McCullough.'

'Shall I fetch it for you, Father?'

'No, no.' He waved his hand irritably. 'I shall go up to the belfry myself.'

He went out and I followed him and watched him going down the central aisle of the church talking to himself. I don't think he realised that he still had the sword in his hand.

# 19

THE NEWBORN LAMB caused so much excitement that breakfast went on too long and we set off late for Mass. But no one seemed to be worried, jubilant as they were about it being Easter Sunday and excited about visiting the shrine the following day.

On the minibus, Mr Belderboss got out his harmonica and had everyone singing 'Come Let Us with Our Lord Arise' and 'Jesus Lives and So Shall I'. Miss Bunce smiled for the first time in days. Mummer sat with her eyes closed, enjoying the rare sunlight that was blessing the coast that morning and giving the sea a deep blue calmness that I'd never seen before. I felt the same sense of hope that I'd felt at Saint Jude's the morning we'd set off. There was nothing to worry about. Parkinson and Collier may have hung the gruesome thing in the wood to scare us, but that seemed to have been the extent of their menace. They were nothing more than oversized children playing knock-a-door-run.

I took everything that was offered that morning – the warm sunlight, the soft shadows on the fields, the spangle of a brook as it wound under some willows towards the sea – and managed to convince myself that nothing would harm us.

Such naivety makes me laugh now.

The small spire of the Sacred Heart appeared and everyone stopped singing so that they could hear the bells. But there was nothing. Only the bleating of the sheep in the field.

'That's odd,' said Mr Belderboss. 'They always ring the bells on Easter morning.'

'I know,' said Farther. 'A full peal too.'

'Why is everyone standing outside?' said Miss Bunce as we pulled up next to the church.

'What's going on, Father?' said Mrs Belderboss.

Father Bernard stopped the minibus and we all got out and joined the rest of the congregation as they milled about in front of the church doors.

The priest came over to meet us.

'I'm sorry, I'm afraid there'll be no Mass this morning,' he said.

'Why? What's happened?' said Mummer.

'An act of vandalism,' he said.

'Oh no,' said Mrs Belderboss. 'Is there much damage?'

The priest seemed lost for words. He could only look back at his flock, gathered around the main door. Clement was among them and when he saw us he waved us over to look.

There on the ground was the wooden Jesus that had hung over the altar smashed and splintered.

'Good Lord,' said Mr Belderboss. 'They've been at it with sledgehammers by the looks of it.'

'Aye, you're not wrong,' said Father Bernard, bending down to inspect the damage.

'Five hundred and ninety years,' said the priest from

213

behind us. 'Five hundred and ninety years that's been hanging over the altar here. And now this. In five minutes of madness. I mean, why?'

'Oh, there is no reason for it with these people,' said Mrs Belderboss. 'They're just mindless thugs.'

'It's their upbringing,' Mr Belderboss said. 'They don't teach them right from wrong at home any more.'

'Will it be kids from the village?' said Mrs Belderboss.

'Yes,' said the priest knowingly. 'There's a few little hooligans that I wouldn't put it past to do something like this. I've seen them spraypainting and littering.'

I saw Clement glance at Father Bernard. It was clear who he suspected, though he didn't say anything.

'Can't you take it inside?' said Farther. 'See if there's any way of salvaging it?'

The priest said nothing but pushed past us and went to the main doors. A huge chain had been passed through the handles and padlocked together. He lifted it up and let it fall back against the doors by way of an answer.

'The side door's the same,' he said.

'What about breaking a window?' Mr Belderboss suggested.

'Break a window?' the priest said. 'The glass is priceless, man, don't be ridiculous.'

'Have you called the police?' asked Mrs Belderboss.

'Yes, of course,' the priest replied.

'It might have been better to have fetched the fire brigade,' said Mr Belderboss.

'The fire brigade?' said the priest, trying to untangle the chain in the vain hope that it might only be an obstinate knot. 'What good would that do?'

'Well, they have things which would cut through that like a knife through butter,' said Mr Belderboss.

'I can't believe anyone would do something like this,' said Mummer. 'Locking people out of the church on Easter morning.'

'What about saying Mass outdoors?' suggested Miss Bunce. 'Like they do at Glasfynydd.'

Mummer made a derisive noise and turned away, but the priest seemed to consider it a decent idea, given the circumstances, and asked the regulars if they agreed. They said little but nodded in supplication and the priest gathered us in front of one of the yew trees and began.

ॐ

The police turned up halfway through and went around the church, inspecting the doors and windows. I noticed that Clement had stopped singing and was watching them anxiously as they squatted down on their haunches to look at the battered crucifix.

After the blessing, the priest seemed a little calmer for having got through the unusual Mass and that the police had arrived. He went around shaking hands and accepting condolences and finally went off to speak to the two policemen who had been standing patiently by, their helmets under their arms, as though they were at a funeral.

'What a disappointment,' said Mummer.

'I thought it was quite nice, really, in the end,' said Miss Bunce. 'Quite liberating.'

'Don't worry, Esther,' said Mrs Belderboss, patting

Mummer's arm. 'It'll be all better when we go to the shrine tomorrow.'

'Yes,' said Mummer. 'I know. I know.'

'You can't let something like this get you down. It's not worth it. It's what these little villains want.'

'I know,' said Mummer. 'You're right. I just wish we could have had a normal service and that Andrew could have taken communion.'

'Come on, Esther,' said Mrs Belderboss. 'Don't be sad. There's nothing more you can do now but trust that the Lord will visit Andrew tomorrow. All the signs are there.'

I saw Clement wave Father Bernard over to the shade of some cypress trees, where he had been lingering as the policemen went around taking statements. Father Bernard excused himself and went over to speak to him. They had a conversation that I couldn't hear. Father Bernard put his hand on Clement's shoulder. Clement nodded, and then Father Bernard came back to where we were standing.

'It's all right if Clement comes back for a bite to eat, isn't it?' he said. 'His mother's out and it seems a shame for him to be on his own today.'

Clement hung behind him, scratching the back of his neck, pretending to scrutinise the inscription on one of the gravestones.

'Well, I don't know,' said Mummer. 'I've not really catered for another mouth, Father.'

She caught Miss Bunce's eye.

'But,' she said. 'I'm sure there'll be enough. It'll be nice to have another guest to celebrate with us.'

We sat down at the dinner table as soon as we got back. If nothing else was going to go right, Mummer at least wanted to eat on time.

Clement had been persuaded to take off his filthy jacket and hang it up by the front door so the smell was at least confined to the hallway. Underneath, he wore a bulging tanktop of red, black and orange chevrons, a khaki shirt and tie that seemed to be strangling him.

Outside, the day had turned overcast and rain was starting to set in again. The room became gloomy enough for candles, which Father Bernard lit one by one.

Mummer, Miss Bunce and Mrs Belderboss came in and out with trays of steaming meat and vegetables, a loaf of bread, sauces in silver boats. A warm plate was set in front of each person and once everyone was sitting down, Father Bernard invited Clement to say grace, not noticing, or wilfully ignoring, the look of horror that Mummer tried to slide discreetly his way, as though on a folded piece of paper.

Without a moment's hesitation, Clement said, 'Lord, we humbly thank Thee for the food Thou hast set before us and ask that Thou bestow on us Thy blessing on this glorious day. Amen.'

There was complete silence as everyone looked at him. It was the most he had ever said in one go.

'Thank you,' said Father Bernard, and Clement nodded and dug his fork into the mound of potatoes.

Everyone watched as he shovelled the food into his mouth and slopped gravy down his tie. Hanny was especially fascinated by him and barely touched his own food for watching Clement eat his.

'How are things on the farm?' Father Bernard asked. 'It must be a busy time of year for you.'

Clement looked up briefly and then went back to his potatoes.

'Not too good, Father.'

'Oh, why's that?'

'We're going to have to sell up.'

'I'm sorry to hear that,' said Father Bernard. 'What's happened?'

Clement looked around the table again and said nothing. Mr Belderboss tried a different tack.

'We were all wondering, Clement, if your mother had had an operation or something.'

'Eh?'

'Well she came with firewood the other day.'

'Oh, aye,' he said. 'Aye, she's had an operation.'

'And now she can see all right?' said Mrs Belderboss.

'Aye.'

'It's amazing what they can do nowadays, isn't it?' she said.

'Aye,' said Clement, without looking up from his plate. 'It is.'

The main course over, Mummer brought out the simnel cake she had made the day before with its sugar paste face of Jesus in the middle and its twelve marzipan balls around the edge representing the disciples.

She placed the cake in the centre of the table and everyone, apart from Miss Bunce, made a fuss over it, praising the detail on Jesus' face, how intricate the thorns were, how the cochineal colouring had made the blood trickling down his cheek so vibrantly red. Hanny picked up the cake slice, but Mummer took it gently from him and went back into the kitchen, returning with a fistful of leaves left over from Palm Sunday.

'It seemed fitting,' she said.

Everyone drew one from her hand. Clement was last and looked around the table before taking one for himself.

'Now,' said Mummer, 'let's see.' And everyone placed their leaves down on the table.

Clement had drawn the shortest.

'What does that mean?' he said.

'It means,' said Mummer, trying to hide her disappointment that he of all people had won. 'That you get to throw Judas on the fire.'

'Pardon?'

'Choose one of the balls on the cake,' said Farther, leaning towards him. 'And toss it into the fire.'

Clement looked at the cake and then at the fire churning in the grate.

'It's all right,' he said. 'Someone else can do it.'

'But you've won,' said Mrs Belderboss.

'Aye,' said Clement. 'But I'd rather not.'

'It's only a bit of fun,' Father Bernard said.

'Go on, son,' said Mr Belderboss, plucking one of the marzipan balls from the cake and handing it to him.

Clement looked at the thing in his hand and then, holding it as though it were a delicate glass marble, he edged his chair back across the stone floor, stood up and went over to the fire. He glanced back at the table and then tipped his hand and sent Judas into the flames. Everyone clapped and for the first time Clement managed a smile, albeit a self-conscious one that made him run his finger round the inside of his collar.

'What was that?' Miss Bunce said through the applause. She half stood up, holding onto the table. The clapping died away and we sat in silence listening to the rain pummelling the yard outside.

'What's the matter, dear?' Mrs Belderboss said.

'Shh,' said Miss Bunce.

A screeching noise came from outside.

Hanny gripped my hand under the table. Everyone turned to look at the window. But there was nothing to see, only the rain beating down.

'Owls,' said Mr Belderboss, picking up the cake slice and handing it to Mummer. 'I'll just have a small piece.'

'No, no, it's not,' said Miss Bunce.

'It was owls,' said Mr Belderboss. 'Barn owls, if I know anything.'

The noise came again, closer this time. The shriek of something in agony.

'You might be right, Reg,' said Farther. 'It certainly sounded like a barn owl.'

Everyone apart from Clement got up and crowded at the window as we heard the sound of barking. In the field beyond the yard, a small white dog was edging backwards, dragging something in its mouth.

'Isn't that your friend's dog, Father?' said Mrs Belderboss.

'Which friend is that?'

'Your pal who helped fix the minibus.'

'I wouldn't call him a pal, Mrs Belderboss.'

'Heavens. What is it doing?' Mummer said.

'Has it caught a bird, Father?' said Mrs Belderboss.

'It's certainly got its teeth into something,' said Father Bernard.

'I told you. It'll have got a barn owl,' said Mr Belderboss. 'They screech like stink when there are dogs about.'

'Don't be silly, Reg,' said Mrs Belderboss. 'How on earth could a dog catch an owl?'

'It's not an owl,' said Miss Bunce indignantly. 'It's much bigger than that.'

'What *is* it?' Mummer said again.

Far away someone whistled and the dog looked up and after a moment shot off across the grass, leaving whatever it had been chewing to die in the middle of the field.

Monro was pining to be let out, lifting himself up and pawing at the door.

'Hey, hey.' Father Bernard went over and tried to calm him down.

'What's the matter with him?' said Mrs Belderboss.

Father Bernard struggled to get hold of Monro's collar.

'It'll be the dog outside,' he said. 'He's not good with other dogs.'

'Oh, get him to stop that awful noise, Father,' said Mrs Belderboss.

Clement was looking anxiously from one person to another.

'Come on, you silly wee beggar,' Father Bernard said gently and put his arms around Monro's neck.

But Monro was still as white-eyed as Clement and jumped out of his grasp and knocked over the small table next to the door on which Mr Belderboss had left the earthenware jar.

It smashed on the floor and its contents spilled everywhere. A few small bones. A piece of leather cut into a crude heart shape. Iron nails pickled with rust. And there was the missing Christ from the nativity set stained the colour of malt whisky.

'Oh, my Lord,' said Mrs Belderboss as her feet were soaked. 'What on earth have you done, you great lump?'

'That smell,' said Mummer, covering her nose with her hand. 'I think your dog's been.'

'It's not Monro,' said Father Bernard. 'It's what was inside.'

A dark yellow fluid was leaking from the jar onto the stone floor.

'What's that?' said Miss Bunce, backing away.

In the puddle of urine there floated what looked like strands of human hair and nail clippings.

Through the commotion, Clement started to call out. Everyone turned back to the table and stared at him. He had left his dinner half finished and had, in the custom of the place, left his knife and fork crossed on the plate. He had his hands flat on the table and was staring at the remains of the jar on the floor.

'I'd like to go home now,' he said.

❧

Clement went out to fetch his jacket. Everyone watched him go and then Mummer swept up the pieces of the jar while Farther laid down some newspaper to soak up the spillage.

'I hope you're going to lock that room up for good,' said Mummer.

'Of course I will,' said Farther. 'I'm sorry, everyone.'

'It was hidden for a reason.'

'I know, I know.'

'You can't leave things alone, can you?'

'Oh, Esther, that's enough,' he said. 'I've apologised. What more do you want me to do?'

'All right,' said Father Bernard. 'Let's not dwell on it. What's done is done.'

'Well I'm still none the wiser,' said Mr Belderboss, 'what that jar was for.'

'I don't know, Reg,' said Mrs Belderboss. 'Perhaps it was a litter bin. Now give it a rest. There are more important things to worry about.' She eyed the door through which Clement had just gone.

'I was only saying.'

'And I was only thinking of poor Clement,' said Mrs Belderboss.

'How do you mean, poor Clement?' said Mummer.

'Well it's obvious, isn't it?' replied Mrs Belderboss.

'What is?'

Mrs Belderboss lowered her voice, aware that Clement might be able to hear them from the hall.

'They've had to sell the farm to pay for his mother's operation, haven't they?'

'They do have the NHS up here, you know,' said Mummer.

'Oh, they'll not have got that done on the National Health so quickly,' said Mrs Belderboss. 'Will they, Father?'

'I shouldn't think so.'

'No, it'll have been some private place,' said Mr Belderboss. 'Very expensive.'

'What a wonderful thing to do for someone though,' said Mrs Belderboss. 'Give everything up like that.'

'Aye,' said Father Bernard.

'I wonder what he's going to do now?' said Mrs Belderboss.

'Leave us alone to salvage what we can of the day, I hope,' said Mummer.

'Esther,' said Mrs Belderboss. 'Don't be unkind. It's Easter Sunday after all.'

'Well,' said Mummer. 'A grown man going all strange at the dinner table like that just over a broken old pot. It was so awkward.'

'He didn't make as much fuss as you,' said Farther, scrunching up the newspaper and feeding it to the fire.

Mummer gave him a look and went back to the conversation around the table.

'His nerves are probably bad,' said Mrs Belderboss. 'He has had to sell his farm.'

'So he says,' Mummer replied. 'But you know what he's like.'

'What do you mean?' said Mrs Belderboss.

'Aye, what is he *like* exactly?' said Father Bernard.

Mr Belderboss leant in towards him and Father Bernard listened, still with his eyes fixed on Mummer.

'He's one of these that tends to exaggerate things sometimes, Father. Doesn't quite live in the same world as you and I, if you know what I mean.'

'But I don't think he's making it up this time,' said Mrs Belderboss. 'I mean his mother can see again. There's no disputing that. They must have got the money from somewhere.'

'I must say, I'm inclined to agree with you, Mrs Belderboss,' said Father Bernard. 'I think we ought to make allowances for the poor man, and if he has had to sell everything then we should perhaps consider what we can do to help. Isn't that the reason we're here?'

'Well, if you think, Father,' Mr Belderboss replied, with a hint of defensiveness.

Father Bernard lowered his voice. 'I don't want to get

on my high horse about it, but can you think of anything worse than losing your home? When I was in the Bone I saw people left with nothing. Good families who had their houses burned down in front of their eyes for no other reason than being Catholic or Protestant. Can you imagine what that does to people?'

'It's hardly the same thing,' said Mummer.

'You must admit it was their choice to sell, Father,' said Mr Belderboss. 'Clement and his mother's. No one forced them.'

'What do you think Wilfred would have done, Reg?' asked Father Bernard. 'He wouldn't have just ignored it, would he?'

'Of course he wouldn't have ignored it, Father. But all the same, I don't think he would have liked us to have got involved. It's nothing to do with us.'

'Isn't it?'

Miss Bunce hadn't said a word throughout, but now she put down her cup and said, 'I think Father Bernard's right. Think of the Samaritan.'

'Hear, hear,' said Farther from the fireplace.

Mr Belderboss smiled at him sympathetically and then at Miss Bunce.

'The thing is, Joan, what you have to understand about these country folk is that they don't want help, and certainly not help from outsiders like us. They're a proud people. It'd be an insult to them. There are times, like Esther says, when the greatest kindness is to leave people be. Isn't that right, David?'

David put his arm around Miss Bunce.

'I think Mr Belderboss is right,' he said.

Miss Bunce looked at him and then down at her tea

cup. Mummer took up the reins and steered the conversation back to Father Bernard again.

'You see when Father Wilfred brought us here it felt as though he was able to draw a circle around us. To keep us focused on our own relationship with God, and allow him to guide us through the days with an attention that he wasn't always able to give us back at Saint Jude's. That was the whole point of being here. It wasn't just a pilgrimage, Father. It was a sanctuary too. It might be worth bearing that in mind.'

Everyone was looking at Father Bernard. He stood up.

'I'll be taking Clement home now,' he said.

'Yes, all right, Father,' said Mr Belderboss.

'Do you want me to come with you?' said Farther. 'Make sure you don't get lost.'

'No, no, Mr Smith,' he said. 'It's kind of you to offer, but I'll be all right.'

'If you're sure.'

'I'd rather you got that fire going for when I get back. The weather looks fair brutal out there.'

'I will, Father,' he said, and began untying the bundles of firewood Clement's mother had brought.

'Mind how you go, Father,' Mrs Belderboss called after him as he went out to get his coat. 'Oh dear,' she said once the door was closed. 'I hope we haven't upset him.'

'I think we did,' said Miss Bunce.

'I was right, though, wasn't I?' said Mr Belderboss. 'I mean no one's persecuting Clement, are they? It's not our fault.'

Mrs Belderboss patted his hand.

'No, it's not,' she said and then shook her head. 'What a mess,' she continued. 'I don't remember it being so – difficult – when we came with Wilfred.'

'He kept everything simple, that's why,' said Mr Belderboss. 'And he didn't go prying into other people's affairs.'

'Still,' said Mrs Belderboss. 'Everything will be better tomorrow, when we go to the shrine. What's that bit from Isaiah? About not worrying about the days that have gone?'

'"Forget the former things; do not dwell in the past,"' said Miss Bunce and finished off her piece of cake.

'That's the one,' said Mrs Belderboss. 'Tomorrow's another day.'

&#8360;

Clement was still waiting patiently on the little chair in the hallway, his walking stick balanced on his knees.

'Can I go home now?' he said.

'I think Father Bernard's just getting his coat,' I replied.

He looked down at the floor.

'I told them not to ring that bell,' he said.

When I didn't respond, he looked up again.

'The bell on Coldbarrow. You know the one up in the old tower next to the house?'

'Yes.'

'It were boarded up for years. But they went out to it.'

'Who did?'

Clement was about to answer but stopped short when a door opened along the hallway. Father Bernard appeared and frowned as he zipped up his coat.

'What's going on?' he said and Clement waved him over and made him sit on the stairs.

'Parkinson and Collier, Father. They went out to

Coldbarrow on New Year's Eve just gone and took the boards off the tower and started ringing that bloody bell. And not a day or two later there were lights on at Thessaly, and then all this business started.'

Father Bernard looked at me and then back at Clement. 'What business?'

'They told me not to come here any more,' he said. 'They said they'd get me sent back to Haverigg, like they did last time. But I had to come and warn you about what they've done. And now that your dog's broke that bottle, it might be the only opportunity I get.'

'That old jar in the dining room? What's that to do with anything?'

'Don't you know what it is?'

'No.'

'They're meant to keep witches away from the house,' he said. 'But you have to keep them sealed. And now it's been opened . . .'

'Clement,' said Father Bernard. 'Is there someone you want us to call? A doctor maybe. Will your mother be in when we get back? Maybe I ought to speak with her. See if we can get you some help with whatever it is that's bothering you.'

Clement lowered his eyes.

'You don't understand, Father,' he said. 'You must keep away from Parkinson and Collier.'

'Why? What is it that you think they've done?'

But Clement didn't have time to answer before someone knocked at the front door with a heavy, rhythmic thud.

Hanny came out of the dining room and grabbed my arm, wanting me to open the door. Gradually everyone was gathered in the hallway and we all listened to the singing coming from outside.

'Who on earth is it?' said Mummer, and she sidled through the throng to see.

# 20

THE PACE EGGERS had always frightened me as a child, looking as they did like things that had crawled out of a nightmare. Each one a mishmash of fairy tale characters, grotesque as Punch and Judy puppets. Natives of some savage tribe as painted by the children of missionaries.

When we'd come here in the past we'd sometimes see them performing on the green at Little Hagby – half a dozen local men, blacked-up like chimney sweeps with only their eyes showing and armed with swords and staffs.

The stink of booze drifted from them as they sang old songs in bass voices; songs that didn't have the predictable, homely rise and fall of the hymns we'd been singing all week, but which tumbled through strange minor keys and moved across intervals that sounded like they might have once charmed the Devil to the surface of the world.

At the front of the pack was Saint George, dressed in a crusader's tabard and banging his wooden staff in time to the song. When it ended he removed his cardboard crown and bowed. Even under all the make-up I could see that it was Parkinson. Collier stood behind him dressed as the character called Brownbags, his dog chained to the gate post outside, straining and yelping.

'We've come as agreed,' said Parkinson to Father Bernard and smiled. Father Bernard glanced at Mummer, who frowned at him.

'And is that Clement you've been entertaining?' Parkinson looked towards the back of the crowd, and everyone turned to see the colour drain from Clement's face. 'Well well. Tha gets about, dunt tha, Clement?'

Mummer still had her hand on the door.

'I'm afraid you must have the wrong house,' she said. 'We weren't expecting you.'

Parkinson looked at Father Bernard and smiled.

'We like to get around all the big houses on Easter Sunday,' he said. 'And we thought tha might appreciate some entertainment what with the weather being so foul.'

'Well, perhaps we could come down to the village and watch you some other time?' said Mummer.

'Oh, we won't stop long,' Parkinson replied.

He seemed to have somehow crossed the threshold without Mummer noticing and she had no choice but to step back and allow the men to enter. Each of them nodded their thanks and wiped their feet on the mat – Saint George, Brownbags, the Turkish Knight and the others, one of whom swept quickly past completely swaddled in a black cloak, leaving Old Ball, the horse, to come in last, wearing a brown smock and holding a real horse's skull on the end of a pole, a set of glass eyes clacking inside. It rolled about, grinning, like the thing we'd found in the woods.

Whoever was under the cloak stooped the nag's head so that it would fit through the doorway to the sitting room.

As it swung down, Miss Bunce stepped back and grabbed at Father Bernard's sleeve.

'Do you think this is a good idea?' she whispered to him when the men had all filed past. 'I mean they could be anyone. Is it some pagan thing?'

'Oh, Joan, it's tradition,' Mummer said. 'We've always watched the Pace Egging.'

'What, here?'

'Well no not here. But, look, it's just a bit of fun.'

'Fun?'

'Yes,' said Mummer, not quite convinced herself, as she followed the men and started to organise a space for them to perform.

℘

She might have been doubtful about letting them in, or embarrassed that she had been doorstepped so easily, but now that the Pace Eggers were here Mummer quickly took charge. She would have them in and out quick sharp.

The room was cleared and Mrs Belderboss was dispatched with Miss Bunce to make sandwiches and tea, while Farther and David gathered up as many of the vulnerable ornaments as they could and took them out into the hall.

I helped Father Bernard shift a table out of the way, carrying it into the bay of the window. He kept his eye on the Pace Eggers as they waited for us to get the room ready. Parkinson waved Clement over and handed him an old curtain, which he strung between two lampstands to form a makeshift wing from which they could enter and exit.

'I didn't think they'd really come,' said Father Bernard.

'What do you mean, Father?'

'I didn't say anything to Clement the other day, but Mr Parkinson had already promised to bring the Pace Eggers up to Moorings. I thought it was just the ale talking. He'd had a fair few, like.'

'Do you think we should have let them in, Father?'

He looked over to where the men were getting ready.

'Why? Because of what Clement said about them?'

'And what we saw in the woods.'

'Look, we don't know that that had anything to do with them, Tonto. Not really.'

He glanced at them again and laughed quietly at their costumes.

'I think they're harmless enough. And in any case how would it look if we asked them to leave now? I think it's best if we just let them get on with it. What are they going to do here?'

'I don't know.'

'Exactly. Don't worry about what Clement said just now. That's between him and them. It's nothing to do with us. All right?'

'Yes, Father,' I said, though I was less convinced than he was.

He smiled at Mummer, who came over with an expensive-looking floorlamp, and set it on the table out of harm's way. She looked at him and went away to help David shift a delicate crystal vase off the mantelpiece.

'What would Father Wilfred have made of these fellers, Tonto?' said Father Bernard.

'I don't know.'

'You don't really talk about him all that much. Did you get along with him all right?' he said, dusting his hands.

'I suppose so.'

'Only suppose so?'

'He did a lot for the poor,' I said, and Father Bernard looked at me and smiled.

'Aye,' he said. 'I know he did, Tonto.'

At Mummer's request, he started to close the curtains.

'I'm only asking, because I know nothing much about the man,' he said. 'I mean, I know he was well respected but was he happy in his work, would you say?'

'I think so.'

'I mean, how did he seem before he died?'

'How did he seem?'

'Aye.'

'I don't know.'

'Would you say there was something on his mind?'

The sound of a bell came from behind the curtain and Mummer turned off the main light.

'I don't know, Father.'

He knew I was being obtuse, but he smiled and turned his attention to the Pace Eggers instead, storing away what I'd said or hadn't said for later.

'Who's your man in the purple there?' he asked in a whisper, pointing to the player pressing his Zapata moustache back into place.

'That's the Turkish Knight,' I said.

'Is he the villain? He looks like a villain.'

'Yes.'

First out of the shadows was Collier, dressed in a frayed kilt, a harlequin shirt and a top hat like a broken chimney-pot. He carried a wicker basket under his arm.

'Who's this?' Father Bernard said behind his hand.

'That's Brownbags,' I said. 'He collects the money.'

'Money?'

'You're supposed to give them some money before they perform.'

Brownbags walked from person to person, as they dug into their pockets for any loose change and threw it into the basket. At each clink of metal, he touched the brim of his hat with his finger and when he had passed along the row he began.

'Give as much as you can spare, we only come but once a year. Build up the fire and let the flames burn. Here are some jolly boys to give you a turn.'

Mummer started clapping and gradually everyone else joined in.

Brownbags went off and was replaced by Saint George and his daughter, Mary.

'Isn't that your man from Little Hagby?' Father Bernard whispered.

I looked again. He was right. Mary was the gangly altar boy from the Tenebrae service, got up in a blonde wig and a white dress which was filthy with mud at the bottom.

Saint George drew his sword from its scabbard and clasped Mary to his side.

'In I come, old Saint George. The champion of Ingyland. My sword was made in God's own forge. A flash of lightning in my hand.'

There was loud cackling from the dark and the Turkish Knight stepped into the circle and drew his sword. Into the spirit of the thing now, everyone booed and hissed on cue, even David, who had let go of Miss Bunce's hand and was watching the play with a face like a child at a pantomime.

The Turkish Knight twirled the end of his long moustache and stepped closer to us.

'I am Sullyman from Turkey Land. I seek to find Saint George the brave. I'll take his life and his daughter's hand. And toss his body in a cave.'

Saint George pulled Mary behind him, shielding her from the Turkish Knight. Mary cowered on her knees, the back of her hand on her brow.

'I am George of Ingyland,' he said. 'My sword is sharp and keen as wind. I will fight you Sillyman. And God will judge you for your sins.'

'Now, Saint George, I will have your life.'

'No, sir, I will strike you dead.'

'I'll take your Mary for my wife.'

'And marry her without your head?'

The two men circled each other, then leapt forward and clashed their swords. Mary screamed, and everyone began to cheer for Saint George, who at last ran the Turkish Knight through, knocking him to the ground where he lay with the sword sticking upright, clamped in his armpit. Mary rushed to the dead knight's side and lay her head upon his chest, weeping.

'Oh, Father, you have killed my one true love.'

Saint George knelt down and put his hand on her shoulder.

'Oh, my poor little turtle dove.'

He turned to us and pleaded, 'Is there a doctor in this town? One that can be quickly found?'

There was a knock at the door. All faces turned to where a small figure appeared, wearing a bowler hat and a coat that trailed on the floor. Everyone was a little startled that he had slipped out unnoticed during the performance.

'Here comes little Doctor Dog,' he said, stopping on the

way to pat the top of Hanny's head. 'Best doctor in the county, sir.'

'Can you cure this knight of Turkeyshire?' Saint George said, taking off the doctor's hat and speaking into it.

'Of what affliction?' said the doctor, removing Saint George's crown and doing likewise. 'Tell me, sir. Confess.'

'Of death, sir doctor, darkest death.'

'Not for five pounds, sir,' the doctor said.

'For ten pounds, sir?'

'For fifteen, sir.'

'Twelve, sir.'

'Yes, for twelve whole pounds and Spanish wine, it shall be done.'

The doctor felt around in the pockets of his huge coat, making Father Bernard laugh louder with each scrap of junk he turned out and dropped onto the floor – toy cars, plastic animals, golf balls, seashells. Eventually, he found a small bottle and knelt down by the dead knight.

'Now, my sleeping Turkey knight, drink this brew of holy breath. Old Doctor Dog will cure you, sir, and call you back from blissful death.'

The dead knight began to cough and then sat upright and clasped Mary to his chest. Saint George embraced the doctor and then flung out his arms to us.

'Rise up, rise up and sing and sing, a song of warm and merry things.'

The knight stood up, touching the wound in his side.

'Once I was dead and now I am alive. God bless Doctor, George and wife. Bring me flesh and oranges and beer. A happy Easter to all our friends here.'

They were about to go off, when a banging sound came from the far end of the room. All their smiles dropped as they sloped away one by one, leaving Saint George who said:

'Yet, there is one who will not sing, or dance about.'

I felt Hanny grip my hand. He had obviously remembered who was coming next.

Another player, the one who had arrived completely swathed in a black cloak, came into the circle holding a single candle at chest height so that it lit up his face. Once he was in the middle of the circle, he reached up and took down the hood. Unlike the others, his face was a postbox red and he had a pair of horns growing out of his bald head. Real buck antlers fastened by some device that was undetectable.

'Ah, now I know this feller,' Father Bernard whispered and nudged me gently in the shoulder.

'In I come to say farewell. Devil Doubt shall take his bow. Come to take your souls to Hell. Where is God the Father now?'

And as he smiled and pinched out the candle I felt Hanny's hand slip out of mine.

✿

I couldn't find him anywhere. He wasn't in the bedroom. Nor was he out in the yard, for it had gone dark now and he wouldn't have gone out on his own. I looked around, checking all the places Hanny liked to hide: behind the ancient upright piano, in the wide bay window on the other side of the curtains, under the tiger-skin rug.

Looking in the kitchen, thinking that he might have gone searching for food, I found Parkinson talking to one of the other Pace Eggers who was at the sink stripped to the waist and scrubbing his face vigorously with a flannel. The water in the bowl had turned to ink. His robes were on the table along with his false moustache and his sword. I put the tray on the table as he patted his face dry with a towel and went to put his shirt back on. I saw that it was the elderly companion of Parkinson and Collier who we had first seen wheezing across the field the day we came to Moorings. Yet now his face was a healthy pink and he radiated the vitality of a much younger man.

'Isn't it wonderful?' he said, holding me briefly by the shoulders, as he went off to join the others. 'Wonderful,' he said to Parkinson, who smiled and nodded and watched him go.

'Dying from the drink, he was, Mr Hale,' said Parkinson.

Hale. I remembered the name from the list in the envelope Hanny had brought back from Thessaly.

I turned to go, but Parkinson spoke again.

'I didn't think a good Catholic boy like thee would dismiss a miracle so readily.'

He walked past me and closed the kitchen door on the laughter coming from the sitting room.

'I hear tha's been over to Thessaly quite a bit,' he said. 'You and your retard.'

I looked at him.

'Oh, I know all about your retard,' he said. 'Your padre's quite a gasbag when he's had a drink.'

'He's not a retard. Father wouldn't have called him that.'

Parkinson smiled.

'How much did he give you?'

'Who?'

'My friend at Thessaly.'

'I don't know what you mean.'

'What was it? Five, ten quid?'

'I told you, I don't know anything about any money.'

He looked at me.

'Twenty,' I said.

'And is that going to be enough?'

'For what?'

'Come on, tha knows what he gave thee that money for.'

I said nothing and Parkinson shook his head and sighed.

'I told him it wouldn't be enough. You see, my friend at Thessaly hasn't quite got the head for business I have. I know people much better than he does. I don't believe people always want money. Not when there's something more important to them. Money you can piss away like ale. What people really want is something that's going to last.'

He put his hands in his pockets and went on.

'I said to him there were a better way of making sure that tha didn't misunderstand what were going on. I said to him that we ought to invite you and your retard to Thessaly, see if there's something we can do to help.'

'Help?'

'Aye, make him better, I mean. Like Mr Hale.'

'I need to go now,' I said.

Parkinson looked at me and then opened the door. The Pace Eggers were singing again. He followed me as I went back to the sitting room.

'He looks after this place well, dunt he, Clement?' he said, patting the wall. 'These old places are a bugger sometimes. Damp as hell. All the wiring shot. Dunt take much for a fire to start in them. You hear stories all the time around here. People burnt in their beds.'

When we came to the sitting room door, he stood and looked in on the singing and dancing. The noise had grown louder.

'We'll be expecting thee then,' he said. 'Tha knows where to come. Or we can come and fetch thee, if tha likes.'

He smiled and went off to join the other men who had linked arms in a circle and were stamping and singing as Hale swung Mummer round in a dance that she pretended to enjoy as much as she could. Father Bernard stood by and clapped along. Mr and Mrs Belderboss looked anxious for the antiques that had been too large to move. Miss Bunce clung to David's arm with a thin smile, as Collier tried to coax her into the circle. Only Clement sat apart, with a protective arm around Monro's neck. Two outcast dogs.

# 21

I FOUND HANNY ASLEEP under his bed with his crayons and his sketch pad. Drawings of Else were everywhere, covering the mattress like a patchwork blanket. He was curled up and snoring softly, a crayon melting in his sweaty hand. I eased it out and, not really awake, he shuffled out from under the bed and put his arms around me.

He had drawn Else in the window at Thessaly, with the bell tower next to it and Leonard's car parked at the side. Else standing outside in the grass under a huge yellow flower of a sun, holding her albino cat. The one he had been working on as he had fallen asleep showed he and Else standing side by side holding hands with a grinning baby between them.

The silly sod thought the baby was his, that, when Else had let him feel it butting her stomach like the lamb had its mother, she was teasing him with a present that she would give to him one day. That was why he wanted to go back to Coldbarrow. He wanted his gift.

But I couldn't take him there. Not after what Parkinson had said.

I removed the pieces of paper and loose crayons from his bed and drew the candlewick over him. He didn't stir at all. He had no idea what was going to happen to him at the shrine tomorrow. He wouldn't remember anything about it until we got there. I watched him sleeping, and wished that his peace could last. I knew what they would make him do at the shrine but he wouldn't understand even if I tried to warn him. I thought about slipping away and taking him down to the Loney to hide when the time came, but there would be no point. Mummer wouldn't let up until she had made him go. I knew that I would be coerced into helping to get him there. Keep him happy and keep him ignorant of what we were really going for. I hated her for that.

᱒

Despite what Mrs Belderboss had said in her confession, Father Wilfred didn't seem all that absent to me. I still felt his hand at work, pushing Hanny towards his role as the touchstone that would prove God's love for the faithful.

I remembered their faces last time we'd been to the shrine. Half fearful, half rapturous that they were about to witness a miracle as Hanny took a mugful of holy water and started to choke. Mummer went to help him, but Father Wilfred held her back.

'Wait,' he said. 'Let the Lord do His work.'

Hanny bent over and gasped for breath. When he stood up his mouth was opening and closing. Father Wilfred held his face tightly, stared into his wide, frightened eyes and began to repeat the Hail Mary until everyone joined in.

'Speak,' said Father Wilfred.

Everyone became silent and listened to the frail note that came out of Hanny's mouth.

'Speak,' Father Wilfred said again. 'Speak.'

He gripped Hanny's head tighter and shook it. Hanny opened his mouth wider but no other sound came out.

Although Father Wilfred looked down his throat with an expression of anguish, as though he could see the miracle disappearing like water down a drain, he still thanked God for sending His spirit down. For showing us His power and munificence. For showing us a taste of the bounty to be had if only we might pray longer and harder.

≈

Now that Moorings was quiet, I could hear the ewe bleating in the field. She was standing alone in the dusk, nosing at the white pile by her feet. When I went outside, she moved away and lay down under a tree. I climbed through the wire and waded through the long grass, feeling my trousers wet and tight against my thighs. There was a strewing of white cotton and limbs, and then I found a small hoof, polished and black, like a mussel washed in on a surge tide. The lamb had been torn to pieces by Collier's dog. I couldn't even find the head.

When I got back to the house, Father Bernard was there, carefully rolling apples out of the bib he had made with the bottom of his coat onto the table. He looked up as I came in and underarmed one of them to me. I quickly took my hands out of my pockets and caught it.

'Where did you get these from?' I asked.

'Outside.'

'Outside here?'

'Aye,' he said. 'Every tree's full of fruit.'

'How can they be?'

'Perhaps they're a type that comes early, I don't know. Aren't you going to eat it?'

'I'm not hungry.'

'Suit yourself,' he said and took a bite from the one that he had been buffing on his sleeve. Juice ran down his chin and he made a cup with his other hand to catch it.

'Was Clement all right?' I asked.

'Aye, I think so,' replied Father Bernard, flicking out a handkerchief. 'He didn't say much, to be honest.'

'Do you think he was telling the truth?' I said.

'What? About witches and lucky charms?' he replied, giving me a half smile as he wiped his chin. 'Come on, Tonto.'

'He seemed frightened all the same,' I said.

'Look,' he said. 'I don't know what's going on with Clement and those other fellers. Probably nothing. I can't imagine why on earth they'd want to intimidate him, or us for that matter. But it's obvious that they're keeping a close eye on what we're doing and I think your mother and Mr Belderboss may be right. It's probably best if we don't get involved. If I were you, I'd stay away from them and from Coldbarrow.'

'Maybe we ought to leave, Father,' I said, taking the opportunity to plant the idea into his head, hoping it might germinate before Parkinson had a chance to pay us another visit. Once we were back in London, they could do what they liked to Moorings. Burn the place to the ground for all I cared.

'You know what, Tonto,' said Father Bernard. 'Between you and me, I'm so exhausted I'd be away back home tonight if I could, but I might very well find myself out of a job tomorrow. And anyway, don't you want to take Andrew to the shrine?'

'I suppose so.'

'There you are then,' he said. 'We'll have to do the full stretch.'

The door to the dining room opened and Mummer was there.

'Father,' she said. 'I'd like a word with you.'

'All right.'

'In private.'

'Now?'

'If that's convenient.'

'Is that all right with you, Tonto?' he said, catching Mummer's eye as he spoke and I nodded, feeling a little awkward that I was caught in the middle.

Father Bernard left with Mummer and they went down the hallway to his room. After a moment I took up my place in the understairs cupboard and waited for them to speak. Neither of them said anything until Father Bernard started to draw the curtain around the washbasin.

'There's no need for that, Father,' said Mummer. 'I've not come for confession.'

'Oh, well would you like to sit down anyway?' I heard Father Bernard say.

'No, I'm fine as I am, Father.'

'Are you sure?'

'Yes.'

'What was it you wanted to talk to me about, Mrs Smith?'

Mummer paused and then said, 'You've not told us much about your last parish, Father.'

'I'm sorry?'

'Your last parish. What was it like?'

'The people or the place?'

'Both.'

'The people were wonderful, the place was terrible.'

'And Belfast, Father?'

'Much the same.'

'Nevertheless, the bishop said you'd worked wonders in these places.'

'I'm not sure anyone works wonders in the Ardoyne, Mrs Smith, but I'll take a pat on the back for trying.'

'Come on, Father,' said Mummer. 'Don't do yourself a disservice. If the bishop said you'd worked wonders then I believe him. Tell me what you did.'

'Look,' he said, laughing quietly. 'The bishopric goes hoopla about the tiniest victories over apathy these days. It doesn't take much to get a gold star. Kick a ball about the cinder fields with some wee rogues and get them to church the next Sunday and they'll consider you for the Vatican.'

'There,' said Mummer. 'You hit the nail on the head, Father.'

'Did I?'

'You said you'd played football with some deprived children.'

'Aye.'

'And they enjoyed it?'

'Aye. More than the Mass I swapped it for, I have to say, but one or two of them kept on coming back.'

'What did they come back for though, Father?'

'Lots of reasons.'

'Such as?'

'What, you want me to pick something out of a hat?

They liked the other people there. The singing. The youth club of a Friday. It was better than being out on the street, throwing bricks at the Saracens. I don't know. Look, is this heading somewhere dark and confined, Mrs Smith? Because I feel like I'm being led into a corner.'

'I just wanted to prove something to you, Father.'

'Prove what?'

'That you were successful in those places because you knew exactly what the congregation needed, what they expected of you.'

'Mrs Smith . . .'

'Wouldn't you say that was the mark of a good priest, Father? Knowing what your parishioners need?'

'Of course.'

'And that a priest ought to respond to those needs?'

'Naturally.'

'Rather than trying to change them?'

'Mrs Smith, if there's something you want to say to me, I'd rather you had it out. It's late and I'm very tired.'

'I want to help you,' she said. 'I know it must be difficult to be thrown into a new parish, but what you need to understand, Father, is that there can only be success in a church when the priest and his congregation are in harmony. If one side wants something different than the other then it all unravels. Father Wilfred knew that.'

Father Bernard sighed and Mummer raised her voice a little.

'He might have been different to you, Father, but he knew how to *be* with us. He knew exactly how to make us feel that God was present in our lives.'

'You mean he told you what you wanted to hear?'

'Yes, Father. Exactly that. We wanted to hear that the

road was going to be difficult. We wanted to be told to pray harder if we wished to be heard. And if we concealed our sins from him, then we wanted to hear that we would be punished. We're all going through a very difficult time, Father,' she went on. 'And I think it's best to keep things the way they were. The way they've always been. It's what everyone knows. We all need a rock to cling to in the storm.'

'Mrs Smith, I'm not trying to change anything.'

'I think you are, Father. Without realising it, perhaps.'

'I'm not. I'm here to listen and guide you spiritually, if I can. That's all. That's the entirety of my remit. I think you must have misinterpreted my interest in wanting to know what happened to Father Wilfred, Mrs Smith. It's not out of some lurid voyeurism. I'm of the opinion that talking about things is the best way to heal the wounds and move on.'

'The wounds are beginning to heal by themselves, Father. All you're doing is opening them up again.'

'Is that what you think I'm trying to do, Mrs Smith? That I'm somehow trying to sabotage everything?'

'Of course not, Father. I just think you can be a little – well – heavy-handed sometimes. It's your age, perhaps. Foisting your own views upon us. All that about Clement and his mother. It's not for us to deal with. Not when we have so many other things to consider. If you want to listen, then listen to what I'm telling you. Guide us by letting us go the way we know best. We know how to get through all this.'

'By standing still?'

'By sheltering, Father. By being patient.'

'And waiting for what?'

'For things to settle again.'

'And if they don't?'

'Look, Mr Belderboss is vulnerable at the moment, Father. He's still confused by everything that's happened and liable to say things that aren't entirely accurate. I don't want you to go back to Saint Jude's with the wrong impression of Father Wilfred. I know you wouldn't mean to, but things can often slip out and rumours start to spread. It doesn't take much for a reputation to be dismantled.'

'Do you want me to leave, Mrs Smith? Is that it?'

'No, Father. I want you to be our priest.'

'So do I.'

'Then hold onto the rock with us, Father. Until the waters retreat.'

'Mrs Smith, I understand that Wilfred's death has been a significant blow to Saint Jude's, but I think you need to face facts if you want to recover from it. He isn't coming back. There's nothing to hold onto any more.'

'There is, Father,' she said. 'We have Andrew.'

'And what does Andrew think about that?'

There was silence and after a moment Mummer excused herself curtly and went out of the room. Father Bernard didn't stir for some time. Then I heard the sound of a bottle opening and its contents going into a glass.

# 22

THE DAY OF the visit to the shrine came around and Hanny was the centre of attention from the moment we got downstairs, where everyone was drinking tea and helping themselves to the apples that Father Bernard had picked the day before. The men had adopted a strange kind of machismo and clapped Hanny on the shoulder and shook his hand, as though they were pages fitting their knight for battle.

Mummer had a basin of hot water ready and she and Mrs Belderboss washed Hanny's face and hands slowly and carefully.

'The Lord will come upon you today,' said Mrs Belderboss. 'I know He will. You're ready. It's your time.'

Father Bernard packed a bag with the things that he would need. Some matches. His stole. A small silver chalice that he had brought from Saint Jude's.

When he had finished he sat at the table with Monro next to him. He said nothing but stroked the dog's head and watched them attending to Hanny, who lapped up the fuss and smiled as Mummer combed his hair and then took a pair of scissors to his nails. He caught my eyes and kissed his fingers. The poor sod thought all this was for Else. Perhaps he thought he was going to marry her. That this was the day she would give him the child and they would be together.

'What does that mean?' said Mummer. 'Why is he doing that with his hand?'

'I don't know,' I said.

'Why don't you tell him where we're going,' she said, nodding at the chair next to her for me to sit down.

I did as I was told and touched Hanny on the arm.

'Hanny,' I said. 'We're going to see God.'

At the mention of the name, Hanny looked upwards and pointed to the ceiling.

'That's it,' said Mummer. 'But we're not going to heaven. God is going to come down here. He's going to make a special visit just for you. Isn't that right, Mrs Belderboss?'

'Yes,' she said. 'We're going to go to a wonderful place, Andrew. It's a secret garden where God makes people better.'

'Now,' said Mummer, inspecting Hanny's nails and knocking his fringe about with her fingers until it was as neat as it was ever going to be. 'I think it's time for Andrew's present. Where's my husband got to?'

'Oh, don't worry, I'll fetch it,' said Mrs Belderboss and she went out and came back a moment later with a cardboard box tied together with an ivory ribbon. She laid it down on the table and everyone gathered around.

'Go on,' said Mummer and gave Hanny the end of the ribbon so that all he needed to do was pull.

Hanny drew back his hand and the bow flopped apart. He opened the lid and put it aside. Inside there was a layer of mist-thin tissue paper. Hanny responded to the hush that had fallen on the room and unwrapped the parcel slowly and gently. Underneath was a new white shirt, the buttons bright and pearlescent, each one etched with a little cross.

'It's beautiful,' said Mrs Belderboss.

'Just the business,' Mr Belderboss added.

'I got it from the shop,' said Mummer. 'It was made in the Holy Land.' And took it out of the box and held it up for everyone to see.

When they had all had a chance to admire it, Mummer gave it to me to hold and made Hanny lift his arms so that she could pull off his vest, taking care not to ruin his hair. Hanny stood and squeezed the fat on his belly between his thumb and forefinger, while Mummer brushed a few loose strands of cotton off the shirt.

'Here,' she said and put Hanny's arm down one of the sleeves and then the other, working his big hands through the cuffs. She moved around the front and pulled it closed across his chest.

'Now when we get to God's special place,' she said, fastening the buttons, 'you mustn't be afraid. You mustn't get upset. Because if you do then God will disappear again. Do as I say and everything will be all right.'

When she had finished doing up his shirt, she ran her hand down the buttons and stood back waiting for the reaction she knew would come. No one had spotted it before, but a large crucifix had been stitched into the front of the shirt, the pleat for the buttons forming the upright and the crossbeam devised out of some delicate embroidery that only showed itself now that Hanny was wearing the garment.

'We have something for you too,' said Mrs Belderboss. 'Reg?'

'Oh, yes,' said Mr Belderboss and he went slowly over

253

to the sideboard and came back with a long thin box, which he gave to his wife.

Mrs Belderboss opened the box and slid out a white candle.

'Here,' she said, passing it to Hanny to hold. 'It's been blessed by the bishop. You can take it with you.'

She hugged him.

'He's looks like a crusader,' she said, noting the way the candle was so long it looked like a sword.

'All he needs is a shield,' Mr Belderboss said.

'He has one already,' Mrs Belderboss replied, patting the cross on Hanny's chest.

ဆ

The morning was damp and cold. Low grey clouds sat over the Loney and kept the woods and ditches full of shadow.

'Nice of you to join us,' Mummer said to Farther, who had appeared at last, rather subdued and distracted.

'Not now, Esther,' he said and cleared his throat.

'Where have you been anyway? Poking about in that room again, I'll bet.'

Farther looked at her.

'It's important that Andrew has everyone with him today,' said Mummer. 'And I don't just mean physically.'

'I know,' he said.

She led the way across the fields with Hanny in tow, fuelling and enjoying his excitement by telling him about the place we were going to.

Quickly, the group stretched and fell apart. Miss Bunce and David negotiated the pools of mud and cow muck hand in hand, Farther followed them, deep in thought and Mr and Mrs Belderboss made up the rearguard, struggling already with the soft, rutted ground and the long detours we had to take around the floodwater.

'Don't let them get lost,' Mummer called back over her shoulder, leaving me and Father Bernard to look after them.

Mr Belderboss leant on his stick, breathing like a dog every few steps. He was determined to walk all the way despite Mrs Belderboss fussing over him.

'Oh, look, woman,' he said. 'If Our Lord did forty days and nights in the desert. I'm sure I can manage a mile or two through a sheep field.'

'I'm only thinking of your heart, Reg.'

He waved her off and carried on.

I found myself walking next to Father Bernard, rather by design than accident. If Parkinson and Collier decided to follow us, as, lying awake in the night, I had convinced myself they would, then I felt safer next to him, no matter how distant he seemed that morning.

I looked at him and he smiled back. His argument with Mummer the night before was obviously still playing on his mind. He brought out a couple of apples from his bag but didn't say anything much until Moorings was out of sight and we stopped by a gate to wait for Mr and Mrs Belderboss.

'Andrew seems fair excited,' he said, nodding up ahead where Hanny was straddling a fence and waving for everyone to hurry up.

'Yes,' I said.

'So does everyone.'

'Yes, Father.'

'Apart from you.'

I didn't reply. Father Bernard leant on the gate with his forearms and watched the Belderbosses coming at a snail's pace; a faint argument.

'If nothing happens today, Tonto,' he said. 'You won't be too disappointed, will you?'

'No, Father.'

'Because I'd hate for you to lose faith in what God can do.'

'Yes, Father.'

'You know, not all miracles are instantaneous. I've never seen one like that anyway. I think it takes a while for them to ripen. If all you look for are Damascus experiences, then you miss all the smaller things that are part of His plan. Do you know what I mean?'

'Yes, Father. I think so.'

He turned and smiled and held the gate open for Mr and Mrs Belderboss, who went through still bickering.

∾

The shrine seemed much further than everyone remembered, but eventually we arrived at a small gravel car park, deserted apart from a mattress and some old car tyres.

The little booth where an elderly attendant had once sold penny information leaflets was gone and there was only the wind and the sounds of sheep far away on the hills.

'You mean we could have come by road?' Miss Bunce said, looking at her muddied shoes.

'We could have come by road, Joan,' said Mummer. 'But I'm not sure arriving in a minibus shows quite the same sense of devotion.'

'Where is everyone?' said Mrs Belderboss as she and her husband finally appeared.

Across the car park was a gate almost completely throttled by the branches of the trees next to it. The gate led to a weedy, gravel pathway that meandered through the trees and came eventually to the shrine itself after another half a mile. All along the path were little figurines half hidden in the undergrowth – Christs and saints and angels peeping around the sides of plastic urns like curious fairy folk.

Here and there were little clearings where grottoes had been set up in honour of various saints and holy men, the trees dressed with the rosaries and rags previous pilgrims had left behind with their transgressions.

Mummer caught up with Hanny who was ahead of us all and steered him well clear of the ribbons, making sure that he passed along the path as quickly as possible. Father Bernard stopped and ran his hand through them.

'Oh, mind they don't come away, Father,' Mr Belderboss said. 'You'll take the sins home with you.'

We came to where Hanny was looking at a statue of Saint Francis that had fallen over and smashed. His head had cracked off and rolled into the undergrowth and wood lice swarmed in and out of his hollow body.

'Oh, Esther,' said Mrs Belderboss. 'It's such a shame.'

'Well, perhaps the groundsman hasn't got round to it yet,' said Mummer.

'I'm not sure there is a groundsman any more,' said Mr Belderboss.

'There must be,' said Mummer. 'They wouldn't just let the place go to seed.'

'But if there's no money, Esther,' said Mrs Belderboss.

'Of course there's money,' said Mummer. 'There's always money. Someone's always got money.'

'I don't think it's anything to do with money,' said Farther. 'It's just that no one comes to places like this any more.'

'What about Lourdes?' said Mummer.

'That's different,' said Farther. 'And anyway, it's like Disneyland nowadays.'

'Well God is still here,' said Mummer. 'Despite what it looks like.'

'Yes,' said Mrs Belderboss. 'Of course He is.'

We walked a little further through a tight kissing gate and then the path was flanked on either side by a tall hedge, as though we were in a maze. The hedge had gone wild and in places had almost met in the middle of the path so that we had to squeeze past the brambles and thorns in single file.

A hundred yards further on, the path ended. Mummer stopped and pulled away some of the branches and leaves to get at the handle of a small iron gate.

'Here we are,' she said, and opened it inwards with one, two, three hard pushes, tearing aside more of the foliage that clung to the railings.

Everyone stopped talking and went through the tangle of rhododendrons until we came to a set of stone steps, damp and black with moss, which led down to where the spring itself bubbled to the surface and could be accessed by opening a small trapdoor in the ground.

Father Bernard helped the ladies down first and they negotiated the narrow, greasy slabs slowly and carefully. When they were safely at the bottom, Father Bernard went back up the steps to help Mr Belderboss. Everyone seemed to hold their breath when he was in the precarious moment between Father Bernard's hands letting go of him at the top and Mummer's hands reaching to him from the bottom.

'You go first, Hanny,' I said, when it was our turn.

He stared down into the shrine and turned to look at me.

'It's all right,' I said. 'Go on.'

Everyone was watching, waiting. He shook his head.

'There's nothing to worry about,' I said. 'I'll come with you.'

I held Hanny's hand and step by step he went down and joined everyone else huddled in the damp.

'I can't believe what's happened here,' said Mrs Belderboss, looking around. 'I'm so sorry for you, Esther.'

'It's all right,' said Mummer.

'The well was always so beautifully dressed,' Mrs Belderboss explained to Father Bernard, who had taken his gold-coloured stole from his bag and was looping it around his neck. 'So many flowers and candles.'

Now, it was an oubliette; cramped and dank and filled with permanent shadow by the yew trees twisting above us. Where the large stones that formed the sheer walls jutted out, there were stumps of wax, which no one could get to light, and so David was designated to hold up a match so that everyone could see the wooden board nailed to the wall on which a scene had been painted of Saint Anne shimmering in white and hovering above the startled peasant children that had first witnessed her apparition three centuries earlier.

Father Bernard knelt down and opened the little trap-door that was inches thick and braced with iron straps.

Everyone gathered round. The holy water trickled past, black and silky-looking with a smell of autumn deadfall and eggs.

I could feel Hanny crushing my hand.

'It's all right,' I said. 'Don't be scared.'

Miss Bunce went first as she was closest to Father Bernard. She took off her coat and handed it to David to hold. Accepting Father Bernard's hand, she knelt down in front of him and bent her head forward. Father Bernard placed his hand gently on her crown, said a quiet prayer, and then reached down into the hole with the chalice to let it fill with water. He brought it up spattering onto the stone and handed it to Miss Bunce. She closed her eyes and drank from the cup and was replaced by David, and then the rest of us one by one.

When it came to Mummer's turn she remained standing. Father Bernard looked at her and then dipped the chalice into the water and stood up to face her.

'Drink this water, the healing balm of Christ,' he said, giving her the invitation he had given to everyone.

'Amen,' said Mummer and sipped until the chalice was empty.

There was only Hanny left. Farther lit the candle Mr and Mrs Belderboss had given him and Mummer took off his coat, so that she could rearrange the collar of his new shirt. Smiling at her son, she tidied his hair and with a kiss on his forehead, she turned him to face Father Bernard.

'He's ready now, Father.'

Father Bernard held out his hand.

'Andrew,' he said, over the sound of the water. 'Come and kneel down here by me.'

Hanny stood clutching his candle.

'Andrew?' Father Bernard said again. And this time Mummer nudged Hanny and pointed to where he should go. Hanny looked at me and I nodded.

Father Bernard held Hanny's hand as he went slowly to his knees.

'All right, Andrew,' he said, pressing lightly on the back of Hanny's head to make him bow down. 'Don't be afraid now. God is with you.'

He kept one hand on Hanny's head and held out the other for the mug Mummer had brought. The one with the London bus on the side. He dipped the cup into the well and brought it out.

'Now, Andrew,' he said, allowing Hanny to lift his head. 'Would you drink this for me?'

Hanny looked at him. I could see his eyes widening. He turned round to find me, but Mummer snapped at him. 'Andrew. Remember what I said.'

'God wants to heal you, Andrew,' Mrs Belderboss said.

'Go on, son,' said Farther. 'It won't hurt.'

Hanny shook his head.

'Just a sip now, Andrew. That's all.' Father Bernard tried to put the mug into Hanny's free hand, but Hanny panicked and knocked it away and the mug smashed against the stone wall.

He got up, threw the candle aside, and made for the steps. Miss Bunce squawked. David tried to stop him, but Hanny easily pushed him aside, and sent him sprawling onto the mossy floor.

Before I could go after him myself, Mummer was up the steps and I felt Father Bernard's hand on my arm.

'Let her fetch him,' he said.

I could hear Mummer shouting at Hanny. She hadn't run after him. She didn't need to.

Farther and Miss Bunce helped David to his feet. His trousers were coated in filth and his lip was cut and bleeding where he had fallen against the wall. Miss Bunce felt around inside the pockets of her cagoule and brought out a tissue and dabbed at his mouth. I could see her face reddening and she was about to say something when Mummer appeared at the top of the steps gripping Hanny's elbow.

'He's going to try again,' Mummer said.

'I don't know if now's the best time, Mrs Smith,' said Father Bernard. 'We're all a bit upset. Perhaps I should bring Andrew on his own tomorrow.'

Mummer smiled thinly. 'No, we can't do that, Father. We're going home tomorrow.'

'Right enough,' said Father Bernard. 'But I can drive Andrew here before we go. I'm sure no one will mind me slipping away for a wee while.'

The others shook their heads.

'I don't mind,' said Mrs Belderboss.

'It might be better to bring the lad tomorrow,' Mr Belderboss said. 'Without everyone watching.'

'We're here now,' said Mummer, aware that Miss Bunce was glaring at her. 'We've made a special effort to come and I'd like Andrew to take the water.'

Farther put his hand on Mummer's back.

'Come on, Esther,' he said. 'Don't upset yourself.'

'I'm not upset.'

'Look,' said Father Bernard. 'Why don't we go back to the house? It looks like it's going to rain any minute.'

'No,' said Mummer. 'I'm sorry, Father, but he is to take

the water and that's that. He is not going to spoil the day.'

'Ah, come on, Mrs Smith, he's hardly doing that now, is he?'

'Isn't he?'

'It's not his fault.'

'Why? Because he's too stupid to know what he's doing?'

'I never said that.'

'Not in so many words.'

'Mrs Smith—'

She grabbed Hanny and took him over to the well, fending off Father Bernard's appeasements with a wave of her hand. She upturned a jam jar of dead stalks and knelt down and filled it from the well. The water spun with sediment and grime.

'Open your mouth,' Mummer said sharply. 'Look at me.'

Hanny looked at up her and started to cry.

'Stop it,' said Mummer. 'What's the matter with you? Don't you want to get better?'

Hanny turned to get away again, but Mummer held his arm and looked over to Father Bernard.

'Well, help me,' she said, but he looked away.

'Careful, Esther,' said Mrs Belderboss. 'You're hurting him.'

Mummer tightened her grip and then more so again, as though she was bringing a wayward dog to heel. Slowly, Hanny opened his mouth.

'Wider,' said Mummer, pinching his cheeks in so that his jaw opened.

'Esther, stop it,' said Mr Belderboss.

'Please, Esther,' Mrs Belderboss cried and then turned away, her eyes full of tears.

'Oh, for God's sake, just drink it,' said Mummer.

Hanny closed his eyes and screwed up his face the way he did when he had to take Milk of Magnesia. Mummer carefully poured the water in, as though she was measuring it. Hanny coughed and choked and then spat the water into her eyes.

Mummer blinked and stretched her face, but said nothing. She found the lid of the jam jar on the ground, screwed it on tight and put the jar in her pocket. Father Bernard was leading everyone quietly out of the shrine. I took Hanny by the hand and followed them. Only Farther stayed behind, staring at his wife.

# 23

DESPITE FATHER BERNARD'S best efforts to persuade them to stay, Miss Bunce and David packed their things and he drove them to the station in Lancaster to catch the sleeper train.

A heavy despondency filled Moorings to the brim and when I couldn't stand it any longer I went to bed, leaving Mummer and Farther and Mr and Mrs Belderboss to talk glumly in the sitting room.

Hanny was fast asleep, exhausted by what had happened at the shrine. I watched him for a while but must have dropped off quickly myself.

I had been asleep for about an hour when I heard someone coming into the room. It was Mummer. She was carrying a steaming cup on a tray. She looked at me and made a motion with her hand that I should lie back down.

'What are you doing?' I said.

'Giving Andrew a cup of tea.'

'He's asleep.'

Mummer shushed me and went and sat on the edge of Hanny's bed. She watched him sleeping for a minute and then took out the jam jar of water. She tipped some of it into the tea and set the cup on the bedside table. The rest of the water she trickled into her hand and, using her finger, traced a cross very gently on Hanny's forehead.

He stirred a little and half woke. Mummer hushed him. Hanny settled again and went completely still, his consciousness sliding back down into the drains of sleep.

She ought to have left him alone. He was so worn out by what had happened at the shrine that he looked dead. His face had the same awful slackness as Father Wilfred's the day Mummer and the others went to wash his body in preparation for burial.

I had been made to go too, to help the visiting priest that had been sent by the bishop to oversee the ablutions. It would do no harm, said Mummer, for the bishop to know she had a capable son when the time came for me to be thinking of a career in the clergy.

They had Father Wilfred laid out in his coffin in the front room of the presbytery. It was a rarely used room and almost as cold as the January day that bristled against the window behind the curtains. A carriage clock futtered quietly on the mantelpiece next to the candles that would be kept lit until the funeral. Everyone stood around the coffin as the priest said a prayer and made the sign of the cross over the body.

Because it *was* a body now and not Father Wilfred at all. Death was a poor draughtsman and had rendered his likeness just a little off-centre, giving him the look of someone who was almost familiar but lacking the something that made him so. Like a waxwork, I suppose.

As a crop of white stubble had spread across his cheeks and chin, his face had taken on the texture of fake velvet. The skin on his arms and legs was like ancient parchment dotted with the ink of moles and liver spots, and beneath

266

the skin lay stringy muscles that had been loosened by the funeral director to make the cleaning easier.

Mummer brought in basins of warm water and a bottle of Dettol and the ladies rolled up their sleeves and slowly opened the folds of linen and began to wash him, gently lifting his arms and turning his legs slightly to get around the backs of his knees. A swirl of a loincloth afforded him some modesty and spared our blushes.

I stood back and held a basin for Mummer. I noticed that there was a brown stain on the satin pillow as she cradled Father Wilfred's head so that she could run a flannel around his face and neck. Water and disinfectant trickled over the hard bow of his clavicle and down the grille of his ribs and when Mummer mopped his brow there remained little droplets among his eyelashes.

When it was done and the ladies were going in and out to sluice the water down the drains, Mummer opened up the newspaper parcel she had brought with her and took out a small bunch of white roses. She crossed Father Wilfred's shrivelled hands over his stomach and interlaced the fingers. Then, careful not to cut him, she lifted his hands and slotted the roses into his grasp one by one.

As they swaddled him again, there was an audible ex-halation. Of pity, I thought, or relief. Relief that it was over. Relief that it wasn't them lying there on the table like meat.

Mummer crossed herself and then sat down on a wooden chair by the coffin with her rosary beads to take the first watch of the vigil. The other ladies said nothing and left one by one.

'Light the candles before you go,' said Mummer as I was putting on my coat.

I did as she asked and watched the light flickering on Father Wilfred's face.

'Is Father in heaven?' I asked.

Mummer looked up and frowned. 'Of course,' she said. 'Why wouldn't he be? All priests go straight to heaven.'

'Do they?'

'Yes,' she said. 'It's their reward for serving God.'

She looked at me a moment longer then went back to her rosary. I knew when Mummer was only half sure about something – like when I came home with algebra homework and Farther wasn't around, or she had to drive somewhere she hadn't been before, the confidence she feigned was tinged with irritation that she didn't actually know the right answer or the right way at all. What if Father Wilfred had gone to Purgatory?

As I cycled home in the snow I tried to imagine what it would be like. Father Wilfred had always described it as a place of closed doors, where sinners were shut off from God until their souls had been cleansed with fire.

What it felt like to have one's soul burnt to purity, I couldn't imagine. It couldn't be a physical pain now that his body was lying lifeless in a box, so was it then a mental torture? Were each of life's hidden sins illuminated and ignited one by one? Was one punished by being forced to live through them all again? All the fear and guilt?

Coming down Ballards Lane past the tube station, I surprised myself and prayed for him. After all, it wasn't his fault. He'd had a shock at the Loney. It was no wonder he went pieces. Anyone would have done the same.

∞

'Andrew,' said Mummer, touching him on the cheek with the back of her hand.

Hanny woke up and looked at her, then coming to consciousness he moved away from her on his elbows. He looked at me and Mummer put her hand on his shoulder.

'It's all right, Andrew,' she said. 'I've just brought you some tea.'

She passed Hanny the cup and he held it like a bowl and sipped.

'That's it,' said Mummer, standing up slightly so that she could check that its contents had all gone. When Hanny had drunk the lot, she put her hand on the back of his neck and kissed him on the forehead. Hanny beamed because she wasn't angry any more.

'Now,' said Mummer. 'Come and kneel down here with me.'

She got off the bed and knelt down beside it.

'Come on, Andrew. Like this.'

He smiled and got down on the floor with Mummer.

'Close your eyes,' she said.

Hanny looked at me and I rubbed my fingers over my eyelids and then he understood.

'That's it,' said Mummer. 'Good lad.'

She stroked his hair and once he was settled, she turned to me.

'Open the door,' she whispered.

'What?'

'Open the door and let them in.'

'Who?'

'The others.'

I got out of bed and went to the door. Farther and Mr

269

and Mrs Belderboss were waiting on the landing. They all turned to face me.

'Is he ready?' asked Mr Belderboss and as quietly as possible, they filed into the bedroom and stood looking at Hanny who had his hands pressed tightly together and his eyes squeezed shut.

'Shouldn't we wait for Father Bernard?' said Mrs Belderboss.

'We'd better start,' said Mummer. 'While Andrew's still settled.'

Mrs Belderboss looked at him. 'Yes, I suppose you're right,' she said.

'You too,' Mummer said to me, and pointed to the patch of floor to her right where she wanted me to kneel.

Farther and Mrs Belderboss knelt on the other side of the bed and Mr Belderboss lolloped over to the chair by the door and sat down heavily, his stick in between his legs and his forehead resting on the handle.

'Lord God,' Mummer began. 'We ask that your healing waters flow through Andrew and bring nourishment to his—'

She broke off as someone else came into the room. Father Bernard stood there in his coat and looked around at everyone. Mrs Belderboss pretended to inspect her fingers. Mr Belderboss smiled at him and then coughed and looked away.

'I thought I heard voices,' said Father Bernard. 'What's going on?'

'We're praying for Andrew,' said Mrs Belderboss.

'Oh,' said Father Bernard, looking at his wristwatch.

'Is that a problem, Father?' said Mummer.

'No, no,' he said. 'I'm just surprised you're all still up.'

'Did Joan and David get off all right?' asked Mrs Belderboss.

'Aye,' he said. 'They caught the train on time. I did try to talk them out of it again on the way there, but they had their minds made up pretty tight about it. It's a shame.'

'It is,' said Mrs Belderboss, and there was a moment's silence before Farther spoke.

'Do you want to join us?' he said.

Father Bernard looked at Mummer.

'No,' he said. 'I'll leave you to it.'

'Come on, Father,' said Mr Belderboss. 'I'm sure your prayers would be worth ten of ours.'

He looked down at what he was wearing. Sodden raincoat. Sodden boots.

'I'm not sure I'm suitable, Reg,' he said.

'It doesn't matter,' said Mrs Belderboss. 'God doesn't mind what you're wearing, so why should we?'

'No, really,' he said. 'I'll be away to my bed and pray for Andrew first thing in the morning when I'm more awake and I can concentrate on what I'm doing.'

'Are you sure, Father?' said Mrs Belderboss, a little disappointed.

'Aye. Praying's like tuning a radio.'

'Come again?'

'You have to be on the right frequency, otherwise all God hears is static.'

'Yes, I see what you mean,' said Mrs Belderboss, smiling sympathetically. 'Well, as long as you're sure, Father.'

'Aye. I'm fairly worn out, to be honest with you. And there's a long drive home tomorrow.'

'Yes,' said Mrs Belderboss with a sigh. 'It has been a bit tiring all said, hasn't it? Nothing's gone quite right. It's all been so difficult. It's such a pity, Father, that you've not seen this place as it used to be.'

'Places do change, Mary,' Mr Belderboss chipped in.

'Oh I know that,' she replied. 'But it's been such a baptism of fire for Father. I mean, Wilfred knew us and he knew this place. He would have coped so much better with all these little problems we've had.'

'True,' said Mr Belderboss. 'He was a firm hand on the tiller.'

'It's no reflection of you, Father,' Mrs Belderboss went on. 'It's rather been our fault, I feel, asking you to take on too much too quickly. I mean, it's like anything, being a priest. It takes time to get things right, doesn't it, Esther?'

'Most definitely.'

Mummer looked at Father Bernard who said nothing more and went out of the room. Mummer resettled herself and noticed that Farther was staring at her.

'What?' she said.

'What's the matter with you?'

'Nothing.'

'Why did you speak to Father like that?'

'Like what?'

'You know what I mean.'

'Do I?'

'Yes,' he said. 'You do.'

Mummer looked at Mr and Mrs Belderboss.

'I'm sorry, Reg, Mary,' she said. 'My husband's obviously a little out of sorts.'

'Out of sorts?' Farther raised his voice and Mr and Mrs Belderboss exchanged looks. 'I think you're the one out of sorts, Esther,' he said.

'And is it any wonder?' Mummer snapped. 'Considering

what we've been through since we got here? This whole thing has been an utter farce.'

'Now steady on,' Mr Belderboss said.

'Esther,' said Mrs Belderboss, eyeing the door. 'He'll hear you.'

'I don't care,' said Mummer, her colour rising in a way I'd rarely seen before. 'I will have my say about Father Bernard McGill. He's a mistake. He's not right for us. I've never met any priest so flippant and carefree with his authority. He makes a mockery of everything we do. I for one will be very glad when he's sent back to Ireland to his own kind.'

Amid the angry voices, Hanny got up and went over to the window. He picked up the stuffed hare and smoothed his hand over its back.

'He's still a young man, Esther,' said Mrs Belderboss. 'He just needs time to mature into someone like Father Wilfred. He will one day. I'm convinced of it.'

'Mary,' said Mummer. 'You were convinced that he wouldn't have gone drinking, but he did. And he invited those louts over.'

'It was only a bit of fun,' said Farther. 'You said so yourself.'

'Fun?' said Mummer. 'You weren't the one being flung around the room like a rag doll.'

'I didn't see you complaining too much,' said Farther.

'And I didn't see you stepping in to stop it,' said Mummer. 'No, you were too busy egging them on with everyone else.

'Good God,' she went on. 'Just listen to what I'm saying. This was meant to be a pilgrimage, a chance for us all to find some peace after everything that's happened and I'm having to worry about strange, drunk men dancing around the sitting room at the invite of the priest who was supposed to be looking after us. What on earth did he think we'd come here for? Larks in the country? To trail around finding lost causes like Clement Parry and his mother? Bringing in every waif and stray he could find? Poking around in business that doesn't concern him or us? Everything's falling apart. I mean, he couldn't even keep us all together.'

'It wasn't his fault that Joan and David went home,' said Farther.

'It was,' said Mummer. 'And he knows it was. That's why he was so late back. Drowning his sorrows in the Bell and Anchor no doubt.'

'Esther!' Farther raised his voice again. 'You can't say things like that. Especially not about a priest. That's how rumours start.'

'Yes, I know,' said Mummer, looking pointedly at Mr Belderboss.

'What?' he said. 'What have I done?'

'The other day you left Father Bernard with lots of questions that I don't really think we want him to be trying to answer.'

'It's not Reg's fault, Esther,' said Mrs Belderboss. 'He was just upset, that's all. His emotions got the better of him.'

'You let Father Bernard bully you,' said Mummer.

'Oh, come on. It was hardly an interrogation,' said Farther. 'I'm sure he was only trying to help.'

'We've got to be more careful,' said Mummer. 'None of us really knows what happened to Wilfred and we're probably never likely to. We can't give in to speculation.

274

If we do that then we're handing over the memory of Wilfred to those who don't care about him like we do.'

'This is Reg's brother you're talking about,' said Farther. 'I think it's up to him what he says about Wilfred.'

'No,' said Mr Belderboss. 'Esther's right. We must keep our suspicions to ourselves. We can't prove anything. I mean if I had his diary it might tell us once and for all.'

'I agree,' said Mrs Belderboss. 'We can't let any rumours spread. It'd ruin Saint Jude's.'

'Well, if there are rumours, I'm sure they're out there by now,' said Farther. 'You can't stop people talking. And anyway rumours come and go. They'll be talking about something else next week. You know what people are like.'

'I'm not sure you've quite grasped how serious this is,' said Mummer. 'People might very well lose interest in gossip and move on, but it's left in their minds as fact. If people have it in their heads that Father Wilfred — you know — then it would turn everything he ever said into a lie. And what would that do to people's faith?'

'Faith's not an exact science, Esther,' said Farther.

'Yes it is,' said Mummer. 'You either have it or you don't. It's quite simple.'

'Esther's right,' said Mr Belderboss.

Mrs Belderboss nodded in agreement.

'Listen,' said Farther. 'I think that if we have even the slightest suspicion that Wilfred took his own life then we ought to report it to the police.'

'And what good would that do?' said Mummer.

'It would be the right thing to do.'

'If we can't prove it, how would they?'

'I don't know. I don't think it matters if they do prove it. Wouldn't it at least take the burden off Reg a little?'

'Well, we can't say anything to the contrary now, can we?' said Mummer. 'How would that look three months down the line?'

'Like we had something to hide,' Mr Belderboss said.

'It sounds like we do,' said Farther.

The apostle clock chimed for midnight. Everyone waited for it to stop.

'Well, Reg and I are a little tired,' said Mrs Belderboss once the last ring had ended.

'It is quite late, I suppose,' said Mr Belderboss. 'We'll see you all in the morning.'

Farther helped Mrs Belderboss to her feet and she held his arm as he led her to the door. Mr Belderboss used his stick to get himself out of the chair. Farther opened the door for them and they said goodnight and went off to their room along the corridor.

Once they were gone, Mummer said, 'Aren't you going too?'

Farther sighed briefly and came and sat on the bed.

'I think you're the one who needs some rest,' he said, taking her hand. 'It's not doing you any good getting so worked up about everything. So things haven't gone all that smoothly, so what? Father Bernard likes a drink now and then, so what? It's really not the end of the world. Don't get so upset about everything.'

'I'm not upset,' she said. 'In fact, in a funny way, I'm glad that I've seen Father Bernard for the inept he is. At least this trip's illustrated that much.'

'Come on, love,' said Farther softly and smiling at Hanny who was still by the window with the hare. 'Leave Andrew be. Let him get some sleep. Come to bed.'

'I haven't finished praying for him.'

He took Mummer's hands in his.

'Esther,' he said. 'I think it's time that we accepted that he is the way he is, and that's how it's always going to be.'

'I can't do that.'

'We're going home tomorrow,' he said. 'And I think that's where we ought to stay. We shouldn't come here again. It's not a good place.'

'What are you on about, not a good place? We've been coming here for years.'

'I mean, I don't think Andrew's ever going to get better here.'

'Why not?'

He looked at me and then down at his hands. 'In that room next to the study . . .' he began and Mummer sighed. 'No hear me out, Esther. It's important.'

Mummer set her face and waited for him to go on.

'Before we went to the shrine, I went to lock it up and I found a name scratched into the plaster by the bed.'

'So?'

'Well I think it was the name of the girl they put in there.'

'It probably was.'

'The thing is,' he said. 'I moved the bed away from the wall to get a better look and there were four other names there as well.'

'So they were all ill,' said Mummer. 'What's that got to do with anything?'

'They all died, Esther.'

'Don't be silly,' said Mummer.

'It's true,' said Farther. 'Each name had a line scraped through it, and . . .'

'And what?'

'I know I've not said anything,' he said. 'And I wasn't going to. But I found some letters.'

'Letters?'

'In a little box under the bed. From Gregson to the children's governess, asking her if the children were better, if they might be able to come home soon.'

Mummer rubbed her eyes. 'Why are you telling me all this?'

'Esther, it wasn't just that one room that was a quarantine,' he said. 'It was the whole house. Gregson didn't build it as a home, but a hospice.'

'Of course it was a home,' said Mummer.

Farther shook his head.

'Gregson never lived here himself; he only built it so the governess could take the children to the shrine.'

Mummer looked at him irritably.

'I still don't know what this has to do with us,' she said.

'Don't you see?' said Farther. 'He kept on insisting that she take them even when it was obvious there was no hope of them getting any better.'

'He had faith,' said Mummer. 'That's all that's obvious to me.'

'It's not about faith,' said Farther. 'It's about knowing when to admit defeat.'

'Defeat?'

'Before someone gets hurt.'

'I'm not giving up on Andrew now. Where would that leave us?'

'Esther, it drove that poor man out of his mind in the end that he couldn't change anything.'

'I know *I* can't change anything,' Mummer snapped. 'I'm not saying that *I* can do anything. I'm asking God.'

Farther sighed and Mummer pushed his hands away.

'Leave me alone,' she said.

'Esther.'

'Leave me alone with my son.'

'Don't do this to him any more. Don't do it to yourself. Let's go home as soon as we can tomorrow. It's not Bernard's fault that everything's gone wrong this week. It's this place. It's sick. It's not good for us.'

'Listen,' said Mummer, grabbing Farther's wrist suddenly. 'Your faith might have crumbled along with Wilfred's but don't try and ruin mine as well.'

Farther tried to prise off her fingers, but she gripped even tighter.

'Do you know what?' she said, smiling a little. 'I think you're scared.'

Farther stopped struggling.

'No,' he said. 'Not me.' And he nodded to the corner of the room, where a gorilla sat under the shelves of pebbles and driftwood with his arms wrapped around his knees.

❧

Hanny has changed beyond all recognition since then, but if I do see anything of the old him it is always through the eyes. There is an honesty of feeling there that betrays everyone, I suppose. And there in that room at Moorings, behind his silly mask, there was a fear that I was to see many years later when I was arrested that night outside his house. A fear that I was going to be taken away and I wouldn't be able to protect him. He has Caroline, of course, and the boys, but he still needs me. It's obvious.

Not that Baxter agrees. He seems to think I was having some sort of breakdown.

'We're definitely getting somewhere, though,' he said the last time I saw him.

It was a wet, blustery day at the beginning of November, a few days before they found the baby at Coldbarrow. The horse chestnut outside his office window was lumbering to and fro, sending its great yellow hands down onto the tennis courts below. They were closed for the winter now. The nets removed and the white lines buried under leaves and seeds. Baxter is a member there, as you might expect. It's that sort of place. Doctors, dentists, academics. He told me that his mixed-doubles partner was doing a postgrad in ancient Hebrew. Lovely girl. Very athletic. Yes, I could imagine Baxter eyeing up her swaying rump as they waited for the serve.

He was standing by the window with a cup of Darjeeling, watching the tree moving in the rain. A clock ticked on the mantelpiece above the fire, which was feeding noisily on a stack of beechwood. He took a sip and set the cup back on the saucer.

'Do you feel the same?' he said.

'I suppose so.'

He looked back outside and smiled to himself.

'Is that a polite *no*?'

'It's a polite *you tell me*.'

He laughed gently and sat down on the leather chair that was facing me.

'You don't have to agree, old boy,' he said. 'Your brother's not paying me to make you jump through hoops. I just rather thought you'd turned a corner lately.'

'In what way?'

'I think', he said, draining his cup and putting it down on his desk, 'that you're beginning to genuinely understand your brother's concerns about you.'

'Am I?'

'Mm,' said Baxter. 'I think you are. I think that if I asked you, you could explain them very eloquently now.'

'*Are* you asking me?'

He interlaced his fingers and then opened his hands by way of prompting me to speak.

I told him what he wanted to hear and he dutifully jotted it down in his notebook. I told him that I understood Hanny and Caroline were worried about me. That sitting outside their house at all hours was unnecessary. That I shouldn't blame the neighbour who called the police. Hanny didn't need me to be his watchman. And the fact that I couldn't identify the particular threats I felt were ranged against him meant that they were unlikely to exist at all. I had invented them so that I still felt *essential* to Hanny, even though he was married and had a family of his own to look after him.

We'd never discussed that last point before but I added it in anyway, knowing that Baxter would be impressed with my self-perception. And I would be a step closer to making him think I was cured.

'Very good,' he said, looking up briefly from his notebook. 'You see, a corner turned. You're a different man to the one that came to me back in March.'

'Is that right?'

'Indeed. I mean there's a way to go yet before you're . . .'

'Normal?'

'Happier, I was going to say. But it's all about little steps, Mr Smith. There's no point in trying to run and all that.'

'I suppose not.'

'And it's not about pressing you into some sort of societal mould either,' he said. 'It's about getting you to a level of understanding that will allow you to interact with others in a more fulfilling, less stressful way.'

He looked down at his fingers and laughed quietly.

'I don't often admit this, Mr Smith, but I actually find myself envying my patients from time to time.'

'How so?'

'It's the opportunity that a crisis can bring, I suppose,' he said. 'To really look at one's place in the grand scheme of things. To identify the things that really matter. It's so easy to bungle through life only experiencing a slender set of emotions and never thinking about why one does what one does. Who was it said, "An unexamined life is not worth living"? Aristotle?'

'Socrates.'

'Ah, yes, of course. Well, it's a sound philosophy whoever came up with it. And one that I'm afraid I cannot live by as well as you, Mr Smith. You are *living* life. You're engaging with the struggle. Not like me.'

'Perhaps you ought to be telling Hanny all this. Then he might understand me.'

Baxter smiled. 'He will in time,' he said. 'You might feel like your relationship is broken, but we humans have an inbuilt urge to fix things. You'll work it out. Your brother is stronger than you think.'

# 24

HANNY SLIPPED AWAY sometime in the night. His bed was empty and his boots and coat were gone. I always slept lightly at Moorings – even more so since Parkinson's visit – and I wondered how he had managed to leave without waking me. But as I got out of bed I realised that he'd laid towels down on the floorboards so that I didn't hear him go.

I felt his mattress. It was stone cold. Even the smell of him had vanished. I couldn't believe he had been so devious and dissembling. It wasn't like him at all.

In the middle of the room, the pink rug had been turned back and the loose floorboard lifted out. I felt around inside the cavity. The rifle was missing and he had taken the bullets from my coat pocket.

I knew where he had gone, of course. He had gone to Coldbarrow to see Else and his baby.

Downstairs in the kitchen, Monro lifted his head and pined when I came in. I stroked his neck to quieten him down and saw that the floor was littered with the treats Father Bernard had brought for him. Clever Hanny.

Monro sneezed and lay down and went back to chewing the bone-shaped biscuits that he discovered one by one in the folds of his blanket.

Outside, a light drizzle, briny and ripe, spread across the fields and its moisture grew on me like fur. The tandem was leaning against the wall, the tyres repaired. That was why Father Bernard had come in so late. He hadn't been at the Bell and Anchor as Mummer said, but out in the yard in the rain fixing the bike.

I pushed the tandem away from the house, manoeuvring it around the puddles and lifting it over the cattle grid so as not to wake anyone. Once I was around the front of the house, I set off down the lane, met the coast road, split the deep puddles that were standing there, and was soon passing through the marshes.

After days of rain they could become six or seven feet deep with no discernible bottom, only a jelly of mud and dead vegetation. I called Hanny's name, strangely hoping that he had stumbled into one of the pools. Better to go that way than whatever Parkinson had in mind.

But there was nothing. Only the hiss of the reeds and the slop of the ink-black water as the wind came across the marshes, bringing a flurry of white flakes.

For a moment I thought it was snowing – it wouldn't have been unheard of there, even in the late spring – but then as I got closer to the hawthorn tree I could see that it had burst into life well before it ought to have done, like the apple trees and the fresh green grass up at Moorings. Each gnarled limb held a garland of petals, the way Father Wilfred had held the white roses as he lay in his coffin.

At the dunes, I had to heave the tandem through the col as the wind had piled sand a foot thick over the road. Hanny's footprints were there, mixed with the impressions of car tyres. Leonard had passed this way and recently.

I called for Hanny again, thinking that he might be

hiding in the marram somewhere. I waited and looked up at the grass bending in the wind, the grey clouds scudding overhead.

The tide was starting to come in. The sandflats were slowly sinking under the water, and way out, almost at Coldbarrow, was a figure leaning into the wind, his white shirt fluttering. It was Hanny. He had the rifle over his shoulder.

I made a cup with my hands and shouted, but he couldn't hear me, of course. And in the event I was glad. The last thing I wanted him to do was start to come back now that the tide was racing in. It was better that he went on and waited.

I left the tandem against the pillbox and began to run across the sand, following the posts as far as I could. In places there was no water at all, but further out in the full blast of the wind, the sand had collapsed into deep gutters, the edges of which fell apart alarmingly as I jumped over each that I came to.

The roar was all about me as the sea thrust itself towards the shore, breaking into foaming crowns when it smashed down into some hidden declivity. Driftwood and weed sped past, rising and falling on the grey swell, turning, breaking, and then sucked under by the currents.

To my right I could make out one of those temporary pathways the water and wind would conjure up at the Loney now and then; long backbones of sand that only became apparent when the high tide left them exposed above the water. I waded over and climbed up to the highest point and saw that it wound in a long, meandering ribbon towards Coldbarrow.

Yet, even that pathway ran out well before I got there.

The ground broke and slipped away, and I was pitched forward into the sea, my legs suddenly kicking into nothingness.

The cold of it took my breath out like a punch and squeezed my scrotum into a walnut. I reached down, swiping my hands through the heavy, grey water, trying to hold on to something, anything, whatever unidentifiable thing of plastic or wood I could grasp – but the tide whipped everything away and there was nothing else to do but swim as hard as I could towards the shoreline of Coldbarrow.

I was a decent swimmer in those days. Quite hardy to the chill of open water and unafraid of the deeps. There weren't many brooks and pools around the Heath that I hadn't explored. But breast-stroking Highgate Ponds was one thing, the Loney was something else. The swell came at me from all sides and seemed determined to pull me under. There was a movement in the water that flowed and gripped and sucked at the same time. I swallowed mouthfuls of salt water and choked it out in bouts of desperate coughing, my throat and my nose burning.

I seemed to be getting no closer and after striking again and again towards land, it occurred to me that I was in the early stages of drowning; in that period of fighting, sinking, resurfacing. And a panic took hold of me. I could barely feel my body. My hands were locked into claws. I would soon get too tired to move. Then what? An ache in the lungs. Silence. Nothing.

Through a burst of blind splashing, the sky, Coldbarrow and the churning horizon were turned vertical first one way and then the other, but through the swing of the world I was aware of a blurred figure on the shoreline. Then, slipping down into the muffled darkness under the water and out again, they were suddenly closer. Something was being thrust out for me to hold. I made a grab for it and felt my fingers close on a frayed leather strap. I felt a pull that countered that of the tide, felt my thighs and knees eventually scraping against the cobbles of the slipway and then the clutch of the sea was gone and Hanny was standing over me. I let go of the rifle strap and he knelt down and touched my face. I could hardly breathe. Words came out juddering. Hanny cupped his hand to his ear, wanting me to repeat what I said, but I pushed him away and he went over to a rock and sat down with the rifle across his knees.

Still shivering, I took off my parka and then my sweater and twisted it into a thick knot to get some of the water out.

'Why did you go off like that?' I said. 'Why didn't you tell me where you were going?'

Hanny looked at me.

'You're an idiot,' I said, looking back across the sands which had now disappeared completely. 'We're supposed to be going home this morning. How the hell are we going to get back? Everyone will be wondering where we are. Mummer will be cross, and it'll be me that gets it in the neck. It's always my fault when you do something stupid. You do know that, don't you, Hanny?'

Hanny patted his pockets. He took out his plastic dinosaur.

'You're always sorry, Hanny,' I said. 'Why can't you just think before you do things?'

Hanny looked at me. Then he bowed his head and

fumbled in his pockets for the gorilla mask. I went over and took it off him before he could put it on.

'You're not frightened, Hanny,' I said. 'You weren't afraid to go sneaking off without me, were you? You weren't frightened of coming all the way here by yourself.'

He didn't know any better, of course, but I was angry with him all the same. More than I should have been. I threw the mask into the sea. Hanny looked at me and then went to the edge of the water and tried to scrape it back towards him with the rifle. He made a few attempts but the mask filled with water and disappeared. He rounded on me and looked as if he was going to hit me. Then he stopped and looked in the direction of Thessaly and kissed the palm of his hand.

'No, Hanny,' I said. 'We can't go and see her. Not any more. We've got to stay away from that place.'

He kissed his hand again and pointed.

'Jesus Christ, Hanny. Don't you understand? If they find us here they'll hurt us. We just need to keep out of sight until the tide turns. No one's going to come this way for now, not while they can't get across. If we stay here they'll never know that we've even been. Give me the rifle. Let me keep watch.'

Hanny turned away from me and held it close to his chest.

'Give it to me, Hanny.'

He shook his head.

'I can't trust you with it. You'll hurt yourself. Give it to me.'

He turned his back to me completely. I took hold of one of his arms and twisted it. He struggled and easily got free and pushed me to the ground. He hesitated for a moment and then swung the butt of the rifle towards me and caught me sharply on the wrist when I put up my hand to protect myself.

Seeing me in pain, he looked momentarily concerned, but turned away and started walking across the heather.

I called him back. He ignored me. I put my sopping coat on and went after him, stumbling through the matted grass and the peat-haggs. I grabbed him by the sleeve, but he shrugged me off and carried on, more determined than I'd ever seen him before.

A dense fog was coming in off the sea now and I thought that he would be too frightened to go much further. But, despite the grey thickening and the silence that fell upon the place, Hanny went on, taking long strides, jumping across the bogs and pools of water, eventually coming to the remains of an old farmhouse or a barn, it was hard to tell what it had been. Only a few ruined walls remained, roughly forming a rectangle that was littered with other rocks and roof slates. Perhaps people had once lived here. Scavenged from the sea. Worshipped at the chapel and tried to pin God to the island like one of the butterflies in our room at Moorings.

Beneath the sound of Hanny's boots going through the debris I could hear something else. Voices, calls. I tried to make Hanny stop so that I could hear it properly and in the end had to kick away one of his feet so that he fell. He sprawled and the rifle clattered away. He went off on all fours to retrieve it and sat down on a rock to wipe off the mud.

I put my finger to my lips and Hanny stopped what he was doing and looked at me, breathing hard with anger.

'Listen,' I said.

The sound of a dog barking came out of the mist, but it was hard to tell where it was coming from or how far away it was. I had no doubt it was Collier's. It was the same harsh barking that I'd heard in the field outside Moorings where the ewe had led her lamb to feed on the new grass.

'Hanny, we need to go back,' I said. 'We can't let them find us here. And I'm cold. Aren't you cold?'

I had started to shiver. My clothes seemed to be wrapped around my bones.

Hanny looked at me and although a flash of concern passed over his face, he turned and clambered over the broken-down wall he was sitting against without waiting for me. I didn't have the strength to hold him back any more. All I could do was follow him as best I could as his form slipped in and out of the fog.

I eventually caught up with him at the edge of a brook that came gushing milky-white down a gully of rocks and slid away through the limp bracken towards the sea.

Something was wrong.

I touched Hanny on the arm. He was staring straight ahead.

'What is it?' I said and, following his eyes, saw that there was a hare sitting on the other side looking back.

It turned its head to one side, sniffed the air, looked back at us, twitched one of its tall spoon ears, and then bolted just a little too late as a dog emerged from the fog, careered into it and tumbled it over in the mud. The hare kicked with its back legs, once, twice, trying to rake off the jaws that were clamped to its neck, but was limp a second later as the dog thrashed it from side to side and chewed out its throat.

This time I got a firm grip on Hanny's arm and tried

to pull him back. If we went there and then I thought we could get away. But he stood rooted to the spot, still looking past me, over my shoulder, not at the hare or the dog but at the two men that had come out of the mist and were standing there watching us.

# 25

IT WAS PARKINSON and Collier. They were dressed in blue overalls and hard boots caked in mud. Scarves wound around their necks and mouths. Their flat caps dripped with the damp.

Collier had a chain over his shoulder. He lowered his scarf and called the dog to him and when it refused he went over and kicked it off the hare onto its side. He raised his hand to the dog and with a well-practised obedience it whined and cowered and Collier got a hold of its collar so that he could pass the chain through it. Parkinson continued to stare at us, cold breath misting around his face.

The brook cluttered over the rocks and bracken.

Still holding Hanny's arm I started to walk away, but Parkinson moved with an unexpected quickness. He sloshed through the water in a few steps and grabbed the hood of my parka, bringing me to heel like Collier had done with his dog. He turned me to face him and gently rearranged my coat so that it no longer strangled me.

'There's no need for thee to rush off,' he said.

He took his hands off me and flicked the wetness from them.

'Hast tha been for a dip?' he said.

He smiled when I didn't respond, amused that I was drenched and shivering. Then he noticed the rifle Hanny was holding and took it off him. Hanny let the rifle slide out of his hands and looked down at his feet.

Parkinson fitted the stock against his shoulder and squinted through the sight.

'Where did you get this from?' he said.

'We found it,' I said.

'It's a bit special is this, for a lad like thee,' he said, glancing at Hanny.

Collier caught the frown I gave Parkinson.

'He means a retard,' said Collier.

Parkinson took the rifle down and pulled back the bolt to open it up. Hanny had loaded it. I could see the top bullet of the clip pressed down inside the receiver.

Now that Parkinson had let go of me, I tried to lead Hanny back the way we'd come, thinking that they might settle for having the rifle off us. But Parkinson quickly held my shoulder again.

'Don't go just yet,' he said.

'Everyone will be waiting for us,' I said.

'Will they?'

'We're going today.'

'Going? Where's tha going?'

'Back home to London.'

'London?' he said. 'Tha wouldn't make it back across to the mainland, never mind London.'

'We can swim,' I said, and Collier laughed.

'Nay,' said Parkinson with mock concern. 'I don't want thee drowned.'

'Look,' I said. 'We're going home today. Do what you

like at Moorings. Take what you want from the place. I don't care. No one will care.'

It was bravado founded entirely on fear and went as quickly as it had arisen the moment Parkinson laughed and turned to Collier.

'I'm not sure I like that accusation. We're not thieves,' he said. 'Are we?'

'Nay,' said Collier.

The sound of a baby crying came from the direction of the house. The dog looked up. Parkinson and Collier glanced at one another. The crying stopped.

'Here,' said Parkinson, serious now. 'It's nowt personal. But we can't let thee go. We're going to have to take out some insurance. You understand what I mean, don't you? By insurance?'

I looked at him and he put his hand on my shoulder again.

'It's the way it has to be. There's nowt you or I can do about it. You just fucked up, that's all. Wrong place, wrong time. Come to the house and we'll get everything sorted out.'

⁊❦

Leonard was loading his car when we got to Thessaly. Clement was there too, fetching and carrying boxes. When he saw us he stopped and looked at us with — what was it? — pity, guilt?

'Carry on, Clement,' said Leonard.

Clement nodded slowly and moved towards the Daimler and slotted the box he was carrying into the back.

Leonard came closer and lit a cigar. Collier's dog started

barking loudly and straining on the chain. Leonard looked at Collier and, capitulating, he took out a frayed leather muzzle from his pocket and fitted it around the dog's face.

'You must love it here,' said Leonard, turning to us. 'You just can't stay away, can you?'

He took a drag on his cigar and looked at Parkinson.

'Are you sure this is necessary?' he said. 'In an hour's time there'll be no trace that anyone's ever been here. If I were you, I'd send them back across when the tide goes out and leave it at that. They've already given their word to keep their mouths shut. What the hell are they going to say anyway? They don't know anything.'

Parkinson answered him with a stare and Leonard sighed.

'Bring them inside then,' he said.

I don't remember either of us trying to run or fight or do anything for that matter. I only remember the smell of the wet ferns, the sound of water churning out of a gutter, the feeling of numbness, knowing that no one was coming to help us and that we were surrounded by those people Father Wilfred had always warned us about but who we never thought we'd face, not really. Those people who existed in the realm of newspaper reports; dispatches from a completely different world where people had no capacity for guilt and trampled on the weak without a second thought.

We went into Thessaly by the back door that led into the empty kitchen we'd seen briefly the first time. On the floor was a metal dish of dog food that smelled as if it had been there for months. Collier's dog nosed at some of the chunks of meat, trying to angle its mouth so that it could eat them through its muzzle.

From somewhere else in the house, the baby cried again.

A desperate bawl that petered out into a whimper that seemed resigned to the fact that no one was going to come and give it comfort.

Parkinson opened the door that led out into the hallway.

'Go on,' he said with a nod of the head.

I hesitated and felt Hanny's hand in mine. He was shaking.

'It's all right,' I said. 'We'll go home soon.'

Collier let his dog out on the chain a little further. Under the grille of the muzzle it growled from its throat and bent its head to try and nip at our ankles.

'Go on,' Parkinson said again.

'It'll be all right, Hanny,' I said. 'Don't worry.'

Once we were in the hallway, Leonard, Parkinson and Collier stopped and looked at the door that led down to the cellar. The door was closed. From the other side came the sound of the baby screaming again. Hanny made kissing movements with his hand.

'What's the matter with him?' said Parkinson.

'He wants to see Else,' I said.

'She's not here any more,' said Leonard.

'Where is she?'

'How should I know? She's nothing to do with me now. She's not my daughter. Laura took her home yesterday. You don't need to worry about them. They both got paid. Everyone's got what they wanted.'

'Apart from you two,' said Parkinson.

'We don't want anything,' I said. 'Just let us go back home.'

Leonard looked at Parkinson and then at us.

'If it were up to me,' he said. 'I'd trust you not to say anything. But I'm afraid Mr Parkinson here thinks otherwise.

And as he's the one with the rifle I'd be inclined to trust his judgement.'

'You know,' Parkinson said to me. 'I think that the problem is that tha doesn't believe that we can help him.'

He nodded to Collier.

'Tell them what your dog did to your 'and.'

Collier held up his hand – he was no longer wearing the black mitten – and drew a line slowly across the back of it with his finger.

'Every fuckin' tendon,' he said. 'Hanging off in rags it were.'

'Five years without work,' said Parkinson. 'Int that right, Mr Collier?'

'Aye,' said Collier. 'There's not much call for a one-'anded drayman.'

'And now?' Parkinson said.

Collier flexed his hand in and out of a fist and then grabbed hold of Hanny's arm, making him jump. He laughed, enjoyed Parkinson's approving grin, and let go.

'I had a cancer growing in the throat,' said Parkinson, pressing a finger to his Adam's apple and then making a star with his hand to show that it had disappeared.

He put his arm around Leonard's shoulder.

'And my friend here looks a proper picture of health, dunt he? Not a sign of arthritis.'

Leonard looked at me and smiled. I hadn't noticed, but Parkinson was right, Leonard's limp had gone.

'Hanny's fine,' I said. 'I don't want you to do anything to him.'

Parkinson laughed and shook his head. 'It's funny, int it?' he said. 'How you church people can have more faith in something that can't be proved than something that's standing right in front of you? I suppose it comes down to seeing what you want to see, dunt it? But sometimes tha dunt get a choice. Sometimes the truth comes along whether tha wants it to or not. Int that right, Mr Collier?'

'Aye,' he said.

Parkinson nodded and Collier grabbed Hanny's arm again. This time he didn't let go. Hanny struggled. I tried to prise Collier's hand away and was so intent on doing so that I only dimly registered Parkinson moving Leonard aside and taking the rifle down.

The shot brought little coughs of dust down from the ceiling and replaced all other sound with a high-pitched whining in my ears. A spent bullet casing skittered away down the hall and Hanny fell onto his side, clutching his thigh which had burst open all over the floorboards.

Parkinson put the rifle back over his shoulder and nodded at Hanny writhing in silent agony on the floor.

'Now tha'll have to have faith,' he said. 'Like it or not. Unless tha wants to take him home a cripple as well as a fuckin' retard.'

Hearing the gun go off, Clement had come inside and was standing next to Leonard, looking on with horror at what had happened. Leonard noticed him gawping and gave him a nudge.

'Don't just stand there, Clement,' he said. 'Get him up.'

Clement started to back away, but Parkinson pointed the rifle at his chest.

'Hey, tha's not delivered full payment quite yet, Clement.'

'Let me go home,' Clement pleaded. 'I've done everything you've asked for.'

'Aye, so far. But tha owes us a few more favours before we're done.'

'Mother will be worrying where I am. I can't stay.'

'I'm not sure tha's got a great deal of choice int matter, Clement. Not if tha dunt want to end up in Haverigg again. You know we could do it. It were easy enough last time. Tha didn't have the wit to get out of it then and I can't see that tha's found any more since. Moorings goes up in flames. Caretaker seen acting suspiciously by local men. What does tha get for arson these days, Clement?'

Clement looked at him and then knelt down at Hanny's side, rolling him gently onto his back so that he could get an arm under his shoulders. Hanny's face screwed up in pain. He was crying like the Hanny I knew as a little boy, his mouth opening and closing like a beached fish. It might have been the time he fell out of the apple tree in the back garden and broke his wrist, or when he came off his bike and left most of his chin on Hoop Lane. I'd always hated it when he cried. When he cried it meant I hadn't kept him safe. I had failed.

'Here,' said Clement and showed me where to put my arm around Hanny's other shoulder.

Hanny opened his eyes and looked at me, completely bewildered, then he sagged and passed out. Between us, Clement and I got him up, snapped him back into consciousness and got him to take his weight on his good leg, while the other bent under him and dragged a trail of blood and fleshstrings along the hallway.

Leonard took a bunch of keys from his pocket and opened the door to the cellar. He went down, shaking them in his hand, turning the baby's cries to screams.

# 26

IT WAS THE first of June and the street outside was breathless and hazy in a prelude to the punishing heat that summer was to bring. Hour by hour the day had been acquiring the tension that comes before a thunder-storm. Everything moved slowly, if it moved at all. The wood pigeons in the plane tree had been quiet and motion-less for hours. On the window ledge a bumble bee sat in the sunlight and didn't stir even when I tapped the glass. The next-door neighbour's cats hunted for shade rather than the mice and finches they usually left on our doorstep.

I was revising *Hamlet* for an exam the following day. It was the final one. And once it was over, school would be done for good. Already the place had become different. Things had stopped mattering so much. No one, not even the teachers, seemed to care any more and I could see it for what it was: an intestinal factory line that was winding down at the end of a particular run of production. Though, what it had produced, I wasn't sure. I felt no different to when I started. Only a little soiled from having passed through its bowels.

What I was going to do next, I didn't know. I would be sixteen in a week's time, but the world didn't quite seem as open as I'd thought it might. When I looked at Farther I saw that work and school were really no different. One merely became qualified to pass from one system to the next, that was all. Routine was a fact of life. It was life, in fact.

She was leaving me alone at the moment, but I felt Mummer prowling around me, waiting for the day of my exam results when she could pounce and drag me away to the life she thought I ought to have. It'd be A levels in History, Latin and Religious Education, then a Theology degree before six years in seminary. I could fight back, of course, assert myself, but without knowing what I wanted to do I'd have little chance against her. I'd be like that hare in the mouth of Collier's dog.

Collier. Parkinson. I had thought about them every day since we'd come back from the Loney. It had been two months now but even with it fresh in my mind, as it were, I still wasn't sure what had happened at Thessaly. What they had done to Hanny for him to be able to walk back up the steps of the cellar by himself and then cross the heath, and go running over the sandflats to meet Father Bernard who had come looking for us in the minibus. How they mended his shattered leg down in that cellar.

When we got back to Moorings, I told Mummer what I'd told Father Bernard – that we'd been across to Coldbarrow to look at the birds and that Hanny had slipped on some rocks and torn his trousers open on a sharp corner. The lie came out easily, without any planning, without any guilt, because I didn't know what the truth was anyway.

Mummer didn't ask anything else. She seemed too exhausted with the worry of where we'd been and so drained by the whole trip that she was just glad to be leaving. Everyone quickly loaded their bags onto the minibus and didn't talk. The only sound was that of heavy fruit falling from the apple trees.

Mr and Mrs Belderboss were still keen to watch the beating of the bounds and although everybody else was tired and desperate to get away from the place, they agreed that they would stop at Little Hagby on the way. Yet when we got there, it was deserted. A warm wind blew across the uncut grass that thrummed with insects woken early from their cocoons. The priest was nowhere to be seen. The crowds that had in the past always gathered on the green with sticks of willow and birch ready to mark out the limits of the parish were shut away in their houses. We drove on.

When Hanny went back to Pinelands, I was glad. I didn't like what we'd brought home from the Loney. He had changed. He seemed not to notice I was there. He was distant and uncommunicative, more interested in everything else around him, which he seemed to examine as though he had never seen it before. He had regressed. Whatever they had done to him at Thessaly had reversed all his learning and turned him back into an ignorant child.

Now that he was back for the Whitsun holiday, he seemed no different. Still the daft grinning all the time. Still the hours of just sitting and staring. I couldn't stand watching him like this, and had spent most of the time since he'd been back alone in my room. He hadn't come up to see me once.

Mummer and Farther were in denial about it all. They could see that something was wrong, that he had changed, but they made no mention of it. Mummer went back to work at the shop, Farther to his office in town. And neither of them could understand why I was so unhappy, why I couldn't just get on with things. Why did I brood so much?

℘

The sun went in and the day became humid. I opened the window as far as the latch would allow, but still couldn't get any air into the room. I watched a car going down the road. One coming the other way. The postman in his shirt sleeves cycling through the shade of the plane trees.

I went back to *Hamlet* and read to the end of Act One. *The time is out of joint. O cursed spite, that ever I was born to set it right.* Then from downstairs I heard the sound of something smashing on the floor and Mummer crying out. I went down to the kitchen and she turned sharply and looked at me as I came in. Her eyes were wide. Her mouth slightly open. Her lips moving, making bits of words. The remains of her best fruit bowl lay around her feet. She looked back at Hanny who was sitting with his hands flat on the table, a cup of tea in front of him.

'What's the matter?' I said.

But before Mummer could reply, Hanny said, 'Nothing, brother.'

℘

Mummer called Farther and he came home at once, hot and flustered, thinking something terrible had happened. When he heard Hanny speak he cried.

Farther called Mr and Mrs Belderboss. Mr Belderboss

303

called the presbytery and got Miss Bunce. The next-door neighbour came round to see what all the fuss was about and she cried too.

One by one they came and Mummer showed them into the kitchen where Hanny was still sitting. She hadn't let him move in case going into a different room might break the spell. They came in tentatively at first, as though they were sitting down with a lion, and took their turn to be with him and hold his hand and marvel.

Seeing that Mummer was still in shock and unsure of what was happening, Mrs Belderboss patted her hand and said, 'It is a miracle, Esther. It really is.'

Mummer looked at her. 'Yes,' she said.

'What else can we call it?' Mr Belderboss said, smiling. 'The Lord has blessed you.'

'Yes, He has,' said Mummer and clasped Hanny's hands in hers.

'It's like the story in Matthew, isn't it, David?' said Miss Bunce.

'Yes,' said David. 'Which one?'

'Nine, thirty-two,' said Miss Bunce. 'When Jesus heals the mute.'

'All those prayers we said, Esther,' said Mrs Belderboss. 'All those years we asked for Andrew to be healed. God was listening all the time.'

'Yes,' Mummer said, looking into Hanny's eyes.

'And the holy water he drank,' said Mr Belderboss.

'Oh, yes, the water too,' said Mrs Belderboss. 'That was the thing that really did it.'

'I'm just sorry that Father Wilfred isn't here to see this,' said Mummer.

'So am I,' said Miss Bunce.

'He'd have been over the moon, wouldn't he, Reg?' said Mrs Belderboss.

Mr Belderboss was smiling and wiping away tears from his eyes.

'Whatever's the matter, Reg?' Mrs Belderboss said and got up to comfort him.

'I can feel him. Can't you feel him, Mary?'

'Yes,' said Mrs Belderboss. 'I can.'

'God bless you, Andrew,' said Mr Belderboss, reaching across the table and taking Hanny's hands. 'It's you that's brought him here. He's with us now.'

Hanny smiled. Mrs Belderboss crossed herself and began to pray. Everyone in the room joined hands and repeated the Our Father until the doorbell rang.

**꿍**

Father Bernard had been out on his rounds of the parish and had only found the note left by Miss Bunce on his return to the presbytery. I saw his form through the frosted glass of the front door as he rang the bell again and waited. When I opened it, he smiled, though he looked – how was it? – a little nervous, a little short-tempered even. I hadn't seen him look like that before.

'Hello, Tonto,' he said. 'How are you?'

'Fine, Father.'

Farther came into the hallway and reached over my shoulder and shook Father Bernard's hand.

'Something wonderful's happened, Father,' he said.

'So I hear, Mr Smith.'

'He's in the kitchen.'

Everyone stopped talking when Father Bernard came

in. They all looked to him to verify the miracle, so that it could be theirs to enjoy properly.

'Father,' said Mummer.

'Mrs Smith,' Father Bernard replied.

The tension between them still hadn't quite dissipated in the months since we'd returned from Moorings.

'Well,' said Farther, sitting down next to Hanny and putting his arm around him. 'Aren't you going to say hello to Father Bernard?'

Hanny stood up and put out his hand. 'Hello, Father,' he said.

℘

Word got around and before long the house was full of people. So many came that the front door was left propped open with a telephone directory.

The hesitancy that had been there earlier, when everyone had been worried that Hanny's speech might disappear as suddenly as it had come, was forgotten now. Hanny had been restored and they let themselves go in the praising of God. They sang around the piano and laughed like children.

Mummer took Hanny from person to person, showing off the gift that had been bestowed upon her, upon all of us. They passed Hanny amongst themselves like a chalice, everyone intoxicated by him. Everyone except Father Bernard who sat alone watching, a paper plate balanced on his knee, chewing the sandwiches I had helped Mummer to quickly prepare.

When I passed him with a tray of empty cups, he said, 'Could I talk to you, Tonto?'

We went outside into the garden, where a few other people from church were standing about smoking and admiring Farther's dahlias. Father Bernard said hello to them and then we walked down to the end where there was a bench under the apple trees.

We sat for a minute listening to the swifts in the waste-ground on the other side of the tube line and saw their black arrowheads whip through the garden now and then for the insects dancing over the greenhouses.

Father Bernard sat down and loosened his collar. The heat was making him sweat and there were rings of dried salt under the arms of his black shirt.

'So, now you know what a miracle looks like, eh Tonto?' he said, looking back towards the house.

'Yes, Father.'

'Quite a thing, isn't it?'

'Yes, Father.'

'How is he? Andrew?'

'I don't know.'

'I mean how does he seem?'

'All right, I suppose. Happy.'

He wafted away a bee that had droned towards him from the apple tree.

'What happened?' he said.

'How do you mean, Father?'

'You know what I mean.'

'God cured him,' I said. 'Like in Matthew. Nine thirty-two.'

He looked at me and frowned.

'When Jesus heals the mute,' I said.

'Aye, I do know the story, Tonto.'

'Well, that's what happened to Hanny, Father.'

'Aye, but do you know the ending?'

'No, Father.'

'You look it up then, Tonto. I have to say I'm with the Pharisees.'

'How do you mean, Father?'

He set his eyes firmly on mine.

'Look, something happened to you and Andrew there at that house on Coldbarrow, and it wasn't anything to do with God.'

I looked at him and then back at the house.

'Why did you go there?' he said. 'I thought we'd agreed to steer well clear of the place.'

'Hanny wanted to see the birds,' I said.

He knew I was lying and couldn't conceal a look of hurt or even anger before he spoke softly again.

'Tonto,' he said, edging forward. 'If you've got yourself mixed up into something that you shouldn't have, I can help you, you know? You mustn't be afraid to tell me.'

'There's nothing to tell,' I replied.

'I don't mean the nonsense that Clement was talking about. There are certain tricks,' he said, 'that clever people can pull to make you believe all kinds of things.'

'Hypnotists?'

'Not that exactly, but something like that. Whatever it is, it's not real, Tonto. It doesn't last. And I'd hate for all this happiness to be ruined.'

'Is that what you think happened to Hanny? That he was hypnotised?'

'Of course not. But you give me a better answer.'

'I don't know what to tell you, Father.'

There was a sudden burst of laughter and we both looked. Hanny was outside now and trying to talk to the churchwardens who were sitting on the bench next to the greenhouse, but a gang of children were dragging him away to play football. Eventually, the children won and Hanny began dribbling the ball around the garden with them all chasing and harrying, trying to dig it out from his feet.

'*Can't* they believe it was God?' I said.

'You mean *let* them believe?' Father Bernard replied.

'Yes.'

'That's called lying, Tonto.'

'Or faith, Father.'

'Don't be a smart arse.'

He looked at me and then we turned to watch everyone up at the house. There was music drifting outside. Mr Belderboss was playing his harmonica. Mummer was dancing with Farther. I don't think I'd ever seen her so giddy with happiness, so much like she ought to be at her age. She wasn't quite forty.

When I think of Mummer and Farther now, I think of them that afternoon, her hands on his shoulders, his hands on her waist. I see the hem of Mummer's skirt playing about her thin ankles. She is wearing those shoes with the cork heels. Farther has his sleeves rolled up, his glasses in his shirt pocket.

Mummer cried out and smacked Farther playfully on the arm as he dipped her.

'There's a different woman,' said Father Bernard.

'Yes.'

'It suits her.'

'Yes. It does.'

He looked down at his hands.

'I'm going be leaving soon,' he said.

'Do you have to go back to the presbytery?'

'I mean the parish, Tonto.'

'The parish? Why, Father?'

'I've decided to go back to Belfast. The bishop's not going to be all that enamoured, but I think it's best if I do. I'm not sure how much more I can do here. Not now, anyway.'

'You can't leave,' I said. 'Who will we get instead?'

He smiled and gave me a sideways look. 'I don't know, Tonto. Somebody.'

He breathed out heavily

'Ah, look, I don't want to go,' he said. 'But I'm not what they want, or what they need. I'm no Wilfred Belderboss, am I?'

He bent down and picked up a fallen apple that lay by his feet. It was full of cinder-coloured holes where the wasps had chewed it. He turned it in his hand and tossed it into the long grass by the fence.

I thought for a moment, then said, 'Father, will you wait here?'

'Aye,' he said and sat back while I went over to the potting shed.

It was warm inside. A smell of old soil and creosote. Farther's tools hung up on rusty nails and above them at the back of some old cracked pots that he was always meaning to glue back together was a plastic bag under a seed tray. I brought it down and took it to where Father Bernard was waiting with one arm over the back of the bench, watching everyone milling around up at the house.

'What's this?' he said.

'I think you need to read it, Father.'

He looked at me and took out the book that was in the bag. He opened it and then quickly shut it again.

'This is Father Wilfred's diary,' he said, holding it out for me to take back. 'You told me you didn't know where this was.'

'I was keeping it safe.'

'You mean you stole it.'

'I didn't steal it, Father. I found it.'

'Take it away, Tonto. Get rid of it.'

'I want you to read it,' I said. 'I want you to know what happened to Father Wilfred. Then you might see that they're all wrong about him. That he wasn't ever the man they thought he was.'

'What are you on about?'

'He stopped believing, Father. Here's the proof.'

'I'm not going to read another man's diary, Tonto,' he said. 'And I'm surprised you have.'

'It doesn't matter now,' I said.

'All the more reason to let him be.'

'Please, Father. Then they might stop comparing you with him.'

He sighed, read for a half a minute and then closed his eyes.

'You need to read it all, Father,' I said.

'I've read enough, Tonto.'

'And?'

'And what? Look,' he said. 'This isn't going to change anything. I think everyone suspects that Father Wilfred stopped believing in God. If they choose to ignore it then there's not much I can do.'

'Do you think he killed himself, Father?'

'Tonto . . .'

'Personally?'

'You know I can't answer that question.'

'But you must have an opinion.'

'It was an accidental death.'

'But is that what you think?'

He put his fist under his nose and breathed in as he thought.

'If they recorded it as an accidental death, Tonto, that's how it was. And it's how it needs to stay if the rumours are to be kept to a minimum. Look, I know people will talk, and that's inevitable, but no one's going to beat their fists on a closed door forever. Sooner or later they'll just accept that he's gone. It won't matter how or why.'

'But that's the truth in there, Father.' I nodded to the book. 'Oughtn't people to know what he was really like? Shouldn't Mr Belderboss know?'

Father Bernard brandished the book at me.

'And what would he know by reading this? How could the ramblings of some poor devil who's clearly lost his mind ever be anything to do with the truth? The best thing you can do is put it on the fire. I'm serious, Tonto. Wrap it in newspaper and burn the bloody thing.'

'And leave Mr Belderboss in the dark?'

'And leave him happy. You saw him inside. He's certain his brother's in blissful peace. Why the hell would you want to try and convince him otherwise?'

He calmed his voice and then spoke again.

'Tonto, the truth isn't always set in stone. In fact it never is. There are just versions of it. And sometimes it's prudent to be selective about the version you choose to give to people.'

'But that's lying, Father. You said so yourself.'

'Then I was being as naive as you. Listen, I do have a bit of experience in these things. It's why I was sent to Saint Jude's in the first place.'

'Experience of what?'

'Managing the truth. You see, that's what your mother didn't understand about me. I wasn't trying to expose anything about Wilfred, I was trying to help them keep the rumours on a short leash. But I couldn't do that if everyone was determined that I should be kept in the dark, could I?'

'Then you do think he killed himself?'

He thought for a moment.

'You remember you once asked me what Belfast was like?'

'Yes, Father.'

'Well, I'll tell you. It's like an ants' nest,' he said. 'An ants' nest that's always being rattled with a stick. People scurry here and then they scurry there. Then the stick comes out again and everything changes.

'The Protestants move out of the Bone to Ballysillan and the Catholics in Ballysillan move back to the Bone. There are too many Catholics in the Bone but they'd rather sleep two to a bed than live in a Protestant street where there are empty houses. So they go across the Oldpark Road to Ballybone and the Protestants in Ballybone go back to the houses that the Catholics wouldn't take. And on the roads that are the fault lines between the estates, they pack up all their stuff, cross the road, swap houses and shout at each other from the other side of the street instead. A street that's probably changed its name half a dozen times, mind you. It's madness.'

'What *is* the Bone, Father?'

It was strange, he'd mentioned the place so many times, and I'd never asked him where it was.

He made a rough shape with his fingers, something like a pentagram.

'Flax Street, Hooker Street, Chatham, Oakfield and Crumlin. But that's just my opinion. Ask someone else and they'll give you a different answer. No one knows where the hell they are in Belfast half the time.'

He looked at me and when it was clear I didn't really understand what he was saying, he sighed and laughed a little.

'See,' he said. 'When you're a priest, you hear all kinds of things. And when you're a priest in Belfast you get told all kinds of things. And when you're a priest in the Ardoyne you wish you didn't know anything. There's always rumours flying around about who's done what to whom and why. Who's an informer. Who's with the Provos. Who's not. Whose son's in the jail. Whose daddy keeps a pistol under his pillow. Who's your friend. Who's your enemy. And they'd look to me to give them the right answer. And that's the trick, Tonto. Making them believe that you know what the right answer is. God knows if I'd been honest about what I knew, the whole place would have gone up in flames. They shouldn't call us priests. Not when we're really firemen.'

He looked back to Mummer and Farther and the others.

'I'm sure they know that you were only trying to help them,' I said.

'Maybe, but it doesn't look as though they need it any more. I don't suppose anyone's going to think badly of Wilfred now this has happened.'

'No?'

'You saw them in the kitchen, Tonto. He's come back and blessed them all. I don't think they really care how he died.'

℅

They couldn't say for certain. It may have been the loose handrail – after all it had come apart in the young policeman's hand when they'd gone up to the belfry. It might have been a simple misjudgement of the first step in the gloom – the bulb over the top of the stairs had blown. It might have been the old floorboards that had warped away from the joists. It might have been all three. It might have been none of these things. The only thing that seemed obvious, or easiest, was that it was a tragic accident.

While it was still dark, there was a phone call from Mrs Belderboss, and even before Mummer had finished speaking to her I knew that Father Wilfred was dead.

Everyone was at the church, she said. Something terrible had happened.

Mummer and Farther and I went and joined the group of people gathered around the doors in the snow. They had taken Father Wilfred away in an ambulance and there was no real reason for us to stand there. But no one knew what else to do.

A policeman was on the steps preventing anyone from going inside. He tried to look intimidating and sympathetic at the same time. A police car was parked at the side of the presbytery. I saw Miss Bunce sitting in the back seat with a policewoman. She was nodding and dabbing her eyes with a tissue.

315

'Poor Joan,' one of the cleaning ladies said. 'Finding him like that.'

Mummer nodded with as much compassion as she could muster, but I knew she was put out by all the attention that was being lavished on Miss Bunce. And for what? The silly girl had gone to pieces.

She had come as usual at breakfast time and, worried that he was nowhere to be seen in the presbytery and that his bed was cold and unused, Miss Bunce had gone looking for Father Wilfred in the church. She searched the vestry and the sacristy and as she made for the book cupboard by the main doors – thinking his recent obsession for tidying and cataloguing might have taken him there – she came across him almost by accident at the foot of the belfry stairs. He was staring up at her, his head broken on the edge of the bottom step and an old sword lying a few feet away from his outstretched hand.

&#8500;&#8500;

It was an open and shut case. It was, as they had first thought, an accidental death. An elderly priest had tripped and fallen. The sword? Had he been trying to defend himself against an intruder? There was no evidence of anyone else having been there. The church was locked from the inside. But then there was the bell that people had heard tolling around midnight. It was strange, certainly, but they had no grounds on which they could grant it any significance. Bells were often rung in churches. The sword and the bells proved nothing and were dismissed. They led nowhere useful.

The funeral took place the day the winter snow began

to thaw. The parish turned out in black and stood under the dripping trees in the Great Northern Cemetery before heading back to the wake at the social centre.

Nobody stayed very long. Miss Bunce couldn't bring herself to eat anything. Mr and Mrs McCullough sat by the cardboard crib the Sunday School children had made, giving Henry accusatory looks between mouthfuls of pork pie, as though they suspected it was all his fault in some way. And the Belderbosses were worn out with the endless condolences offered by the other churchgoers who had turned up to pay their respects – not quite as grief-stricken as they, but nervous and bewildered all the same about the ripple that been sent across their pond. What would become of Saint Jude's now?

They shook Mr Belderboss's hand and kissed Mrs Belderboss on the cheek and went off to sit in huddles in their coats, eating their sandwiches quickly and letting their drinks go flat.

In the end, Mummer, Farther and I were the only ones left, and uncertain what else we could do, we started to clear away the plates of uneaten sandwiches and half-empty glasses of beer. Once the tables had been wiped clean, Mummer draped the dishcloth over the tap in the kitchen, Farther switched off the lights and we went out into the slush. It seemed an absurd ending to a life.

∽

While the bishop was arranging Father Wilfred's replacement an ancient priest came to Saint Jude's for a few weeks to plug the gap. He was functional and nondescript. I can't even remember his name. Michael. Malcolm.

Something like that. He had no responsibility other than to take Mass and receive confession, and perhaps feeling a little insignificant because of this he took his role as caretaker rather literally, sending us altar boys out to weed the beds in the presbytery garden or touch up the paint in the vestry.

After Mass one Sunday, he dispatched me to the belfry to check that there were no pigeons nesting there. He had had a great deal of bother with pigeons nesting in the belfry at a church in Gravesend, he said. Their muck played merry hell with the mortar on these old buildings. If pigeons were found, he would have to inform the bell-ringers to ring Erin Triples. Only Erin Triples would shift them. He was quite mad.

The belfry stairs had been made safe. The handrail had been replaced and a new bulb screwed into the light fitting. A heavy rug had been thrown down over the buckled floorboards while they waited on a carpenter.

There were no birds nesting there, of course. It was completely silent. The bells hung motionless in their frame. I went to look out through the small grimy window that faced south for the light. It was February. The snow had been washed away by the rain and the streets all around were slick with it. It being Sunday, the roads below were quiet. A car would occasionally go down the street with its lights on but that was all. Beyond, there were other streets, houses, low-rise flats, belts of diffused greenery and then the grey monoliths of the taller buildings in the city. I was struck by the sudden thought that my future lay amongst all that somewhere.

I was about to go back down when I noticed the stack of colour in the corner. Father Wilfred's robes. The purple that he wore at Lent, the red for Pentecost, the workaday green, and the white he had latterly put on for Christmas. The police hadn't noticed them. I suppose they looked like the kind of junk that ended up in belfries, which were only really loud attics when all said and done. But the robes hadn't been dumped. They had been neatly folded, the creases smoothed away. His crucifix was lying on the top along with his Bible and his white collar. And his diary.

# 27

EVERYONE WAS STARTING to go inside the house. Farther came down the path to where Father Bernard and I were sitting.

'Will you come, Father?' he said. 'Andrew's going to read for us.'

'Aye, of course, Mr Smith,' Father Bernard replied.

'Isn't it wonderful?' said Farther and shook Father Bernard's hand again before he went back to the house.

A train rushed past, leaving a skirl of litter and dust, and then the rails returned to their bright humming. In the scrubland beyond, the swifts were darting over the tufts of grass and the hard-baked soil with its beetroot-coloured weeds. We watched them turning on their hairpins deftly as bats.

'You will get rid of that book, won't you, Tonto?' said Father Bernard.

'Yes, Father.'

'Then we'll be all square, won't we?'

'Yes, Father.'

'We'd better go,' he said and waved back to Farther who was beckoning us to hurry.

☙

I knew that Father Bernard was right and that I ought to get rid of the diary for Mr Belderboss's sake, but I didn't, and I never have.

I've read it so many times that it has become inked onto my brain like a well-known fairy tale, especially the day that everything changed for him.

It began like any other at Moorings. There was the usual carnival of weather. The gathering for prayers in the sitting room. The various shades of gloom moving about the house like extra guests. But after supper, an unexpected burst of evening sunshine had drawn him out of the house and he had been taken by a sudden urge to go down to the sea.

For a number of reasons, he noted, he had never been there before. He had always been rather put off by the local stories about the vagaries of the tides, and in any case, to reach the sea meant traversing the marshland by a road that seemed to be barely there, inundated as it was by overspill from the rain-swollen pools. And when he got to the shoreline, what would he find? Surely there would be little of interest. Only sludge and what the sea had left behind. He feared it would be a waste of time, which led him to consider the other main reason why he had never gone. Time was his gift to his parishioners when they stayed at Moorings and it wouldn't be fair of him to take it back. It was important that he was on call, so to speak.

But, the compulsion to go to the sea wouldn't leave him. It felt as strong as any demand he had ever had from God. There was no option, then, but to put on his coat, take his notebook and go and answer Him. It was, he supposed, the mere fact that he had never been there before that made the call so powerful. For wasn't it the responsibility of Christians to seek, to move forward, to be missionaries? Not to take God with them to new lands like a trading commodity, but to make Him manifest there. To raise Him out of the land. God was already everywhere. People needed only to notice Him.

He was sure that God would walk with him on the sand, give him His guidance and explain the lessons he needed to take back to Saint Jude's. He would tell him what he needed to put into the spiritual alms boxes of those who hadn't been able to come on the pilgrimage and had missed out on the special attention God had conferred upon those who had made the effort. Surely for the good of the parish, his fellow pilgrims wouldn't begrudge him an hour alone. They would understand the importance.

He thought of himself as a shepherd in one of those pre-Raphaelite paintings, drowsing under the dapple of an ancient tree, his thoughts taken away by the flowers and the dancing insects to higher things or nothing. His sheep down the hillside out of his immediate protection but safe enough to roam the pastures for a time unattended. Yes, they would understand.

But if it was God's will that he should go to the sea, what was that apprehension that still dogged him as he started off across the marsh road? It was the feeling that he had disturbed something. The growing unease that the marshes were somehow aware of his presence. It was, he wrote, a dark and watchful place that seemed to have become adept at keeping grim secrets; secrets that were half heard in the whispered shibboleths that passed from one bank of dry reeds to the other.

It reminded him of an illustration of the Styx in the book of Greek history and legend he had had as a boy – his only book, fatter than the family Bible on the mantelpiece. And what stories he had found between the pasteboard covers. Perseus, Theseus, Icarus. What about Xerxes the Persian king, who had tried to bridge the Hellespont in order to crush the Greeks? Or Narcissus, kneeling by his woodland pool? Or Charon, the pilot of Hades? He would have felt at home here, old Charon. Drifting through the marshes in his coracle.

He inspected his feelings again – that was, after all, why he had come – and found that he was not actually afraid, nor was he really apprehensive. It was more a nervous excitement. Whatever lay in wait here, watching him, was nothing so malevolent. It was evidence of God. He scribbled down a quote from Psalms that came to mind: *Let the heavens be glad, and let the earth rejoice; let the sea roar, and all that fills it.*

There was nothing here that should make him wary, only glad. This corner of England was theirs, something they alone had discovered and had been blessed in the finding. In the springtime God was in the wheat fields and the pasturelands; He was in the rain and in the sunlight that followed and glossed every dripping leaf and branch. He was in the cry of the lambs and in the little cups of life the swifts built in the eaves of old barns. And down here on the beach, even though it was bleak and deserted, God was still at work. Here was the wild God who made nature heave and bellow. The violent shadow that followed Jesus through his tender ministry and could test men in an instant with water and wind. But if the weather should turn, there was nothing to be afraid of. There would be a goodness in His purging. A better world made from the wreck of the old.

Once he realised this, the marshes seemed to let down their guard. He noted the birds that he would not normally have seen up at Moorings, and never in London. Coots. Shelducks. An egret, brilliantly white, dipping for the water snails he had seen clinging to the bullrushes.

Further out over the marsh, he saw a cuckoo being mobbed by a squabble of little brown birds. Reed buntings, most likely. He had read that cuckoos liked to use their nests most of all for their arch deception, secluded as they were and woven so beautifully into soft chalices that kept the eggs from the worst of the weather.

As it turned out, the road was not nearly so flooded as it had looked from the house. The water had only washed across the surface and it was clear and still, like a thin mirror reflecting the icy horseheads of cumulus above him, their edges crisp against the blue. If he stood still long enough, he observed, one had the sensation of looking down into the sky, with infinity under one's feet. A strange sense of vertigo that he disturbed after a moment by breaking the puddle with his toe and moving on.

The shadow cast by the dunes was lengthening and he found himself walking in shade well before the tarmac give way to sand.

There must be something about sand that invites a person to put themselves directly into contact with it. To walk on it in boots or shoes seems a waste almost. He saw fit anyway to make a note of the fact that he had taken off his shoes and turned up the bottoms of his trousers.

Picking a route that wound through the sprouts of

marram grass, he climbed up the slope, feeling the wonderful collapse of it under his feet. The burn it put into his thighs. The coldness of the sand when he broke the surface. He was seventy-three years old, but he felt like a child again.

When he reached the top, he was quite worn out with the effort and stood catching his breath and taking in the panorama. He recalled the instruction given to him years before by his tutor at Saint Edmund's College – a keen amateur naturalist, like him.

'Look first,' he had told him. 'And then see. Be patient and you will notice the workings of nature that most people miss.'

It was a piece of advice that he had taken as it was meant – as a metaphor for focusing on the interdependencies of God's world, yes, but also one that he could apply practically in his role as a priest.

He had learnt to watch his parishioners closely, to monitor their progression through the sacraments so that he was better able to correct any deviation from the road that would lead them to heaven. It was his duty. It was the fulfilment of his calling. Their road was his road also. If they found peace at last, then so would he.

He watched and waited and began to see the way the grass moved in the wind, the way the wind came with all the subtleties of a voice. He started to see how the colours of the sea changed as light followed shadow across its vast surface. Turquoise, cobalt, slate, steel. It was quite beautiful. As was the natural geometry of the horizon as it bisected the sea and the sky and invited the eye to be drawn along its length – from the distant industry spiking out of the Fylde peninsula to the south, across to Coldbarrow with its empty heath and its empty house – across to the Furness shipyards faint and grey.

There were the genteel seaside towns full of white houses further away up the coast, and beyond them the Cumbrian mountains rose in severe crags that bared their teeth in the lowering sun.

It was the gulls that made him look back to the beach. He hadn't noticed their noise before. In fact he hadn't been aware of them at all. He had startled them away, perhaps, as he blundered up the sand dune and now that he had been standing there for a few minutes and they knew he was no threat they had returned to feed on the stuff that had rolled in with the seaweed and driftwood and marked the stretch of the tide. It was going out now. Little by little. With each break and foam and hiss it lost its grip on the land and slipped further back. It had been a high tide, he noticed. It had come as far as the old pillbox and left a skirt of wetness around its base.

They were stupid creatures, seagulls. There was something vile about them. As there was with brattish children. The way they screeched and fought over the same scraps, even though the place was an embarrassment of riches.

They were like the people who lived in that esurient underworld, from which he had separated Saint Jude's and its congregation successfully enough for it to seem a place of vivid contrast. The people of that Other world were not the same. They walked in darkness. They were to be pitied. And shunned, if they would not change.

He carried no guilt about such defensiveness. In Romans, Paul talked about associating with the lowly, but it seemed like idealistic nonsense now. Paul's world had gone for good and had been replaced by a vacuum. The sinful no longer worried that they would be punished by God, because God to them did not exist. And how could they be punished by an absence? Wrath and fury, when they came, were no longer attributed to any kind of divine retribution but to natural freakishness and bad luck – and so it was up to him to interpret and judge the world as it truly was. Not to play God – never to do that – but to make it clear for his parishioners by drawing divisions between their world and the Other that God was still present and in authority.

In their world, cause and effect continued. If they sinned, they confessed and were absolved. If they performed good deeds they would be rewarded in heaven. In the Other world there was nothing but inconsequence. Oh, there were people jailed and so on – he had, in his younger days visited them all: rapists and murderers and incorrigible thieves – but for most it was only a temporary withdrawal of their liberty. They cared little, if at all, about their eternal freedom or incarceration. A manila file of forms in an office somewhere to be pulled out at the next offence was the only legacy of their sins. No heed did they pay to the entry that had been added to the greater book of reckoning.

It had been Paul's decree that neighbour should love neighbour and this he stuck to – but only within the world he had created at Saint Jude's. The people of the Other world would care little if he loved them or not, if he rejoiced with them or wept with them or pitied them. Paul had warned of the dangers of judging others – that only God was fit for the task – but those in the Other world needed to be shown up for what they were. And he felt qualified to judge them; they had made it easy for him to do so. Despite what Paul said, his sins – such as they were – were not like theirs. Their sins came from a greater depth entirely.

He had never left a child to die in its own filth as a mother had done in one of the high-rise estates not long ago. He had never poured petrol through a pensioner's letterbox and tossed in a match for fun. He had never come stumbling out of a vice club at four in the morning. He had never stolen anything, destroyed anything. Nor had any of his flock. He had never lusted after anything or anyone, as people in that Other world seemed to encourage and applaud.

He knew what such people would think of his relationship with Miss Bunce. She couldn't be his housekeeper without being his lover also. It was impossible that he would have no carnal desire for her, she being so much younger than he and at his beck and call. He loved her, yes, but not in the way that the Other people understood it, for whom love could not be separated from intercourse.

Galatians, Ephesians, Peter and John. He could have picked a weapon from a vast arsenal to defend himself and show them that it was possible, an act of devotion in fact, to express God's love in the loving of a brother or sister in Christ.

She was the most pious girl he knew. She was a beacon of light in the presbytery. She was untainted by the world that lay outside, and the proof that he had made a difference.

Indeed, all his parishioners deserved to feel like Miss Bunce. Different, loved, guided and judged. It was their reward for being held to ransom by a world that demanded the right to engage in moral brinkmanship whenever it pleased.

People talked about a permissive society, but, as he knew it, permission was something one asked for. No, this was what it was – an assault. They were being beaten into submission by morals that were the reverse of their own. He had lived a long time and had seen the world regressing. With each year that went by it seemed that people were no better than children in their petulant demands.

And children themselves were changing. Youth still had the natural rebelliousness that had been there since the time of Moses, but it seemed to have had something added to it, or forced into it – a fearlessness. No, more a detachment. He had seen it in the youngsters he had caught one evening smashing gravestones with bricks they had knocked out of the churchyard wall, a kind of emptiness in their eyes. They had looked at him as though he wasn't quite real, or what he was saying wasn't quite real. They had been no more than eight years old.

These weren't just the jittery fears of an ageing priest, it was a genuine feeling that all goodness and simple humility – for who on earth was humble nowadays? – had been excised from the hearts of men. He alone, it seemed, had noticed the apparent descent from depravity to depravity that had taken that Other world to a place that was unique and irreversible. There was no darkness now that couldn't be explored or expressed.

Only a few weeks ago had he watched them all coming out of the Curzon at midnight from some horror film that the paper said involved jack hammers and acid. They were laughing. The girls with their hands in the back pockets of the men.

It had been the same night a homeless lady had been kicked to death under Waterloo Bridge. And while the two things weren't connected in any literal sense, he felt certain that they occupied the same pool that had formed when the wall between sick imagination and the real world came down.

It was against this potent mixture that they protected themselves at Saint Jude's and could, ironically, practise the very freedoms the Other people claimed to enjoy, the freedoms that were bandied around as being somehow the looked-for end result of millennia of social cultivation. At Saint Jude's they were free to think; they were free to examine the meanings of love or happiness, unlike the Other people, for whom happiness was the accumulation of objects and experiences that satisfied the simplest of desires.

The Other world had equality now, they said, but what they meant was that everyone had the means to exhibit their own particular unpleasantness. There had been people shot dead in Londonderry and women blown to shreds in Aldershot in the name of equality. And they were always marching. He had seen men marching for the right to sleep with other men. He had seen women marching for the right to rid themselves of their unborn children without reproach. He had seen them marching to Trafalgar Square with their heavy boots and their Union Jacks. Oh, the black shirts might have been hidden under suits and donkey jackets but they were the same men who had infected the place where he had grown up.

Equality. It was laughable. It wasn't equality at all. Not what he understood by the word. Only in the eyes of God were people equal. In the eyes of God each person had the same opportunity to be rewarded with everlasting peace, even the most hardened sinners. They could all walk the same path together if the people of the Other world would only repent. But they never would.

He detested leaving Saint Jude's or the presbytery and dreaded any meeting that would necessitate the use of the tube, which at rush hour really did seem to be a place from Hell.

The only way to cope was to think of himself as Dante, documenting evidence of this Other world's iniquities to share with his flock on his return. That way, as he was swept along in its currents, he might lift himself out of the tide of filth that pressed up against the doors of the train, the way the gulls were pressing against one another now to get at whatever it was that had become such a prized catch.

§⃝

At first it was an old fishing net rolled up by the sea into a cocoon; no, a beached seal, he decided, when a gull lifted off and he caught a glimpse of pale skin.

But then he saw the boots tumbling in the edge of the water.

He went down the dune, slipping and almost falling, grasping the marram and feeling it hold firm for a moment before it came loose in his hand. At the bottom he took his shoes from around his neck and started across the sand, running for the first time in years, shouting and waving his hands, scattering the gulls.

It was as he had feared. The man was drowned. The thought that he might yet be saved had crossed his mind as he ran towards him, but it was far too late for that. The gulls had pecked deep holes in his neck and slit the tattoos there, but had drawn no blood.

The man's hair was half covering his face, but when he knelt down and bent his head close to the sand he could see that it was the old tramp they had been talking about at the dinner table. The wretch he had seen asleep in bus shelters and leaning against the gates of cattle fields, his body limp with drink, his eyes slow to follow what was passing. Well, now his eyes were as blank as mushrooms.

A fresh wave broke and surged up the beach and washed under the body, leaving little bubbles in the tramp's hair and in his beard as it ebbed away.

Dying was so easy. A brief, salty sousing and it was done.

The next wave came soon after and as it retreated again the sand gave way and broke into little runnels, the grains pouring down into the gouges.

He looked around, but there was no use in calling for help. Not here. There was no one. He thought about going back up the dune and waving his arms to try and attract their attention back at Moorings, but it was unlikely they would see him. He would seem a tiny figure to them, obscured to shadow by the sun. And if they did see him what would they think? Would they come? If they came, what use would they be? There was nothing they could do now. And was it fair to compel them to see what he had found? The women especially. It would cast a shadow over the whole trip.

Faster and faster the sand was liquefying around the tramp's body, running away from under him and making him turn slowly on to his side. A larger crack appeared, running out of the top of his head to where Father Wilfred was kneeling. The water filled it on the next wave and widened it so that a great cake of sand broke and the body suddenly rolled and fell and floated. He hadn't realised it until now, but the tramp had been lying at the very edge of a deep trench.

What made him reach out and grab the shirt, he wasn't sure. It was instinctive, he supposed. He caught a sleeve and taking it firmly in his grip he dragged the body towards him, feeling for the first time – and with a shock that made him take hold with his other hand as well – the strength of the sea as it was pulling away from the land.

As the water in the trench lowered, the walls became apparent. They were made of a grey substance that was neither sand nor mud. He slipped down, dug in his feet, and slipped further. The outgoing water was moving apace, its speed increasing as it neared the narrowing bottom of the gulley, where he now found himself up to his knees. A section under his foot gave way and disappeared and he fell and ran the side of his face down the wall, tasting the gritty sulphur of the sludge. He let go, floundered, felt the water sucking him, tried to regain his grip, but the body was hurried away. He pushed himself upright and waded after the body a few paces before it was clear that it was pointless and although it was washed back towards him a few times as the tide engaged in its last ebb and flow, it was with the same mockery as a child who holds out a ball for its playmate only to snatch it away. Eventually the body sank out of sight.

He got out of the water and went up the beach and crossed the line of weed. He leant against the pillbox and wiped the mess off his face and stared at the sea, wondering if anything might reappear. But already it seemed that what had happened was unreal. That only minutes before he had been clinging to the sleeve of a corpse. There was no evidence of the old tramp at all now. Even his boots had gone.

It was shock, he supposed, the cold that was making him shiver, but he was terrified. He had almost been dragged into the sea, yes, but it wasn't the sea that he was afraid of.

He felt alone.

More alone than he had ever felt in his life. It was a kind of nakedness, an instant disrobing. His skin prickled. A cold eel slithered in his stomach. Feelings that he thought he had left behind in childhood on those nights he had cried himself to sleep over another dead brother or sister surfaced and spread and overwhelmed him.

Was it pity? No, he felt nothing for the tramp. He was from the Other world and had got what he deserved. Wasn't that so?

Why, then, did he feel so altered? So abandoned?

It was the place itself.

What was it about this place?

And then it came to him.

He had been wrong about everything.

God was missing. He had never been here. And if He had never been here, in this their special place, then He was nowhere at all.

He tried to dismiss the thought as quickly as it had come, but it returned immediately and with more insistence as he stood there watching the gulls flocking for the crustaceans left behind, and the clouds slowly knotting into new shapes, and the parasites swarming in the carcass of some thing.

It was all just machinery.

Here there was only existence coming and going with an indifference that left him cold. Life here arose of its own accord and for no particular reason. It went unexamined, and died unremembered.

He had fought with the sea for the dead drunk's body with the same futility with which Xerxes had flogged the Dardanelles with chains. The sea had no concept of quarrel or possession – he had only been a witness to its power. He had been shown the perfect religion. One that required no faith. Nor were there any parables to communicate its lessons, because there were none to be taught. Only this: that death was blank. Not a doorway, but a wall, against which the whole human race was mounded like jetsam.

He felt like a drowning man himself, flailing about for something to hold on to. Just one thing that might help him stay afloat a little longer, even if it was bound to sink in the end.

After what seemed like an age, he put on his shoes, and walked for an hour back and forth, as the dusk settled, from one end of the beach to the other, searching the dunes, the rock pools, the deep channels.

Finding nothing.

# 28

Mummer had corralled everyone into the sitting room to listen to Hanny read. The elderly folk sat on the sofa. The rest stood behind them. The armchair that Father Bernard had been given that rainy night when we'd first decided to go back to Moorings, was now set out for Hanny instead. He sat down and Mummer kissed his face and handed him our Bible.

Hanny smiled and looked around the room. He opened the Bible and Mummer knelt down at his side.

'There,' she said, turning a few pages and pointing.

Hanny looked around at everyone again. They were all waiting for him to begin.

He stared down and put his finger on the page and began to read. It was from the end of Mark – the passage that Father Wilfred often branded onto our mortal souls as we sat in the vestry after Mass.

The disciples had refused to believe that Jesus had risen from the dead, but we were not to be like them. We could not be afraid to see Him in all his glory.

'"These signs will accompany those who believe,"' Hanny read. '"In my name they will drive out demons; they will speak in new tongues; they will pick up snakes with their hands; they will place their hands on sick people, and they will get well." '

As Hanny spoke, a murmur of excitement ran through the room, and they knew that God was among them. Mummer was sobbing. Farther went over and put his arms around her. Mr and Mrs Belderboss had their heads bowed and were praying quietly, encouraging others to do the same. Miss Bunce and David stared as Hanny read slowly and carefully, but never once faltered on a single word.

Father Bernard glanced over at me. One day I thought I might be able to explain to him, to everyone, what had happened, or have to, but what I would say I didn't know. I would only be able to give them the facts as I remembered them, as I'm writing them now.

ॐ

I've left this part until last, but it must be set down as well as everything else. When they come asking questions, as they surely will, I'll need to have things straight, no matter the horror.

Doctor Baxter says I ought to worry less about the minutiae of life and look at the bigger picture, but I have no choice and the details are important now. Details are truth. And in any case, I don't care what Baxter says. I saw what he scrawled on my notes. It was only a few words that I glimpsed before he closed the file, but it was enough. *Some improvement, but continues to exhibit childlike worldview. Classic fantasist.* What the hell does he know anyway? He wouldn't understand. He doesn't know what it means to protect someone.

ॐ

I've walked down those cellar steps again and again for the last thirty years, in bad dreams and small-hours insomnia. I know every footfall, every creak of wood. I can feel the damp plaster under my hand as I did on that foggy afternoon as Clement and I inched down in the dark, holding the wall, holding Hanny.

He had lost consciousness by the time we reached the bottom and we had to drag his full weight to a mattress in the middle of the floor that had been freshly stained around the buttons. He slithered from our grip and fell heavily. Clement knelt down and placed a grubby pillow under his head.

There was a smell of burning. A table by the mattress was covered in a black cloth, and the bunches of mistletoe hanging from the ceiling were turning in the heat from the candles. The air was thick and stagnant and the walls glistened with condensation. Here and there, thin stalactites had formed and roots of weeds sprigged through where the mortar had dissolved. It was nothing more than a cave clad with white bricks. It was the place Elizabeth Percy had taken all those sea-weary sailors to be bludgeoned and eaten.

By the mattress was a heap of dirty towels and an enamel bowl of instruments coated in blood that had turned dark and resinous: a scalpel, scissors, a pair of forceps. Else had given birth down here. The child had never seen the daylight.

At the end of the room was a wicker basket, which shook as the baby kicked and screamed itself hoarse. Clement put his hands over his ears. In the low room, the noise was terrible. Parkinson and Collier stood against the wall. The dog lay with its chin on its paws, its frightened eyes looking up for some comfort. It whimpered once and was silent.

Under the screaming there was another sound, a soft thudding coming from somewhere, something like thunder heard from a distance. It rolled and scattered and returned. And I realised that it was the sea pounding the rocks under Thessaly.

'You can go back upstairs now,' Leonard said to me as he went over to the basket and took out the baby which was wrapped in a white sheet.

'No,' I said. 'I want to be with Hanny.'

I bent down and squeezed Hanny's hand, but he couldn't open his eyes. He had been sick down his new white shirt. His whole body was shaking as his leg seeped blood. He was dying moment by moment.

'Clement,' said Leonard.

Clement put his hand gently on my shoulder.

'Come on,' he said. 'Tha'd better do as they say. There's nothing tha can do for him now.'

'I want to stay.'

'Nay,' said Clement, his voice almost at a whisper now. 'Tha doesn't. Believe me.'

I knew Clement was right and that I had to go with him, but I didn't want to leave Hanny alone with them.

Leonard came past me with the bundle. The baby was still screaming in a ferocious way, terrified and violent, like a trapped animal. It was so strong that Leonard had to hold it close to his chest.

'Go on,' said Leonard, raising his voice. 'You can't stay.'

I felt myself being pulled out of the room as Clement dragged me up the stairs and out into the hallway, where he stood against the door so that I couldn't go back down.

'They'll tell you when it's been done,' he said.

'When what's been done?'

'When he's better.'

'What will they do to him?'

'Them?' said Clement. '*They* don't do anything.'

'I don't understand.'

Clement looked at me in a way that suggested he didn't either.

How long I waited there, I don't know. An hour, two maybe. The fog pressed close to the house and the hallway was filled with a pallid light. All the while Clement stood with his back to the door, eyeing me nervously, until finally we heard Leonard calling us down.

Clement stood aside as I went down the steps two at a time into the darkness. The main bulb had been turned off and the cellar was lit only by the candles placed around the rim of a chalk circle that had been drawn on the floor. Leonard, Parkinson and Collier were standing inside the circle. Collier's dog lay by his feet shivering.

Outside the ring, Hanny was lying on the mattress, the baby next to him. Both of them were motionless – Hanny curled up with his hands around his knees as he had been when I left him, the baby half wrapped in a sheet.

The swaddling clothes had come apart, and although Leonard quickly stepped out of the ring to draw the sheets back over the child, he wasn't quick enough. I saw the baby's blind grey eyes. Its shrivelled yellow face. The grotesque swellings on its neck. The mangled claw of a hand.

I say baby. I'm not sure that it was human.

Leonard knelt down by Hanny and shook him gently by the shoulder. Hanny woke blearily. He rubbed his face with the backs of his hands and sat up. After a moment he seemed to recognise me, though his eyes were still half closed and drooping, and Leonard helped him to his feet. The bleeding had stopped and he came to me without a limp.

'Now what dost tha think?' said Parkinson from the gloom beyond the candlelight.

I felt Hanny put his hand into mine. It was warm and heavy.

Parkinson laughed quietly to himself. Seeing my expression of disbelief, Collier laughed too. The dog barked once and shook its collar.

Still the baby didn't stir. It lay there with its eyes half open staring at the ceiling.

The sea thumped against the rocks and faded and returned but more faintly now than it had been before.

'The tide's going out,' said Leonard.

'The sands will be clear by two,' said Parkinson.

'The fog won't lift though,' said Collier.

'No?' said Leonard.

'It's cold as you like out there,' said Collier. 'Especially with all t'flood water. Frets will sit well inland all afternoon.'

'Good,' said Leonard. 'Then there should be fewer people on the roads.'

He looked past me at Clement, who had come down the steps without me noticing.

'Is everything ready?' he said.

'Aye,' replied Clement.

'Well then,' said Leonard. 'I think we ought to conclude our business here.'

'Gladly,' said Parkinson and he took a candle to the end

of the room, returning with the palm leaves Mummer had used on Easter Sunday. He had evidently stolen them from the kitchen when he'd come to Moorings with the Pace Eggers.

Setting the candle down, he pushed the leaves into his fist and offered the first draw to Leonard.

'Oh no,' said Leonard with a quiet laugh. 'You know full well I was never part of the disposal, Parkinson. We agreed that from the start.'

Parkinson looked at him and then moved on to Collier, who took a leaf and glanced sidelong at Clement.

'Go on,' said Parkinson.

Clement shook his head and Parkinson smiled and drew one for him anyway, placing it into his hand and closing his fingers around it.

Clement began to cry, and I was so taken aback to hear him sobbing like a child that I didn't realise that Hanny and I had been given a leaf each until Parkinson was ready to draw the lot.

'Let's see then,' he said and everyone showed their leaves.

Parkinson smiled and Collier let out a breath of relief.

'The best result eh, Parkinson?' said Leonard.

'Aye,' he said, grinning at me. 'Couldn't've been better.'

Clement sniffed and wiped his nose on his arm.

'You can't do this,' he said, holding Hanny by the shoulder. 'He's only a lad.'

'Nay,' said Parkinson, holding out the rifle for Hanny to hold. 'Fair's fair. He drewt shortest straw.'

'Come on,' said Clement. 'Tha knows tha tricked him.'

'You sawt straws, Clement. There was nowt amiss.'

Still dazed, Hanny took the rifle and looked at it curiously before he slipped his hand around the small of the butt and placed his finger lightly on the trigger.

'Draw it again then,' said Clement, turning to Leonard, thinking that out of the three of them he might have some pity.

'Fuck that,' said Collier anxiously. 'It's been done. It's not right to do it again.'

'Don't worry,' said Parkinson, reaching into his jacket and taking out one of his butcher's knives – a cleaver that looked as though it could split a pig in one blow. 'The lad's not going anywhere until everything's been cleared away.'

'Leave him alone,' said Clement. 'Look at him. He's still out of it. He dunt understand what tha wants him to do.'

'Oh, he will,' said Parkinson.

Clement swallowed hard and after hesitating for a moment, he took the rifle out of Hanny's hands.

'Go home,' he said. 'Go on.'

Collier looked at Parkinson again. Parkinson dismissed his worries with a little shake of his head and put the knife away.

'Such nobility, Clement,' he said. 'I never knew tha had it in thee.'

'It can be something of a false victory, though, nobility,' said Leonard, who came out of the gloom wiping his brow with a handkerchief. 'Wouldn't you say?'

He slowly folded the handkerchief and put it back in his pocket as he looked down at the baby on the mattress.

'I mean it might seem as though Clement's relieved your brother of an awful task, but I'm afraid it doesn't really matter who drew the short straw. And I'd hate you to think that his graciousness has somehow taken the pair

343

of you out of the equation. You're down here with us like it or not. We could lay the blame at your door whenever we wanted to. But I think you know that.'

'And they wouldn't like prison much, would they, Clement?' said Parkinson.

Clement looked down at his feet and Leonard went over to him and held him by the shoulder.

'No one's going to prison,' he said, looking from one person to the next. 'Not if everything that's happened here is buried away for good. Right, Clement?'

Clement looked at Leonard and then extracted himself from his hand and took Hanny and I by the arms towards the stairs.

'Don't listen to them,' he said. 'None of this has owt to do with you. You don't belong down here.'

He gave Hanny and me a shove.

'Go on,' he said, fretful that we were taking so long to leave. 'You'll be able to cross now. Go home.'

He nodded up the stairs and then went back over to Leonard who was waiting for him by the mattress. Leonard clapped him on the shoulder and Parkinson gripped him playfully round the back of the head.

'Don't worry, Clement,' he said. 'Dog'll eat whatever's left.'

Clement closed his eyes and began to pray and his voice followed us up the stairs as he begged God for mercy and forgiveness.

But there was no one listening.

# 29

COLDBARROW IS STILL all over the television.

I saw yesterday morning that they had erected a tent on the sands close to where I almost drowned all those years ago. They were working quickly to collect as much forensic evidence as possible before the tide turned, though there can't have been much left. Not now.

The reporter was standing on the mainland, shouting over the driving gales and sleet. The police had now launched a murder inquiry, he said. Two elderly local men had been taken in for questioning, and they were searching for a third.

Things were gathering apace. But I was prepared. All those evenings I'd spent writing everything down hadn't been wasted. Everything was clear now. Everything was straight. Hanny was safe. It didn't matter what anyone said to the contrary. Leonard, Parkinson and Collier wouldn't have had the wit to plan as I had. They had been too reliant on each other's silence and hadn't reckoned on the Loney revealing everything they'd done.

I waited for as long as I possibly could before I had to leave for work, with one eye on the news and the other on the weather outside. A blizzard had been raging since the dark of the early morning and the street outside was becoming lost under heavy drifts of snow. It was starting to come light but only just. A grey colour spilled across the sky, pale as dishwater.

Walking down to the station I outpaced the cars that were waiting to get onto the North Circular in a long line of exhaust fumes and brake lights. People stood huddled at bus stops or in shop doorways which were still shuttered and dark. Even the Christmas lights they had strewn along the high street were out. The city was grinding to a standstill, it seemed, and the crib outside the church on the corner was the only thing of brightness.

They set it up every year – a kind of garden shed crammed with life-sized shepherds and wise men and Mary and Joseph kneeling before the plump little Christ in the hay. Music plays on a loop all day and night, and as I paused to cross the road, I caught the tinny trickle of 'Joy to the World' before the lights changed.

The tube was packed, of course. Everyone steamed and sneezed. Coldbarrow was headline news on most of the papers. Each had the same syndicated photograph of Thessaly tumbled to ruins on the beach. Some had grainy images of people in white boiler suits stooped over the rubble. I wondered how long it would be before I saw Parkinson or Collier or even Clement blazoned across the front page. They would be in their seventies now, perhaps their eighties. About to be jolted out of the complacency of old age.

At the museum, I let myself in through the back door. It was so quiet that I wondered if there was anyone else there, but going through the staff kitchen there were a few others standing around in their coats drinking tea, in a kind of holiday mood, thinking that it was very likely the museum would be closed for the day. And they were probably right. I mean, who was going to risk life and limb or a bout of the flu to come and see an exhibition of pewter or Edwardian millinery?

'Hey, I wouldn't get settled,' said Helen jovially, as I gave them all a cursory good-morning nod and headed to the basement.

I know they think me rather odd and talk about me when I'm not there. But I don't really care. I know who I am and I've worked out all my failings by myself a long time ago. If they think I'm fastidious or reclusive then they'd be right. I am. And so where do we go from there? You've worked me out. Well done. Have a prize.

Helen gave me a frowned smile as I undid the security grille. She looked as though she was going to come over and speak to me but she didn't, and I pulled the shutters aside and went down the stairs, unlocking the door at the bottom that, once closed behind me, meant that no one was likely to bother me for the rest of the day. There is a phone but if I get any correspondence it's through email. They understand that I need quiet to work. They've learnt that much about me at least.

A waft of warm air met me. It's always warm in the basement. A dry heat to stop the damp getting to the books. It can be a bit oppressive in the summer but that morning I was more than thankful for it.

I switched on the strip lights and they pinked and flickered and lit up the long rows of bookshelves and cabinets. The homes of many old friends. Ones I've got to know intimately over the last two decades.

When I have a moment, which is becoming rarer these days, I like to visit Vertot's *History of the Knights of Malta* or Barrett's *Theorike and Practike of Moderne Warres*. There's no better way to spend an hour or two once the museum has closed than reading these volumes as they were written – in quiet reflection and study. Any other way is worthless. Having them spread open in a display case upstairs for people to glance at in passing is an insult if you ask me.

I generally work at the far end of the basement where there's a computer I use for research and a wide desk where I can keep all the bookbinding equipment and still have plenty of elbow room.

I don't know why I felt the urge to do it, and it makes me feel like someone out of a Dickens novel, one of Scrooge's clerks perhaps, but a while ago I moved the desk under one of those glass grids they have at street level where I could look up and watch the shadows of feet going past. I suppose there was something comforting about it. I was down there warm and dry and they were out in the rain with people and places to hurry to and be late for.

But today the glass was opaque with snow, making the basement even gloomier. The strip lights don't do much apart from create shadows, if I'm honest, and so I switched on the anglepoise lamp and sat down.

For the past few weeks, I had been working on a set of Victorian wildlife books that had been donated from the sale of some laird's estate up in Scotland. Encyclopaedias of flora and fauna. Manuals of veterinary science. Copious volumes about badgers and foxes and eagles and other reprehensible predators. Their habits and breeding patterns and the many ways to cull them. They were in a reasonable condition, given that they had been languishing in a gillie's hut for years, but the leather covers would have to be replaced and the pages re-sewn if anyone was ever going to read them again. Someone would. There was always someone who would find such things fascinating. Academics might take pains to go through all the details, but what was of interest to the museum, the bit of social history they could sell to the public, was the handwritten marginalia. The little insights of the anonymous game-keeper who had stalked the moors of the estate and kept his master's animals safe for nigh on fifty years.

Notes about the weather and nesting sites were strewn around the sketches he had made of the things he had had to kill in order to protect the deer and the grouse. A fox caught in a snare. An osprey spread-eagled by shotgun pellets. They seemed at first glance, gruesome, boastful things, no better than hanging trophy heads along a hallway, or rats along a fence, but the detail of feathers and fur and eyes that he had taken time to render with his fine pencil made it clear that he loved them dearly.

It was, to him, no different to pruning a garden, I suppose. The gillie hadn't hated these animals for following their instincts of survival any more than a gardener hates his plants for growing. It was a necessary mastery that he exercised over the estate. Without him, there would have been nothing but chaos, and I suspect that it's reverted back to wilderness now that there's no one looking after it any more.

I worked for an hour or more until I heard the doors at the other end of the basement opening. I put my glasses down on the desk (I have become short-sighted in recent years) and looked around the shelves. Helen appeared, her coat over her arm.

'Are you there?' she called, making a visor with her mittened hand and peering through the shadows.

I got up from the desk.

'Yes? What is it?'

'Good news. We can go home,' she said.

'Home?'

'They're going to close the museum because of the snow.'

'I've got work to finish off.'

'You don't have to do it,' said Helen. 'Everyone else is leaving.'

'All the same. I'd like to get it done.'

'It's really coming down out there,' she said. 'I'd get going if I were you. Otherwise you might be stuck here all night. If you need a lift, I can take you as far as Paddington.'

She had come further towards me now and stood at the end of the 990s: *history of New Zealand* to *extraterrestrial worlds*.

'I don't mind,' she said.

'It's out of your way,' I replied.

'It doesn't have to be.'

I looked back at the book on the desk.

'I've too much to do to go home,' I said. 'Haven't you?'

She looked at me, gave me that frown-smile again and zipped up her coat.

'I'll see you on Monday,' she said and went back towards the door. The basement became silent again apart from the steady tick of the central heating.

I returned to the book and gently removed the stitching from the spine of McKay's *Prevention of Galliforme Diseases* with a pair of tweezers before dropping the brittle strands of thread into the bin. No, it was better that I stayed here. It wasn't fair to ask Helen to drive a mile out of her way in this weather. And they would only start gossiping again if they saw us together in her car.

&#8449;

I didn't stop working until hours later. It was three in the afternoon. I hadn't eaten any lunch, but I wasn't hungry, and I often lose track of time down there in the basement anyway, separated as I am from the world of scurrying feet above. A day could sometimes easily pass without me once looking up from what I was doing.

I switched on the kettle to make tea and as it boiled I looked up at the glass panel. It glowed with a buttery light and I wondered if it had stopped snowing at last and the sun had come out. Whatever, it would be going dark before long.

I sat back down at the desk but hadn't taken a sip before there was someone knocking at the door. It wasn't Helen come back to rescue me, I knew that. She had keys. Most likely it was Jim, the caretaker, who I'd fought tooth and nail to keep out of the basement with his anti-bacterial sprays and his polish and his propensity for throwing things away. He'd always been a little abrupt with me since I'd had his key off him, and rattled the ones he had left in a plaintive way, it seemed, as though without the full set he felt somehow emasculated.

Don't get me wrong. I don't dislike him. I'd just rather it was me who kept the place clean and tidy. Jim doesn't really get the idea of an archive, keeping things. I quite admire him in many ways and had half-expected him to have stuck around that afternoon. He's a stubborn old sod like me and wouldn't have gone home just because it was snowing.

I put the cup down and went to open the door. Jim stood there – brown overcoat and navy tattoos – his mace-head of keys hanging from his belt.

'Yes?'

'Visitor for you,' he said, stepping aside.

'Hanny?' I tried to sound surprised, but I knew with all this business at Coldbarrow that he would come to see me sooner or later.

'Hello, brother,' he said as he sidled past Jim and shook my hand.

'I'm locking up at four,' said Jim pointedly and wandered off up the stairs, jangling his keys.

'What are you doing here?' I said and gestured for Hanny to go down to my desk as I closed the door. He was damp with snow and his scarf was caked in ice.

'I rang the flat, but there was no answer,' he said. 'I must admit I thought you'd be at home today.'

'I've too much to do,' I replied.

'You work too hard.'

'Pot. Kettle.'

'Well, you do.'

'Is there any other way to work?'

He laughed. 'No, I suppose not, brother.'

'Tea?'

'If you're having one.'

I made Hanny a cup as he draped his wet things over the radiator.

'Don't you get lonely down here, brother?' he said, looking up at the glass panel.

'Not at all.'

'But you do work alone?'

'Oh yes.'

'You said that with some conviction.'

'Well, there was someone else once.'

'What happened to them?'

'She wasn't quite suited.'

'To what?'

'To detail.'

'I see.'

'It's important, Hanny.'

'It must be.'

'It's not easy staying focused all day,' I said. 'It takes a particular type of mind.'

'Like yours.'

'Evidently.'

Hanny took the cup of tea off me and pressed the back of his thighs against the radiator. He looked up at me, went to say something, but stopped short and changed tack.

'How are things going with Doctor Baxter?' he asked.

'Baxter? All right, I suppose.'

'He said you were making progress last time I spoke to him.'

'I thought our sessions were meant to be confidential.'

'They are, you fool,' said Hanny dismissively. 'He didn't give me any details. He just said you'd turned a corner.'

'That's what he seems to think.'

'And have you?'

'I don't know.'

'You seem happier.'

'Do I?'

'Less anxious.'

'You can tell that about me in just a few minutes?'

'I do *know* you, brother. I can see it, even if you can't.'

'Am I that transparent?'

'I didn't mean that. I meant that it's hard to perceive things about yourself sometimes.'

'Such as?'

'Well, I can see that Baxter's making a difference. And that our prayers are too.'

'Oh yes, how are things at the church?' I said.

'Couldn't be better,' he replied.

'Still packing them in every Sunday?'

'Sunday, Monday, Tuesday . . . We've been very blessed, brother. We light a candle for you every day.'

'That's good of you.'

Hanny laughed quietly. 'God loves you, brother,' he said. 'Even if you don't believe in Him, He believes in you. It will end. This sickness will leave you. He will take it away.'

Perhaps it was the light down there, but he looked old suddenly. His black hair was still thick enough to have been tousled into a nest by his woollen hat, but his eyes were starting to sink into the soft cushions of the sockets and there were liver spots on the backs of his hands. My brother was slowly slipping towards pension age and I was following like his shadow.

He embraced me and I felt his hand on my back. We sat down at the desk and finished the tea in silence.

Having circled around what concerned him and run dry of small talk, he looked troubled now, frightened even.

'What is it, Hanny?' I said. 'I'm sure you didn't come all this way to ask me about Doctor Baxter.'

He breathed out slowly and ran his hand over his face.

'No, brother, I didn't.'

'What then?'

'You've heard the news about Coldbarrow, I take it?' he said.

'I could hardly have missed it, could I?'

'But have you heard what they're saying now?'

'What's that?'

'That this poor child was shot.'

'It was on the news this morning, yes.'

'And they reckon it was some time ago. Thirty or forty years. Back in the seventies.'

'Yes?'

'When we were there.'

'So?'

His hands were trembling slightly as he brought them to his face again.

'I've been having this memory,' he said. 'They sometimes come back to me out of the blue but I don't always know what they mean.'

'Memories about the pilgrimage?'

'I suppose they must be.'

'Like what?'

'A beach. A girl. An old house with ravens.'

'Rooks. That was Moorings.'

'Moorings, yes that's right. And I vaguely recall going to the shrine, but that might just have been Mummer putting things into my head. She was always talking about it, wasn't she?'

'Yes.'

It was all she talked about.

'And there are other things, brother, things that are just

355

feelings or images. A door. A tower. Being trapped and frightened. And . . .'

'And what, Hanny?'

He looked at me, blinked back a few tears.

'Well, this is it. This is the memory I've been having since I saw Coldbarrow on the news.'

'A memory of what?'

'A noise close and loud. And something thumping against my shoulder.'

He looked at me.

'Like a gunshot, brother. Like I'd fired a gun.'

'What are you saying, Hanny? That you think you did it? That you killed this child?'

'I don't know.'

'Why would you? It makes no sense.'

'I know it doesn't.'

'It's a trick of the mind, Hanny,' I said. 'We were always playing soldiers on the beach. That's what you're remembering.'

'But it seems so real.'

'Well it isn't. It can't be.'

His head sagged.

'What happened to me, brother? I've prayed so many times for Him to show me, but there's nothing but shadows.'

'You were healed by God. Isn't that what you believe?'

'Yes, but . . .'

'Isn't that what everyone believes?'

'Of course . . .'

'Isn't that what brings them to the church every day, Hanny?'

'No, no,' he said, raising his voice a little. 'Something else happened that Easter.'

356

'What?'

He breathed out and sat back in the chair, nervously thumbing his bottom lip.

'I've never really talked about it, brother, not even with Caroline, and I suppose I've tried to push it down inside me, but if I ever think about the pilgrimage, there's always something else there in the background.'

'Something else?'

'Behind all the euphoria.'

'What?'

'A terrible guilt, brother.'

I shook my head and touched him on the shoulder.

'I feel as though I'm going to drown in it sometimes,' he said and his eyes glistened again.

'It's not real, Hanny.'

'But why would I feel like that, brother, unless I'd done something wrong?'

'I don't know. Perhaps you don't feel as though you deserved to be cured. I understand it's quite common in people who have been saved or rescued from something. Don't they call it survivor guilt?'

'Maybe.'

'Look, I may not believe in what you believe, Hanny, and perhaps that's my loss, but wherever it's come from, even I can see that you've not wasted the opportunity you've been given. You're important to people. You've brought so much happiness into their lives. Mummer, Farther. Everyone at the church. If anyone deserved to be released from the prison they were in, it was you, Hanny. Don't throw all that away now. You're a good man.'

'If only Mummer and Farther were still around.'

'I know.'

'I just wish I could remember more,' he said.

'You don't need to. I can remember everything as it was. I'll speak for you if the police come.'

'Will you?'

'Of course.'

'I'm sorry to have to rely on you, brother, but I just can't remember anything clearly.'

'Do you trust me?'

'Yes, yes of course I do.'

'Then you needn't be troubled any more.'

He wept now and I put my arms around him.

'Those nights I spent outside the house,' I said. 'I didn't mean to scare you or worry you. I just wanted you to know that I was there.'

'I'm sorry.'

'I'm not ill.'

'No, no, I know that now.'

Jim knocked on the door again. I heard him coughing and rattling his keys.

'We'd better go,' I said.

'Yes, all right.'

'Once Jim sets his mind on something there's no getting around it.'

He looked me square in the eyes. 'Thank you, brother.'

'What for?'

'Watching over me.'

'That's all I've ever wanted to do, Hanny.'

'I'm sorry that I didn't let you.'

'It doesn't matter now,' I said.

Jim let us out and then closed the main doors behind us.

'Did you come in the car?' I asked as we wound scarves and fitted gloves at the top of the steps.

'No, I couldn't face the traffic. I got the tube.'

'I'll come with you some of the way then.'

Hanny looked at me.

'Why not stay on and come back to the house?' he said.

'Are you sure?'

'Yes,' he said. 'I'm sure.'

'What about Caroline?'

'I'll talk to her. She'll understand.'

It had stopped snowing and had gone dark. The sky was clear and full of hard stars. Everything had been whitened and thickened and there was a crust of ice over the drifts. Road signs were buried and street edges dissolved. Hanny went down the steps and hesitated at the bottom.

'I think I've lost my bearings, brother,' he said, looking back up at me with a smile.

'This way,' I said and took his arm and led him along the road to the station.

&#8422;

We sat opposite one another on the tube, my faint reflection hanging next to his face. We couldn't have looked more different (I have become a little gaunt around the cheeks these last few years, a little thin on top) but we were brothers nonetheless. Bonded by the business of security and survival.

Like Father Bernard said, there are only versions of the truth. And it's the strong, the better strategists who manage them.

Who were the police going to believe fired the rifle? Hanny? Pastor Smith? The dumb boy healed by God? My gentle, middle-aged brother sitting across from me, swaying with the rhythm of the train?

No, they would believe what I would tell them. That we were nowhere near Thessaly when it happened. That we were running back across to the mainland, stumbling through the water channels in the fog, when a single gunshot echoed around the Loney, and was lost in the silence of the sands.

CAPSTONE

# Stay Smart!

*Smart things to know about...* is a complete library of the world's smartest business ideas. **Smart** books put you on the inside track to the knowledge and skills that make the most successful people tick.

Each book brings you right up to speed on a crucial business issue. The subjects that business people tell us they most want to master are:

*Smart Things to Know about* **Brands & Branding**, JOHN MARIOTTI

*Smart Things to Know about* **Business Finance**, KEN LANGDON

*Smart Things to Know about* **Change**, DAVID FIRTH

*Smart Things to Know about* **CRM**, DAVID HARVEY

*Smart Things to Know about* **Customers**, ROS JAY

*Smart Things to Know about* **Decision Making**, KEN LANGDON

*Smart Things to Know about* **E-Business**, MICHAEL J. CUNNINGHAM

*Smart Things to Know about* **E-Commerce**, MICHAEL J. CUNNINGHAM

*Smart Things to Know about* **Growth**, TONY GRUNDY

*Smart Things to Know about* **Innovation & Creativity**, DENNIS SHERWOOD

*Smart Things to Know about* **Knowledge Management**,
TOM M. KOULOPOULOS & CARL FRAPPAOLO

*Smart Things to Know about* **Leadership**,
JONATHAN YUDELOWITZ, RICHARD KOCH & ROBIN FIELD

*Smart Things to Know about* **Managing Projects**, DONNA DEEPROSE

*Smart Things to Know about* **Marketing**, JOHN MARIOTTI

*Smart Things to Know about* **Partnerships**, JOHN MARIOTTI

*Smart Things to Know about* **People Management**, DAVID FIRTH

*Smart Things to Know about* **Scenario Planning**, TONY KIPPENBERGER

*Smart Things to Know about* **Strategy**, RICHARD KOCH

*Smart Things to Know about* **Teams**, ANNEMARIE CARACCIOLO

*Smart Things to Know about* **Your Career**, JOHN MIDDLETON

You can stay **Smart** by e-mailing us at **info@wiley-capstone.co.uk**
Let us keep you up to date with new Smart books, Smart updates, a Smart newsletter and Smart seminars and conferences. Get in touch to discuss your needs.

CAPSTONE

# Smart

## THINGS TO KNOW ABOUT

## Culture

DONNA DEEPROSE

First Published 2003 by
Capstone Publishing Limited (a Wiley company)
8 Newtec Place
Magdalen Road
Oxford
OX4 1RE
United Kingdom
http://www.capstoneideas.com

CIP catalogue records for this book are available from the British Library and the US Library of Congress

ISBN 1-84112-418-4

Typeset in 11/15pt Sabon by Sparks Computer Solutions Ltd, Oxford, UK (http://www.sparks.co.uk)
Printed and bound by T.J. International Ltd, Padstow, Cornwall

# Contents

*Acknowledgments*                                                        vii

*What is Smart?*                                                          ix

Introduction                                                              1

**Part I – What is Corporate Culture?**                                   5

1  In a Nutshell: Definitions                                            7

2  Hidden Culture: Values and Beliefs                                    13

3  Culture Revealed: Practices, Behaviours and Symbols                   21

4  Name that Culture: Various Models                                     41

5  Rebellious Offspring: Subcultures                                     51

**Part II – Why Culture Matters**                                     **61**

  6  Impact on the Organization                                        63

  7  Impact on You                                                     81


**Part III – The State of Culture Now**                               **97**

  8  Ghosts of the Past                                                99

  9  Destabilizing Forces                                              109

 10  The Rise and Fall of Cyberculture                                127


**Part IV – Seeking Better Cultures**                                 **143**

 11  The Textbook Model                                               145

 12  Variations on a Theme                                            161

 13  Creating Your Own Culture of Success                             181


**Part V – Fixing a Dysfunctional Culture**                          **191**

 14  Five Good Reasons to Change and One Doomed to Failure            193

 15  How to Change a Culture Without Really Trying                    199

 16  You as a Change Agent                                            209

 *Index*                                                              217

# Acknowledgments

Several people generously shared their ideas, experiences, and their time with me as I prepared to write this book. I'd especially like to acknowledge the help of two pioneers in the field of corporate culture: Terry Deal, who was ready with insights and stories whenever I called, and Ed Schein, whose e-mail correspondence made me bless the creation of that medium. Thanks, also, to David Matthew and Eloy Bizet-Cruz, who talked to me about working within – and sometimes against – the cultures of different organizations, and Marlene Kess, who has created a culture of her own. And to others who described their experiences in some troubled cultures, but prefer to be anonymous, my thanks to you; you know who you are.

I am lucky enough to have a cadre of smart supporters, who are always generous with encouragement and advice (when I ask for it) that's right on target. Once again, thanks to all of you.

# What is Smart?

The Smart series is a new way of learning. *Smart* books will improve your understanding and performance in some of the critical areas you face today like *customers, strategy, change, e-commerce, brands, influencing skills, knowledge management, finance, teamworking, partnerships.*

*Smart* books summarize accumulated wisdom as well as providing original cutting-edge ideas and tools that will take you out of theory and into action.

The widely respected business guru Chris Argyris points out that even the most intelligent individuals can become ineffective in organizations. Why? Because we are so busy working that we fail to learn about ourselves. We stop reflecting on the changes around us. We get sucked into the patterns of behaviour that have produced success for us in the past, not realizing that it may no longer be appropriate for us in the fast-approaching future.

There are three ways the Smart series helps prevent this happening to you:

- by increasing your self awareness;

- by developing your understanding, attitude and behaviour; and

- by giving you the tools to challenge the status quo that exists in your organization.

Smart people need smart organizations. You could spend a third of your career hopping around in search of the Holy Grail, or you could begin to create your own smart organization around you today.

Finally, a reminder that books don't change the world, people do. And although the *Smart* series offers you the brightest wisdom from the best practitioners and thinkers, these books throw the responsibility on you to *apply* what you're learning to your work.

Because the truly smart person knows that reading a book is the start of the process and not the end ...

As Eric Hoffer says, 'In times of change, learners inherit the world, while the learned remain beautifully equipped to deal with a world that no longer exists.'

*David Firth*
*Smartmaster*

# Introduction

Early in my business writing career, I took a job as an editor in the corporate communications department of a large company. Shortly after I arrived, the company president held a briefing for the department, urging participants to ask anything they wanted. New and eager, I peppered him with questions and was delighted with his willingness to respond. But as I came down in the lift with my colleagues, one of them fixed me with a frown and sneered disapprovingly, 'You certainly asked a lot of questions.'

I caught on. It wasn't written anywhere, but one had to earn the right to take as much airtime as I'd claimed. As a newcomer, I was perceived as being pushy.

Lots of the key rules for thriving in organizations are unwritten; often they are even unstated, and sometimes they

> **Smart quotes**
>
> 'Cracking the culture code reveals the real stuff that lurks just under the surface of everyday life. You understand more, and you can cope better – or know when it's time to leave.'
>
> Lee Bolman and Terrence Deal, *Escape from Cluelessness*[1]

hover below the level of consciousness. Nobody told me that day I should sit quietly and defer to my more senior colleagues; my boss didn't chastise me for my behaviour. But I had inadvertently branded myself as a show-off and a non-team player among some of my co-workers.

Rules like that one are embedded in the culture. As I grew to understand it, I realized that what happened that day was reflective of the value the organization placed on longevity and loyalty. You had to be around a while and prove yourself to earn the respect of your colleagues.

The rebuke in the lift felt like a blow at the time, but in fact cultural norms are seldom intrinsically good or bad. They are ways of behaving that have worked consistently enough to become ingrained within the organization. They worked originally because they supported the organization's basic assumptions about what kinds of people, products, activities, relationships, and management and marketing styles added value to the organization. They continue to work because people who abide by them thrive, earning favour among colleagues and those higher up in the organization, and because they provide a degree of security. It's comforting to be able to depend upon the certainty that action A will elicit response B throughout the organization.

Eventually, cultural norms simply become habits. Few people question them or wonder why they endure. Each generation passes them on to the next, sometimes through instruction but often just by example.

While cultural norms are inherently neither good nor bad, they do sometimes outlast their usefulness to the organization. As markets, the economy and the broader society change, organizations have to rethink their goals and their methods if they are to survive. Cultures that once sustained the mission of the organization now appear quaint, out-of-touch and incapable of supporting movement in a whole new direction.

But ingrained as they are, and providing the comfort that they do, corporate cultures don't change easily, especially since organizations in transition often go through several disruptive altercations. Seeking security in the midst of this chaos, employees cling tenaciously to their old beliefs, old behaviours and old ways of solving problems. Still, cultures do adjust, sometimes out of inspiration, stirred by new leaders with new visions and new assumptions, and sometimes out of desperation, when employees accept – however reluctantly – that without change the organization will flounder (or the individuals will be cast aside). In some companies, such as GE in the early years of Jack Welch, inspiration and desperation both played a part.

Actually, strong cultures are never static. Over time, cultural changes occur even in organizations that appear to sail unsullied through economic and market upheavals. The basic assumptions of the organization may remain the same, but the behaviours that support those assumptions – such as encouraging ethnic and gender diversity – evolve in response to societal standards as well as technological and organizational innovations.

Whether you are a leader (or aspiring leader), manager, or individual contributor, the culture of your organization will affect your career because:

- *It can support or constrain organizational progress.* This can increase or restrict your opportunities.

- *How well you fit into the culture will affect your sense of comfort and belonging.* If you fit like a glove, you may soar to organizational heights or you may get so comfortable you miss warning signs of danger ahead. If you are a duck out of water, you'll have to decide whether to adapt, bolt or work to makes changes – perhaps to create a subculture in your corner of the company.

- *We are in a tough economy and an era when downsizing is common even in good times.* Many companies are in transition, leaving their cultures in disarray. In these organizations nobody is comfortable.

- *Finally, your organization's culture will have an impact on your own ability to innovate, respond to change and get things done in a timely fashion.* It will also attract other people to work with you, either from inside or outside the organization.

For all these reasons, it's important for you to understand the culture and subcultures in your own organization, as well as the social and technological changes that have radically affected the cultures of all organizations over the past two decades and what the lasting influences of these are. And in a world that is constantly changing, it's almost a given that sooner or later you will be involved in that most difficult of tasks, a culture change effort. The more you know about what's involved with that endeavour, the better.

The goal of this book is to help you understand these things and give you tools to make the most of your knowledge, in order to support the success of your organization and the growth of your career.

## Notes

1  Bolman, LG & TE Deal (2000) *Escape from Cluelessness*. AMACOM, New York.

2  Schein, E (1992) *Organizational Culture and Leadership* (2e). Jossey-Bass, San Francisco.

# Part I
# What is Corporate Culture?

Scholars, writers and management gurus have answered that question in a phrase and in multiple paragraphs. To lay a common groundwork for the rest of the book, this part defines culture, lists its components, helps you classify cultures in focused and meaningful ways, and concludes with the role subcultures play in creating a total organizational culture.

Chapter 1 defines corporate culture. It starts with a quick and dirty – but quite workable – definition, then expands on that until it provides a more thoughtful, inclusive version that focuses on *why* as well as on *how* people behave.

Chapter 2 looks into the heart of organizational culture: the values and beliefs that drive behaviour and give rise to other cultural expressions.

Chapter 3 examines the many ways culture is expressed, including management practices, employee behaviours, communication, celebrations, stories and architecture.

Chapter 4 summarizes a number of culture models: classifications of cultural components into generic cultural types that provide focus and give meaning to what is otherwise a random list of characteristics.

Chapter 5 explores the depth and breadth subcultures add to an organization and the threats they sometimes pose to its stability.

# 1
# In a Nutshell: Definitions

If you've read anything about corporate culture, you have undoubtedly come across this quick, breezy definition:

*The way we do things around here.*[1]

It's glib, but it's useful for several reasons.

First, it refers to something observable: the way people do things. We can get a grasp of an organization's culture by identifying those behaviours and processes that are consistent throughout the organization. For example, if we see that people regularly gather together to work out their differences and come to joint conclusions, we can deduce that it is part of this organization's culture to make decisions by consensus.

Second, there is an inference in this definition that everyone in an organization contributes to the culture and shares in responsibility for it. It's the way *we* do things, not something *they* do. ('They' usually means some vague upper management group too removed to relate to.) In fact, there have been numerous examples of organizations where the way people do things was so out of management's control that all efforts to change it failed.

Third, it describes something powerful enough to have a profound influence on business outcomes. How people do their work has a big impact on the success or failure of the organization.

Finally, defined this way, culture also influences your own career. For every person, questions arise. Do I fit here? Is this the way I work best? If not, should I adjust, should I leave, or should I try to change the organization? Can this culture support the goals of the organization and, if so, how can I contribute? If not, what happens to me if the organization fails? Can this culture support my pursuit of my personal career goals? If, for example, I wanted to work independently on a project of my own, could I do that here? Conversely, if I wanted to pull together a team to tackle a problem, could I do that? How would I – or my team – be recognized if the effort was successful?

As a definition of culture, *the way we do things around here* covers a lot of ground. It's a great tool to jumpstart our thinking about corporate culture. And yet, it's not the whole story.

For one thing, it's a bit vague, begging a lot of questions. The way we do *what* things? The way we run our equipment or the way we run our meetings? The way we handle finances or the way we handle each other? Which things fall into the category of culture and which don't? And what about the things that everyone does differently? Toss that definition into a group and you'd probably get as many interpretations as you have people.

But more importantly, it misses some key ingredients. Culture is more than behaviours and systems – what corporate anthropologists call artifacts – it

Smart
answers to
tough
questions

is also values, beliefs and assumptions that give rise to the aspects of culture
we can observe. In fact, these less observable elements of culture may be
the most important. Not only are they at the core of existing behaviours,
they also determine how the organization and people within it will react to
new situations and what new behaviours will be chosen to deal with new
problems and opportunities as they arise.

So let's look at some more inclusive definitions offered by some of the leading thinkers in the field.

Here's one that neatly sums up the components discussed above:

*It's an organization's – the corporation's, the division's, the team's – com-
mon values, symbols, beliefs, and behaviors. Culture comes down to a common way of thinking, which drives a common way of acting on the job or
producing a product in a factory.*[2]

That definition comes from Rob Goffee and Gareth Jones, who identified four styles of corporate culture that we'll look at in Chapter 3. Their definition not only focuses on what people do, but also hints at why: because they share common values and beliefs – a common way of thinking.

It answers some questions and raises another. Why do people in an organization, many of whom don't even know each other, share a common way of thinking?

That's the issue at the heart of culture. And it's the issue that author, academician and consultant Edgar Schein focuses on in his definition:

*A pattern of shared basic assumptions that the group learned as it solved its problems of external adaptation and internal integration, that has worked well enough to be considered valid and, therefore, to be taught to new members as the correct way to perceive, think, and feel in relation to those problems.*[3]

So *the way we do things around here* is driven by our shared assumptions or, in the terminology of Goffee and Jones, our common way of thinking. We weren't all born with those assumptions, nor were they forced upon us. We, or those who preceded us, learned them by discovering what worked and what didn't work in solving organizational problems, in much the same way as our earliest ancestors learned that a fire kept a cave warm, but you had to avoid direct contact or you would get burned. In the cave and in the corporation, when a solution worked consistently enough to be proven valid, it became absorbed into the group's knowledge bank and was passed on to new members: this is what works, so this is the way we do things around here. Eventually an assumption becomes so ingrained that it slips below the conscious level and is taught primarily by example.

Underlying the way we do things is the bigger assumption that this way of doing things works. It facilitates the success of the organization and the success of the individuals within the organization. Schein has described culture as 'the residue of success.'[4]

## The smartest things in this chapter

- *The way we do things around here* is the most common definition of corporate culture.

- But culture is more than behaviour; it is also the shared values, beliefs and assumptions that drive what we do and the way we do it.

- Those values, beliefs and assumptions are learned, based upon what works to solve problems, and are passed on to succeeding generations within the organization.

## Notes

1   In their book *Corporate Cultures* (1982, Addison-Wesley, Reading, MA), Terrence E Deal and Allan A Kennedy attribute this definition to Marvin Bower, author of *The Will to Manage*.

2   Goffee, R & G Jones (1998) *The Character of a Corporation*. Harper-Business, New York.

3   Schein, EH (1992) *Organizational Culture and Leadership* (2e). Jossey-Bass, San Francisco.

4   Schein, EH (1999) *The Corporate Culture Survival Guide*. Jossey-Bass, San Francisco.

# 2
# Hidden Culture: Values and Beliefs

You could say that an organization's culture is the sum total of all the elements that go into it: values, management practices, behavioural norms, communication (both words and channels), stories and legends, ceremonies and rituals, and architecture. But that suggests those elements are independent of each other, and, of course, they are not. The organization's deep-seated values and beliefs about what it stands for and what make it successful are what drive all the other cultural components.

Most companies have well publicized values statements. They hang them on walls, encase them in plastic paperweights, publish them in newsletters and tout them to the press. Many of these statements follow a familiar pattern: they pledge allegiance to providing the best return for shareholders, excellent products and services for customers, and respect and opportunities for employees.

These are what Edgar Schein calls 'espoused values.'[1] They are either spelled out in formal lists or they are culled from manifestos issued from time to time by a strong leader who calls for people in the organization to take personal responsibility, show initiative or support the team.

In the best situations, the practices of management and workers in an organization directly reflect these espoused values. Although it happened 20 years ago, everyone's favourite example of values in action is the behaviour of Johnson & Johnson during the Tylenol scare of 1982, when an unknown person laced several bottles of Tylenol capsules with cyanide, resulting in seven deaths. Law enforcement authorities quickly determined that the bottles were tampered with after they left Johnson & Johnson plants, that the perpetrator had probably purchased them in several stores, poisoned them, and then slipped them back onto store shelves. Nevertheless, Johnson & Johnson immediately removed all their product from store shelves everywhere, launched a broad communication campaign urging people not to use any Tylenol capsules they had at home, and offered to replace any previously purchased Tylenol capsules with uncontaminated Tylenol tablets. The actions cost the company well over a hundred million dollars and, in the minds of some pundits, put the Tylenol brand at risk forever.

But these actions were in complete concurrence with the Johnson & Johnson credo, first written in 1943, that places customers first and shareholders last in the list of those to whom the company is responsible. (Employees come second, by the way.) People at Johnson & Johnson know that fol-

SMART PEOPLE
TO HAVE ON
YOUR SIDE:

EDGAR SCHEIN

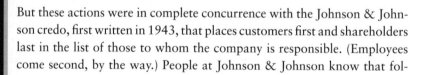

Edgar Schein, author, consultant and professor emeritus at the Sloan School of Management at MIT, is often called a founding father of corporate culture. One of the reasons for that distinction is his model of three levels of culture:

- *Level 1 – Artifacts:* the things you can see, hear and feel when you walk into an organization. They include architecture, the way people dress, the language they use, the stories they tell about the organization, rituals and ceremonies, and the way people behave in relation to each other and their work. These are the manifestations of the culture, but observing them tells you little about why people behave as they do.

- *Level 2 – Espoused Values:* the official version of the values that steer the company, found in documents stating its vision, mission, values and philosophy. These are the values top management describes in speeches and recruiters relate to job applicants. In an ideal world, these would explain the artifacts, but in the real world there is often a noticeable contradiction between the two. Espoused values may be a wish list or, worse, they may reveal the leaders' lack of understanding of the underlying assumptions that really drive the organization.

- *Level 3 – Basic Underlying Assumptions:* what truly drives the organization. These shared values, beliefs and assumptions began with the founder or key leaders who originally imposed them on the organization. Because they worked, allowing the organization to succeed, people learned them, internalized them, and passed them on to succeeding generations. Eventually they were taken for granted and accepted as truth. Though often unconscious, they are strong enough to make it inconceivable for people to behave in a way not supported by them.

Schein described the three levels in his books *Organizational Culture and Leadership* (2e, 1992) and *The Corporate Culture Survival Guide* (1999). In these works, he also outlined a culture change methodology, which is the basis for the process presented in Chapter 15 of this book.

The author of 14 books, he has written extensively in the field of organization development, including the books *Organizational Psychology* (3e, 1980), *Process Consultation Vol. 1 and Vol. 2* (1969, 1987, 1988) and *Process Consultation Revisited* (1999).

lowing their credo is good business. Far from killing the Tylenol brand, the company's actions in 1982 saved it, and Johnson & Johnson shareholders have always fared well.

There are plenty of more current, if less dramatic, examples of scripted values at work. Royal Dutch/Shell Group of Companies espouses only three core values: respect for people, integrity and honesty. The evidence that these are more than catchwords is in the details: things like flowers and clean bathrooms at Shell stations, and support networks for spouses of globetrotting Shell employees.

But carefully crafted values statements are not always the real stimulus for corporate culture. For one thing, they are often a little too vague to translate into consistent behaviour. What does it look like to 'support the team', for example? Does it mean offering your best ideas, listening openly to the ideas of others and working through to consensus? Or does it mean never disagreeing with the prevailing group opinion even if you know it will lead to disaster? It's easy to see that two very different cultural attributes can fly under the same banner.

Second, values statements became trendy. Jumping on the bandwagon, organizations too often hammer out versions that reflect what executives think they 'oughta' value, or perhaps what they 'wanna' value – if only they trusted everyone in the organization to work productively that way. So these statements are sometimes more effective as public relations pieces than as codes to live by. Or, to express it more positively, formal statements are often expressions of idealized values, rather than operating values.

In the worst case scenario, where values statements are really oughta-be or wanna-be documents, operating values can actually be at odds with espoused values. Plenty of employees have learned, for example, that a new values statement espousing respect for employee knowledge and initiative isn't really an invitation to recommend an action that runs counter to a management directive. They've tried it once, been shot down, and gone back to assuming their ideas don't count.

## Values the organization lives by

Operating values are often so ingrained in the organization that insiders are barely aware of them consciously. Yet they are the basic assumptions that people in the organization share about what the organization stands for and what makes it successful. They reveal to insiders the real meanings of generic-sounding values statements, so that everyone in an organization somehow – miraculously, it seems – interprets a platitude in the same way.

Imagine two hypothetical companies, Company A and Company B. Both have values statements that laud their employees for 'taking personal responsibility'. In Company A, people all 'take personal responsibility' by proposing their own ideas, working on them individually and seeing them through to completion, basking in glory if they succeed and accepting blame if they fail. The underlying assumption is that each person is accountable for a defined, individual task or project. But in Company B, people 'take personal responsibility' by adopting a team goal as their own and giving their all, even beyond their own role descriptions, to bring the team goal to fruition. The underlying assumption is that each team member is individually accountable for the result of the team's efforts. Each company may also have its own assumptions around the meaning of accountability, including the expected impacts of success or failure.

In the beginning, organizations operate according to their founders' beliefs about the value of product quality, ethical business practices, customers' concerns, and employee development. Some visionary leaders spell out their values, live by them consistently and insist on everyone else in the organization doing the same.

Bill Hewlett and David Packard did just that in 1957 when they crafted the famous *HP Way*, which explains the approach to profit, customers, fields of interest, growth, people, management and citizenship that would guide the company's actions for succeeding decades.

Few founders have the foresight to record their values and beliefs for immortality. But they reveal them just as clearly through spoken words and even more clearly through their actions. They strengthen the message by hiring people who share their values. As the company profits and grows, these values and beliefs are validated. Throughout the company, people not only accept them as 'right', they internalize them as their own.

Of course, even underlying values evolve somewhat over time, as the company adjusts to new markets, new technologies, and new demands of both customers and employees. Very occasionally a larger-than-life new leader comes along and remakes a company in a new image. But that's the exception. What's more remarkable is the degree to which the original values stick through good times and bad, influencing the organization's response to economic, technical, social and environmental changes.

They stick because, as time passes, they slip so far into the collective unconscious of the organization that they are barely verbalized, let alone questioned. Acting in concert with them is normal and comfortable. Defying them is an unspoken taboo. Yet the words to define them are often elusive. While it's true that values drive behaviour, sometimes you have to study the predominant behaviours and infer from them what operating values or basic assumptions would consistently lead to actions of this kind. The next chapter describes what to look for: the management practices, behavioural norms, and other symbols that suggest the values and express the culture of the organization.

## *The smartest things in this chapter*

- Shared values drive the practices, behaviours and symbols that express the organization's culture.

- While some companies, like Johnson & Johnson, are noted for living their stated values, many companies' values statements are more platitudes than guiding principles.

- Values reflecting the beliefs and assumptions of the founders have tremendous staying power throughout the life of the organization.

- Operating values are often at a deeply buried level that can only be assessed through behaviours and other cultural artifacts.

## *Notes*

1  Schein, EH (1992) *Organizational Culture and Leadership* (2e). Jossey-Bass, San Francisco.

2  Neuhauser, P & R Bender 'Does Corporate Culture Really Matter in Start-ups and Small Young Companies?' at www.culturedotcom.com.

# 3
# Culture Revealed: Practices, Behaviours and Symbols

Values may be at the heart of it all, but when most people talk about culture, they describe the way people behave, the way they do their work, how they treat each other and customers, how they communicate, what and how they celebrate, and the kind of environment – physical, social and psychological – in which they work. These are among the expressions of culture this chapter delves into.

## Management practices

Perhaps more than any other culture indicator, management practices that are consistent and pervasive throughout an organization shape and perpetuate the corporate culture, influencing the behavioural norms of employees. Depending upon the organization's prevailing management practices, when you work for a company your managers will expect you to:

| | | |
|---|---|---|
| Work alone | or | Work in a team |
| Do assignments they give you | or | Find work that needs to be done and arrange to do it |
| Work under close supervision | or | Report your progress toward goals and ask for help when you need it |
| Report to one manager only | or | Work on several projects with different project managers |
| Stick with tried and true methods and do them right every time | or | Take calculated risks, with the expectation that you will learn from your failures |
| Communicate through channels | or | Communicate freely with anyone |
| Suffer consequences for delivering bad news | or | Suffer consequences for hiding bad news |
| Suffer public humiliation if you make a mistake | or | Receive private counselling if you make a mistake |
| Work assigned hours | or | Work the hours and schedule necessary to get your tasks done |
| Prove your worth by following established procedures better than your peers | or | Prove your worth by being more innovative and creating something new |
| Rise up in the organization by blending in | or | Rise up in the organization by standing out |
| Go into purgatory if you fall short of expectations | or | Learn from your mistakes or leave if you fall short of expectations |

If your thought now is, 'I want to work for the company in the second column,' hold onto your CV for a moment. First of all, few companies look like either entire column. You can work in a culture that offers freedom and opportunities to be creative and still get dressed down publicly for your mistakes. In that culture you may be expected to have a thick skin. In another culture that appears to be risk-aversive, you may suddenly be surprised to see a big promotion go to the maverick who had the guts to buck the system, do something different and win. In most companies, the prevailing management practices are a few from Column A and a few from Column B.

Second, everything in Column A isn't inherently bad. There are times in anyone's life when close supervision is comforting, when it's difficult to measure one's own progress, identify one's own problems and figure out when it's time to ask for help. Sometimes being left to one's own devices feels like abandonment, not empowerment. And working assigned hours may translate into working reasonable hours, while determining your own schedule may really mean 24/7.

Nevertheless, it's true that a lot of what's in Column A reflects what management theorist Douglas McGregor, in 1960, called the Theory X style of management. According to McGregor, Theory X managers base their behaviours toward employees on the assumption that people are basically lazy, will do the least necessary to get by, and need to be motivated and controlled with carrots and sticks. On the other hand, McGregor said, Theory Y managers assume that people are self-motivated, want to do their best and contribute to the organizations they work for. These managers function by pointing people in the right direction and supporting them as they progress.[1]

So you could say that management practices are dependent upon a basic Theory X–Theory Y orientation. But that isn't the whole story. A manager needn't assume employees are lazy to expect them to follow established procedures or to communicate through channels. These may reflect a comfort with structure more than any negative assumptions about people.

Whatever the prevailing management practices are in an organization, they tend to be perpetuated because they work. That doesn't mean that in the long run they ensure the success of the company. It means that, by copying them, each new generation of managers earns rewards and promotions, moves into more powerful positions, and passes the prevailing practices on to those that follow.

## Behavioural norms

If management philosophy drives the culture, then behavioural norms express it. When you describe how people typically behave in an organization under a variety of circumstances, you are describing the culture.

Behavioural norms are the accepted ways of acting and expressing feelings in situations that arise at work. From how to dress to when to show up for meetings, to when to speak up or remain silent, every organization has slightly different patterns to which most people adhere.

There are norms that guide how people in an organization perform tasks, how they produce innovations, how they socialize, even how they express individuality. The lists below describe some of the variables.

### Performing tasks

Each organization has its own accepted ways for members to:

- *React to deadlines and budgets.* Are they sacrosanct? Are they often ignored? Are they flexible if situations change?

- *Handle problems.* Do people hide them or announce them? Are people comfortable asking for help?

- *Respond when someone else needs help to perform a task.* Do colleagues pitch in? Would offering to help be appreciated or deemed threatening or insulting? Do others ignore the needy person and concentrate on their own work?

- *Share information.* Is information hoarded or passed out freely? Do individuals acquire power by keeping their information to themselves or by sharing it? Do people accept or ignore information that comes from others? What are the typical conduits for sharing information: one-to-one, public arena, face-to-face, e-mail?

- *Deal with time and schedules.* Do most people arrive at work early or late? Do they leave early or late? What does on time mean: on the dot or somewhere within a 10–15 minute spread? Do 9 a.m. meetings really start at 9 a.m. or at 9.15?

- *Handle conflict.* Do colleagues deal with conflict openly? Do they attack or look for solutions? Do they stifle conflict? Do they look to a third party for resolution?

- *Express feelings about task success.* Do people announce their accomplishments or would that be considered unseemly bragging? Do they congratulate their colleagues and openly admire each other's work?

- *Deal with failure.* When something goes wrong, do people hush it up or analyse it for lessons learned?

## Innovating

Most companies are convinced they have to innovate or they'll die, run over by changing tastes, changing economics and changing technology. Yet for employees, there is an unwritten rule book in each organization that tells them how to:

- *Act when they have a new idea.* Should they act on it independently and ask forgiveness if they screw up? Should they ask their boss's permission to try it out? Should they pull together a team to develop it, test it and seek funding to implement it? Should they put it aside assuming no one would pay any attention to them anyway?

- *Respond when someone else has a new idea.* Do they put it down? Do they challenge it? Do they encourage the other person, even volunteer to help the other person implement it? Do they contribute ideas to it and suggest other sources of aid? Would such contributions be appreciated or perceived as a threat to the owner of the original idea?

- *React to new technology.* Do they actively seek it out and push the organization to acquire it? Do they enthusiastically learn and use it when it's available? Do they ignore it as long as possible, clinging to old equipment and systems?

- *React to change in processes and structures.* Do they take on new roles and apply new methods energetically? Do they go through the motions without contributing input of their own? Do they drag their feet, waiting for a signal that this time the change will last?

## Socializing

Within the organization, is it typical for people to:

- *Visit each other for informal chats within the workplace?* Do people drop in on each other just to shoot the breeze for a few minutes? Do they talk about personal things? Does the workplace encourage or discourage such discourse?

- *Go out together after work?*

- *Socialize in work unit groups or in peer groups?* Do managers socialize more with other managers, for example, or with the people who report to them?

- *Bond with team members?* Do work teams develop into social groups? Do they become exclusive on and off the job?

- *Exclude people based on personal friendships?* Do they prefer to work with their friends rather than with people they don't socialize with?

## Expressing individuality

Culture isn't just about conformity. Within a given culture, there are also acceptable and unacceptable ways of demonstrating individual tastes, ambitions and personalities. For example, to what extent does the organization tolerate individuals who:

- *Dress differently?* Do people look like clones or individuals? Are eccentricities in dress frowned on or smiled at? What would it take to generate disapproval: an earring (for a man) or tongue stud? Bare legs or a bare midriff?

- *Buck the socialization codes?* Are loners tolerated? What about corporate social climbers, who curry favour with upper management?

- *Try out different lifestyles?* Would the organization encourage and welcome back someone who took time off to travel around the world with a backpack?

Corporate cultures are defined as much by the behavioural norms of the rank and file in an organization as by those of the top executives. Who determines what those norms will be? To some extent they may be dictated by management (or union) policies, but largely they evolve as people discover what behaviour works best for them. What helps them get ahead? What keeps them out of trouble? If taking initiative earns kudos, people will do that. If ideas get ignored or shot down, people won't express them. It's often subtle rather than overt management behaviour that influences the behavioural norms of the people in the organization. But once people catch on that a particular way of behaving leads to comfort and security or positive recognition, they learn those patterns of behaviour and teach them to newcomers. Eventually behavioural patterns may become so entrenched that they are self-perpetuating, barely associated any more with any perceivable management practices.

## Communication: words and channels

### Language

Phrases, metaphors, idioms, quotes and jargon that are coined within an organization and popularized throughout it are like the passwords and secret phrases that bestow membership and belonging to members of a club. Knowing them makes you one of the in-group. Using them differentiates you from outsiders.

### Communication channels

Just as the words used are expressions of the culture, so too are the channels through which they pass. Both the sanctioned routes by which messages

Language that resonates can become a rallying cry within the organization. When Katherine M Hudson became president and CEO of Brady Corporation, she found a company of people who were cautious, risk-aversive and afraid to collaborate with each other. Among her efforts to change that attitude was an off-site meeting to discuss how to bridge gaps between divisions and locations. In response to one participant's especially insightful comment, someone else in the audience shouted out, 'Yo'.

Although it hadn't been a word with much coinage at Brady in the past, people responded to it with good humour and enthusiasm. 'I said it seemed like we were describing a journey from no to yo,' Hudson wrote in the *Harvard Business Review*, 'and that became our cheer for the meeting and the company.'

Cultural-specific language contains messages that are absent from more generic expressions. For instance, while 'no to yo' translates broadly into a change from negative to positive, at Brady it says even more. For Brady people, it affirms that they'll take more risks, they're moving toward a goal, and they're having fun doing it. The company even created a 'Double Yo Award' – a yo-yo – 'to imprint on people's minds the spirit we're trying to encourage at Brady.'[2]

travel and the media that carry them say a lot about the culture of the organization.

## Routes

Got a question that only someone outside your department – or someone in top management – can answer? Have you picked up some information you think top management should know? Or do you have a suggestion you are sure would improve business if you could just get top management to listen? Depending upon your organization's culture, getting your message to the right person might be as easy as sticking your head in the person's door and asking for a few minutes of her time. Or you might need to send

Early in her career in corporate communications, an editor needed to write an article about one of her company's star operating divisions. So she sent a memo to the executive vice-president who headed up the division, requesting an appointment. Eventually, she got the memo back with the appointment confirmed, but running along the margins were signatures and comments from the full line of command of both her own and the other division. The implicit message was that there are appropriate channels to go through. Nobody had explained that to her, and nobody chastised her for breaching accepted behaviour, but she got the hint and didn't need to be reminded again.

After that, she sent her communications to senior executives through the system. It rankled a bit at first, feeling like a waste of time. But she came to realize that communicating through channels in that company worked fairly efficiently and kept everyone appropriately informed. The system had one other plus. If someone high up noticed your work and liked it enough to compliment it, that compliment also went through the lines of command, with every other executive en route scribbling an echoing kudo in the margin. It could get you recognized throughout the organization and remind your own management that you deserved recognition at home too.

your message through all the layers in the formal organization chart. Or you may need to cultivate an expediter, someone with a vast informal network who seems to have miraculous access to the most influential people in the organization.

## Media

Cultural norms prescribe not only the accepted routes for communicating with others, but also the media used. Do interactions take place most often in person, by phone, on paper or by e-mail? Is it OK to stop by spontaneously for a face-to-face meeting, or is it more acceptable to set up such a meeting by phone or in writing. Most typically, traditional companies put a lot of stock in face-to-face meetings, set up in advance by going through channels. Companies with wide open landscaping where the president sits out in the open with everyone else often encourage drop-in face-to-face dialogue. At SEI Investments, for example, founder/chairman Al West doesn't even have a secretary to shield him from visitors and callers. Hi-tech companies often rely heavily on e-mail. Microsoft is famous for the deluge of e-mail messages from employees that Bill Gates answers every day.

It's important to recognize that neither the choice of language nor the preferred channels determine the quality of communication throughout an organization. You may go through a tedious process of sending a message up the line of command and down again – and get your answer back too late and too incomplete to be of value. Or you may operate through the same channels and find that your message gains credibility and authority as it goes along, resulting in a faster, better decision at the top. You may find that the fastest, most effective way to communication is via e-mail, allowing writers and responders to devote their full attention to the subject at a convenient time, unpressured by other, conflicting demands. Or the convenience of the system may seduce people into sending offhand messages based on thin information, devoid of the nuances and deeper understanding that face-to-face contact might provide.

Like most expressions of culture, the language and the communications channels that predominate in an organization can help you understand how people work and interact – but not necessarily how well.


## Corporate anthropology and archaeology

Anthropologists who study obscure cultures put a lot of stock in ceremonies and rituals, as well as the society's stories, myths and legends. Corporate cultures have all these characteristics. Archaeologists patch together portraits of ancient cultures from their artifacts, among the most telling of which are the remains of their buildings. Similarly, it's interesting to examine how much the buildings and decor of corporations reveal about the cultures of the organizations housed within.

## Celebrations, ceremonies and rituals

Special events draw attention to what the organization and the people in it consider significant. A quarter of a century ago, when people still expected to spend their entire career with one company, some of the most meaningful ceremonies celebrated employee anniversaries: 5 years, 10 years, 20 years, 25 years. The attending hoop-la swelled as the years added up, as did the accompanying honorarium, which evolved from perhaps a bronze pin for the earliest occasion to the inevitable gold watch for the true lifers. People wore their insignia with pride.

Fewer companies commemorate employee longevity with the same fervour today, but you can still learn a lot from what they do celebrate and perhaps even more from *how* they celebrate.

Does the brass and the bubbly come out to mark new product introductions? The completion of projects? Promotions of individuals? You can get an idea of what the culture values by what it commemorates.

The nature of celebrations provides insight into how formal or informal the organization is, the nature of the relationships between people, and changing company priorities. Are celebrations formal occasions marked by speeches and polite applause? Do people from across the organization join together to salute each other for their achievements? Or are celebrations more local, kept within a tight work unit? Is there an 'in' list of people who get invited to special events? Or are there big, informal events when people

Smart things to say about culture

congregate, enjoy each other's company and recall similar occasions in the past? Are the events even similar to those in the past?

The advent of the digital age brought with it a ritual that was born in the burst of hi-tech start-ups by college-age technophiles: the Friday afternoon beer blast. It was a celebration of hard work, high hopes and togetherness. Where you find the remaining vestiges of such events now, you have to look deeper to discover if people are still sharing that exuberance or if they are simply taking a quick break before working late and into the weekend.

Another ritual that expresses company culture is associated with employee departures. When a respected person leaves the company, do colleagues wave him on his way with good wishes and some fanfare? Barely notice his departure? Strike him from their collective memory as if he never existed? Or guiltily rejoice that a job opens up or an outplacement doesn't have to happen? One individual recalls making two departures, 20 years apart, from the same company. The first time, as a 20-something about to become a new, stay-at-home mother, she'd been toasted, roasted and gifted by her entire department at a long, giddy lunch in her honour at her favourite restaurant. The second time, leaving a department decimated by changing priorities and recurrent downsizings, she had a quiet lunch with the last remaining member of the department and slipped away.

The style of its celebrations usually reflects the degree of formality, stratification and friendliness that distinguish the culture of an organization. What it celebrates can tell you a lot about the importance of people, milestones and achievements. But celebratory events can become artifacts of another era or can be mere window dressing, so the energy and enthusiasm people put into participating in them can tell you even more about current culture.

## Stories, myths and legends

In the autumn and winter of 2001, a new story took hold at AXA Financial Inc., which is headquartered in New York City and owns The Equitable Life Assurance Society of the United States. In a period of economic downturn with its accompanying threat to jobs, people took heart and focused with pride on The Equitable's response to the September 11 terrorist attack. Within a week, the company announced a programme to expedite the payment of claims and provide other complementary services to families of victims of the attacks.

It set up 'disaster relief' claims and information centres in midtown Manhattan and near Washington, DC for life insurance beneficiaries to receive immediate, on-site payment as well as professional grief counselling. The company also committed to extending the grace periods for life insurance premiums and expediting the processing of loans taken against life insurance policies.

Especially for long-term employees, these actions resonated with the legend they'd been brought up on, the one that was always told to prove how much The Equitable cared about people. In World War II, the company paid death claims for all insured service-people killed in action, even though its policies excluded the company from that obligation.

Stories, myths and legends are the tales that are told and retold to illustrate characteristics or expectations of people in the organization. They may be about exploits of founders, leaders or other heroes; the misdeeds of villains; or, as in the Equitable story above, pivotal events in the life of the organization. Implicit or explicit in each story is a moral that implies what the organization and the people within it value around work, relationships and treatment of colleagues and customers.

## Architecture (and how people use it)

As 2001 drew to a close, Hewlett-Packard's high-profile chief executive Carleton S Fiorina fought the Hewlett and Packard heirs over her proposed merger with Compaq, waging battle not from an elegant, high-floor private office, but from a second-floor space that had never broken trust with HP's beginnings in the original Silicon Valley garage. The *New York Times* described it as 'a kind of first-among-equals version of the classic Silicon Valley cubicle, a large corner space marked off by beige, shoulder-high partitions.'[3]

The open landscape of the Hewlett-Packard offices symbolizes its celebrated 60-year-old culture based on trust, openness and consensus, and founded on a participative management style that became immortalized as the *HP Way*. But even well-entrenched cultures are open to differing interpretations and the merger battle was largely about culture. Fiorina, who was recruited to turn around the company's recent flagging performance, insisted that the merger was in keeping with the founders' vision. 'This company has never been about looking in the rear-view mirror,' the *Times* article quoted her as saying.

Her opponents saw it differently. Already dismayed by her eight-figure pay package and her expansion of the corporate jet fleet, both employees and heirs looked askance at this departure from the company's tradition of – as the *Times* described it – growing organically.

Like Hewlett-Packard's, most corporate architecture is intended to facilitate the current or the desired predominant culture in the organization. Open environments are meant to stimulate interaction among people, encouraging the exchange of ideas, and to downplay rank and privilege.

On the other hand, private offices with doors that close signal that the organization values individual work, giving people quiet, private places to think alone and to produce. Of course, that's only half of the message. Often those offices range from closet-sized spaces, where anyone but the most antisocial of beings would suffer screaming claustrophobia, to ballroom-sized suites. When they are assigned according to title and rank, people scramble for them as much to acquire status as to enjoy the comfort of a larger, better positioned office.

SMART VOICES

SEI Investments' headquarters in Oaks, Pennsylvania doesn't look like a financial centre. What it resembles is a factory complex. Its low brown and grey clapboard buildings are studded with red-trimmed windows and joined to each other by flyways spanning pedestrian walks.

Inside each building is a vast open space, filled with furniture on wheels grouped in various arrangements, each desk topped by a computer whose cable hook-up dangles in red coils from the soaring ceiling. The whole space is bathed in natural light streaming through the windows.

The space and equipment are designed to make rearrangements easy. To move one person or a whole group requires no packing – just unplugging the equipment, rolling the furniture off to its new location, and plugging it all in again.

'The physical plant is saying, "Look, we're open-minded",' says Mark Samuels, Senior Vice-President, Corporate Marketing and Communications. 'You work with a team, you can arrange your desks however you want. If you are going to take a temporary assignment, we'll make it easy for you to move your stuff. If a group bulges, maybe the group next to it can contract a bit to make room.'

The plant also says a lot about the organizational structure at SEI, which *Fortune* named one of the best companies to work for in 2001. At about the same time as it moved into its current office space, SEI dropped six or seven layers of management from its organization chart and scrapped the position of secretary entirely. So even executives type their own letters and no one – not even the founder and chairman, Al West – has a 'gatekeeper' to hide behind.

SEI people relish the opportunities for communication that the environment provides. 'It used to take two meetings – back and forth between secretaries – to set up a meeting,' Samuels says. 'Now I can walk over to the person's desk and have that meeting when I think of it. It's way more productive.'

The different rules of etiquette also mean not abusing the open space. Just because you can see people doesn't always mean you can talk to them. If someone is busy, Samuels uses hand signals, gesturing 'Call me'.

It's hard to know whether the environment at SEI contributes to or results from a characteristic you don't often read about in connection with the investment world, but Samuels stresses it. 'People at SEI,' he states emphatically and without embarrassment, 'are *nice*.'[4]

Whatever clues to culture architecture gives, it's important to look past the surface to discover how people are really using the space in which they work. Individual offices don't always close people off from each other. If you see people moving in and out of each other's offices, clustered together in one office to work out a joint problem, or simply standing in doorways talking, that's evidence that the walls aren't separating people. And in some organizations, offices are assigned not by rank but to best accommodate the work of the occupants.

Wide open spaces don't always promote interaction either. Some people find them too noisy and claim conference rooms to work in whenever possible. Other people stay tucked down within their low cubicle walls, with their backs toward the doorway. And arrangements with offices around the windows and cubicles in the centre of a floor often intensify the stratification of people. It's important to remember that newly designed space often reflects the ideal rather than the actual culture. It's what people do with it that expresses the true culture of the organization.

## Attitudes and emotions: cultural undercurrents

Attitudes and emotions are another organizational component that's hard to ignore, although talking about them in a book on corporate culture is skating on thin ice. There's a big overlap here with another concept called organizational climate. The purists maintain that culture – shared values and behaviours – is quite separate from climate, which measures 'how it *feels* to work here'. Many organizations measure their climate every year or so with climate surveys, often called employee satisfaction surveys. While culture is persistent and slow to change, climate is much more susceptible to upswings when employees feel they are being treated well and downswings when they feel put upon. It is, in fact, a measure of one level of employee attitudes and emotions.

But attitudes and emotions can also become deeply embedded, resist change, and heavily influence the way people behave. Cultures reflect whether people operate from fear or from security, whether they trust or distrust management, whether they are cynical or they believe personally in the mission and goals of the organization. You can't get a solid grip on a culture if you ignore these undercurrents.

## The smartest things in this chapter

- Management practices and expectations reflect and reveal organizational values and shape the behavioural norms of employees.

- Behavioural norms regarding everything from how to dress to when to disagree with your boss provide employees with comfort and security as well as a perceived recipe for success.

- Talking the language of the organization is like knowing the passwords and secret phrases that bestow membership and belonging to members of a club. Communicating through accepted channels adds efficiency.

- Celebrations, ceremonies and rituals draw attention to what the organization and the people in it consider significant.

- Implicit or explicit in stories, myths and legends are morals that imply what the organization and the people within it value around work, relationships and treatment of colleagues and customers.

## Notes

1 McGregor, DM (1960) *The Human Side of Enterprise*. McGraw-Hill, New York.

2 Hudson, KH 'Transforming a Conservative Company – One Laugh at a Time' in *Harvard Business Review*, July–August 2001.

3 Lohr, S 'Hewlett's Chief is in a Battle for Her Deal and Her Career', *New York Times*, 10 December 2001.

4 Adapted from 'Open Environment Reflects Open Culture at Investment Company' by D Deeprose, which appears at MWorld, the membership website of the American Management Association.

# 4

# Name that Culture: Various Models

There are lots of reasons to diagnose a culture: to decide if it's right for you, to determine how best to work within it, to convince someone else to join your organization, or even to try to change it if the organization is in trouble. First you need to understand it, to be able to explain it to yourself.

One way to explain the culture of a specific organization would be to identify all the characteristics described in Chapter 2. You'd have a long list – too long perhaps. Instead of shouting, 'Eureka, now I understand what this place is all about,' you might shake your head in bewilderment, trying to puzzle out the contradictions (because there are bound to be some) and decide which of the multitude of characteristics are most important. The problem with a list of characteristics is that it lacks focus. It's easy to miss the forest for the trees.

KILLER QUESTIONS

How can I capture the essence of my company's culture in just a few words?

Scholars and consultants have tried to remedy the problem by developing culture models. They've each selected the dimensions of culture they believe best differentiate one organization from another. From those dimensions, they've developed typographies of corporate cultures. Because they've chosen different sets of dimensions, their types are different too. You'll find each of them is a lens for looking at an organization in a new and interesting way.

## Risk and feedback

Corporate culture was a new concept just beginning to get airtime when Terrence Deal and Allan Kennedy introduced a model of four cultures in their 1982 book, *Corporate Cultures*.[2] They based the model on two variables: 'the degree of risk associated with the company's activities, and the speed at which companies – and their employees – get feedback on whether decisions or strategies are successful'.

The combinations of high/low risk and high/low speed produced four possibilities – four generic cultural types – which, the authors found, tend to concentrate in characteristic industries. The four types are:

- *Tough-guy/macho culture* – high risks and fast feedback. A world of individuals each out to become a star. The stars bond only with each other, and the losers fall by the wayside, causing heavy turnover. Cultures like this are often found in advertising, investment banking and throughout the entertainment industry.

- *Work hard/play hard culture* – few risks and quick feedback. Persistence and remaining upbeat are the keys to success. This is typically the culture of sales organizations, where it's all a numbers game: you won't sell every prospect, but the more you persevere the more successful you will be. There are individual stars, but, Deal and Kennedy maintain, it's the team that counts because the team produces the real volume.

- *Bet-your-company culture* – high risks and slow feedback. People make big stakes decisions, then wait years to find out whether they were right or wrong. As a result, in this kind of world, people are very deliberate. The focus is on the future. Deal and Kennedy found this culture prevalent among firms in the mining and oil industries, capital goods companies, and large systems businesses.

- *Process culture* – low risk and little or no feedback. No individual transaction is going to make or break the company. In fact, it's difficult to identify the outcome of a single transaction. People toil away without knowing how what they do affects the success or failure of the organization. Since it's too hard to determine if they are doing the right things, people concentrate on doing things right – on processes. The organization values technical perfection.

At one time, you could find process cultures in many industries: banking, insurance, retail, government agencies, and utilities among them. But these days, with the emphasis everywhere on short-term, measurable results, you might be hard pressed to find an example of a pure process culture in any company with an ounce of life in it.

## Sociability and solidarity

Now change your lens to look at corporate culture from a different viewpoint. In their book *The Character of a Corporation*, Rob Goffee and Gareth Jones outlined a framework of four cultures based upon two dimensions they called sociability (focus on friendliness and relationships) and solidarity (focus on tasks).[3] To understand these four cultures, it helps to acknowledge the pluses and minuses of each of the 'S words'.

*Sociability*, say Goffee and Jones, promotes high morale and *esprit de corps*, fosters teamwork and sharing information, and makes it likely that people will put in extra effort to help their colleagues look good and succeed. On the dark side – and yes, there is one – sociability also makes it hard for employees to criticize each other, sometimes leading to tolerance of poor performance. And at its worst, sociability degrades into cliques and informal networks that circumvent or even undermine 'due process'.

*Solidarity* encourages relationships based on common tasks, mutual interests and shared goals, rather than friendship. That suits customers and investors just fine; they couldn't care less whether the people who do the job like each other, just that they get it done. For workers who like clarity and knowing exactly what's expected of them, solidarity is a blessing. At the extreme, however, high-solidarity cultures can be oppressive and brutal.

High/low sociability and high/low solidarity combine into the following four cultures, each having both a positive and a negative version.

- *Communal culture* – high sociability and high solidarity. It sounds like an unbeatable combination: caring deeply for each other, intensely passionate about the product, and determined to beat the competition. These cultures live their values; they don't just hang them on the wall. Legends abound about superhuman feats of the leaders. But this culture is hard to sustain beyond start-up, when the founder and a few hand-picked people who share the same vision comprise the entire company. Still, the authors found some communal examples among large corporations, notably Johnson & Johnson.

In its negative shape, the communal culture degrades into extreme or counter-productive versions of the very qualities that provide its strength: dedication to the communal family wreaks havoc on workers' real families. Determination to outdo competitors corrupts into disdain for them. Commitment to the leader distorts into 'surrender to the leader', permitting no dissent, say Goffee and Jones.

- *Networked culture* – high sociability, low solidarity. The atmosphere is relaxed; the rules are a bit vague and open to interpretation. Performance targets and standards are negotiated. People like each other, trust each other and help one another without looking for a payback. Information moves fast and fluidly.

  On the downside, poor performance may be tolerated. It's hard to censure friends' bad performance or to pass judgement on their excuses for it. Strategic focus is fuzzy. People are more concerned with means than with ends, and sometimes they never get there. In its worst form, Goffee and Jones warn, sincere friendship degenerates into 'an insidiously political and manipulative place to work'.

- *Mercenary culture* – low sociability, high solidarity. Work takes precedence over everything – seven days a week. Trust in co-workers is based on the assumption that everyone has the same goal. Goals must be met, with little time spent in agonizing over how. Competitors are enemies to be destroyed, not just beaten.

  In a negative mercenary culture, the focus on goals degrades into concentration on the next short-term target, ignoring long-term consequences. The enemy isn't just the competitor, it's inside too – someone down the hall or in another department. It's OK to trample over people whose activities seem to intrude on yours. If your efforts or needs create problems for others in the organization, that's their tough luck. It's no longer the organization's goals that count; it's only your own.

- *Fragmented culture* – low sociability, low solidarity. Ideas count more than individuals. The only requirement for individuals is output. They don't have to show up eight hours a day; they don't have to play softball with their co-workers. They don't have to buy into some corporate vision or mission. But they do have to produce. Goffee and Jones found this culture occurring in newspapers, law firms, consulting companies and universities.

  In the dysfunctional version, people not only don't play with their co-workers, they attack them. They're well past not buying into the corporate vision; they sabotage it. And they pare their output down to just enough to survive. The author's two favourite words for this version of fragmented: nasty and brutish.

## Equality vs. hierarchy, and people vs. tasks

Here's another take on corporate cultures, this one developed by Fons Trompenaars, who is best known for his studies of national cultures and their impact on global business. Acknowledging that organizations had cultures of their own, Trompenaars defined four generic ones, distinguished by two sets of variables:[4]

- *Equality/hierarchy.* Is the organizational structure flat or vertical?

- *Orientation to the person/orientation to the task.* Does status depend upon who you are or what you know and can do?

The two sets of variables combine to produce:

- *Family culture* – hierarchical, people-oriented. The dominant feature in the family culture is the attitude toward the leader, who is viewed as a caring father who knows what's best for everyone. That reverential attitude toward the leader extends to the leader's anointed representatives.

Smart things to say about culture

Power is vested in people – ordained by the authorities – rather than in roles and tasks. Once ordained, prominent members are supported by the organization, which colludes to ensure their success, since their loss of face would threaten the group's coherence. In such an organization, pleasing one's boss is reward enough for working. In fact, people are more motivated by praise than by pay for performance, which can threaten family bonds.

- *Eiffel Tower culture* – hierarchical, task-oriented. The structure of the organization is a classic pyramid, with the responsibilities and functions of each job determined before anyone fills it. Each level on the pyramid (or tower, in this case) is responsible for what goes on in the levels below. Each square in the organization chart bestows its accompanying authority and status on the person filling the job. That status stays in the office. As Trompenaars puts it, 'If you meet the boss on the golf course, you have no obligation to let him play through.'

  Eiffel Tower cultures fill jobs by carefully matching skills to requirements; you won't get a job on the strength of your charisma. People in Eiffel Towers consider conflict irrational, and avoid it. (Why should it happen if everyone is following the same rules?) Change is difficult because it requires massive rewriting of manuals, job descriptions and all the other rules of the organization.

- *Guided missile culture* – egalitarian, task-oriented. Guided missiles aim at a defined target and do whatever it takes to reach it. The typical work group is a project team, pulled together temporarily with no roles fixed in advance. The leaders are temporary too, and they treat the experts on their teams with respect. Criteria for team membership is how well a person performs and contributes to the joint outcome. Although teams are the preferred vehicle for working, it's a culture of individualists who develop a close relationship around a particular project, then disband and go their separate ways. What motivates them is the excitement of each project.

- *Incubator culture* – egalitarian, people-oriented. This isn't a business incubator; it's an incubator for self-expression and self-fulfilment. Incubators provide a sounding board for innovative ideas and the resources and support needed to implement them. People work long hours because they love what they are doing, but they'll change what they do quickly because, Trompenaars explains, the problem itself is open to redefinition. Organizations with this culture have almost no structure beyond that required to provide logistical support. Relationships are voluntary, built around shared enthusiasms and superordinate goals, and perhaps because of that they are marked by intense emotional commitment. Leadership goes to those whose ideas and progress impress co-workers.

    Silicon Valley provided the prototype for incubators, but Trompenaars found it also among professional groups, such as doctors' group practices, law partners, or, as he describes them, 'any group of professionals who work mostly alone but like to share resources while comparing experiences'.

### Should you name it?

Did you recognize your organization's culture among any of the styles above? If so, then you may have some new insight into what you can expect in the workplace. Did you identify the culture you'd like to work in? Then

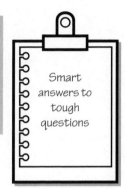

you may have some new thoughts about where you'd fit in best and do your best work. But here's a caveat. These 'pure' cultural styles are neater on paper than in reality. Looking back at the cultural types they defined in 1982, Deal and Kennedy acknowledged in 1999 that no company they knew of precisely fitted any of their categories.[5]

Few organizations have cultures that narrowly defined or that consistent. Perhaps they did once, but years of restructuring, technological revolution, globalization, downsizing and the notion that change is the new constant have destabilized the cultures of countless organizations.

That doesn't render any of the styles invalid. Any of them can still predominate throughout an organization, and can exist in a pure form in a pocket – one work unit or one geographic location, for example. But this caveat is a reminder not to get locked into an expectation that you can wrap yourself in a specific, comfortable culture for the rest of your working life. It doesn't work that way.

## The smartest things in this chapter

- If you find a long list of cultural characteristics is more mind-boggling than enlightening, you might get a clearer picture of an organization's culture by applying the framework of a culture model.

- Applying different models lets you look at a culture in new and interesting ways, just as different camera lenses lend new focus to an object being photographed.

- Few organizations have cultures as 'pure' as those described in any model.

- Certain cultural characteristics correlate to some degree with specific types of businesses or industries.

## Notes

1  Hofstede, G (1997) *Cultures and Organizations*. McGraw-Hill, New York.

2  Deal, TE & AA Kennedy (1982) *Corporate Cultures*. Addison-Wesley, Reading, MA.

3  Goffee, R & G Jones (1998) *The Character of a Corporation*. Harper-Business, New York.

4  Trompenaars, F (1993) *Riding the Waves of Culture*. The Economist Books, London.

5  Deal, TE & AA Kennedy (1999) *The New Corporate Cultures*. Perseus, Cambridge, MA.

# 5
# Rebellious Offspring: Subcultures

Imagine the birth of a brand new company. Sticking to the mythology of modern entrepreneurialism, let's assume it's started in a garage by two life-long friends who shared a dream while they invented a new technology. The founders dazzle the first potential customers by their sheer passion for the product. To get the company going, they surround themselves with a few like-minded individuals. Their work styles are similar. The employees are few in number, similar in ambition, and joined together in their mutual admiration for and trust in the founders, whose work style they happily emulate. This is a very homogeneous culture. Soon, as the company becomes known, its culture is recognized in national magazines.

Now let's assume that success forces the company to add reinforcements to the small group. The founders are so busy keeping their clients happy they hardly have time for creative work any more so they hire a couple of engineers to streamline the product. And while they easily garnered their first clients – who shared their fervour – the founders are not sure how to get out there and expand the market. So they add a dedicated marketing professional and a couple of salespeople. Then they discover that their growth has exacerbated rather than relieved their money issues, so they bring in a financial hotshot along with a new accountant and an assistant.

Unlike the first group, who shared everything, these people aren't joined at the hip. Rather, they are single-minded in their devotion to their specific functions. They spend more time talking to other people in their own functional worlds than they do to the core group at headquarters. The sales and marketing people work differently from the engineers, who find the financial types a big constraining force. And none of them is quite sure what the original group does besides 'yes' the founders.

Then the more laid-back of the two founders gets restless, cashes out his share in the company and retreats to the Mojave Desert, where he supports ecological causes and dabbles in wind-power technology. Those who were closest to him bemoan his departure, miss his easy-going style and form an enclave dedicated to recapturing the good old days.

Now what's happened to the company's much-lauded culture? People still recite the same values, which combined idealism and honesty, and captured the public imagination: changing the world a bit, making some bucks and having a good time. But there seem to be some real differences in opinion about what changes, how many bucks and how to have fun.

Looked at through the Goffee and Jones sociability/solidarity lens, described in Chapter 3, this company started with a communal culture, but the new parts of it look more like mercenary cultures. If you apply the Trompenaars model, it looks like an incubator with pockets of guided missiles. Are these culture clashes? Can an organization survive these fissures?

What's really happened is the same thing you'll find in any organization: the company has developed a number of subcultures, groups of people inside the organization with behavioural norms, rituals and certain values that are noticeably different from those of the overall corporate culture. Some subcultures are inevitable, some are necessary, some are irritating but useful checks on the corporate conscience and some are seditious. While some represent cracks in the mortar that binds the organization together, others give it strength and flexibility to respond to new issues and operate in a variety of environments. These subcultures emerge in a number of ways.

## Natural childbirth

As a company grows, needs arise for sophisticated specialized functions to support the core business. It's only natural that subcultures grow up around each of these functions. It takes a different mindset, different behaviours and different processes to sell a product, for example, than it does to build it. Building it requires tenacious attention to technical details – alone, or in concert with others as thrilled as you are by its idiosyncrasies; selling it

'R&D encourages bet-your-company characteristics (high risks and slow feedback). Sales evokes the work/play culture (low risk and quick feedback). Accounting epitomizes the process outlook on life (low risk and no feedback). And the top echelon executives shine as the stars of the tough- guy culture (high risk with quick feedback).'

Terrence Deal and Allan Kennedy, *Corporate Cultures*[2]

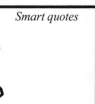

demands tenacious pursuit of people who can barely grasp the product's potential let alone its wizardry. And keeping the organization from financial disaster calls for resolute devotion to numbers and meeting the bottom line.

While people in every function are equally dedicated to their own versions of changing the world, making a buck and having fun (to use our hypothetical company as an example), the builders also value creativity and innovation, the sellers value outside relationships, and the numbers people value structure and discipline. Despite their differences, in the best of all worlds the functions live in peace with each other. The builders know they can't change the world if no one buys their product, and they can't sustain the business unless someone keeps the finances in good shape. The salespeople need a product to sell and the assurance they'll get paid on schedule. And without a product and someone to sell it, the numbers people wouldn't be in business; they'd be doing theoretical maths.

So, while they all grumble a little over the obstacles each group is convinced the others create, for the most part functional subcultures tolerate each other with equanimity and occasional appreciation.

In a healthy organization, the subcultures keep each other in balance. In worse scenarios, however, they can become a problem, especially if they get secretive, shutting out people from other parts of the organization, usually with a superior sounding, 'Oh, you wouldn't understand,' or if they aggressively undermine each other, or, most of all, if one group actually does rise to ascendancy and force its style on everyone else. When you see that happen – for real, not just the complaint of someone who didn't get the budget she'd hoped for – you're looking at a company in trouble.

## Cloning

First, our hypothetical operation overflowed the garage, and a group of people moved into a basement down the street. Later it opened up production facilities in several locations around the country. Eventually it started operations in several countries around the world – each time recreating itself, but inevitably with a few differences.

Each location develops a subculture as it adapts to the different assumptions and expectations of the local managers and employees, customers and suppliers; to different business conditions; and to the local physical surroundings, be they urban high-rise, suburban industrial park or rural isolation. Even with travel and the miracle of hi-tech communication, local facilities feel cut off from headquarters and often out of the loop, so they focus inward. The heroic exploits of the founders are of less concern than the style of the local managers; headquarters stories and myths are just that – stories, not metaphors for how to behave. Each location develops its own heroes and myths.

Geographical subcultures are as inevitable as functional ones. They are even necessary if the facility is to thrive in the local business and social environment. But they do provide a challenge to leaders to ensure that the organization's core values and basic assumptions are as clear and as relevant in Tokyo as in Telford or Topeka, even though they may manifest themselves in different behaviours. If they are not, loyalty to the organization erodes and the organization splinters philosophically or even structurally.

## Extended families

It doesn't always require geographical distance to refocus loyalties and re-define leadership. The same thing can happen when the family tree develops

'Different business units
have different strategic and
product imperatives, and
different functions rely on
different kinds of employees
with different skills and ways
of working. Imposing unifor-
mity can blur the organization's focus on product and
functional excellence.'

Mohanbir Sawhney, 'Don't
Homogenize, Synchronize',
*Harvard Business Review*,
July–August 2001

new branches by organizing into semi-autonomous divisions. And as the greater group of employees get more
and more removed from corporate management, they
look for heroes, role models, and work/social groups
within an organizational unit of a size they can relate to,
whether that's division, department or immediate work
unit. All of these can evolve into distinctive subcultures,
sometimes operating side-by-side in the same facility as
their colleagues in other part of the organization.

The family tree, or organization chart, draws attention
to other subcultures too – based on levels. Top management, middle management, supervisors and workers all
have issues and interests in common with their peers that
differentiate them from other levels and pull them into hierarchical subcultures. These are effective support groups
and become dangerous only if they become so tight they
begin to blind their members to needs of the rest of the
organization.

At the worker level, many organizations accommodate another subculture
– unions. These legitimize themselves on the very basis of their opposition
to management. Often, working with this subculture is less a matter of
integration and more one of negotiation.

## Generation gaps

As the years go by, differences grow up between the history, habits and expectations of long-term employees and those of newcomers. Generational
subcultures become apparent. That's fine, even advantageous, when the
groups learn from each other, each gaining a broader perspective than they

would have surrounded only by peers. It's destructive, on the other hand, if the formation of subcultures hardens the resistance of each to understand and accept each other.

## Marriage and adoption

Predominant cultures are downgraded to subcultures when organizations join through merger or acquisition. But these aren't subcultures in the same way that Finance or IT is a subculture within the larger culture of 'BigCorp', operating from a common set of core values, separated by functional or geographic peculiarities. These are groups of people whose very way of life is at stake, whether their company has been acquired or they are struggling to retain their identity in a merger. The road to resolution of differences is as potentially rocky as the marriage of two strong personalities or the adoption of a feisty teenager. Furthermore, Deal and Kennedy warn that as former colleagues get together to rehash the old days and complain about the new, they cultivate 'a hodgepodge of secret subcultures held over from the latest merger'.[3] One of the greatest challenges for leaders of merged companies is to take advantage of the strengths of these groups while drawing them into the evolving culture of the new organization.

## One big happy ...?

Well, maybe not always. Subcultures pull at the ties that bind people together in an organization. They have different expectations, different goals and different ways of pursuing those goals. Sometimes they clash with each other and a subculture dies, draining the organization of some vitality, or it goes underground, undermining the organization's very foundation.

*Smart quotes*

'We have met cases in which 20 years after a merger the cultural traces of the merged parts could still be found.'

Geert Hofstede, *Cultures and Organizations*[4]

But more often, especially in organizations with effective leaders who emphasize common core values and joint problem solving, subcultures lend needed diversity and a breadth of outlook that is necessary for survival in today's rapidly changing marketplace. For individuals, subcultures often make it possible to find a comfortable place to work and make a contribution within an organization whose broader culture leaves them feeling like a fish on a bicycle.

## The smartest things in this chapter

- Subcultures are groups of people inside the organization with behavioural norms, rituals and certain values that are noticeably different from those of the overall corporate culture.

- Such subcultures develop in distinct functional groups, geographic areas, divisions and organizational levels.

- They may share the organization's core values but express them in ways that are particular to the business needs of their unit, strengthening the organization by giving it resources to respond to varying needs in the rapidly changing marketplace.

- Subcultures created through mergers and acquisitions often have different core values and are difficult to integrate.

- When subcultures compete for dominance or subvert other groups, they undermine the stability of the organization.

## Notes

1   Davis, SM (1984) *Managing Corporate Cultures*. Ballinger, Cambridge, MA.

2   Deal, TE & AA Kennedy (1982) *Corporate Cultures*. Addison-Wesley, Reading, MA.

3   Deal, TE & AA Kennedy (1999) *The New Corporate Cultures*. Perseus, Cambridge, MA.

4   Hofstede, G (1997) *Cultures and Organizations*. McGraw-Hill, New York.

# Part II
# Why Culture Matters

Any top executive, manager or front-line worker who ignores the culture of his organization does so at his own peril. His decisions, actions and relationships – however logical in his own mind – may fail miserably and leave him forever wondering why.

Culture matters because it can support or inhibit the performance of the organization. Chapter 6 talks about the many ways it does that.

It matters because it can turn the workplace into a source of satisfaction, even joy, for those who toil there. Or it can drain their energy, creativity, and individuality. Chapter 7 looks at the impact of corporate culture on the individual, starting from the moment she begins a job hunt through the ups and downs of her career.

# 6

# Impact on the Organization

This chapter and the next contain arguments for paying close attention to organizational culture. Truth told, separating these arguments into 'Impact on the Organization' and 'Impact on You' is an organizing trick that makes it easier to arrange them in digestible chunks to chew on and mull over and consider how each affects you. But, in fact, all of Part 2 – this chapter as well as the next – is about why culture matters to *you*.

While the next chapter tackles individual career issues, surely one of the biggest career issues of all is the success of the organization (or, more likely, organizations) for which you work. It's pretty hard to have a successful career in a failing company. This chapter looks at how culture affects organizational results, focusing on its impact on performance, strategy and change. And since recent history suggests there's a fair chance that, whatever company you work for, it will either acquire or be acquired by another while you are there, this chapter also examines the impact of culture on the outcome of mergers and acquisitions.

## Impact of culture on performance

In January of 2002, Starbucks Corp. reported record-breaking revenue and earnings results for its previous quarter. Apparently someone forgot to tell Starbucks there was a recession going on. Undoubtedly there were plenty of factors contributing to Starbucks' success; maybe it even got a boost from the newly unemployed hanging out drinking coffee. But Starbucks has always attributed its achievements largely to the commitment of its people – and that's a cultural phenomenon. In 1999, authors Deal and Kennedy quoted former CEO (now Chairman) Howard Schultz: 'If people relate to the company they work for, if they form an emotional tie to it and buy into its dreams, they will pour their hearts into making it better... I pour my heart into every cup of coffee and so do my partners at Starbucks.'[1]

In several studies tracking companies over a period of years, researchers found that companies with 'strong' cultures outperformed their competitors. In 1999 Deal and Kennedy looked back at the companies they had cited in 1982 and found that their stock market performance over those years was nearly double the Standard & Poor's average.[2] James Collins and Jerry Porras examined the track records of 36 companies, starting as far back as the '20s, and concluded that, since 1926 the stock market performance of those companies they called 'visionary' outdid the market average by about 14:1.[3] Their definition of visionary has a lot in common with the concept of a 'strong' culture.

So, just what is a strong culture? If you search the literature on corporate culture, you'll find plenty of references to so-called strong cultures, often assuming everybody knows what that means. Although you may have to read between the lines to pin it down precisely, the authors seem to be agreeing that in strong cultures members have consistent values, adhere to unwritten rules of behaviour, and share a sustaining vision.

'We needed people to have a sense of ownership and urgency around the business, to welcome innovation and take risks. But in the existing culture, people dutifully waited for marching orders and thought of their bosses' needs before their customers'.'

So wrote Carol Levin Bernick, Vice-Chairman and Director of the Alberto-Culver Companies and President of Alberto-Culver North America, in the June 2001 issue of *Harvard Business Review* ('When Your Culture Needs a Makeover'). Daughter of the company founders, Bernick told of confronting flattened sales and slipping margins by 'recruit[ing] everyone in the battle and get[ting] every single person focused on the same goals'.

People working in organizations with strong cultures enjoy a sense of community and are secure in their knowledge of what they must do. They don't have to waste time figuring out what their next move should be or wait for the boss to tell them. In that atmosphere, they work harder and more effectively.

## But is a strong culture enough?

Talk about heroes and legends! In the annals of American business as the twentieth century came to a close, one of the great heroes was CEO Aaron Feuerstein of Malden Mills in Lawrence, Massachusetts, makers of Polartec®, the fleecy wonder fabric we all love in jackets, vests and blankets. Feuerstein saved the town the first time in 1981 when he rescued its bankrupt mill and began to turn it into a modern, profitable operation, in defiance of the direction most American textile makers were taking, moving their operations offshore. But he really took on heroic proportions in 1995 when a fire burned the mill to the ground, and instead of immediately laying off his 3000 workers he paid them through the first months of rebuilding and brought them all back when the factory finally reopened.

Feuerstein told a reporter for *Parade Magazine*, 'The fundamental difference is that I consider our workers an asset, not an expense... I have a responsibility to the workers, both blue-collar and white-collar... I have an equal responsibility to the community. It would have been unconscionable to put 3000 people on the streets and deliver a death blow to the cities of Lawrence and Mathuen.'[4]

There were more Feuerstein stories, the reporter discovered: big ones like the heart bypass operations for employees that he'd arranged, and little ones like the free soft drinks and breaks he provided workers in the summer heat.

In a workplace like that, you'd expect loyalty and commitment, and Feuerstein got it. After the fire, plant production rose. He told the reporter, 'Our people became very creative. They were willing to work 25 hours a day.'

## And now for the bad news

For a few years, Malden Mills was a poster child for good corporate citizenship, exemplary leadership and employee commitment. Its story was as warm and fuzzy as Polartec® itself. So when the problems crept in, perhaps no one noticed the first warning signs.

At any rate, even Feuerstein admits the company didn't react fast enough to the appearance of cheaper fleece fabrics, produced in countries where labour is cheap and costs are low. Malden Mills' share of the market slipped. Even Britain's foot and mouth disease epidemic had an impact, as hikers stayed home in droves and sales of fleece outerwear dropped. And then the recession set in and the entire market contracted. (Who knows – maybe the company even suffered from its own success. When a product lasts seemingly forever, how many do you need? I've got perfectly good 15-year-old Polartec® garments I'm still wearing happily.)

By the fall of 2001, the company's financial troubles were overwhelming and it had no choice but to file for Chapter 11 bankruptcy, a condition demanded by creditors to tide the company over with a new loan. Hard-nosed critics blamed the situation on Feuerstein's good heart, pointing out that the emergency loan he was seeking exactly matched what he'd paid to sidelined workers after the fire. But the company's employees didn't see it that way. Its 900 union workers responded to this crisis in the manner their leader had modelled a few years earlier: in a new contract negotiated after the bankruptcy, they agreed to give up their paid personal days in 2002 and accepted a wage freeze until 2003.

It didn't appear to be a grudging concession. The *Christian Science Monitor* quoted workers' reactions to the contract: 'I would never leave him at a time like this,' one said. 'Malden Mills is where I want to be,' asserted another.[5]

But whether Malden Mills' family culture can survive this latest blow remains to be seen. For one thing, a company in bankruptcy has to put its creditors ahead of its employees. Second, Feuerstein disclosed his plan to sell an equity stake in the family-owned mill.[6] And at the urging of his main creditor he hired a new chief operating officer, who came from a management consulting firm. How all these changes will affect this lauded workplace in the years to come awaits another chapter in the ongoing Malden Mills story.

Is a *strong* culture enough to keep an organization's bottom line strong too? The Malden Mills story isn't over yet, but it certainly leaves that question open. A strong culture is essential to success, but maybe it's not sufficient. When you look at the annals of companies that have fallen in the past few years, you find examples to support that thesis.

When Metricom, a San Jose, California, pioneer in wireless data, self-de-structed in autumn 2001, it wasn't for lack of a strong culture. In fact, it personified the best of the Silicon Valley ideal of creativity and high-inten-sity work ethic.

'Metricom created confidence, a feeling that "I can do that",' Venkat Suresh, a former Metricom staff engineer told *Forbes* magazine.[7] 'We learned from our own mistakes. We were constantly honing the technology. Everyone had the same attitude. That's how it got built.' In fact the culture there was so strong that, according to *Forbes*, ex-Metricomers: 'still believe in the promise of technology and in their own ability to make a difference. They have a deeper faith in their fellow workers, tapping a lifelong network of professional friends for help in finding the next opportunity. And with the gritty determination of early settlers, they believe in the future.'

But not even that degree of mutual commitment to shared values could save the company when its strategy of rapid expansion, riding on ever-increas-ing venture capital, suddenly went bust, and its 'zig-zagging marketing strategy,' as *Forbes* described it, failed to produce revenue that matched its engineering zeal.

## The link between culture and strategy

Unlike Metricom, Malden Mills may yet prove that it's possible for a strong culture to save a company when its strategy fails, but that only works when the culture and a compelling new strategy are in sync. While the literature on corporate culture extols strong cultures, it also em-phasizes the importance of a strategically 'appropriate culture'.

An appropriate culture can provide the energy needed to implement an effective strategy. The EZI story [on page 70] confirms that.

A strong, but inappropriate, culture can limit strategic possibilities, blinding strategy makers to ways of thinking and behaving that don't match their assumptions and unwritten 'rules'. According to some veterans of Metricom, this may have happened there. A culture that worked for engineers, they suggest, was ill-equipped to support successful marketing.

*Identifying cultural glitches*

Matching culture and strategy isn't always obvious. At Marriott International, the hotel chain, managers and employees prided themselves on always being there for their customers even if that meant working 50 hours a week. But when Marriott began to find it difficult to recruit talented people and some of its best managers quit, the company knew it had to make changes before it was too late. What had to change was not the strategy of good service, but those long hours that led to burnout and turned off good people. So Marriott implemented a programme to reduce work hours and stress. The results were gains in productivity with no slippage in customer service.[9] (There's more on Marriott's culture change in Chapter 15.)

## Impact of culture on change

With such a linkage between culture and strategy, what happens to an organization with a tight culture/strategy fit when top management sets off on a radically different strategic path? Plenty of companies attempted just that – with varying results – during the '80s and '90s, when unprecedented technology, globalization and changing customer expectations found them losing market to swifter upstarts. Their ability to reinvent themselves

A CULTURE/STRATEGY MATCH THAT CONFOUNDS COMMON WISDOM

Egon Zehnder International (EZI), a worldwide executive search firm, bases its strategy on supporting its clients with its entire network. That requires co-operation among EZI partners and professionals, bucking the cultural norm in an industry where individual recruiters typically guard their own clients zealously.

In a *Harvard Business Review* article, founder Egon Zehnder described how the company supports co-operation, rather than competition, with a compensation plan that defies common wisdom.[10]

Most professional partnerships reward partners according to their individual billings. But EZI pays all partners a base salary that varies only from location to location (but not from partner to partner within a location) and divides a portion of each year's profit equally among all partners. So it is to the partners' advantage to send potential clients and recruits to a colleague in another location if that's likely to result in a match.

EZI also puts high value on company experience. So it distributes another portion of the annual profit according to seniority and ploughs the final portion back into the firm. Since all partners have equal shares, the longer they stay the more the value of the shares is likely to grow.

Non-partner consultants receive bonuses based on how 'partner-like' they have been. That has nothing to do with billings, but plenty to do with behaviours like supporting colleagues, publishing articles, and being active in associations – activities that benefit EZI's reputation.

Supported by its unconventional compensation plan, EZI has built a culture in which:

- People are highly collaborative, enthusiastically sharing information about existing and potential clients and executives who might meet clients' needs.

- People are there for the long term so they have time to build large networks of contacts. Annual turnover among partners is 2 per cent, Zehner said, compared to an industry average of 30 per cent.
- People have common values and common expectations worldwide. 'The people in our Boston office think and act the same way as the people in our British and Brazilian offices,' Zehnder asserted in *HBR*.

hinged to a large degree on how well their corporate cultures could adapt to strategic change.

Imagine a traditional company, populated by people who perform the same tasks day after day, take great pride in doing their tasks well and are rewarded for doing just that. Now imagine that a hotshot planner convinces top management to embark on a strategy of innovation and risk-taking, betting the health (if not survival) of the company on developing new products and pitching them in new markets. In that environment, does such a strategy have a hope of succeeding?

Now imagine the frustration of a group of heady dot-commers asked to count paperclips to keep expenses down and to forego the installation of Version 5.0 and put aside the development of 5.1, because customers haven't figured out 4.5 yet. This mismatch is as hopeless as the one in the previous paragraph. Trying to pull off a business strategy in an inappropriate culture is worse than mixing oil and water. It's more like trying to stick together the wrong ends of a pair of magnets. They repel each other.

So here's one more answer to the question: Why does culture matter? Culture matters because, depending upon how adaptive it is, it can either help or hinder an organization's efforts to update, innovate and meet changing market demands.

Lots of things influence a culture's ability to adapt to change, including:

- *Size.* It's just a lot harder to reach thousands of people, persuade everyone, and keep them all in sync than it is to convince 100 people that it's important now to do things differently. A few cynical or recalcitrant managers or influential informal leaders can smother each pocket of change-enthusiasts that spring up in a giant organization.

- *Age* of organization – or more accurately some frequent effects of age. In a new organization the primary cultural force is the founder and behavioural norms adjust to whatever direction the founder moves in. But after a few generations pass, organizational culture depends less upon the leaders and more on tradition. In an organization that has experienced minimal change over the years, tradition can get pretty rigid. Behaviours take on values of their own with the assumption that they are inherently the 'right' thing to do. Of course, it's not inevitable that a culture becomes rigid as an organization ages. Many companies grow and become strong precisely because adapting to environmental and market changes is a basic value that underscores their culture throughout the life of the organization.

- *Goal orientation.* A culture that's focused on goals adapts to change much more easily than one that is fixed on means. People working toward a goal will recognize that something has to change if their current way of working isn't moving them toward goal accomplishment. And if the goal changes, they may not be happy about it, but they will recognize that their behaviours have to change too. But in organizations where the goal is hazy or barely relevant to the great majority of employees, it's hard for people to make a connection between the way they work and organizational success or failure.

If you want to see an example of the impact of culture on change, attend some company-sponsored training programmes. You'll see people, ostensibly sent on the programme to learn new behaviours, resist trying something different, stating, 'We don't do it that way here.'

Smart things to say about culture

The past two decades have brought plenty of examples of companies struggling to change in the face of non-adaptive cultures. There's a fairly typical pattern. Leaders in organizations that have always rewarded employees for conforming to one set of behavioural norms take a close look at the bottom line and suddenly have an epiphany: they have only two choices, change or die. They announce two moves: downsizing and strategic change (which will now be forever linked in the minds of employees, creating another reason to resist change). However, since these leaders are themselves products of the culture in which they operate, their first change efforts are fumbling and unsuccessful, often leading to their own demise and reaffirming the suspicions of people throughout the organization that the whole idea of change is misguided and their best bet for saving themselves is to hunker down and follow the old norms even more stringently.

But the organizational change effort doesn't end. Next come the outsiders, brought in to turn the company around. Knowing their job is to do what internal people failed at, they underestimate not only the potential of existing employees but also their power, and charge forward without consulting or even informing the people who have to implement their decisions. To survive, the troops learn the new language, but they go right on working the way they always have, simply giving it new labels. Once again, the disconnect ensures failure. And the cycle starts again.

OK, that's a pretty dreary scenario and obviously many companies break out of it when leaders from the inside or outside succeed in tapping the culture's strengths and modifying its stultifying characteristics enough to support necessary change. But there are still many organizations that fit the scenario described.

One such company is a training and consulting firm that, for anonymity's sake, I'll call National Training and Consulting Corporation (NTCC).

## A culture in disarray

If architecture can reveal culture, then the offices of NTCC tell you that this company values quiet, hard work and conformity. Each floor has a warren of cubicles, designed not so much to encourage interaction as to provide as much privacy as possible for their inhabitants even though they share air space above shoulder level. Around the cubes are as many individual offices for middle managers and mid-level professionals as can be squeezed into the space. They are small, many windowless, with sound-proofed doors, and all fitted with identical modular furniture. For a visitor, it's hard to find your way through the maze, and it's hard to know when you've reached your destination because there's so little to differentiate one location from another.

Toward the corners some spaces are different, boasting larger, more grace-ful offices reserved for higher level managers. In the past few years, those corner spaces have housed a revolving group of tenants, most of whom have failed to leave a lasting mark on the organization as it struggles to remain relevant in a business thrown into turbulence by new technological and global influences and rapidly shifting trends in management. Customers that once went to NTCC for tried and true management practices now seek solutions from each new management guru.

But NTCC was slow to recognize the erosion of its market.

'Right into the early '90s, complacency existed because we had been perceived as providing exactly what the business world wanted,' explains one
long-term NTCC manager. But what that world wanted in the early years
('50s, '60s and '70s) was what she calls 'textbook management', a style she
defines as 'carrot and whip' or 'tell them what to do, tell them how well they
did it, and give them a raise'. By the '80s, that credo had less currency; by
the '90s, it was deemed hopelessly inadequate by many. Still, it wasn't until
the late '90s that a customer survey drove home the reality that NTCC was
sliding in its strongest traditional market: supervisor and middle manager
training.

In an organization devoted to providing the same service for 40 years, innovation wasn't high on the list of driving values. It wasn't that the company
never created new products; it offered new seminars, new workshops, and
new publications fairly regularly. But these followed a mould. Radical ex-
perimentation usually ended in failure.

For the most part, people went on, year after year, doing what they'd done
before. As long as they worked hard, they were rewarded with annual bonuses. While everyone had incentive goals, they weren't stretch goals, the
manager explains. They were goals for doing what the job entailed.

'People still think they deserve a bonus just because they work hard,' she
says. 'They're not connecting their own fortunes to that of the company.
Their attitude is, "My fortune is connected to how hard I work, not to the
success of the company."'

After pushing a company expansion, which some considered unwise, the
CEO left in the late '90s. By then there was a group in upper management
panting for radical change, and the company brought in a new CEO to lead
it.

But, says the manager, 'Instead of looking at our strengths and weaknesses, he had a grandiose scheme to eliminate the training side of the business and make NTCC into a cutting-edge consulting firm.' The first step was to purge NTCC of leaders who didn't fit the new strategy and hire a whole new group of people to drive the change.

But there was little contact between this group and the rank and file who were expected to implement it. The new group didn't look for input from the veterans, and the veterans didn't offer it. Instead they protected their own turf and prayed that the new regime would go away. Predictably, it did. It wasn't long before the new CEO, the in-house change-agents and most of the new hires were gone.

Chastened by the fracas, the board called on a former employee – one of the old school – to serve as acting CEO. The rank and file breathed a sigh of relief, but their respite was short-lived. Afraid perhaps that this new leader was more backward- than forward-looking, the board bypassed him and brought in another outsider to take over.

'The new CEO is reclusive,' says the manager. 'People worry about what exactly is happening. What is happening is that he is doing a lot of things that he doesn't share until they are ready for implementation. But not getting input – that's an issue for a lot of people.'

After years of turmoil, how would she describe the culture now?

'It's in disarray,' she says. Yet, despite numerous layoffs, she states that the biggest expectation of long-time employees is 'to stay, but not to make a difference'.

Do new people think they can make a difference?

'The Gen-Xers do,' she replies. 'They have yet to have it knocked out of them.'

## The impact of culture on mergers and acquisitions

If you work for a large organization and you haven't yet experienced a merger or acquisition, count on it – you will. At the rate companies are marrying and divorcing, it's bound to happen to you.

Whether such a union is successful or not depends in large part on the cultures of the organizations involved. Are they compatible? Is at least one of them adaptable? What will happen if the dominant one runs roughshod over the other: quick adjustment, demoralization or pockets of subversive resistance? If the organizations are going literally to merge two operations into one, it's important that people understand each other's language and have the same attitudes toward customers, schedules, quality, innovation and manager–employee relationships. If one organization is going to supply or support the other, they need to share the same expectations for how they will work together. Only if the two organizations continue to operate completely separately, under the umbrella of a merged parent, is there a chance that two totally different cultures can live cheerfully side-by-side. Even that lasts only until a new generation of leaders or a new parent company strategy takes a more hands-on approach in the hopes of profitable synergy.

Organizations that understand how important their culture is to their performance will look for areas of cultural compatibility and incompatibility before they ever agree to merge, and will take great pains to resolve major cultural differences from the outset. If they don't, they're in for rocky times ahead.

'Even now, mere mention of Quaker Oats' acquisition of Snapple causes veteran deal makers to shudder... The debacle cost both the chairman and president of Quaker their jobs and hastened the end of Quaker's independent existence.'[12]

What happened? In a *Harvard Business Review* article, writer John Deighton goes on to explain: 'There is a vital interplay between the challenge a brand faces and the culture of the corporation that owns it. When brand and culture fall out of alignment, both brand and corporate owner are likely to suffer... Some processes are best entrusted to managers with cautious, prudent temperaments while others flourish in the hands of risk takers.'

Quaker was full of cautious, prudent types, but, says Deighton, 'Some brands just want to have fun, and from birth Snapple was one of them.'

Quaker rationalized distribution of the beverage, cut out many quirky flavours, replaced Snapple's edgy ads with bland corporate ones – and suffered as sales drastically declined. Finally, Quaker sold the brand to Triarc Beverages for less than a quarter of what it originally paid. A few years later, Triarc sold its jazzed-up Snapple brand to Cadbury Schweppes for a very handsome profit. Triarc's CEO Mike Weinstein, who now runs the Snapple operation for Cadbury, told Deighton, 'To Quaker, new products were seen as a risk. We perceive them as the opportunity. It's the most fun part of the business.'

'The magic is back,' proclaimed Triarc as it pitched the rejuvenated brand. (And for one die-hard Snapple fan there was more good news: cranberry-flavoured iced tea came back too.)

## The smartest things in this chapter

- Organizations with strong cultures, where members have consistent values and adhere to unwritten rules of behaviour, typically outperform their peer companies.

- A mismatch between culture and strategy can make effective implementation very difficult, if not impossible.

- Companies need adaptive cultures to survive in a world of constant change.

- The success or failure of a merger or acquisition depends in large part on the compatibility of the cultures involved.

## Notes

1 Deal, TE & AA Kennedy (1999) *The New Corporate Cultures*. Perseus, Cambridge, MA.

2 Ibid.

3 Collins, J & J Porras (1994) *Built to Last*. HarperBusiness, New York.

4 Ryan, M 'They Call Their Boss a Hero' in *Parade Magazine*, 6 September 1996.

5 Associated Press 'At Malden Mills, one good turn deserves another' in *Christian Science Monitor*, 19 December 2001.

6 Browning, L 'Private Sector: Bankruptcy Court Fault Lines Between the Good and the Bad, in the *New York Times*, 30 December 2001.

7 Corcoran, E 'Digital Diaspora' in *Forbes*, 18 February 2002.

8 Goffee, R & G Jones (1998) *The Character of a Corporation*. Harper-Business, New York.

9  Munck, B 'Changing a Culture of Face Time' in *Harvard Business Review*, November 2001.

10 Zehnder, E 'A Simpler Way to Pay' in *Harvard Business Review*, April 2001.

11 Kotter, JP & JL Heskett (1992) *Corporate Culture and Performance*, Free Press, New York.

12 Deighton, J 'How Snapple Got Its Juice Back' in *Harvard Business Review*, January 2002.

# 7
# Impact on You

When you go to work for an organization, you take on not only a job, but a way of life for eight or more hours a day. How well you fit into that way of life influences your job satisfaction, your career progress and your happiness.

In fact, the match between your personal style and the organization's culture began to affect you even before you were hired. It influenced the employer's decision to hire you and, consciously or subconsciously, it informed your choice to take the job. And if you leave and join another company, there will be a carry-over effect, because your expectations will have been shaped by what you experienced.

This chapter examines how corporate culture affects your work life, starting from the moment you begin a job search:

*Smart quotes*

'We have a right to ask of work that it include meaning, recognition, astonishment, and life.'

Studs Terkel, *Working*[1]

- how it shapes the courtship between you and potential employers

- how it influences your life on the job, and

- how it pushes you to make certain decisions as you adapt – or not – to the culture of the organization where you work.

## Opening the gate to a new culture

You may not even have been conscious of what you were doing when you nervously went on your first job interviews, but right from the start of your career you were reacting to elements of the culture. Did the receptionist smile and offer you coffee? Were you kept waiting? Were people in suits or casual clothes? Was the workplace neat or untidy? Quiet or noisy? Were people working alone or in clusters? Were you thinking, 'This is a scary place,' or 'Hey, this is a cool place'?

Here's conventional wisdom: if you want to get a job, then look and act like the people who work in the company where you are applying. It's typical for a job applicant to assess the culture and determine, 'Do I fit this company?' But it's just as important to decide, 'Does this company fit me?' and if it doesn't to ask, 'Do I really want to work here?'

## Knowing yourself

Terrence Deal, co-author of *Corporate Culture* and *The New Corporate Culture*, gets downright passionate when he talks about selecting a place to work out of love, not out of duty or desperation:

'One thing people don't think enough about is that when you choose a place to work you choose a way of life. Job hunters are so bent on impressing that they don't pick up signals. It's amazing that so many smart people do so many dumb things.

'People are so worried about the quality of paper of their resume and what's in vogue, they never get around to asking, "Who am I? What kind of life do I want to live?" There's a country song that goes, "The heart has a mind of its own." If you listen to your heart, it helps.'

Smart quotes

'Believe it or not, in some places you will be labelled as "too different to be one of us" if you are even wearing the wrong colour or style of suit, tie or shirt.'

Alison Blackman Dunham, *You Are the Product*[3]

If you are on the verge of a job hunt, ask yourself what kind of culture you need in order to do your best work. Here are some questions to start with:

- Does it matter to me what I wear? Do I feel more professional in a suit or cut-offs?

- Am I willing to work 24/7 on a project I really love or would I resent anything beyond eight hours a day?

- Do I work better alone or in a team?

- Do I want my co-workers to become my friends off the job as well as on?

- What's my attitude toward deadlines – flexible or fanatic?

- Do I need a lot of freedom to make my own decisions about my work?

- Am I happier following a routine or always working on something new?

- Can I jump from project to project or is it important to me to see a job through from beginning to end?

When you know what you want, then you also know what to look for when you start your job search. Through research, by observation and by asking the right questions of the right people, you can find out whether your potential employer offers a culture in which you would flourish.

## Getting to know the company

How do you get the low-down on a company's culture in advance? You can get the most obvious information, such as how people dress, just by asking the person who sets up the interview. You can also ask how many interviews you can expect and with whom. That alone tells you something about whether this company makes decisions by mandate or by consensus.

If you know somebody who knows somebody who works there, or you can find out where employees hang out after work, you can ask more penetrat-

'Take the example of an IT company that recruited a senior consultant, from Arthur Andersen, as a senior manager in business development. HR spectacularly failed in hiring this recruit… They had not gauged the cultural mismatch. From Arthur Andersen to a chaotic IT organization that had no systems/procedures, this was a major cultural shock for the consultant. An excellent performer in his previous role as a consultant, he failed to live up to the expectations of him in the new company. His first day at work, he was shocked to find this leading IT company did not have proper IT infrastructure, leave alone state-of-the-art technology for employees to use. And from there on it was downhill.'

Hanif Kanjer, www.coolavenues.com

ing questions, like, 'What skills does one need to succeed?', 'What does it take to get promoted?', 'How do you find out what's going on in the company?' Remember, of course, that you are only getting the perceptions of a few people, but it's all input into your understanding of the culture of the organization.

You can ferret out more online and in the library. Look for magazine and newspaper articles about the company. Have books been written on it? Scour the website. But don't get too taken in by the website's description of the company culture. They all read pretty much the same: innovative, empowered people having fun creating value for stockholders. Still, a savvy reader can ferret out some differences. A *Fast Company* article says to consider the language emphasized in print and by executives when they describe the culture.[4] Companies that predominately use words like 'compensation, bonuses, prestige, resources, and rewards' are telling you something quite different from companies that stress 'communication, relationships, creativity, and growth.' They're all good words. But a different emphasis creates a different culture.

Once you start interviewing, look for evidence that verifies, discredits or adds to what you've already learned. Nobody can complain if you arrive 15 minutes early for an interview, and that gives you time to observe the surroundings and how people interact with each other. You can even chat up the receptionist. It's OK to ask, 'What do you like most and least about working here?' You can ask your interviewers that too. Nobody's likely to air the organization's darkest secrets, but you can pick up hints, and you can learn what people think is good about the place. In addition, you'll find out as much about the people you ask as you will about the organization, and those are the people you'll be working with.

Armed with all that knowledge about the organization's culture, you'll be in a better position to decide if the company is right for you. And you'll know what you're getting into when you do take a job.

## Living within the culture

At least you'll know some of what you are getting into. Once you are on board, you'll find yourself dealing with myriad cultural influences – some expected and some unanticipated. The culture will affect:

- *How many hours you spend each day with your family or enjoying personal activities.* If you love your work you may be willing to spend long hours at it, but when you're actually doing it you'll discover there's a big price to pay.

- *Whether you and your colleagues co-operate or compete with each other.* In some organizations, people hoard information; in others they share it. In some, they work together toward a goal; in others they compete to reach that goal first. If you're the competitive kind in a co-operative organization, you'll be frustrated and you may be ostracized. If you're the co-operative kind in a competitive organization, you'll get left in the dust. In an organization where working individually is the norm, you might be viewed as shirking your job if you try to enlist others to help you. But if teamwork is the norm and you go off in a corner, people may think you're trying to hoard the glory.

- *How much you interact with your fellow employees both on and off the job.* There's interaction around shared projects and there's social interaction. Some companies encourage socializing, on the grounds that people who care about each other personally work better together. Other companies give off a strong signal that business and friendship don't mix, fearing people won't be able to make tough decisions that adversely affect their friends.

- *How much input you have into decisions that affect you.* Some companies seek input from their employees before making broad organizational changes. Others discourage front-line employees from taking any actions that aren't spelled out in a manual. Between those two extremes, you'll have a range of decision-making authority that depends in part on cultural norms.

- *The degree of supervision you'll get and give (if you are a manager).* If your method as a manager is to delegate and step aside, you'll do well in a culture where the norm is for everyone to step up to the bat and run. But if you're in an organization where close supervision is the norm, you'll find your delegated tasks go nowhere. And if you move full speed ahead on a project assigned to you, you may find yourself dubbed insubordinate.

- *Your ability to innovate, respond to change, and get things done in a timely fashion.* The organization's attitude about itself – conservative and set in its ways or constantly on the lookout for new products and new processes – affects your opportunities to be creative. So do the expectations and style of your managers and people you work with.

If you read the clues well before you took the job, you should be comfortable with these facets of your company's culture. There will be some surprises, but most of us are flexible enough to adapt to a situation that's a little short of ideal.

## But what if the fit is really bad?

What if you missed some really important culture clues and you are miserable? What if you thought you could ignore the culture because the work itself was so perfect – but now the culture is getting in the way of doing the work you love? What if you just plain needed the job and worrying about culture seemed like a luxury? The reality is that other issues can override your concerns about culture when you get the job offer. Countless people, for one reason or another, find themselves taking jobs in alien cultures, only to ask themselves later, 'What have I gotten myself into?' If you're one of those, sooner or later you'll find yourself facing the same decisions you might have made before you took the job.

*Can you conform and become what the organization wants?* If you do, you may become successful, powerful and financially secure. In time, you may look back and laugh at the youthful fantasies that fomented your discontent. Or you may become bitter or burn out. Of course, if the differences are superficial, most people adapt with little more than amusement over the situation. One businesswoman laughs, remembering her first job as a California transplant in a conservative New York publishing house. 'Nobody talked to me for the first few weeks,' she recalls. 'Then one day the boss's secretary invited me to go swimming and took the opportunity to tell me tactfully that my pointy-toed, turquoise shoes were not 'in style'. That afternoon I went into a shoe store and bought new shoes. Everyone talked to me after that.'

*Could you compromise, conforming in most ways in return for the right to flaunt your individuality in other areas?* ('I'll follow the dress code and speak the company jargon if I can pursue this project I've been dreaming about for years.') If you can walk such a fine line long enough to pull off that project and a few more, you might become a company legend yourself, so no one will dare criticize your peccadilloes. Or you might be marginalized or tolerated only until the company perceives it no longer needs your special skills.

*Should you quit while you still have some energy and self-esteem?* Maybe, especially if you know now what you do want and have a plan for how to go after it.

You also have one more choice now that you're on board. *Should you try to change the culture?* Frankly, it's highly unlikely that a successful organization is going to change the way it works just because you'd rather work in some other way. This book has already emphasized that cultures resist change. Even very strong leaders at top levels succeed in orchestrating organization-wide culture changes only if not changing poses a clear and dangerous threat to survival. But if you like a challenge, you're not powerless in your own corner of the organization. If you can demonstrate that your preferred way of working will solve a business problem, you might inspire a subculture within your own area. And if you sense a hint of change in the air at top levels, you and like-minded peers can play a role in implementing it. Chapters 14, 15, and 16 take a closer look at culture change.

## A cultural journey

If you ask yourself those questions throughout your career, you'll probably come up with different answers at different times. You may look back later and decide that some of your answers were right and some were wrong, but they'll lead you on quite a journey. Here's one example.

At different times in his 20-year career as a systems manager, Eloy Cruz-Bizet tried conforming, compromising, quitting and leading change. Now a partner in a small Brooklyn printing company, he says, 'I finally came to the realization that I had a career in a field that can only exist in a large corporate environment and I'd never really fit in there. So I decided to leave.'

For Cruz-Bizet, the road to that turning point began when he was a teenager enraptured with computer technology in the '60s. He obtained a high school internship at IBM. The culture shock was enormous.

First, he was a black teenager in a sea of blue-suited, white men. 'In any cross-cultural situation,' he says, 'you come with a sense of who you are that you have to deny enough to fit in. Now the organization wants you to become this third thing, a company clone.'

He tried, although looking back he realizes he had hardly a clue about what a corporation meant. But the gains were tremendous: for six months he worked in the development library, where he relieved employees on their lunch breaks and got a chance to work on many programs. That, he recalls, was an advantage over regular employees who were typically assigned to just one.

'After six months, I had unmatched credentials. By the mid-seventies, after college and a couple more jobs, I had a resume that got me in even though I looked a little different. I grew a ponytail and wore comfortable shoes, but otherwise, I wore the three-piece suits.'

He loved the work, so much so that he never questioned that a big corporation was the place to be, despite his self-described 'leftist, anti-corporate feelings'.

'Remember, at that time mainframes were the only game in town and they cost many millions of dollars. That meant only large corporations could afford them.' With the promise that the company had five mainframes, he joined a major investment firm as a systems manager.

'But I was naive to think all they wanted me to do was wear a suit. Corporate politics were of little interest to me. So when someone said Vice-President Joe Snow's computer is down, I said, "OK," and added the job to the pile of work to do. Others understood that doing this man's job first was the correct political gesture.

'They didn't know what to do with me, so the pressure mounted. I started getting excluded from meetings so I wouldn't embarrass my manager. But if you don't get included, people in positions to advance you don't get to know you.'

Finally, he was fired. But Cruz-Bizet had a skill that was in great demand. He was a conversion expert in an era when companies were converting from old, outmoded computer systems to faster, more powerful, more sophisticated ones. In the '80s, he was a rarity, a person who could straddle both systems and understood the conversion process.

There followed a series of jobs that followed a pattern. He'd manage the conversion, and when that was over, the company and he would find they could no longer tolerate each other.

Eventually he decided he didn't want to be a manager any more and took a job as a conversion specialist for a large urban hospital. There he was in for another culture shock. The IT group was so loose and laid back that 'the manager dressed like a clown'. In comparison, wearing a suit (even with bushy ponytail and comfortable shoes) led him to be mistaken for a doctor.

Once that mistake got him the offer of a desk worth thousands of dollars instead of the basic $200 models his peers were assigned to.

Now he suffered the frustration of working in a shop whose only goal was to do the least possible. Convinced that a non-profit organization would never fund the $40 million required to do a conversion, the manager would regularly draw up a proposal requesting about $6 million. And every time the board of directors turned it down.

'The board members came from for-profit companies. They knew you couldn't do a conversion for that,' Cruz-Bizet explains. Each turn-down reinforced his manager's conviction that the money would never come, so the group went on doing work-arounds, massaging an antiquated punch-card system into the late '80s.

Then, the hospital hired a VP-level person to take over the systems group. 'He was a bigot, but he was strong and knew how to get things done,' Cruz-Bizet states.

The vice-president referred to a group of black workers as 'afro-heads', and in response to an African-American job applicant snorted, 'We're not a training ground for the third world.' But his first day on the job, having read everyone's resumes and employment histories, he got rid of the clownish manager and put Cruz-Bizet in charge. With mixed reactions, Cruz-Bizet found himself back in management.

The new VP drew up a $40 million conversion proposal and won board and state approval for it. Cruz-Bizet still marvels at his boss's political savvy.

'He prioritized by following the money. Finance was first; payroll was second; radiology wasn't even on the list.' But he got the resources to get the work done fast. A telephone conversion that had been predicted to take three years was completed in six weeks.

Cruz-Bizet learned a lot from his hard-nosed boss. One day the vice-president demanded that a major change be made by the next Friday. Expecting disastrous employee resistance, Cruz-Bizet responded, 'Do you realize this is a union shop?'

His boss handed him the union contract and told him to take it home and read it. 'I discovered the union didn't protect its members from being fired. You could get rid of people if you followed a due process.'

So he went straight to his worst employee and demanded some work. The worker responded by losing his temper and cursing Cruz-Bizet, who wrote him up for intemperate behaviour and abusive language. When the worker stormed back and shouted, 'What did you write me up for, you stupid f***?', Cruz-Bizet wrote him up again. A couple of quick meetings later, with union reps in attendance, the handwriting was on the wall. Word quickly got back to the rest of the crew that the worker was going to be fired. The job got done by Friday.

But eventually, Cruz-Bizet and his boss came to a standoff. 'I was told the vice-president wanted me to come in the middle of the night to fix a problem,' he recalls. 'I assigned someone else. The next day I was told, "He wanted you. You're out."'

He'd been at the hospital for five years, and thanks to an employee file full of letters of recognition for his work, Cruz-Bizet left with a tidy severance package. Still, he wasn't ready yet to take his money and flee corporate America. There were a couple more corporate jobs before the realization dawned that, although he loved the work, the conditions under which he worked just weren't worth it to him.

Supporting himself with some consulting jobs, he dropped into a print shop one day to order new business cards. A few weeks later, the cards still weren't ready.

'You need someone to set up some systems here,' he told the proprietor, who responded, 'Do you want to help?' They worked out terms, giving Cruz-Bizet a 50 per cent partnership.

'I don't have the same salary or prestige,' he says, 'but I have my self-respect. We've got goals to make, real customers, and a real reason to do the job well, because if we don't, it shows in that week's bottom line. There's something satisfying about that that didn't exist in a large corporation.

'I've been here eight years now. That's the longest job I've ever had.'

## What's right for you?

Cruz-Bizet found his cultural match in a small organization where he could focus on the work, the customers, and the results instead of large company politics. That doesn't make his choice right for everyone. It probably wouldn't even have been right for him earlier in his career.

Whatever your job choices – and there will undoubtedly be more than one in your career – you will find that the culture of the organization has as much impact on your satisfaction and your success as the work you do. If you've chosen your job well, your work style and that of the organization will mesh and you'll have the foundation to accomplish your work goals. If you're not so lucky, and find yourself floundering in an alien sea, you're up against these choices: conform, compromise, leave or make it your job to change the organization.

## The smartest things in this chapter

- The match between you and the corporate culture influences a company's decision to hire you and should also affect your choice of what job to take.

- Through research, questions and nosing around, you can (and should) learn a lot about the culture of a potential employer.

- On the job, you'll fare better if you are comfortable with cultural norms around issues like work hours, teamwork, friendships, decision-making processes, delegation, and innovation and change.

- If the culture fit is bad, your choices are: conform, compromise, leave or – most challenging – change it.

## Notes

1   Terkel, S (1997) *Working*. New Press, New York.

2   Goffee, R & G Jones  (1998) *The Character of a Corporation*. Harper-Business, New York.

3   Dunham, AB 'You Are the Product' – for information see www.advicesisters.com.

4   Rothenberger, C 'Consulting Culture: Two Companies Uncovered' in *Fast Company* (Web only), November 2000, at www.fastcompany.com.

5   Kotter, JP & JL Heskett (1992) *Corporate Culture and Performance*. Free Press, New York.

# Part III
# The State of Culture Now

Cultures are unique to each organization. And yet every company is influenced now by a set of cultural phenomena that distinguish this era. The next three chapters examine these.

Chapter 8 takes an unsentimental look at the disappearance of cultural features that used to characterize many companies, but are fast fading from today's workplaces – things like job security, paternalism and the sense of family.

Chapter 9 examines a number of destabilizing forces that challenge the very concept of corporate culture: downsizings, loss of loyalty and the disappearance of face-to-face contact, as companies go virtual or disperse around the globe.

Chapter 10 reviews the rise and fall of our era's most extraordinary companies, the dot-coms, and examines the continuing influence of the culture they spawned.

# 8

# Ghosts of the Past

It was my first job in New York: assistant editor of an internal publication for The Equitable Life Assurance Society of the United States. After I'd been there a year the department secretary brought me a form to sign to authorize deduction from my pay cheque of my contribution to the pension plan. I was 24 years old. I couldn't imagine being old enough to draw a pension and I certainly didn't want any more deductions from my pay cheque. So I refused.

The secretary looked at me with scorn and declared, 'This is the way we do things in this country.'

And indeed it was. It was the way people did things then in other countries too, including Canada, the not-so-foreign land from which I'd come. That pension plan was a symbol that, since I'd survived a year, the company was now inviting me to spend the rest of my working life there.

There are still a few companies that promise job security. EZI, the international executive search firm profiled in Chapter 6, has a seniority-based compensation system, encouraging people to stay with the organization for their entire careers. But it's a professional partnership organization, and partnerships are much more typically lifelong than are employment contracts in business corporations.

KILLER QUESTIONS

How many people do you know in your parents' generation who worked for one employer for at least 20 years? How many people in your generation will do the same?

Among big corporations, Southwest Airlines is almost unique in its no-layoffs policy, which has held since the company started in 1971. (For more on Southwest, see Chapter 12.) In early 2002, the *New York Times* located some smaller companies that were holding out against the inclination to trim staff in tough times. One was Maurice Villency, a furniture chain with 200 employees in the New York area. 'For us, firing people would be like committing suicide,' Eric Villency, the company president, told the *Times*. 'Cutting somebody would be like getting rid of a mother or an uncle. We just can't do it.'[1]

But in most organizations, the era of lifetime employment has long passed, even in Japan, the country that championed it most famously. For example, in January 2002, Hitachi announced it would eliminate 4000 jobs by 30 June, following 16,350 job cuts in 2001.[2]

## Ghost 1: the ghost of security (past)

When people took job security for granted they might (and probably did) grumble about the salary, the boss, and the missed promotions, but the job was a given.

Certainly not all employees and employers were joined at the hip. Seeing greener pastures, employees could pick up and leave any time – and move into another organization that offered the same promise of security. Yes, companies did fail, putting all their employees out of work, or fall on hard times and lay off part of their workforce. But those were the unlucky ones. The 25-year pin, the gold watch and the pension were a reality for many. Certainly they were real for enough people to give the impression that these prizes were possible, even likely, for everyone who worked hard, worked regularly and did what the boss said to do.

That kind of security was not only part of the corporate culture, but, after World War II, it fed developments in the broader culture as well. People with secure jobs could finance cars and get mortgages, and thus suburbs were built. They could take vacations. They could save some money and send their kids to better schools than they went to. They could buy life insurance, and extend their security even further. And when the time came to collect those pensions, they created a cohort of senior citizens who were better off financially than their predecessors had ever dreamed of. In the '80s and '90s, whole new industries, such as travel for seniors, grew up in response, and retirement villages mushroomed in friendly climates.

You didn't get to be an employee-millionaire in the era of job security, but you didn't expect to. You expected your living standard to improve steadily over time, and for many people it did. You expected a secure retirement, and many people lived to enjoy it.

But even security could have its dark side. Ralph H Kilmann, another of the culture pioneers, wrote that, 'Culture is to the organization what per-

Yes, she still had her job, an executive at a large company told a friend after the organization's most recent round of layoffs. 'But you know what?' she added with an uncharacteristic, hard edge to her voice. 'It's only a matter of time. If they didn't get me this time, they'll probably get me the next time. And that's OK. I'm thinking that it'll be an opportunity to rethink what I want to do with the rest of my life.'

Almost the sole survivor of a department that had been absorbed by a high-profile vice-president, she was still employed but she felt almost invisible, ignored by her new boss and colleagues who were little more than half her age. They seemed to assume she was a relic who couldn't possibly have anything valuable to contribute in the new environment. It was, of course, only a matter of time before they would discover that she'd survived a succession of layoffs because she was extraordinarily good at what she did and was as current in her approach to her work as she was familiar with the history – and what had once been the traditions – of the company.

But now, she felt, the company had no traditions. It was reinventing itself every few years as a new regime swept in and tried to remake it in the image of the last organization the new leaders had worked for. During previous downsizings she'd been sad to lose colleagues and uneasy about what new direction the company would take. But this time, after about 20 years, she just felt disconnected.

sonality is to the individual.'[4] Like personality traits, culture facets can express themselves either positively or negatively. While in one company, job security may have given employees the freedom to innovate and explore, in other organizations it dulled those drives. Unthreatened, unchallenged, people had little motivation to be creative or improve their products and processes. So the dark side of security was complacency, even stagnation.

## Ghost II: the (mostly) benevolent father figure

If job security had both a bright and a dark side, so too did the second ghost from not-so-distant past, the paternalistic organization whose implicit messages to its employees were:

- We'll take care of you.

- Trust us. We know what's best.

- Don't question us.

- Just do as we say.

Often a carryover from a strong and caring founder, paternalism became embedded in the hierarchical structure and a top-down decision process. Eventually the organization itself became the father figure, through processes and practices that perpetuated the model of stern but loving parents and dependent child.

- *We'll take care of you.* In the early days of the company, when the number of employees was small and the founder was active, 'We'll take care of you' could mean anything from a companionable arm across your shoulder to a quiet advance on your salary in a time of crisis or a visit to your home if a family member was sick. As organizations grew, the personal touch was replaced by company credit unions, company scholarship programmes for employees' children, and employee assistance programmes. But the message was fundamentally the same: the organization as benevolent parent, capable and willing to meet all your needs.

    As a benevolent parent, the organization loved all its children equally and strove to treat them fairly by family standards. Salaries

'I remember working in an electronics company, in the department that oversaw progress chasing. Part of my job was to accompany the boss around the site twice a day… He knew every nook and cranny of the site, every piece of equipment and how it worked. But even more impressive was the fact that he knew all the human beings that operated the equipment, by name… Conversations he had with his employees were mostly not about electronics. They were about their outside interests, their hobbies, their families, and of course – since the love of gossip is inherent in all human beings – about their fellow workers' exploits… There was an unwavering loyalty to the firm and an expectation that the firm would provide for its workers.'

David Varney, former CEO of British Gas[5]

– like allowances – depended more on position and seniority than on individual achievement, and increases were fairly consistent across the board. Promotions went to the person 'in line' for the next rung up the ladder.

- *Trust us. We know what's best.* Like parents, management made decisions about what to do, who should do it, when to do it and what resources to use, without seeking input from employees. Workers either assumed management knew what it was doing or – and here's the dark side again – learned quickly that their own suggestions were unwelcome. Like children they were best seen but not heard.

- *Don't question us.* Things like finances, profitability, competitiveness and strategic direction were solely the domain of management, who didn't offer up the information or encourage employees to ask. In fact, many employees didn't think about those things. They focused on their tasks and willingly colluded with management to keep the thinking and the doing sides of the business quite separate.

- *Just do what we say.* 'Here's your task. Do it exactly this way. Don't try anything new or different. If you think you have a better idea, keep it to yourself. Your job is to do what you are told.' The good part from the employees' point of view was that as long as they did exactly what they were told, they were never responsible if the outcomes were disappointing.

If you're thinking as you read this that there are still plenty of companies where directives are handed down from on high and employee input is neither offered nor wanted, you are certainly right, although more and more organizations are encouraging worker involvement. What's disappeared is the other side of the paternalistic equation, the side that promised, 'We'll take care of you', the side that made stifling creative ideas and original thinking a worthwhile trade-off for many people. As former British Gas CEO David Varney said, 'There are many employees who feel they have lost something of real value. We have lost a powerful social connection.'[6]

## Ghost III: one big happy family

People still make friends with their co-workers. Some companies still have picnics in the summer and holiday parties in the winter. But the 'powerful social connection' is gone. It takes more years than people have together now to create the family feeling bred by lifetime employment in a paternalistic organization. If you worked with someone 8 hours a day for 25 or 30 years, you saw more of that person than you did of your children and maybe even your spouse. People took care of each other in ways that were healthy (helping each other) and not so healthy (covering up for each other).

As in any family, there were people you knew you could depend upon, people you knew better than to turn your back on, people who took care of you and people you took care of. They were as familiar to you as your spouse or siblings or in-laws. You celebrated together and suffered together, had squabbles and made up. All in all, they were part of your reason for going to work each day, part of what gave meaning to your job.

In most companies, the family is a ghost now, replaced by revolving teams and frequently restructured work groups.

For many people, the ghosts of the past still haunt their workplaces. And they will continue to do so until people find new constants, new consistencies to replace what they have lost.

## The smartest things in this chapter

- Job security has gone, but complacency and stagnation are disappearing along with it.

- Paternalism in organizations is rare now, releasing worker creativity but destroying social bonds and the sense of being cared for.

- Job transience and the loss of father figures have whittled away at the sense of family that once added meaning to the workplace.

## Notes

1  Ligos, M 'The Opposite of Layoffs: Ties of Loyalty' in the *New York Times*, 20 January 2002.

2  Reported by K Belson in 'World Business Briefing/Asia: Japan: Job Cuts at Hitachi' in the *New York Times*, 31 January 2002.

3   Harris, J (1996) *Getting Employees to Fall in Love with Your Company*. AMACOM, New York.

4   Kilmann, RH (1985) *Beyond the Quick Fix*. Jossey-Bass, San Francisco.

5   From a speech to the Windsor Leadership Trust. Found at www.danarubin.com.

6   Ibid.

# 9
# Destabilizing Forces

Is culture without stability an oxymoron?

Edgar Schein has written that: 'Culture refers to those elements of a group or organization that are most stable and least malleable.'[1] With all the destabilizing forces that have battered organizations in the last decade or so, one can't help questioning, in cynical moments, whether there is much corporate culture left. Or has it become a victim of downsizing, restructuring, and trends like telecommuting and globalization? This chapter examines the impact of these forces on organizations today.

KILLER QUESTIONS

Can culture survive downsizing, restructuring, telecommuting and globalization?

## Pared-down organizations

Sometimes they call it downsizing, in the idiom of the '80s, or restructuring, which gained popularity in the '90s, or just plain layoffs, the blunter word that's currently regained coinage, preferred over the euphemisms that never succeeded in softening the impact. By any name, companies have been paring down their workforces through successive cuts in staff for nearly two decades. They trimmed bloated headcounts in the '80s, chopped desperately in the economic downturn of the early '90s, then kept right on pruning through the high-rolling '90s with the discovery that Wall Street loved them for it. With the shaky economy of the new century, layoffs took on new momentum.

In January and February 2002, the business press reported layoff announcements almost daily. Some of the bigger ones in the United States (reported by CNNmoney at www.money.cnn.com) included Boeing's plan to cut 10,500 jobs, BellSouth's announcement that it would lay off 3000 workers, and Lucent's new round of 7000 cuts, part of a reduction in force from 123,000 in 2000 to an expected 55,000 by summer 2002.

In Europe the same thing was happening. British Airways reported it would cut 5800 jobs. In February, TIMEeurope reported layoffs of 12,000 at the Swiss firm ABB; 5000 at the chipmaker Infineon; and 2600 at Ericsson, the Swedish telecom equipment provider.[2] And these were just the tip of the iceberg.

In the United States, the outplacement firm Challenger, Gray & Christmas reported that the total number of jobs cut in 2001 was nearly 2 million, the highest number since the firm began been collecting data on job losses in 1993.[3] Interestingly, the second highest number of layoffs for any year in that period was in 1998, when the technology-fuelled economy was going strong. The recession-spurred job cuts may be record-breaking, but they are also a mind-numbing continuation of a trend that's become endemic to good times and bad.

*The toll on corporate culture*

People who work in an organization with a strong culture have the advantage of being secure in their knowledge of what their roles are, what you must do to fulfil them and how to relate to other people in the company. Layoffs rock that security. As the organization reshuffles to adjust to its new leanness and shifts the survivors into new slots, cohesion and confidence give way to the following.

### Role confusion
If you've been through a downsizing – and who hasn't? – you know what it feels like. Previously, you understood what your responsibilities were. You'd figured out what your boss expected of you and, if you had people reporting to you, what they needed from you. You knew how much leeway you had in defining your own projects and choosing your own tasks. After a downsizing, none of those givens remain true. You know your responsibilities have changed, but neither you nor anyone else seems to know just what your new responsibilities are. You probably have a new boss who is as confused as you are about what's going on. People reporting to you expect far more answers than you have the knowledge and resources to provide. You don't know yet how much control you're going to have over your own job.

In the midst of all this, it's pretty hard to get a handle on corporate culture. Things work themselves out in time, but often just in time for the next upheaval.

### Goal confusion
If your work unit has been ravaged by layoffs and you've got a fraction of the headcount left, are you still expected to achieve the same goals? If so, how will you do it? If not, what's important now? Will you have any say in setting the new goals, or will they be mandated by a new management

group that has little understanding of your capabilities? Perhaps, in the re-organization, your unit has been combined with another and you are now responsible for meeting those goals too. These are just some of the questions that undermine security and cohesion in the wake of a downsizing. It's hard to maintain a cohesive culture when you don't know what the goals are or if they keep changing.

### Broken communication channels

In a stable culture, people know how to manoeuvre through the communication channels. They might have to wait for big news to work its way slowly down through levels of management or they might get it quickly from a direct source. Getting approvals to take action may be an arduous process of sending data up the ladder step by step and waiting for a response to come down rung by rung. Or it might involve an e-mail to one person. But as long as they know the processes, people work them successfully, be they rigidly hierarchical or free-flowing 360 degrees.

People also take advantage of the informal communication networks, the ones where news and feedback flow miraculously unhindered. They know which workplace gossips can be trusted to have the straight scoop. They develop relationships with key people who can open doors to the secret passageways that bypass the most cumbersome formal routes. They know whose ear to whisper in if they need to send a message that might cost them their tongue if they were to deliver it directly.

Downsizings decimate both formal and informal communication channels. Invariably, the organizational structure changes, and it takes time for information to start flowing through the wires of the new organization chart. People barely know whom they report to and who reports to them. They certainly don't know how much information each of those people wants and needs. They become unwitting bottlenecks. Throughout the organization there are people who are new in their jobs and don't know yet the significance of the data they receive. They become information roadblocks or, worse, purveyors of misinformation. The informal channels fall into equal disarray if the news sources or door-openers are laid off or moved into another part of the organization. And even if they survive, they lose their effectiveness if their sources are shunted off or their centres of influence shattered in the restructuring.

Without communication, can culture exist? Or is an organization just a series of disconnected cells, each struggling to survive?

### Awaiting the next shoe's drop

Like the layoff survivor whose story appears in the previous chapter, people can experience only so many downsizings before, emotionally at least, they disconnect. Some leave, while they can still control their own departure, and others wait for the severance package they'll get if they're on the list next time. Among those who stay, the timid ones look for places to hide, where they won't rock any boats or ruffle any powerful feathers. The bold ones go after projects and titles (ever noticed how job titles get fancier after downsizings?) that will shine up their resumes. The practical ones do what's needed to get good performance ratings and look for fulfilment outside the workplace. But, anticipating the inevitable next round of layoffs, all of them are thinking *me*, not *we*. They're asking themselves, 'What can I get out of this?' not 'How can I make this organization more successful and a better place to work?' They know that even if they could have such an impact, it would most likely dissolve in the next restructuring.

## *Loyalty? What's that?*

Loyalty used to mean a pact between employer and employee. From employer to worker, the tacit understanding was: You have a safe job here as long as you perform up to par. From worker to employer, there was a cor-

Q: Can you downsize without killing the culture?

A: Sure – with care, sensitivity and honesty, and especially if top management isn't raking in the millions while low-paid minions are losing their jobs. Malden Mills, whose story is in Chapter 6, is one example. Another is Agilent, a spin-off of Hewlett-Packard, which made *Fortune's* 2002 list of best companies to work for after laying off 8000 workers.[4]

*Fortune* magazine tells the story of Cheryl Ways, whose husband had to beg her to come home at 9 p.m. on her last day on the job. Ways was thinking about her co-workers still with the company.

'This was my gift to them,' she told the *Fortune* reporter, 'to leave my job in the best way possible.'

A producer of chips, electronic components, and testing and measurement devices, Agilent fell victim to the severe economic downturn that affected its chief customers, the telecom companies. With the support of its fanatically loyal employees, the company cut costs to the bone and even won employees' agreement to an across-the-board pay cut before finally acknowledging the inevitability of slashing staff.

'Agilent,' *Fortune* says, 'considers itself the true keeper of the *HP Way* ... The *Way's* key precept is that workers will give their best if they're treated honestly and listened to.' There's nothing in the *Way* that covers how to lay off employees – in fact, it's the antithesis of the *Way's* original intent – but, given no choice, Agilent executives did their best to apply its precepts to the situation they were forced into.

Their main tool was to communicate, communicate, communicate. Through e-mails, newsletters, 'coffee talks' between managers and employees, and CEO speeches, they shared all the information they had with employees all along the way. 'Managers were told to be as honest as possible, to keep the door even more open than usual, and to field every question lobbed.'

> The first downsizing was announced in August 2001; by November the company was forced into a second round. Still, neither those that were forced out nor those that stayed felt the company had broken faith with the Way. And if layoffs don't become a habit, they too will keep their faith in Agilent and with the Way.

responding unspoken agreement: I'll stay here as long as you treat me fairly. In that environment, culture took shape and stabilized.

With companies repeatedly downsizing, the tacit pact is no more. Companies lure talent with the offer of challenge and opportunity – for now. Individuals promise to give their all – until something better comes along. You might call it situational loyalty; it lasts until the situation changes.

What have been sacrificed are trust and commitment to shared values, the very bedrock of a strong culture. The part in each company's values statement about respect for its employees is pretty hard to swallow if the company is regularly cutting jobs to please Wall Street. Not only do they distrust the organization's commitment to its employees, when they see how expendable that so-called value is, employees get pretty cynical about the other values too.

But the demise of loyalty can't all be blamed on job cuts. Although we're quick to blame downsizings, there's been another contributing factor. Over the past two decades an increasing number of jobs have been in the field of computer technology. The technological revolution and the demand for the whizz kids who were devoted to it modelled a different kind of work loyalty: loyalty to one's function, not to one's employer. With their passion

*Smart quotes*

"'I stay loyal because the company has been loyal to me," said Norman Tenenbaum, an associate manager of Maurice Villency's Madison Avenue store, who has been with the company for 20 years.'

Melinda Ligos, 'The Opposite of Layoffs: Ties of Loyalty', *New York Times*, 20 January 2002 focused on their technical work, all they need from an employer are the resources to do it. If another employer offers better resources, then, for them, it's logical to move on. During the '90s it was easy for the digital wizards to jump from employer to employer seeking greater challenges, more opportunities to innovate on the cutting edge, and, of course, more of that phenomenal amount of money that was dangled in front of them.

It's hard to sustain a culture when the players keep changing.

## Virtual companies

If it's hard for a culture to survive when people don't stick around long enough to buy into it and perpetuate it, then what happens when the employees aren't there at all? According to a 2001 survey by the International Telework Association and Council, about 28 million United States employees are teleworking.[5] In Canada, there are an estimated 1.5 million teleworkers, estimates Statistics Canada.[6]

Those numbers overestimate the impact somewhat since they include people who split their time between the office and home or travel. But there are a growing number of people whose primary connection to their employer is via computer and telephone. And they are not all telemarketers. Telecommuting expert June Langhoff, who has written several books on the subject, lists a vice-president of a telecommunications company, some nuclear engineers, a health care manager and even a police sergeant among the sampling of telecommuters described on her website.[7]

Telecommuters working from home are immune to a number of workplace behavioural norms. They don't have to worry about dress code; they can work all day in their pyjamas if they feel like it. While they may have to be available by phone at certain times, they can largely set up their own work

Can there be a unified culture in an organization like this?

It's 10 a.m. on payday. That's when Robin from the postroom delivers pay cheques to data processing. On this occasion, Robin has just two cheques to drop off, although the department employs eight people. Lisa, the administrative assistant, hands one cheque to Jill, the manager, who has only time to smile a thank you, being in the middle of a 'meeting'. Then Lisa walks past an empty cubicle to give the other cheque to Tony, who is glued to a computer.

Jill's meeting is online with the staff, the rest of whom are telecommuters working at home. The empty cubicle is for the rare occasion when one of them must be on-site.

Lisa herself doesn't get a pay cheque today because she actually works for a temporary staffing agency.

Down the hall in information systems, Robin doesn't have many pay cheques to deliver either. The space is crowded with people, but most are independent contractors.

In fact, Robin, the post clerk, doesn't get paid today either. Postroom operations, although located in the corporate office, was outsourced a few years ago to a firm that specializes in postroom management.[8]

This hypothetical, but not atypical, company illustrates the forces that divide people in today's organizations.

schedules – so long as they get the work done. These are neat advantages, but they are practices that set them apart from the culture of their office-bound colleagues. There are social factors with the potential to isolate telecommuters even more, such as being cut off from workplace dialogue. In a workplace shared by tens or hundreds of people, there is an incredible amount of information that gets shared around the metaphorical water cooler. Important decisions get made as a result of spontaneous meetings in the hall. And relationships meld over birthday cakes or champagne toasts to mark project milestones. The small building blocks of culture are hard to maintain by e-mail only.

While telecommuting is moving employees out of a common workplace, temps and independent contractors are filling those same spaces with people whose ties to the corporation are tenuous and short-term. These people are business nomads. Culturally, they live on the fringes of the organizations where they take on temporary assignments. They have neither the time nor the inclination to develop emotional ties to any workplace. While they are in one organization, they apply themselves to their tasks and expect to finish their projects. When they move on, they leave few footprints behind.

### And now for the good news

This workplace displacement sounds like a death knell for corporate cultures, but miraculously – or more likely through good planning and careful implementation – virtual companies aren't all dissolving into cultural wastelands. In fact, many companies are building new cultures around telecommuting. In its 2001 survey, the International Telework Association and Council found that, 'An overwhelming majority (almost 80 per cent) [of teleworkers] feels a greater commitment to their organization and most say they plan to stay with their employer. Notably, almost three-quarters of at-home teleworkers reported a major increase in productivity and work quality.'[9]

### Globalization: dispersion on the grandest scale

Expanding internationally poses a cultural challenge of a totally different nature from the other destabilizing factors discussed in this chapter. Every

Cohesive cultures don't happen by chance in organizations where people spend most of their time working at home or on the road. At AT&T, where telecommuting is a way of life for many managers and workers, managers get training in how to:

- *Select good candidates for telecommuting.* It's not for everyone. Good telecommuters work well independently, don't need plenty of face-to-face contact with colleagues, and are good at planning and scheduling their own work.
- *Track performance, concentrating on results.* Telecommuters need clear goals and performance standards, mutually agreed-upon methods of monitoring results, and plenty of focused feedback.
- *Stay in touch with telecommuters.* Telecommuting isn't like taking an occasional work-at-home day when the unspoken message is: 'Don't bother me.' It's important for managers to phone or e-mail telecommuters as often as they'd call or drop in on an employee down the hall.
- *Avoid micromanaging.* Good telecommuting arrangements are based on trust.
- *Maintain work group synergy.* At AT&T, they developed virtual water coolers, where people get together electronically to share information.
- *Avoid overloading non-telecommuters.* This can by done by planning work in advance, taking into consideration everyone's schedule.[10]

time a company opens a branch in a different part of the world it faces a potential clash between its corporate culture and the national culture of its host country. If you've taken an international assignment, you've undoubtedly experienced that clash personally. If there's a move abroad in your future, you should expect to.

Western fashion and music may be ubiquitous around the world. Fusion cuisine (or the Big Mac) may have given us all global palates. Mobile phones may have connected the most faraway places. But those are superficial compared to the deeply embedded attitudes and beliefs we absorb, usually unconsciously, as children. These constructs help us understand others within our own culture but create mystifying obstacles to relating to people of other cultures. And despite centuries of travel, relocation, even domination of one culture by another, these national, ethnic and regional differences still exist. Behavioural norms that promote understanding between people in one culture can be totally incomprehensible to people in another part of the world.

To understand why, Geert Hofstede, who founded the Institute for Research on Intercultural Cooperation at Tilburg University in the Netherlands, studied IBM employees around the world. From his research he identified five cultural dimensions, which he published in 1980 and has updated since then. If you are trying to transplant a corporate culture from one part of the world to another, examining it against these dimensions might help you understand why you're having problems. Hofstede's five Cultural Value Dimensions[12] include:

1  *Power distance* – what employees expect from those in authority. In high power-distance cultures, bosses tend to be more autocratic and

*Smart quotes*

'In America, we think hiring on merit is good; nepotism and cronyism are bad. But in Thailand, they do nepotism and cronyism. So a Thai guy says to me, "Look at this through my eyes. You have an important job to fill, you post it, and you hire a stranger to do it. I'd hire my cousin. I've known him for 30 years. I know he won't let me down. He won't cheat me." You leave the room thinking, "Why don't I hire my cousin?" It gets bewildering.'

Steve Kerr, Chief Learning Officer and Managing Director at the Goldman Sachs Group in New York and former Vice-President of Leadership Development at GE.[11]

employees expect to be told what to do. In low power-distance cultures, employees expect their bosses to consult with them before making decisions. (Hofstede identified Latin America, France, Spain, and most Asian and African countries as regions with high power-distance cultures and the US, Britain and most northern European countries as low power-distance.)

2   *Individualism/collectivism* – 'Which comes first, me or the team?' People in individualistic cultures expect to take care of themselves and make decisions based on their own needs. In collectivist cultures, people value loyalty to the group, base decisions on the group's needs, and expect the group to take care of them. (Countries with individualistic cultures include the US, Canada, France and South Africa. Japan, Mexico and Greece are examples of countries with collectivist cultures.)

3   *Masculinity/femininity* – what motivates people's behaviour? Is it the more 'masculine' goals of achievement, advancement and recognition, or the more 'feminine' needs of co-operation, security and good relationships. (Hofstede rated Great Britain, the US and Japan among the highest on masculinity. Sweden, France and Indonesia were among the top-ranked countries on the femininity scale.)

4   *Uncertainty avoidance* – how comfortable people are in situations where the outcome is unknown. People who are high on uncertainty avoidance prefer to live by rules that minimize the occurrence of unexpected results. People low on uncertainty avoidance want opportunities for innovation and creativity and may even be energized by the risks inherent in a project with an uncertain outcome. (Hofstede's research placed Korea, Japan and Latin America high on the uncertainty avoidance scale and the US, the Netherlands and Britain among those countries on the low end.)

5    *Long-term/short-term orientation* – willingness to make trade-offs be-
    tween short- and long-term gratification. (China, Japan and India rated
    high among countries having cultures with long-term orientation and
    Britain, Canada and Germany were among countries with short-term
    orientation.)

## *The meaning of time*

One big cultural divide is the meaning of 'on time'. Around the world, cultural differences range from 'within 30 seconds with no excuses', to sometime within the decade if nothing else comes up. At the risk of stereotyping,
there seems to be a North/South variation here, with Northern cultures
viewing time more precisely and Southern ones taking a more leisurely
attitude. Exporting behavioural norms around time from one culture to
another can be an exercise in futility.

## Back to the question: can corporate culture survive?

Despite this chapter's emphasis on the threats to corporate culture, the
answer to the question, 'Can it survive?' is: 'Of course it can. And it will.'
Maybe not in the warm and fuzzy – but occasionally smothering – forms
of the past. But people are culture builders. We need culture to make sense
of our own place in our surroundings. Adapting to the destabilizing forces
may result in cultures that are more temporary, but on the positive side they
will most definitely be more responsive to change.

Globally, there are models of vast organizations that operate everywhere
and, like Royal Dutch/Shell (See Chapter 2), remain true to a basic set of
values while welcoming diverse behaviours locally and, on a worldwide
level, encompassing those behaviours that work best.

Here's another set of cultural dimensions that impact the corporate cultures of any organization that expands internationally.

Author/consultant Fons Trompenaars identified seven dimensions that account for the differences in cultures around the world.[13] (Formerly with one of the world's most global companies, Royal Dutch/Shell, he had plenty of opportunity to experience cultural differences first hand, but he based his work on surveys.) His dimensions divide into three categories: relationships with people, orientation to time and relationship to nature. The first five dimensions fall into the first category:

1 *Universalism vs. particularism.* Is there one right way or are right and wrong dependent upon the situation? Hiring is a good example: do the same eligibility requirements apply to all or are friends and family in a special category.
2 *Individualism vs. collectivism.* What takes precedence, the individual or the group? Does the individual exist to support the group or does the group exist for the benefit of the individuals within it?
3 *Neutral vs. emotional.* Do we keep our emotions in check or is it acceptable to let them show?
4 *Specific vs. diffuse.* Is a business deal confined to the terms of the contract or is it a broad, personal relationship among those involved?
5 *Achievement vs. ascription.* Are people judged on the basis of what they do (their achievements) or who they are (factors like age, gender, social status, education, profession)?
6 *Sequential vs. synchronic.* How do people manage time? Do they follow carefully scheduled plans or juggle several balls at once? Time has an additional aspect – are people rooted in the traditions of the *past*, concentrating on the immediate rewards of the *present*, or focused on the potential of the *future?*
7 *Internal vs. external control.* Does nature control us or do we control it? Are people more dominating and comfortable standing their ground in a conflict or are they more flexible and willing to compromise?

As to the cultural devastation of sequential downsizings, there is no denying the toll has been steep. Where cultures rebuild most quickly is around individual work units or functions – groups that are small and cohesive enough to have shared values and common behaviours and to have rebuilt trust. Organization-wide cultures reform as management brings these groups together in pursuit of a common corporate goal.

## The smartest things in this chapter

- Repeated downsizings have produced role and goal confusion, severed communication links and resulted in a mindset more focused on 'me' than 'we'.

- Loyalty to function has largely replaced loyalty to organization.

- Virtual workplaces have made face-to-face contact rare among their employees, yet teleworkers profess increased commitment and loyalty to their employers.

- Clashes between local societal norms and corporate cultures pose challenges to global organizations.

## Notes

1 Schein, EH (1992) *Organizational Culture and Leadership* (2e). Jossey-Bass, San Francisco.

2 Wallace, CP 'Blood, Sweat, Toil and Tears' in *TIMEeurope*, 22 February 2002, at www.time.com/time/Europe.

3 Reported in 'Fewer Job Cuts in December' in *CNNmoney*, 3 January 2002, at www.money.cnn.com.

4 Roth, D 'How to Cut Pay, Lay off 8000 People, and Still Have Workers Who Love You' in *Fortune*, 4 February 2002.

5 'Number of Teleworkers Increases by 17 Percent', a news release dated 23 October 2001, reported at www.telecommute.org.

6 Reported by InnoVisions Canada, at www.ivc.ca.

7 See www.langhoff.com/faqs.html

8 'Staffing in the '90s', supplement to the January 1997 issue, *Getting Results*, American Management Association.

9 See note 7.

10 These recommendations are based on 'AT&T Trains Managers to Supervise Telecommuters', supplement to the January 1997 issue, *Getting Results*, American Management Association.

11 From Deeprose, D (2002) *Global HR*. Capstone, Oxford, England.

12 Hofstede, G (1996) *Culture and Organizations: Software of the Mind*. McGraw-Hill, New York.

13 Trompenaars, F (1993) *Riding the Waves of Culture*. The Economist Books, London.

# 10

# The Rise and Fall of Cyberculture

In the late '90s, you couldn't avoid the endless stories in the press about those oh-so-cool dot-com companies. The scenarios they painted were consistent: long-haired kids in cut-offs, barely old enough to have work permits, their excitement so intense that the air crackled as they worked zealously on the next great Internet breakthrough. Suddenly at 2 a.m., their eyes red with either fervour or exhaustion, they would leap from their workstations and head for the real heart of the workplace, the foosball table. Whooping and hollering, they'd play off their weariness, then hang around the table afterwards for an impromptu discussion about someone's work problem, generating enough solutions to start a whole new line of business. Reinvigorated, they would head back to work, fuelled by handfuls of snacks, lattes and caffeine-spiked soft drinks from the office kitchen. Later, before wandering off home as the sun came up, they might drop in at the company massage room for a rubdown.

*Smart quotes*

'What the dot-coms did was bring fun to the workplace.'

Lewis J. Goetz, CEO of Group Goetz Architects, quoted in *Business Week online*[1]

'Fun and games vie with attempts to create near-religious experiences as the cornerstones of explicit culture.'

Rosabeth Moss Kanter, *eVolve!*[2]

As we read about it, this was the brave new world of the New Economy. It banned the creativity-sapping relics of the Old Economy: rules about what to wear, regular work hours, hierarchical work structures and jobs with defined tasks. The pundits began to apply the word organic to work relationships, meaning people identified and did the work that needed to be done, rather than performing pre-defined tasks. Spontaneous teams formed, disbanded, and reformed as needed.

Gone were old-fashioned notions about the value of experience, which reserved the top positions for old guys and ensured that young people would have all the zest beaten out of them before they would be considered mature enough to lead. What good was experience in a world that was changing by the hour? Nobody had experience in what was going to be important tomorrow.

Gone too was the whole notion of separation of work and life. Work was life! You didn't go to work to earn money to buy food, put a roof over your head, and enjoy personal pursuits in your non-working hours. You went to work to pursue a personal vision. People talked about 'building experiences' rather than filling jobs.[3]

Whatever they called it, for the technically savvy there were plenty of jobs to fill, and plenty of headhunters out there luring them from job to job with ever increasing perks.

But the confluence of work and fun was only one side of the dot-com revolution. Based on the amazon.com model, the basis for measuring success was different from the start. Growth (and perceived potential for growth), not profits, fuelled soaring stock prices. Young companies went public with IPOs that made overnight millionaires out of entrepreneurs and their administrative assistants alike, while the companies plunged forward with new initiatives funded more by additional injections of venture capital than by revenues.

Especially as the era progressed, the whole purpose of building companies and doing work radically changed. Where Jeff Bezos and friends at amazon.com had a vision for changing the way the world bought books (and just about everything else, eventually), in the latter years of the dot-com era, the driving force behind many Internet start-ups was not so much better living through Internet technology as get rich quick. Thousands of dot-com wannabes had visions that had nothing to do with changing the world and everything to do with launching an IPO and becoming gazillionaires. The people who flocked to work for them did so less for the fun of creating new technology and more for their share of the windfall when the company went public. Everybody knew somebody who'd become an overnight millionaire by being in the right company at the right time. And everyone was convinced it would happen again, and again, and again.

In pursuit of the almighty IPO, there were plenty of Internet start-ups that flunked the fun test. If there were rotating teams, it was more because the players passed quickly through the company on their way to the next big 'experience' than because they completed one phase and regrouped for the succeeding one. Far from empowering their employees to innovate, many dot-com founders trusted no ideas but their own. With no experience in project implementation, they micromanaged the execution of their ideas and were prone to decision making by decree with scant thought to weeks of work laid to waste by capricious changes in plan. While the press reported big salaries paid to young techies, there were countless start-ups where the majority of workers were rewarded more with the promise of IPO riches than with fat pay cheques in hand.

Despite visions of the Promised Land, even during the headiest time there were scores of companies that fell by the wayside before they ever floated the vaunted public offering. In the dot-com heyday, that was OK. The entrepreneurs dreamed up a new idea, went after new venture capital and started again. The legions of workers posted their resumes online and moved on. No one had expectations of a long-term relationship between employer and employees, anyway. That was just another relic of the Old Economy, one that had proven itself to be a false promise.

## And then ... reality

The bubble burst and the venture capital well ran dry in 2000. If you were among the stunned refugees from defunct dot-coms, you may have been indelibly marked by the experience. You probably reacted in one of two ways. Having tasted the heady mix of freedom and creative power that drove the dot-coms, you vowed you'd never work any other way; you'd never get stuck in the humdrum of a rigid, uptight Old Economy business.

Or, battered and bruised by your ride on the crashing rollercoaster, you sought out the relative calm and security of an organization that had been around a while, one where everyone had an assigned role and a designated place in the structure.

But whatever your inclination, chances are you'll be living with the cultural legacy of the dot-coms for years to come.

## A ROCKY RIDE ON THE DOT-COM ROLLERCOASTER

The vibrancy, the excitement, the electricity in the air. You couldn't help being struck by those things from the minute you walked into the building occupied by WebHouse Club in early 2000. The space seemed to soar with exposed steel beams surrounding an atrium, where small groups of buoyant workers gathered around tables. The executive I was visiting – a refugee from a company so mired in Old Economy values he'd given up trying to polish off the mental dust – walked lighter and smiled broader than he had in the hushed, formal surroundings of his former company.

Just a few months old, WebHouse Club was already beginning to overflow its workspace, so his office was small and crowded, a far cry from the richly upholstered and curtained space he'd previously occupied. But he loved it. He was invigorated.

WebHouse Club was the brainchild of Jay Walker, a New Economy titan so bold he had the audacity to patent the business model used by priceline.com, his first major venture into the Internet, which offers name-your-price travel services. Walker founded priceline.com, then turned over its daily management to others and concentrated on Walker Digital, an intellectual property incubator, and starting new ventures such as WebHouse, which licensed the priceline.com model and applied the name-your-price model to groceries and petrol.

At WebHouse, Walker was a legend in his own time.

'The myth of the company was that if Jay talks to somebody, he'd convince them of anything,' the executive recalled two years after those heady early days.

Over the course of a few months, 400 people happily hitched their career hopes to Walker's shining star. The company was cash rich, thanks to Walker's personal investments and a healthy dose of venture capital. With priceline.com, then an Internet powerhouse, WebHouse had the broad shoulders of a strong big brother to smooth its path. And if anything went wrong,

Jay could make it right, everyone was convinced. WebHouse Club was surely on the fast track to a successful IPO that would make them all rich. Anticipating that, they willingly threw themselves into typically long dot-com workdays.

'We'd kill ourselves eight days a week,' the executive exclaimed, modifying his claim slightly with: 'Well, at least six. You'd come in at eight and leave at eight and work at least one weekend day.

'In the beginning, everyone loved it. As long as we felt like the company was going somewhere, people worked with energy and enthusiasm.'

The goal was growth, growth, growth. The idea was that, 'the more quickly you could grow and grab market share, the more likely you'd be profitable in the future.' Employees who bought into that – which in the early days included pretty much everyone – were acknowledged and rewarded for their efforts. Walker and company managers recognized dedicated employees at all-hands meetings and handed out mementoes to symbolize accomplishments. Starting in the Metropolitan New York area, WebHouse Club expanded into the 48 contiguous states within nine months, signing up most of the major supermarket chains to fill WebHouse Club customers' online orders. There were regular champagne parties to herald the achievement of each growth target.

People felt important and successful.

So why did WebHouse Club last only a year, while priceline.com hangs on (though it's far from the Internet powerhouse it promised to be)? The reasons were financial, strategic and cultural.

Financially, 2000 was the year venture capital dried up for dot-coms, and WebHouse Club's backers locked up the strong box. At the same time, the value of priceline.com stock tanked, taking a big bite out of Walker's personal fortune and eliminating him as a financial saviour for his fledgling company.

Strategically, the former WebHouse executive maintained, the company blew it by ignoring its customers' requests for making the service easier to use. 'We didn't get as much repeat business as we wanted,' he stated. 'That's the basic reason we failed. If the customer says it's too hard to use your website and you don't make changes, that's not listening to the customer.'

There were people in the organization who noticed that customers weren't coming back. But the company culture kept their voices from being heard. It was a basic tenet of the organization that communication was to be informal. People were expected to move freely in and out of each other's offices to solve problems. And they did a lot of that.

'But you were often missing something in that process,' the former executive recalled. 'You'd have two people solving a problem but you probably needed three others who weren't present.'

Formal channels of communication were almost non-existent. Top executives met weekly, but much of what they decided never got pushed down through the ranks.

'Once,' the former executive remembered, 'someone tried to call a meeting of everyone at the next level down. That was resented.'

Without pipelines that fed information down, it was equally difficult to push feedback up. And no one at the top was looking for bad news. Ideas that didn't match Jay Walker's were discarded. 'If it wasn't Jay's idea, it probably wasn't good,' was accepted wisdom. So warnings about losing customers fell on deaf ears. For WebHouse leadership: 'It was all about signing up new people, not holding on to the customers we had. Our leaders would say, "They're getting a 30 per cent reduction on groceries. What more do they need?"'

By autumn 2000, it was too late to figure that out. Financiers, like customers, weren't coming back. WebHouse closed its doors and shut down its web site.

Looking back on a hectic year in the dot-com world, the former executive mused, 'If you don't put in the right processes and business practices, you won't be able to sustain the culture. High energy turns to chaotic energy. Spirals of despair result when the leaders are no longer respected.'

And yet he added, 'Though, on the very last day, people said it hadn't been fun in recent months, but they wouldn't have missed it!'

EBAY: THRIVING IN DOT-COM LAND

While dot-coms crashed around it, eBay, the online auction giant, just kept on growing.

In a critical respect, it is the quintessential e-commerce company, selling not a product but a 'business model.' Unlike traditional auction houses, it doesn't hold items to be auctioned off, but rather facilitates deals between sellers and buyers. But in another respect, eBay stands almost alone among dot-commers. It has always been profitable and has always funded its operations on cash flow, rather than depending upon venture capital.

Ironically, for one of the most successful of all pure-play dot-commers, eBay credits its triumph to its old-fashioned way of doing business. Company spokesperson Kevin Pursglove told the *E-Commerce Times*: '[CEO] Meg Whitman has committed to running eBay by Old Economy rules. While [e-commerce companies] competed for first-mover advantage and market share, Meg ensured that expenses did not outpace revenue and that every dollar invested returned at least a dollar.'

Founder Pierre Omidyar, who started eBay in his tiny apartment in 1995, was an atypical entrepreneur from the start. But his idiosyncrasies would facilitate all the most positive features of the celebrated dot-com culture: openness, empowerment, community. Venture capitalist Bob Kagle, who provided eBay with a modicum of capital and an abundance of solid business advice, said of Omidyar: 'He had a high listen-to-talk ratio and was keen on what was right for the company even if that meant bringing in someone else to run it.'[5]

Omidyar and his partner, Jeff Skoll, sought a CEO with solid experience in running traditional companies. In 1998, they coaxed Meg Whitman to leave her job as general manager of the pre-school division of Hasbro, Inc. and cross the country to San Jose to take over running the fledgling dot-com phenomenon. She exemplified their ideal leader – 'a strong and decisive executive, though not one with a need-to-dominate personality.'[6]

Whitman fitted right into eBay's culture – 'one that was open to the voices of customers and other employees. The ideal eBay executive, in their collective view, understood the importance of consensus, of listening, of giving employees a long leash, and of the company's caring environment.'[7]

But you can't really talk about eBay's culture just in terms of its employees, because what eBay is really about is its community of users, who number in the tens of millions and range from occasional sellers to small companies that do all their business through eBay. The company's key to success is keeping them happy and loyal. There have been glitches, such as the time eBay tried to change its checkout policy and ran into thundering resistance, forcing it to make the new policy optional rather than mandatory. But the company has succeeded for the most part in keeping its finger on that community's pulse through chat rooms, bulletin boards, a newsletter, focus groups and visits to eBay headquarters.

An important part of being an eBay employee is understanding that you, too, are part of that community. Employees meet with visiting users and are encouraged by Whitman 'to be collectors themselves and to think like customers. Most desks at eBay corporate offices hold a collection of some sort – a reminder of eBay's origins'.[8]

From the start, Omidyar encouraged employees to speak out if they thought the leaders were straying from their espoused values of honesty, openness, equality, trust, mutual respect and mutual responsibility. Those were the basis for building the user community, and Omidyar expected employees to be watchdogs of the values internally, saying he looked to the employees 'to maintain those values among themselves and the management team'.[9]

The dirty little secret among many dot-com start-ups was that, while they claimed to value employee input, they heeded only feedback that matched the founder's own ideas and sidelined independent thinkers. By contrast, eBay nurtures a 'no-penalty operating culture in which fear of making a mistake, or fear of being on the wrong side of an issue, will not muzzle employees or subvert ideas that challenge the status quo'.[10]

## *The dot-com legacy*

The dot-coms are dead. Long live the dot-coms! What's different about the new Internet players is that preceding each dot and com is often the name of a familiar Old Economy company. The bursting of the dot-com bubble didn't signal the end of the Internet; it simply made way for earth-anchored companies to pick up where the pure-play dot-coms left off.

While traditional companies eventually dominated the Internet, many aspects of dot-com culture survived – by influencing the values and practices in companies once firmly grounded in the Old Economy. E-commerce culture characteristics sidled into traditional companies in a variety of ways:

- First, during the dot-com heyday, traditional companies had to compete for the best talent against these gilded emporia of fun, glory and fantastic (or fantasized) wealth. They had little choice but to grit their teeth and make similar offers.

- Second, it turned out that the best aspects of dot-com culture – the emphasis on innovation, teamwork and speed – translated into improved productivity in traditional organizations.

- Third, as the former dot-commers moved into other settings, they took with them a way of working that included characteristics like respect for knowledge over status, openness to others' ideas, determination to act on their own initiative and willingness to work long hours.

In truth, the pure-play Internet companies didn't invent most aspects of the so-called dot-com culture. The hi-tech pioneers of Silicon Valley were famous for their Friday afternoon beer blasts and their jeans and bare feet dress code long before anyone ever heard of a dot-com, let alone settled on a convention for spelling it. At WL Gore and Associates, the Gore-Tex® people, new associates (never known as employees) have been responsible for choosing their own projects for 40 years. (For more on the culture at WL Gore, see Chapter 12.) Office walls had been coming down in Old Economy companies since the '70s, although in those days everyone admitted it was to save space. Progressive manufacturing companies had been replacing the old plant hierarchy with self-directed work teams since the '80s. And Abraham Maslow has had people seeking self-actualization through work since the '50s.

But it was the dot-coms that caught the imagination of the press and the public and gave high visibility to a way of working that, outside a few isolated examples, had received more exposure in business books than on the shop floor or in office suites. So the dot-coms deserve some credit for mainstreaming once-radical practices, including:

- *Business casual* – the ubiquitous dress code that was unheard of 15 years ago. Of course, most traditional companies draw the line at frayed jeans

Harvard Professor Rosabeth Moss Kanter wrote the book *eVolve!* right at the time the dot-com era peaked and crashed. She began her research as the dot-coms were approaching their zenith, leaving Old Economy behemoths in their wake and capturing the imagination of the public, the awe of the pundits, and the cash of the venture capitalists. She finished her manuscript as hosts of pure-play, e-commerce wonder-firms crumpled under the weight of their own ambitions and traditional companies with innovative ideas began to move in on the Internet. It was perhaps the perfect time to capture the essence of e-culture.

Some of her findings, expressed in *eVolve!*:[11]

- At the heart of e-culture is community: 'shared identity, sharing of knowledge, and mutual contributions'.
- E-culture reverses the generational roles. The young mentor their elders: 'But it's not youth that leads the way, it is new ideas executed with discipline and traditional values.'
- The models for the future are the pacesetting 'wannadots' (Kanter's term for existing companies venturing onto the Internet), which share the e-culture characteristics of 'organizational curiosity and the desire to innovate'.
- Four best practices, derived from e-culture, are necessary for excellence:
  - When you don't know the outcome in advance, 'treat strategy development as improvisational theatre'.
  - 'Nurture networks of partners.'
  - 'Reconstruct the organization as a community.'
  - To attract and retain the best talent, 'treat people as volunteers who renew their commitment periodically through the three Ms of mastery, membership, and meaning'.

Kanter is the Ernest L Arbuckle Professor of Business Administration at Harvard Business School. She specializes in strategy, innovation and leadership for change. She became a household name with her first book, *Men and Women of the Corporation*, in which she demonstrated the crushing effect of corporate bureaucracy on individual potential. With *The Change Masters*, she made her reputation as one of the leading experts on corporate change. In all, she has written or edited 15 books and advises corporations and governments worldwide.

and rocker T-shirts. And khaki pants and blue shirts can be as stifling of individuality as dark suits and striped ties.

- *Faster decision making* – people with the best expertise, not the highest rank, make decisions, which require a minimum of approvals to come into effect.

- *Flexible responsibilities* – rather than being locked into a fixed job description, people's roles change, often in response to what needs to be done to meet organizational goals.

- *A new view of conflict* – seeing it as creative rather than disruptive.

- *Networked communication.* Everybody's connected to everyone else so information can flow directly, bypassing the old, hierarchical pipeline. That's a great advantage, but it's got a downside too. What many companies are struggling with now is information overload, with a shortage of interpretation, translation and explanation of why this data is important to each person who receives it.

- *Flexible (and longer) working hours.* Of course the movement to staggered start and end times and experiments with fewer, longer days started long before the e-commerce era, but the dot-coms were notorious for employees who roamed in and out 24 hours a day, accelerating flexibility even more and giving cachet to the concept that the person who works the longest hours wins. The eight-hour day has probably joined the type-writer as a relic of business past.

- *Team problem solving.* Most of the dot-coms were too young and too small to develop functional or departmental silos, so when decisions had to be made anybody with relevant expertise got tapped for a temporary team to handle the issue. Traditional companies are increasingly discovering they can solve problems faster by working the same way.

- *New responses to employee expectations and impatience.* Young people who moved into traditional companies from start-ups fully expected their new employers to give them important, innovative work from day one. They had little interest in working their way slowly up a corporate ladder. Undoubtedly many had rude awakenings. But some companies recognized a competitive advantage in the newcomers' strong technical skills and eagerness to make a difference and created roles based on skills and knowledge, not on hierarchy.

- *Appreciation for change.* Looking forward to new challenges rather than bemoaning a lost sanctuary.

## What about the playful perks?

By 2000, the masseurs were going mainstream, showing up among companies on *Fortune* magazine's list of best companies to work for. But two years later, in the midst of an economic downturn, the *Fortune* list was more focused on companies that avoided layoffs or at least treated laid-off workers generously and with compassion. Yet *Fortune* did report that many companies were hanging on to 'frilly perks', from free coffee to MBNA's (*Fortune's* number 26) $500 gift to each employee on his or her wedding day.[12] But don't look for the foosball table to replace the conference table in big business boardrooms.

## The smartest things in this chapter

- The dot-com myth was that everyone would become a millionaire. Reality was that many toiled for peanuts, awaiting an IPO that never came.

- Another myth was that everyone was empowered to innovate. In reality, often only the founder's ideas counted.

- The strongest dot-coms, such as eBay, mix employee empowerment with Old Economy virtues like depending upon profits, not venture capital.

- The strengths of the dot-coms – such as innovation, teamwork and speed – transferred to the traditional companies that took over as Internet leaders.

## Notes

1 'Legacies of the Dot-Com Revolution' in *Business Week online*, 20 March 2001.

2 Kanter, RM (2001) *eVolve!* Harvard Business School Press, Boston.

3 'I don't look for jobs. . . I ask myself, "What kind of experiences can I build around my core values?"' in *Business Week online*. See note 1.

4 See note 1.

5 Bunnell, D & R Luecke (2000) *The eBay Phenomenon: Secrets Behind the World's Hottest Internet Company*. Wiley, New York.

6 Ibid.

7 Ibid.

8 See note 2.

9 See note 5.

10 See note 5.

11 See note 2.

12 Levering, L & M Moskowitz 'The Best in the Worst of Times' in *Fortune*, 4 February 2002.

# Part IV
# Seeking Better Cultures

The disappearance of old values like job security and the demise of the dot-coms with their promise of a brave new culture leaves one asking: 'Isn't there something better out there?' This part of the book suggests places to look for solutions to cultural disarray.

Solution one, in Chapter 11, is in the recommendations of management experts who have studied the practices in high-performing organizations that involve and empower their workers.

Solution two, in Chapter 12, is in examples – three companies that serve as models and one that profoundly demonstrates what not to do.

The third solution, in Chapter 13, is found within ourselves. This chapter is about creating a 'personal culture' that provides stability in any environment.

# 11
# The Textbook Model

Smart answers to tough questions

The corporate anthropologists insist there is no best culture for all busi-nesses. Rather, for each organization, there is a strategically appropriate culture, i.e. a unique culture that best supports the organization's strategy.

But the management and leadership gurus, from the venerable Peter Druck-er to the cool Tom Peters, offer amazingly consistent advice on how best to run a company, especially the people part. One could argue that their advice is more of a management model than a culture model. But if you pick up a book on management and another on corporate culture, you'll find an awful lot of overlapping content. So, arguably, the experts are purporting a model culture, at least in the following respects:

- involved employees

- empowered employees

- shared sense of ownership throughout the organization

- flattened organizational structure

- teams as the primary unit of work

- support for risk-taking

- emphasis on continuous learning

- diverse workforce

- shared customer focus.

Put them all together and they sound a lot like a culture, don't they? Certainly practising these sincerely and consistently until they became rooted in an organization's unconscious would have profound impact on the organization's culture.

Here's what each of these 'ideal' practices looks like.

## Involved employees

Involved employees at all levels contribute to any decisions that will affect them. They have input into planning, organization of work groups, and scheduling and assigning work. In some organizations they have even participated in downsizing decisions and determining what jobs to eliminate.

Since employees actually do the work, it only makes sense that they have knowledge about the work that no one else has. They know when work slows down because resources aren't available. They know when their work is held up because a prerequisite task isn't done yet. They often know when an adjustment to a schedule, a machine, a form or a list of people invited to a meeting would speed up a process or improve the quality of output. Organizations that involve their employees tap all that knowledge and feed it into the decision-making process from the outset.

Employee involvement isn't really a new idea. The Drucker quote above dates back to 1973 and even the Peters quote below is from 1987. But at the same time, Peters also quoted Frank Borman, former chairman of Eastern Airlines, as declaring, 'I'm not going to have the monkeys running the zoo.'[3] So, new or not, it is pretty revolutionary to involve employees in what many consider management prerogatives.

To make it work, management must start by sharing all the information employees need to give relevant input and make informed decisions. That includes strategy, goals, financial realities, and internal and external threats and opportunities. When Carol Lavin Bernick took over as president of Alberto-Culver North America, she invited every employee to a two-hour 'state of the company'

*Smart quotes*

'His knowledge, his experience, his needs are resource to the planning process. The worker needs to be a partner in it.'

Peter Drucker[1]

*Smart quotes*

'I am frustrated to the point of rage – my files bulge with letters about the power of involvement… Truly involved people can do anything!'

Tom Peters[2]

'Allowing employees to be the "boss" in certain situations – actually helped me lead.'

Robert A Eckert, chairman and CEO of Mattel.[4]

address that has become an annual event. At the first one, she shocked the troops by revealing that their proudest achievement, VO5 shampoo, earned the company exactly one cent profit on each bottle and that, in fact, the company was being carried by what many considered a mere sideline business, a chain of beauty supply stores.[5] Armed with that knowledge, the troops took a new interest in the beauty store business and, at the same time, looked for ways to increase the profit on their flagship shampoo.

There are many ways to collect input from throughout the organization. Alberto-Culver has a group of 70 growth development leaders (GDLs) who are conduits between top management and the work groups. About every six weeks Bernick meets with the GDLs, who usually each bring a group member as a guest. They discuss questions, concerns and solutions. 'At this point, our employees are nailing every major business problem we have,' wrote Bernick in the *Harvard Business Review*.

Robert Eckert, chairman and CEO of Mattel, gets a lot of his employee input informally by eating in the company cafeteria. Sometimes he arranges to eat with a group of employees. Sometimes one or a few will drop by his table to talk about what's on their minds.[6]

Listening to worker input into organization-wide issues is one aspect of employee involvement. The other part is giving them control over their own work and work groups. Back in 1973, Drucker wrote, 'The responsibility for job design and work-group design belongs to those who are responsible for output and performance. And that is the worker and the work group.'[7] Why give employees this responsibility? For Drucker the answer was elementary: with respect to the individual job, the worker is 'the only expert'. That principle still drives the employee involvement concept today.

In organizations where employee involvement is ingrained in the corporate culture, work groups set their own performance goals, based on organizational goals, and hold themselves accountable for meeting them. Work groups decide how the work will be done and who will do it. They also take responsibility for improving their processes, their tools and their output. The most obvious manifestation of this form of involvement is the self-directed work team. But supervisor-led work groups can function the same way – they call it participatory management.

## Empowered employees

Empowered employees have the right to take decisive actions on their own even if those decisions require a commitment of money, other resources or organizational goodwill that is not formally authorized by their job descriptions.

An empowered customer service representative can commit the organization to a replacement *and* a refund delivered overnight to a customer who had a particularly frustrating experience. The same representative can refuse to deal with an abusive customer. An empowered technical support person can hop a plane and travel halfway around the world when phone and e-mail fail to solve a distant co-worker's computer problem. Tom Peters, who has a story for every situation, tells of a FedEx employee who hired a helicopter to fly him into the mountains after a blizzard and drop him on a mountain top so he could fix a downed phone line and get FedEx up and running again.[9] (Obviously there's more to empowerment than spending company money.)

> *Smart quotes*
>
> 'When you empower your employees, you give them not just tasks to do. You give them areas of responsibility and decision-making authority to deal with situations that arise daily.'
>
> Florence Stone and Randi Sachs, *The High-Value Manager*[8]

Like employee involvement, empowerment is management's acknowledgement that in any job, the person with the most expertise for handling unusual situations is the person actually doing the work. But that's easier to say than to live by.

The essence of empowerment is trust and knowledge. Empowerment only works when management trusts that employees won't abuse their power, won't give away the store and have the ability to make crucial judgement calls. To warrant such trust, employees need to understand organizational goals and constraints so they can make decisions that may be unusual but do advance the goals and don't overstep absolute constraints.

The price managers pay for empowering employees is being held accountable for their employees' decisions and actions. For many, that's a pretty scary if not totally outrageous contract. So large-scale employee empowerment is not yet as prevalent in reality as it is in words and values statements. But for organizations that jump the hurdle – via a lot of preparation for both managers and employees – the rewards are speedier outcomes, better quality results and higher customer satisfaction. Not to mention increased respect going two ways between the workforce and management – and that's a culture thing.

## Shared sense of ownership

Employees can share ownership in a number of ways. Obviously, there's equity ownership thanks to occasional employee buyouts and, more frequently, employee stock ownership plans. Such plans are a bit tarnished these days, due to the ongoing Enron disaster, where employees have lost their life savings rather than become worker-millionaires. Nevertheless, in plenty of companies, workers are building nest eggs while adjusting to their role as owners, not detached wage earners.

But the kind of ownership the experts are promoting is more psychological than financial. It's ownership in the sense of responsibility and pride. While equity ownership can contribute to these feelings, getting people to act on them takes more than stock options. Workers who are involved in decision making feel a sense of shared ownership in the outcomes of those decisions. Worker teams who plan their own work, determine their own schedules and assign roles within the team, own the results of their efforts, whether that result surpasses or falls short of expectations. They own the accolades of success and they own responsibility for making improvement where necessary. Individual workers own their own jobs when they can decide for themselves how best to do them even if 'best' requires occasional extraordinary actions.

Owners are seldom satisfied with mediocrity, so this kind of ownership often leads to both incremental and transformational improvements in processes, tools and outcomes.

## Flattened organizational structure

In the '80s, a vice-president of a large corporation counted the number of levels between him and the president/CEO. There were five. Yes, you read that right. A vice-president with *five* more vice-presidents, senior vice-presidents, and executive vice-presidents separating him from the chief executive. Just imagine how many levels down there must have been between him and a supervisor. No wonder the company moved slowly.

All those layers disempower everybody, not just front-line workers or low-level managers. Everybody's got a boss, who has a boss, who has a boss… Decisions get stuck in the wires between the boxes on the organization chart. Critical information gets lost making its way through the maze.

In organizations that empower their employees to plan, organize and monitor their own work, all those layers of management are totally redundant. So progressive organizations are getting rid of them. Tom Peters calls for three layers maximum in one facility. There are factories with only two layers: the plant manager and everyone else. In such facilities, 'everyone else' is grouped into work teams with rotating leadership roles. But the manager doesn't assign those roles. The workers do, taking turns so everyone learns the skills involved in each role.

*Smart quotes*

'I insist on five layers as the maximum. Three layers… should be tops for any single facility.'

Tom Peters[11]

Collapsing the hierarchy not only speeds the decision-making process and puts more power at the lower levels, it also strips the remaining rungs on the ladder of some of their mystique. With only a few levels, even the people on the lowest rungs are likely to know everyone between them and the top – not personally perhaps in a large organization, but at least who they are and what they are there for. And the people at the top have a much better grasp on what happens on the front lines when they are not protected by five layers of vice-presidents.

## Teams

If two heads are better than one, think what seven could do. It's not that simple, of course, but the basic concept behind the growing popularity of teams in organizations is that a small group of people working in concert *toward a shared goal* will outperform individuals working separately. There's ample evidence that teams can do just that. One example – after reorganizing into self-directed work teams, a GE plant reduced its cycle time to a fraction of what it had been. When it took over the manufacture of one part from a sister plant, the team-based facility beat the other plant's production time in its first week. Over a longer term, it bested the other plant's annual average cost by 28 per cent.

Here's an example of a different kind. A Wisconsin insurance company charged a cross-functional project team with the task of lowering the time it took to adapt to changing state regulations for one of its products. The team slashed the time to a maximum of 60 days from an average of 220.

Organizations use teams effectively both for ongoing work and for one-shot projects. The team vehicle of choice for ongoing work is the self-directed work team (variously called autonomous work team, empowered work team, shared leadership team or self-managed team). This team is a permanent work unit. What makes it different from other work units is that the team assumes traditional supervisory responsibilities: setting goals, planning how work will be done, scheduling, assigning tasks, and in some cases even hiring and firing. Leadership roles rotate among team members. Because the teams take over duties that used to go to supervisors and managers, conversion to self-directed teams is often a part of restructuring to reduce management levels in an organization.

Project teams, on the other hand, are temporary, existing only as long as it takes to achieve their goal of solving a defined problem or exploiting a specific opportunity. Members are selected because they have specific skills and expertise. Project leaders have the double-edged task of facilitating synergy among the various experts in the team and controlling progress toward the project goal.

Organizations such as Procter & Gamble, Citibank, American Express and EDS organize important parts of their business around projects rather than ongoing functions. They call it managing by projects or enterprise project management. Rather than committing themselves to one permanent work unit, employees move in and out of teams as project teams form, perform their mandate and close down. By contrast with life in a traditional, functionally-based organization, it is something of a peripatetic work style. Managing by projects, like implementing permanent teams, is a powerful influence for reducing organizational levels. There are just fewer entrenched operations for layers of management to stick to.

Whether permanent or temporary, successful teams share common characteristics and responsibilities. As Jon Katzenbach and Douglas Smith explain in *The Wisdom of Teams*, 'They shape a common purpose, agree on performance goals, define a common working approach, develop high levels of complementary skills, and hold themselves mutually accountable for results.'[12]

Working that way is a big change for many, both for the timid, who would eschew that kind of accountability, and for those who grew up with the western myth of the rugged individualist. Does convincing such people to embrace teams change the underlying culture? Not quickly, the evidence shows. Titeflex Corporation in Springfield, Massachusetts, did such a good job of converting its flexible hose plant into a team-based operation that the general manager and union chief steward went on the lecture circuit together to share their experience. But five successful years later, the operations manager – an ardent team champion – assessed the depth of the conversion. 'This company has about ten cheerleaders for teams,' he said. 'Without them, the company would revert to its old style in a year.'[14]

## Risk-taking

Taking risks – pursuing opportunities despite some possibility of failure – wasn't very popular among employees in paternalistic organizations. For sure, they would be punished if they failed. Even if they didn't fail, they might be punished just for attempting something they weren't formally authorized to do. Since risk-taking definitely wasn't in their job description, they were never formally authorized to do it.

That worked in the old days when corporations could go on for years doing exactly the same thing and make money at it. It doesn't work any more because tastes and technology are moving so fast that organizations have to change constantly just to keep up. And as P&G says, 'zero risk equals zero change.'

Ideal organizations (if not all *real* ones) recognize that what empowering employees really means is allowing them – even encouraging them – to fail. Every new initiative carries with it some danger of failure. Every successful initiative carries with it the ghosts of unsuccessful efforts that preceded it, each one revealing new information that that made the next attempt work better. Companies have always had failures of this kind, but they only allowed them at the top.

The new model supports risk-taking at all levels. In return for eating some failures, the organization spurs multitudes of small innovations everywhere that add up to major improvements in products, services, tools and processes. It also profits because small failures no longer get hidden, only to turn into later disasters. Instead, sometimes they get fixed or, at worst, they get milked for all the learning they can provide.

In the annals of business legends, there's an oldie-but-goodie featuring Thomas J Watson, IBM's formidable early leader. According to the story, a junior executive lost $10 million of the company's money in a doomed venture. Expecting the worst, the young man offered his resignation to Watson, who roared, 'You can't be serious. We've just spent ten million dollars educating you!'

Watson understood the value of taking risks.

## Continuous learning

With the recognition that change was inevitable came the realization that to stay out in front, organizations and the people in them had to keep learning – continuously. No one would ever be in a position to say, 'OK, now I know all there is to know about my job.' For one thing, the tools, technology and processes of every job are going to keep changing. For another thing, every job is going to become obsolete – as will the incumbent who hasn't learned what's necessary to move on to the next. And for a third thing, performing any job requires continually learning more and more about the environment in which that job operates because no job functions in isolation and the environment keeps changing.

Continuous learning is as much about learning from working on new projects, from watching and listening, and from making and correcting mistakes as it is from skills training and higher education. It's equally important for employees to figure out how to use what they have learned to improve their own performance and that of the organization.

Organizations that truly value continuous learning make formal learning available, while encouraging employees to participate in projects and activities that broaden their skills and knowledge. Some organizations even give employees pay rises for acquiring new knowledge and skills, whether or not there is an immediate opportunity to apply them on the job.

## Diverse workforce

Once there was affirmative action in the United States. Forced into it, companies rushed to hire and promote minorities and women – largely into support staff positions. For companies in most other parts of the world, it was still pretty much a non-issue.

That's changing everywhere as organizations discover that not only women and minorities, but others – such as the physically disabled – who had also been excluded from the workforce, all have knowledge, skills and new perspectives that can be a competitive advantage.

You'll find plenty of corporate values statements that profess to 'value our diverse workforce', but whether that's real, ideal, or a rainbow face on a bedrock white male culture you'll only learn by digging deeper than the company website.

## Customer focus

The top three items in most values statements are customers, shareholders and employees – not necessarily in that order, but usually customers come first.

In companies that practise the ideal of organization-wide customer orientation, a passion for quality, service, responsiveness and timeliness pervades the entire organization. 'How will this affect the customer?' is as much on the mind of programmers as salespeople. Executives and managers model this attitude when they identify what customers truly value, focus resources on that, and eliminate any wasted effort on things customers care little about. They extend and perpetuate the passion by empowering front-line employees to solve problems on the spot.

And if they are really radical, they concentrate on *serving* their employees on the grounds that if you treat your employees really, really well, they'll treat the customers really, really well. After all, Max DePree, one of the prophets of the new ideal, wrote, 'The first responsibility of a leader is to define reality. The last is to say thank you. In between the leader is a servant.'[17] That approach is a big step toward defining a culture.

## The smartest things in this chapter

- The culture experts say there is no ideal culture, but the management gurus agree on a comprehensive list of practices for improving organizations.

- Involving employees in decision making and empowering them to take action on their own initiative gives the organization full and fast benefit of their knowledge, skills and insights.

- Shared ownership – psychological and equity – promotes improvements in processes, tools and outcomes.

- Organizations that replaced layers of management with teams of workers have registered quantifiable performance improvements.

- By encouraging risk-taking and learning from mistakes, organizations make transformational improvements.

- The first step toward serving customers well is serving employees.

## Notes

1 Drucker, PF (1973) *Management: Tasks, Responsibilities, Practices*. Harper & Row, New York.

2 Peters, T (1987) *Thriving on Chaos*. Alfred A Knopf, New York.

3 Ibid., quoting the *Washington Monthly*, June 1986.

4 Eckert, RA 'Where Leadership Starts' in *Harvard Business Review*, November 2001.

5 Bernick, C 'When Your Culture Needs a Makeover' in *Harvard Business Review*, June 2001.

6 See note 4.

7 See note 1.

8 Stone, FM & RT Sachs (1995) *The High-Value Manager*. AMACOM, New York.

9 See note 2.

10 DePree, M (1989) *Leadership is an Art*. Doubleday, New York.

11  See note 2.

12  Katzenbach, JR & DK Smith (1993) *The Wisdom of Teams*. Harvard Business School Press, Cambridge, MA.

13  Quoted in Deeprose, D (1995) *The Team Coach*. AMACOM, New York.

14  Ibid.

15  Found at Procter & Gamble's website at www.pgcareers.com/apply/how/risk.asp.

16  Senge, P (1990) *The Fifth Discipline*. Doubleday, New York.

17  See note 10.

# 12

# Variations on a Theme

The previous chapter described characteristics of an ideal organization, according to the consensus of influential management thinkers. It hedged a bit on whether the combination of those characteristics comprised an ideal culture, concluding only that they would have a big influence on the culture of any organization that practised them.

Influential, yes. But a cookie cutter, no.

This chapter looks at the cultures of some companies that have been recognized for modelling the practices described in Chapter 11. Two of them, Microsoft and Southwest Airlines, dominate their industries (for Southwest, in terms of profitability, if not size). One, WL Gore and Associates, is so far ahead of the pack in its interpretation of these practices that, after 40 plus years, it's still somewhat of a maverick, although the rest of the corporate world is slowly catching up. The fourth, Enron, is a whole different story, but it bears a look because before its cataclysmic fall it was a poster child for the New Economy corporate culture.

You'll see some significant similarities and some marked differences among the four.

### *Microsoft's free-wheeling culture and the discipline required to sustain it*

Two prominent magazines, the *Harvard Business Review* and the *Atlantic Monthly*, recently published different perspectives on life at Microsoft.[1] In the *Atlantic Monthly*, a writer, James Fallows, described the Microsoft culture as he saw it during a six-month stint as part of a team developing the next release of Microsoft Word™. In the *HBR* article, Robert Herbold, former Microsoft CEO, wrote about the organization-wide systems installed during his tenure to bring sanity to a mind-boggling proliferation of processes that threatened to strangle the very innovation and spontaneity that had created them.

Together, the two articles provide fascinating insights into how a worldwide organization of more than 30,000 employees sustains its legendary entrepreneurial culture. They also reveal that some aspects of the culture can look very different to different people. Those differences in perception seem to result mainly from the expectations they brought to Microsoft, formed by the cultures from which they came. These two articles are the basis for this profile.

## Bottom-up decision making

Who decides what goes into Microsoft software programs? The people developing them, with surprisingly little interference by management, Fallows discovered. 'If there is something you love or hate about Microsoft programs,' he wrote, 'don't thank or blame Bill Gates; some specific member of the Microsoft team decided to "own" that feature and include it in a program.'

If you are a program developer at Microsoft and you've got an idea for the software you are working on, you don't have to go through an agonizing approval process to get your feature included. Instead, Fallows wrote, the process is like this: '1. Persuade your colleagues that a certain feature will be popular, and that it can be created, and 2. Create it.'

Of course some projects need top-level approval – such as launching a whole new software program. But even those don't suffer micromanagement, Herbolt confirmed. Shortly joining Microsoft, he attended a meeting where a program manager proposed a new project to Bill Gates. After it was over, Herbolt asked Gates what the next steps would be. Coming from Procter & Gamble, he expected memos, reviews, modifications and eventually final approval from on high. But Gates responded, 'No, that's it. The key decisions got made. Now his group better hustle to implement things – or else.'

> *Smart quotes*
>
> 'With the fiercely independent culture of Microsoft managers and developers, however, it is rare that Gates tries to mandate anything; according to Sinofsky [a former Gates technical assistant], the "numbers of those things are so small that they have a reputation all their own".'
>
> Michael Cusumano and Richard Selby, *Microsoft Secrets*[2]

## Face-to-face or e-mail?

When Herbolt arrived at Microsoft's Redmond, Washington, campus at 7 a.m. on his first day on the job, he was surprised to find the place empty.

When his assistant finally arrived he asked her what the hours were. As he remembers it, her reply was, 'Oh, there aren't any specific hours, but that doesn't matter. Most work is done by e-mail.'

Not surprising, you may think, for one of the world's pre-eminent technology companies. What's more surprising is that this characterization doesn't match Fallows' impression at all. What he observed was that, 'Microsoft relies as heavily on face-to-face contact as any organization I've ever seen… To make a difference one must be at the headquarters, must come to the office, must sit through meetings.' What he saw at the Redmond campus were offices full of people constantly moving through scheduled and spontaneous meetings.

Which is correct? Both perhaps, depending upon the basis of comparison. If you come from a traditional company like Procter & Gamble, where it's normal to arrive at 7 a.m. for a long day at the office, then at any given time Microsoft's offices might look pretty empty. Microsoft employees have the freedom to make their own hours and the tendency (which even Fallows observed) to hide away to work alone on tasks only they can do.

But if you come from a magazine environment, where reporters are off pursuing individual stories, which they can write and e-mail from anywhere, then the Redmond campus would look like a buzzing beehive.

### Workaholic or slow pace?

The assistant who responded to Herbold's question about office hours also told him that 'everyone is a workaholic'.

But Fallows found the pace at Microsoft headquarters slow, although his friends there didn't agree with him. He observed that Microsoft employees averaged fewer hours per week and less all-nighters than did people in places like banks, law firms, election campaign offices or even newspapers. His Microsoft colleagues assured him there were lots of times when everyone worked non-stop, 'that if I stayed for a whole development cycle, over two or three years, I'd see the pace pick up'. But, as a magazine writer, Fallows was used to shorter cycles and the Microsoft pace felt luxurious.

His conclusion was that Microsoft cares more about effectiveness than efficiency. When the right time comes, he wrote, 'they all do what needs to be done'.

## Interpersonal relations among Microsoft people

There's a perception that technology companies of the Silicon Valley era are hotbeds of unbridled confrontation as colleagues ruthlessly attack each other's favourite ideas, never personally, of course, but always in search of the most elegant solution. Fallows didn't find that at Microsoft. In fact, the words he used to describe people there were 'nice', 'congenial' and 'non-backbiting'. Their exchanges about features or strategy, he said, were 'nothing compared with the way lawyers, journalists, or politicians snap at one another'.

## Shared ownership

At Microsoft, shared ownership is literal, with stock options a big part of the compensation package. Fallows and Herbold agree this influences the way people at Microsoft behave, encouraging them to buy into others' ideas because of the potential for big reward. Herbold felt it helped reduce resistance to the organization-wide systems he introduced that resulted in cost savings. 'After all,' he wrote, 'their stock options were tied to Microsoft's share price.'

But ownership is more than money. It's reflected in the way developers 'own' their parts of the programs they work on. It's reflected in employees' propensity, noticed by both Fallows and Herbold, to wear clothes decorated with the Microsoft logo. And it's reflected in their conviction, according to Fallows, that: 'Microsoft has prospered strictly because it builds great software.' Not even the ongoing, high-profile antitrust case against Microsoft has diminished that.

## Prospering with LUV and fun at Southwest Airlines

Geographically and technologically, the Texas-based Southwest Airlines is miles apart from Microsoft. Since the mid-nineties, it seems as if no book on culture or management is complete without a profile of Southwest. And for good reason. Southwest Airlines, the fifth largest airline in the United States, continues to stand out as the company that succeeds by putting its employees first. What better evidence than this: after the terrorist attacks on September 11th 2001, Southwest was the only US airline that made a profit in the fourth quarter of that year and the only one that did not lay off a single employee.

In fact, in its 30 years of existence, Southwest has never failed to make a profit and has never laid off anyone – not through oil crises, recessions or war.

### The company based on love

In most organizations, talking about love would be unbearably corny, but co-founder Herb Kelleher has made a big deal of it. The airline's symbol on the New York Stock Exchange is LUV; its headquarters is at Dallas' Love Field Airport; its company newspaper is called LUV Lines. Somehow, at

Southwest it rings true. From its no-layoff policy to its pride in having more than 800 married couples on staff,[3] Southwest acts out its message.

It also demonstrates that LUV is more than a three-letter word by:

- *Trusting its employees to do what they think is right on their own initiative.* A Southwest manager thought it was right to arrange overnight delivery of hundreds of teddy bears from a Chicago toy manufacturer to Oklahoma City for distribution at a community meeting after the tragic bombing there.[4]

- *Soliciting employee input into problem solving and decision making.* Early in the airline's life, it was employees who figured out how to maintain the flight schedule with fewer planes by decreasing the turnaround time on the ground.[5] That turnaround speed remains a Southwest competitive advantage.

- *Maintaining the business world's most famous open-door policy.* Employees drop in on any executive to talk about what's on their mind. There are no suggestion boxes at Southwest. Herb Kelleher thinks any manager who needs a suggestion box to get employee input isn't doing the job very well.

- *Sustaining an atmosphere where people are always pitching in and helping each other.* Southwest is a heavily unionized company, but that doesn't stop employees from going way beyond what's in their job descriptions. It's common for pilots to help out with baggage, checking in passengers or even cleaning the cabin between flights.

- *Publicly putting employees first – even ahead of customers.* Customers who abuse employees get invited not to fly Southwest again. Still, Southwest's 'positively outrageous customer service' is legendary. The legend isn't based on providing amenities. Southwest provides no meals and assigns no seats in advance. Instead, it's always been built on the premise that when you treat employees right, they'll treat customers right, with friendliness, warmth and extraordinary care. Stories abound to back that up. There's the one about the agent who babysat a customer's dog for a week so the customer could travel. There's another about a customer service representative who spent a night in a hotel with a frightened elderly woman whose flight was grounded in fog.

### Laughing all the way to the bank

As if loving each other weren't enough, at Southwest Airlines they are deter-mined to have an uproariously good time doing it. Not just a pleasant time, but a knee-slapping, guffawing time. The pilots and flight attendants are famous for their jokes. Have you heard the one about the flight attendant who got all the passengers to lean inward so the pilot could check the rear-view mirrors? And for their games, like rolling toilet paper down the aisle and offering a prize to whoever could guess the number of squares. Then there's 'guess the gate agent's weight' inside the terminal. Back at the office, Herb Kelleher has been known to arrive at meetings in drag and livened up the place by riding his motorcycle (a gift from employees) through the hall until the noise drove everyone crazy and they asked him to stop.

It's all part of the Southwest philosophy: people work better when they are having fun.

*And in return ...*

In return for the love, the fun, the promise of no layoffs (and the stock ownership plan), Herb Kelleher and his fellow co-founders of Southwest expected employees would be loyal. Their expectations have been borne out. Southwest's employee turnover rate is about half the industry average. The company's 10-year contract with its unionized pilots is unheard of anywhere else. Making a profit consistently isn't always easy and when the company asks for belt-tightening, employees oblige. On the eve of his retirement as CEO in 2001, Kelleher told *Fortune* magazine that in 1999 he began to worry that the company was getting too dependent on cheap oil prices, so he asked Southwest people each to save $5 a day. They did, helping cut costs by 5.6 per cent.[8]

*Culture by committee*

All this mutual love and respect among everyone at every level doesn't happen by chance. In fact, it's carefully engineered. Southwest even has a culture committee, set up by Colleen Barrett, who is now company president and was always Kelleher's right-hand person. People from all areas and all levels sit on the culture committee. One of their initiatives is to improve cross-functional co-operation throughout the company. As a result of their efforts, Southwest has had a policy for years of sending all the executives into the field once a month to work a front-line job, like loading baggage or checking in passengers. It's just one of the company's efforts to keep management and workers on the same team.

*Shining up your resume?*

So, you're thinking you'd like to work at Southwest? You and a couple of hundred thousand other people, all vying for a few thousand jobs each year. But you'll have an advantage if you remember this: Southwest hires for attitude, not skills. The company's position is that it can develop your skills, but you have to bring the attitude. So here's how to demonstrate you've got the Southwest attitude:

1   When someone else is talking, pay close attention; ignoring other people's ideas is not the right attitude.

2   Be friendly and polite to everyone. If you are rude to any Southwest person on your way to an interview, you haven't a chance.

3   Laugh. At Southwest, they like the sound.

## What if there were no bosses?

Chaos or Nirvana? WL Gore & Associates of Newark, Delaware, manufacturers of Gore-Tex®, the breathable, waterproof lining material, and other polytetraflouroethylene (PTFE) products, has proven that an organization without bosses doesn't have to be chaos. You'll have to decide for yourself whether or not you think it's Nirvana.

When he and his wife, Vieve, founded the company in 1958, Bill Gore was convinced that if you freed people from bureaucracy and hierarchy, they would produce outstanding results. As his company grew, you could say he turned it into an experiment to test that hypothesis. He built a lattice organization, where there were no reporting relationships and everyone had a direct line of communication to everyone else. The organization chart was a scattergram of little boxes, each one connected to every other one. Forty years later, with the founders' son, Bob, as president, the organization still looks the same, although it's been duplicated in locations around the world as the company grew to employ over 6000 people globally.[10]

The system works fine, the company found, as long as the organizational unit is fairly small, no more than about 200 people. So units are kept to that size. If a division starts to bloat, it gets divided into two units small enough for everyone to know everyone else.

## So who runs the place?

Gore's mission is all about innovation – developing and exploiting new applications for the polymer PTFE. Every Gore plant is comprised of teams organized around technology or market opportunities. The teams set their own goals, create and pursue their own plans, and obtain their own resources. They are guided by a set of principles that are much more than fancy words on glossy paper. There are only four:

1 Fairness to each other and everyone with whom we come in contact.

2 Freedom to encourage, help and allow other associates to grow in knowledge, skill and scope of responsibility.

3 The ability to make one's own commitments and keep them.

4   Consultation with other associates before undertaking actions that could impact the reputation of the company by hitting it 'below the waterline'.[12]

Below the waterline means something with the potential to seriously damage the reputation or financial health of the company – thus sinking it. Notice that the guideline doesn't call for passing such a proposal past any executives – just knowledgeable associates.

## Who's an associate?

At WL Gore, everybody is an associate. Sure, sure, you've heard it before. Nobody's an employee any more, everybody's an associate; but other than the words, nothing much has changed. Well, nothing much has changed at Gore either, but that's because there have always been associates there rather than employees. In fact, it's the Gore lead the other companies have been following as they adopt the term. The difference is that since Gore doesn't have bosses, the term 'associate' really means something.

The first responsibility of every new associate is to choose a task or a project to commit to. Naturally, it's got to be something useful to the team, but there's a range of possibilities for every newcomer, who is helped in learning the ropes and making a commitment by a sponsor. Anyone can be a sponsor; usually it's someone who has the most to gain by the new person's success. Taking on sponsor duties means accepting responsibility for the development and growth of the associate. Sponsors provide encouragement, offer guidance on how to get along at Gore, give performance feedback, provide help in obtaining resources and serve as advocate for the associate in compensation discussions.

*But who's got the big picture?*

It's all very well, you may be thinking, for teams to set goals, associates to make commitments and sponsors to support them, but somebody's got to have a big picture and make sure all the projects co-ordinate and meet organizational goals. There are leaders to handle those responsibilities: line leaders, business leaders, functional leaders, task force leaders, divisional leaders, etc. The ideal is for leaders to rise organically, based upon the willingness of others to follow them. In fact, at WL Gore that ideal works pretty well, and leaders change naturally as projects and situations change.

*An ideal place to work?*

Certainly *Fortune* magazine likes the culture at WL Gore, assigning it a perennial spot on the 'Best Companies to Work For' list. For an achievement-oriented self-starter who is a great team player, WL Gore offers a unique environment (and a stock ownership plan; associates are the majority owners and the Gore family minority owners). But life without bosses is no piece of cake. It's no place to decide to coast for a while. Thriving at WL Gore requires each individual to take the initiative to make continued contributions to the company. That's brought home in the performance rating and compensation process. Associates rank their peers, based on their contributions, and those rankings are the basis for salary actions.

That much empowerment isn't everybody's cup of tea.

### Enron: flying too close to the sun

In the fast-paced world of the '90s, Enron epitomized the New Economy. The Houston-based firm transformed itself from a stodgy pipeline company to a high-flying energy trading company. In its own mind, it went from being the 'leading energy company' to simply the 'leading company'. Analysts and academicians fell in line to agree. Its stock soared. Business schools studied it. Harvard wrote a case study based on it.

It wasn't just *what* the company did that drew attention, but *how* it did it. Enron seemed to embody the best of what the management authorities touted:

- It rewarded creativity and risk-taking.

- It empowered employees to make important decisions and take actions on their own initiative.

- It provided plenty of opportunities for movement and growth.

And, oh, the perks. For many employees, these were what characterized the culture in the good days:

- free laptops and hand-helds

- expensive office furniture

- lunches on the tab at the best restaurants, and limousines to get there

- $100 bills dropped on everyone's desk to celebrate a milestone

- ski trips for executives

- Waterford crystal for secretaries on Secretaries' Day

- lavish parties, where executives rode in on elephants or motorcycles.[13]

The good things never came easy. Top performers worked incredibly long hours. One employee told the *Washington Post* he'd worked 14–16-hour days without lunch breaks. But according to his wife, 'he came home from work "energized".'[14] Another reported to the *New York Times* that three-day business trips could turn into three months.[15]

The performance review system terrorized everyone. Like many other companies (WL Gore, for example), Enron had a peer-review system. But Enron people believed that if you crossed one of your reviewers, you'd get zapped. Performance ranking determined bonuses and stock options, and the differences in rewards for highest and next highest ratings were tremendous.

All in all, though, people at Enron were energetic, optimistic and confident their future was in good hands.

When the blow came, it came hard. In fall of 2001, Enron announced it had overstated earnings by $600 million from 1997 to 2000. Unable to sell the Enron stock in their retirement portfolios, many employees lost their life savings. Top executives, who got rid of much of their Enron holdings months earlier, didn't share their fate. The company declared bankruptcy in December, facing allegations of questionable accounting and unlawful trading by executives and investigations by the Department of Justice, the Securities and Exchange Commission, the House Energy and Commerce Committee, and a Senate committee. All that was left of Enron was a shell, trying

*Smart quotes*

'The environment was an extreme rush. Very busy, very progressive and innovative. I've never worked with more talented people in my life and I'm so grateful I had the opportunity.'

A letter from a former Enron contractor to *HoustonChronicle.com*, 4 December 2001

*Smart quotes*

'People were afraid to get crossways with someone who could screw up their reviews. How did managers ensure they passed muster? "You didn't object to anything," says one former Enron executive. The whole culture at the vice-president level and above just became a yes-man culture."'

*BusinessWeek online*[16]

'In addition to feedback from your supervisor, anybody and everybody could offer feedback on you. Plus you knew that the bottom ten percent were going to get axed. This changed the entire atmosphere at Enron. It became a den of back-stabbers and snitches.'

A letter from a former employee to *HoustonChronicle.com*, 4 December 2001

desperately to pick up some pieces. All that was left of its vaunted culture was a memory.

Looking back at the culture with the benefit of hindsight, the analysts are asking questions:

- *Was the culture to blame?* Was the freedom so great and the pressure to perform so high that stepping outside good business practices – if not outside the law – was inevitable?

- *Was it all a sham?* Were Enron's stated values of respect, communication, excellence and integrity never any more than pretty words?

  In 2000, then-CEO Jeffrey Skilling, one of the masterminds of Enron's meteoric rise, made a videotape emphasizing, 'People have an obligation to dissent in this company.' He exhorted employees, 'I have no idea what's going on down there, so if you've got a problem with it, speak up.'[17] Yet, in the wake of the company's collapse, Enron managers and executives have insisted their efforts to warn Skilling of the dangers of Enron's financial manoeuvres were either rebuffed or ignored.

  Skilling left Enron just in time, resigning in August 2002.

- *Or, perhaps, was it all just too good to be true?* The analysts, business schools and other companies will be asking that question for a long time.

## The smartest things in this chapter

- It's possible for companies to share characteristics, such as empowered employees, yet have very different cultures.

- At Microsoft, the focus is on contributing program features and meeting deadlines.

- At Southwest, the keys are love, laughter and no layoffs.

- WL Gore associates are so empowered they have no bosses, but they are accountable for contributing to company success.

- At Enron, the marriage of empowerment and excess dissolved in disaster.

## Notes

1 Herbold R 'Inside Microsoft: Balancing Creativity and Discipline' in the *Harvard Business Review*, January 2002 and Fallows J 'Inside the Leviathan' in the *Atlantic Monthly*, February 2000 (digital edition found at www.theatlantic.com).

2 Cusumano, MA & RW Selby (1998) *Microsoft Secrets*. Touchstone, New York.

3 Reported by Sheila McNulty in 'Southwest Airlines: Short on frills, big on morale' in the *Financial Times*, 30 October 2001.

4 Harris, J (1996) *Getting Employees to Fall in Love with Your Company*. AMACOM, New York.

5 Neuhauser, P 'Southwest Airlines: How to Build a Culture with Speed as One of the Key Characteristics', found at www. culturedotcom.com.

6 McNulty, S 'Southwest Airlines: short on frills, big on morale' in *FT.com*, 30 October 2001, at www.financialtimes.com.

7 Quoted at www.iflyswa.com/careers.

8 Brooker, K 'The Chairman of the Board Looks Back' in *Fortune*, 28 May 2001.

9 Freiberg, KL & JA Freiberg (1996) *Nuts!* Bard Press, Marietta, GA.

10 Most of this description of the organizational structure at WL Gore is based information found on the company's website at www. gore.com.

11 See note 10.

12 These principles have been reported in various articles, including Anfuso, D '1999 Innovation Optimas Award Profile: W.L. Gore and Associates, Inc.' in *Workforce*, March 1999.

13 These items were reported in Banerjee, N, B Barboza & A Warren 'At Enron, Lavish Excess Often Came Before Success' in the *New York Times*, 26 February 2002.

14 Ahrens, F 'Life After the Crash' in the *Washington Post*, 1 March 2002.

15 See note 13.

16 'At Enron, "The Environment Was Ripe for Abuse"' in *Business Week online*, 15 February 2002.

17 Reported by Dewan, SK 'A Video Study of Enron Offers a Picture of Life Before the Fall' in the *New York Times*, 31 January 2002.

# 13

# Creating your own Culture of Success

There's a popular slogan making the rounds: 'You are the CEO of your life.'[1] Well, if you are, then go ahead and found your own culture.

This chapter isn't about changing the culture of a whole organization, or even a whole work unit. (Those await succeeding chapters.) It's about the culture of you, about creating your own stable and supportive personal environment.

## Your own culture: what's that?

Your culture is the sum total of your values and the way you express them in your behaviours and your relationships with others.[2]

Hanging an irreverent cartoon on the wall of your office is an expression of your own culture. So too is telling the cleaning staff that the neat and sparkling condition of the conference room made it a pleasure to hold a meeting there. Even if saying thank you and recognizing people's efforts isn't part of the corporate culture, there's nothing to stop you from doing it if it fits into your personal culture.

## So what?

Will actions like these make a dent in the overall culture of the organization where you work? Maybe, maybe not. You never know where the ripples will spread when you drop a stone in the organizational water, but that's not the point here. The point is that acting in concert with your own values will make you feel better about yourself and your work, whatever the environment in which you operate. It may even lead you out of a toxic environment and into a refreshing one of your own making.

In the early '80s when the first books devoted to the subject appeared, the corporate culture mavens touted culture for providing security and stability. But repeated downsizings in the intervening years have dashed that. We live in a world of short-term contracts – in jobs, in marriage, even in friendships, as people move frequently to new neighbourhoods, new cities or new countries. Creating one's own culture produces an antidote to that by:

- *Providing a constant in a world of change.* Your most deeply held values are portable. They can travel with you wherever you go. Living true to them provides the stability you are unlikely to find in any company.

- *Creating meaning in the here and now.* Buying into the espoused values of an organization or a society can mean deferring personal satisfaction or postponing what's meaningful for you. That feels like risk-avoidance, but it's really a big life risk. I used to have a neighbour, a gentle, kindly man who was retired from a successful sales career. After caring for his wife for years as her health declined, he reluctantly placed her in a nursing home, then spent most of his time visiting her. He told me one day, sadly, 'You spend all your life working hard so that you can enjoy your retirement, and then this is what happens.' If you identify your deepest values and live true to them now, you won't have to wait until it's too late to enjoy yourself.

## Platitudes or possibilities

It's true: talking about living one's values is a lot easier than doing it. But plenty of people have figured out how.

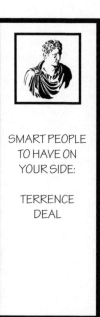

SMART PEOPLE
TO HAVE ON
YOUR SIDE:

TERRENCE
DEAL

Terrence Deal and his co-author, Allan Kennedy, pioneered the field of organizational culture with their book *Corporate Cultures*, published in 1982.[3] In 1999 they revisited the topic in *The New Corporate Cultures*, taking a hard look at what was left of corporate culture in an era of downsizing, mergers and acquisitions.[4]

In *The New Corporate Cultures*, Deal and Kennedy took sharp issue with companies that repeatedly lopped off portions of their workforce to produce short-term cost reductions and curry favour in the stock market. 'The traditional tie between employees and their employers, a bond central to the evolution of strong cultures, was severed in the 1990s,' they wrote. 'And it may take decades before strong and cohesive cultures can once again become the driving force behind long-term business success.'

Pretty pessimistic words. Yet when you talk to Terry Deal, what strikes you immediately is his exuberant optimism. Yes, corporate culture as we knew it

– a security blanket of sorts – is a thing of the past, but Deal sees a new kind of culture arising from the ashes. 'There are signs that things are not quite right,' he says, 'but that can never diminish the human spirit.'

## NEW KIND OF LOYALTY

'I think we're going to see a different form of people's loyalty to a company,' he insists. This new form isn't based on guaranteed lifetime employment; it's much more personal. It's founded on people's desire to make a difference. 'Sure they want to make a buck,' Deal contends, 'but they also want to make a difference. They have a yearning for work to have a higher calling.'

Deal, a consummate storyteller, makes his point with the case of an airlines worker who spoke up at a full-staff meeting with the president. 'How did you find the hangar when you walked in?' the worker asked.

'It was fine,' the president replied somewhat diffidently.

'But how did you find it?' the worker persisted.

'It was fine,' the president repeated, not quite sure what this exchange was all about.

'I'm the person who cleans it,' the worker said finally. 'I just wanted to know how you found it.'

Then Deal adds another illustration. This time it's about a bus driver, who described his 'real job' as seeing that the kids have a good attitude while they are travelling to and from school.

Deal's examples are of people striving to create their own cultures where work has dignity and nobility, where it's more than just a job. 'Whatever you do,' Deal stresses, 'you've got to have a belief that it's important.'

## SHORT-TERM BUT MEANINGFUL

'There's no lifetime security, but I think there can be a wonderful robust tie without that,' he maintains. He uses his own experience to illustrate. 'I arrived at Harvard in 1977. There were no tenured slots; it was not a possibility. So I went to the dean and said, "Let me see if I have this right. We're going to have a marvellous affair and treat each other with great respect, but we're never going to get married. Is that right?" I was right, and I had a great time for six years.'

In fact, as a professor, Deal has since been in both tenured and non-tenured positions. Ironically, for someone whose writings mourn the shattered tie between employers and employees in corporations, he's found himself more comfortable under contract than under tenure. Of course, he's had an unusual career, from the time he worked as a school teacher and moonlighted as a policeman, through the period at Harvard, his years as a tenured faculty member at Vanderbilt, and his position now as the Irving R Melbo Professor of Education at the University of Southern California. Add to that his consulting work and his writing (26 books and still counting), not to mention the wine he makes from the grapes he grows at his home in San Luis Obispo, California.

In an odd sort of way you could say Deal's come full circle from those early years as a cop. In 1961, he pulled over a car going 75 miles an hour in a 55 mph zone. As he tells the story: 'The driver jumped out and started banging on the patrol car. I motioned him to get back in his car, told him I was sorry, but I had to issue him a citation. When I asked him his name, he said, "I told you, I'm Irving R Melbo, dean of education at USC.' I asked him if that was the University of Santa Clara and he yelled at me that he would ruin my career!'

That was the only time he ever met the man in whose honour Deal now holds his position at USC. Terry Deal, who still harbours an irreverent attitude toward authority, enjoys the irony.

Take David Matthew for example. He's a partner now in The Research Board Inc. in New York, an international think tank that provides trend analysis, strategic research and networking services to chief information officers of 100 of the world's leading corporations. Matthew, who is passionate about cutting-edge technology, is in his element. But in the '80s, Matthew worked for the American Management Association (AMA), better known at the time for its dedication to traditional values than its technological innovations.

At least that's how most people who were associated with AMA then remember it, but Matthew recalls it differently. He remembers introducing educational teleconferences; developing interactive video disks, a precursor of Internet-based training; and introducing the personal computer as a training aid. When he confronted people who hadn't a clue what he was talking about, and who certainly had no cultural antecedents for adopting strange new ideas, Matthew used ingenuity.

'The way I got the first PC into the organization was kind of funny,' he recalls. 'I talked to the controller and told him, "You know, there's this thing called the personal computer and it's only about this big, and there's this program called VisiCalc that would let you do your own reports and analyses." Of course there was no budget for a personal computer so we bought an 'Apple typewriter'. I showed him how to use VisiCalc and he was a convert.

'It was a big organization and slow to move in some areas. So I did what any entrepreneur would do. I went where there was the most leverage and the least resistance. I fought the battles where there was ground to be won.'

## Winning ground

There's always ground to be won. Claiming it – and stamping your culture on it – may not necessitate pitching a battle, but it will require you to:

- *Assess your own values.* The problem is that, as individuals, we're almost as prone to kidding ourselves or co-opting the maxims of the day as organizations are. If it's cool to wear tongue studs we'll do it and attribute it to valuing our right to express individuality. Unless you are inhumanly self-aware, you probably won't get to your true values by making a list on a yellow pad. So try this:
  - For a while, pay close attention to when you feel good, when you are energized, when you feel useful and when you feel appreciative.
  - Each time you experience one of these good feelings, acknowledge what is causing it. Are you more content when others pitch in and help you or when they leave you alone to solve a tantalizing puzzle? Is it more satisfying to help others reach their personal goals or to direct the work of others toward an organizational goal? Does time fly faster when you are working with machines or numbers or people? Take special note of when you feel guilty satisfaction in something that is not currently in vogue. Keep a record of these revelations.
  - Pay attention to what other people appreciate in you. Ironically it's often the deep-down values you've tried to squash (unconsciously, perhaps) because you've deemed them uncool or not relevant. A friend tells a story about when her financial consultant retired. Dismayed, she told him how much she'd miss him, and he assured her he was turning her over to someone who was better at the job than he. Surprising herself, she exclaimed, 'But money isn't everything,' to which he replied in bemusement: 'That's what all my clients are saying.'
  - Look for patterns that reveal what you value in your heart and soul. It might be innovation. It might be achievement. It might be solitude. It might be friendship. It might be the opportunity to improve the world. It might even be money, but if that's the case, dig a little deeper to uncover what money symbolizes to you: freedom from want? status? beautiful things? confirmation of your worth? What you hope money will get you tells a lot about what you really value.

- *Find ways to express your values.* If you are working in an alien culture, you've probably stopped putting yourself out to do things nobody appreciates, whether it's performing a simple act of kindness, sharing your expertise or volunteering for an unusual project. But this is your personal culture we are talking about here. When you behave in concert with your values, what matters is that you appreciate it. In addition, seek out people who share your values, and show your appreciation for them. In time you'll build a culture bubble of your own. It won't isolate you from the predominant culture of the organization, but it will help you float above it.

Some people find another way. They live their values through an avocation, satisfied to have a job that is just a way to support what really matters to them. New Yorker Marlene Kess founded and runs KittyKind, a rescue operation for cats and kittens. She's paid her bills by working in the health insurance field, but she devotes herself to KittyKind. Asked why, she responds, 'This is my life's work.'

- *Build a power base from which to act.* If you want to make a difference, or just be different, you need a source of power. Having authority helps, but more important than power *over* [others] is power *to* [act]. To acquire that kind of power:
  - Become an expert in something you consider important. People respect expertise, especially when the person having it shares it generously. If you hoard it, people will ignore you or resent you. You gain power by sharing it, as David Matthew shared VisiCalc back in the days when, to the uninitiated, spreadsheets were as mysterious as astrophysics.
  - Earn trust and credibility. Without these, personal power is non-existent. Earn trust by keeping your promises, maintaining confidentiality, meeting your obligations, acting on your values consistently and sup-

porting others who share them.

- Build relationships. Even if all you want in life is to be left alone to solve your own problems, you're going to need the support of others to earn that right. Building and maintaining relationships entails:
  - taking the needs of others into account before you take any actions that affect other people (and most actions do)
  - opening yourself up to points of view that are different from your own
  - helping people even at times when it's inconvenient or a burden
  - accepting help even when you'd rather go it alone
  - making your own needs known. Don't expect people to read your mind
  - showing appreciation in ways that are appreciated. Forget the golden rule and remember George Bernard Shaw's advice in *Man and Superman*: 'Do not do unto others as you would they should do unto you. Their tastes may not be the same.'
  - confronting and discussing barriers to the relationship. When you try to ignore it, a piece of grit will grow into an insurmountable mountain
  - seeing yourself through others' eyes. You'll probably discover you've been beating yourself up for faults they don't see and patting yourself on the back for a few virtues no one's noticed you have. Invite and appreciate feedback from others. 'How am I doing?' might just get you polite platitudes, but 'How could I do better?' will probably inspire some surprising responses.
- In an ideal world, every organization would provide a culture that nourished and created meaning for its employees. But in the real world, your chances for long-term satisfaction are better if you accept that responsibility for yourself.

## The smartest things in this chapter

- You are not totally a slave to your corporate culture. You can create a personal culture based on your own values and expressed in your behaviour and relationships with others.

- Some people find their true life's work in an avocation, rather than depending upon their jobs to give meaning to their lives.

- Expertise, trust and relationships help you build the power base you need to act according to your own values.

## Notes

1  In his book *Brand You 50* (1999, Knopf, New York), Tom Peters attributes this statement to a Discover Brokerage ad campaign. Most writers treat it as if it's in the public domain.

2  This definition and portions of this chapter are based on unpublished work by Rosalind Gold of Gold Consulting, an organization and training consultant who specializes in business communication and project management. She is also a clear thinker and frequent channeller of universal truths.

3  Deal, TE & AA Kennedy (1982) *Corporate Cultures*. Addison-Wesley, Reading, MA.

4  Deal, TE & AA Kennedy (1999) *The New Corporate Cultures*. Perseus, Cambridge, MA.

5  Senge, PM (1990) *The Fifth Discipline*. Doubleday, New York.

# Part 5

# Fixing a Dysfunctional Culture

First of all, what is a dysfunctional culture?

The early part of this book emphasized that a 'good' culture is one that supports the organization's mission and strategy and can adapt when the strategy needs to change. A company that consistently meets its goals, thrives in its marketplace and is prepared to meet the future, isn't going to be worrying about a dysfunctional culture. In that organization, there may be aspects of the culture you, as an individual, don't like. But there's no denying that it works at that time for that company.

But what about a company whose performance is not so stellar – a company that has never quite lived up to expectations, one that has very low expectations or one that has taken a nosedive and can't pull out of it? Any efforts to make improvements will have to contend with a culture that is geared to support the existing, sorry state – in other words, a dysfunctional one. Is it time to declare the culture out of date and change it? And if change is called for, what's the best way to go about it? This part of the book tackles those issues.

Chapter 14 answers the question 'Why change?', because it takes a really good reason to capture the hearts and minds of people who are emotionally vested in the existing culture.

Chapter 15 offers a process for change designed to enlist support, reduce resistance and minimize the 'Oh no, here we go again' syndrome.

Finally, Chapter 16 is for those who aren't CEOs but are asking, 'What can I do to make change happen in my organization?'

# 14

# Five Good Reasons to Change and One Doomed to Failure

It's been repeated several times throughout this book, and you'll see it in anything you read on the subject: changing a culture is *hard*. It takes a long time. It can be very destabilizing, and, if you go by the odds, there's a good chance it won't work.

It's something you don't even want to try without a very, very good reason. And there are good reasons. In fact, there are situations in which culture change is more than just desirable; it may be imperative. Here are five.

Smart answers to tough questions

Q: What makes culture change worthwhile?

A: Poor performance.

1 *Business is rotten.* It's been getting worse and worse. People here work as hard as they can. Our output is of high quality. But nothing we do seems to matter. We've lost a lot of customers and we're losing more every day.

2 *The competition is ruining us.* We used to have this market sewn up, but lately some new competitors have taken our market by storm. They're faster and cheaper, and they're picking off our customers one by one.

3 *We're growing too fast to keep up.* We can't hire and train people fast enough to keep up with demand. Customers are complaining that we are not meeting our commitments.

4 *We're not meeting our goals.* There are all kinds of reasons – people aren't pulling their weight; we can't get all the resources we need; the goals are impossibly ambitious; the goals keep changing. But the bottom line is we're just not cutting it. People don't even pay attention to goals any more since they know we never meet them anyway.

5 *Customers are screaming mad.* We're inundated with complaints about poor quality, poor service, even lack of common courtesy.

And here's a sixth reason – not quite so pressing perhaps but worthwhile nevertheless – *We're doing OK, but we'd like to do much better.* There are great possibilities out there, but we just don't seem to know how to exploit them.

You may be thinking, 'Those are business issues, not cultural ones.' If so, good. Because the one reason that doesn't work is: *We need a new culture.*

Utter those words and people will do one or more of the following:

- scream 'aieeeeeehhhhh!' and run out of the room

- raise their eyebrows, looking knowingly at each other, and mutter, 'Here we go again'

- dig in to protect their turf

- agree with everything you say and go right on doing the same as always, maybe tacking some new labels on old processes and behaviours.

*Smart quotes*

'People follow easily the leader who undertakes meaningful changes clearly connected to strategy. This is not always easy, but I've never looked on ease as an incentive.'

Max DePree,
*Leadership Jazz*[1]

## The sure-fire wrong way to change a culture

Frankly people have every reason to respond negatively to the suggestion that there is something wrong with their culture and that it needs to change. First of all, it's insulting. Telling people their culture is bad is like telling them their baby is ugly. Culture is very personal. It's deeply ingrained, a part of them. It's what they stand for. If this culture is inferior, then they must be inferior too.

Second, it's confidence-shattering. They've spent years fitting into the existing culture because they were taught that it was correct. If it isn't correct, then what is? If the founders and managers and colleagues who taught them the old way were wrong, then who is right? Why should they believe in some new ideology and its latter-day prophets?

Third, it's threatening. Culture change is often accompanied by restructuring, which usually means job losses. And even if they survive, what if they can't fit in to the new ways? Worse yet, what if they do fit in and then next year or the year after that, someone decides to change the culture again?

Fourth, unless they were born yesterday, they've been through this before. Culture change for its own sake was heady stuff in the '80s. Fixed on the shining beacons of technology and finance, companies tried to remake themselves in the image of Wall Street stars during the '90s. But in most cases, after great disruption and reshuffling of jobs, things settled back into old norms. So when you say 'culture change' to the veterans, their reaction is that it's a waste of time, money and effort.

Finally, culture for its own sake is not really the issue. After all, a place of business is not a social club. A corporate culture evolves to support the business purpose. It should only need to change if the purpose is not being realized. That takes us back to our five good reasons for change. Confronted with any of these situations, people will acknowledge the need to make business changes. These aren't personal. They may be somewhat threatening, but if they are given all the information, people will recognize that doing nothing poses an even larger threat.

IBM's once hallowed, service-oriented culture was a bad joke about a has-been by the '90s. But Big Blue didn't metamorphose from a complacent, sluggish dinosaur into a nimble, cutting-edge Internet forerunner by pushing through a culture change. It reinvented itself because then-CEO Lou Gerstner and other IBM executives supported a couple of early-Internet enthusiasts who saw a place for IBM in this new strange new world. They didn't start out with a plan to make over the company; they just wanted to take advantage of what this new technology offered. But they started a groundswell. As told by Gary Hamel in the *Harvard Business Review*, they built 'a community of Web fans that would ultimately transform IBM'.[3]

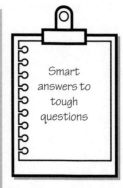
Q: But what if the company is succeeding spectacularly while intimidating its employees, treating them with no respect and generally creating a toxic atmosphere?

A: Let's just say you have been hired as the CEO of such an organization, and you're determined to change it. Are you going to demand, 'All managers will treat their employees better…or else?' Hardly a good example for what you want to achieve. Rather than call for a culture change, you'll make more progress by modelling the behaviour you want people to emulate. As others catch on and copy you, you reward them for it. You give the best jobs with the most people reporting to them to those who work the way you do. You ease the tyrants into places where they can't spread their poison. Eventually, you change the culture by example. The same process works in a single department.

Whether you are the CEO of a company being hammered by the competition, or the manager of a business unit that is not meeting its goals, you have a much better chance getting people to agree to make business changes than to make culture changes. But to solve those business problems, people will have to do some things differently. When the new ways of doing things work, people will repeat them in new situations. When they work again and again, they eventually become norms. When you have enough new norms, you've got a changed culture.

## The smartest things in this chapter

- The best reason to change the culture is to solve a performance problem.

- Focusing on the culture, not the business issue, puts people on the defensive.

- Changing work practices to solve a business problem leads to new norms and eventually to a culture that supports company goals.

## Notes

1  DePree, M (1992) *Leadership Jazz*. Doubleday, New York.

2  Abrahamson, E 'Change Without Pain' in *Harvard Business Review*, July–August, 2000.

3  Hamel, G 'Waking up IBM' in *Harvard Business Review*, July–August 2000.

# 15
# How to Change a Culture Without Really Trying

OK, you can't change a culture without any effort. But you can change it with more success and less anguish if you focus more on solving a business problem than on 'fixing' the culture. And if you don't have a business problem to solve, then why would you be messing around with the culture anyway?

During the '80s, when the first books about corporate culture hit the business bestseller lists, every company wanting to call itself progressive and innovative launched a culture change programme. Usually, when the formal programme ended, people thankfully slipped back into their old ways. The culture experts don't place much stock in those kinds of programmes any more. Deal and Kennedy call them 'a lot of bollocks', insisting that: 'Cultures change only when they need to and are damned well ready to change.

'It may be hard for an egg to turn into a bird: it would be a jolly sight harder for it to learn to fly while remaining an egg.'

CS Lewis, *Mere Christianity*[2]

They change when their collective intelligence recognizes that the world has changed and that the culture better adapt in order for the business to survive.'[1]

The need to survive is key to the change process below. It is based on *The Corporate Culture Survival Guide*, in which Edgar Schein outlines a culture change process built around resolving a business problem. Schein's process, adapted from a model by Beckhard and Harris,[3] includes:

1 *Determine: why change?* Occasionally a new leader will come along who is so charismatic that people in the organization will toss aside old assumptions and follow, spellbound, into new ways of thinking and behaving. But more often, real culture change will only happen in response to a business problem so severe that it threatens survival.

2 *Define the desired future state.* To solve the business problem, what new ways of thinking and working will be required? This question has to be answered in specific, behavioural terms. Broad statements like 'share more information' won't do. Schein argues for spelling out what that means in statements such as: 'After every project there will be a full review by all the participants at which time you give one another frank feedback on what worked and what did not work during the life of the project.'[4]

3 *Assess the current state.* Schein advocates bringing together small groups of people, preferably with a facilitator, and to focus the discussion on the business problem. After reviewing the three levels of culture, artifacts, espoused values and basic underlying assumptions, the steps are to:
   • identify lots of artifacts

- identify the organization's espoused values
- compare values with artifacts
- determine what assumptions are driving the behaviour and other artifacts where they contradict espoused values
- assess the assumptions. Focus first on those elements of culture that will help solve the business problem. Then identify those that may get in the way.

4  *Determine the work that needs to be done to get from the current to the desired state.* Define the gaps by stating specifically how work is done now and contrasting that to how it must be done in the future. That requires the same kind of specificity as described in Step 3. This process is bound to reveal additional cultural assumptions that may lead to more required changes.

5  *Manage the transition.* There's no pat plan that covers every transition. This is organization-specific and may include education, large system interventions, coaching or a variety of other actions to get the organization from where it is to where it wants to be. In a large organization, the original change leaders will have to turn much of the work over to other groups, but they will need to continue to monitor what's happening and to model the new behaviours and processes themselves.

> **Smart quotes**
>
> 'Change is not a decision; it is a campaign.'
>
> Rosabeth Moss Kanter, *eVolve!*[5]

## The change process at work

Until the late '90s, Marriott International was happy with its culture of '"face-time" – the more hours you put in, the better'.[6] Marriott people took pride in always being available to meet their customers' needs. But when the best managers began to leave and it got hard to recruit more, Marriott acknowledged it had a business problem. Marriott Vice-President Bill Munck described how Marriott addressed that problem, in *Harvard Business Review*.[7] His story illustrates the steps in Schein's change model above.

- *Reason to change.* First, Marriott recognized that without top-notch managers and staff it would not be able to sustain its service excellence. That was reason enough to make some changes.

- *Desired future state.* The company's objective was a better balance between the professional and personal lives of its managers. It would measure its success by four criteria: 'Reduced work hours, less job stress and burnout, no adverse impact on Marriott's financial performance, and sustained high quality of service to guests.' Marriott already had procedures in place to measure performance and service.

- *Current state.* Marriott found its existing behaviour norms were in sync with its stated value of providing excellent service in the short term, but were undermining it over time. People were working 50–60 hours a week. Even worse, they were hanging around at work when they really didn't even need to be there, just to avoid criticism or jokes about bankers' hours.

  But there were other norms that would help Marriott meet its goal of equal performance with less stress. 'For one thing,' Munck wrote, 'the company rewards employees for taking prudent risks.' So when the leadership team at the Copley Marriott in Boston was offered a chance to pilot a programme to solve the retention and recruitment problem, most of them jumped at the opportunity. And Munck was confident that Marriott people were so dedicated to customer service they would never sacrifice that.

- *Work to be done.* Using focus groups, Marriott identified the tasks ahead, including reducing the frequency of some business reports, eliminating some meetings, reducing the one-hour overlap between front-desk managers' schedules and providing better tools, such as e-mail access to customers and better IT support.

- *Transition.* At the Copley, the first high-profile step was to eliminate the departmental and monthly financial review meetings. 'Our culture was such that some of those meetings were considered sacred cows,' Munck wrote. 'So eliminating them was like committing a big taboo – one that was noticed by everyone.' The hotel also provided Internet access to managers and hired an on-site systems manager. And the change leaders began to act as role models, purposely going home early when business allowed.

- *Outcome.* The proof of the change effort was in the results. In the *HBR* article, Munck stated that at the end of the pilot, participating managers reported working an average of five hours less per week. The number of managers who felt their jobs infringed on their ability to handle personal responsibilities dropped from 77 per cent before the pilot to 36 per cent after. There was no change in the measured quality of service, and productivity gains (new customers) more than made up for the cost of computers and Internet access.

## Good advice

Experiences at Marriott and other companies illustrate a number of other points change experts stress when they give advice on how to implement a culture change programme.

- *Start small.* It's easier to manage a pilot than a full-company press. A pilot is also an opportunity to find out where the glitches are and make course corrections before expanding the programme. And it's a lot easier to convince the rest of the organization to make similar changes when you've got proof that they work. Marriott started with a three-hotel pilot and measured the impact of that before going organization-wide.

- *Stage a dramatic event.* Grabbing attention is an effective way to initiate change – especially when the impact is positive. Munck and his team got noticed by cancelling meetings that were viewed as sacred cows. At IBM in the mid-nineties, before the company had any Internet presence, a small group of Internet aficionados signed the company up for the biggest booth at an early Internet world trade convention. It cost thousands of dollars. John Patrick, the manager who spearheaded IBM's drive to Internet supremacy, told Gary Hamel for the *Harvard Business Review*, 'It was money I did not have, but I knew I could find it somehow. If you don't occasionally exceed your formal authority, you are not pushing the envelope.'[8]

- *Enlist others.* By recruiting a team of like-minded thinkers before you move forward with a formal program, you spread your base of support, benefit from the ideas of committed people and probably win over some who would resist if they thought the changes were being forced on them without their input. At Marriott's Copley Hotel, Munck got the full management team behind the effort before taking action.

- *Develop trust.* Even if you are promising a change everyone wants, it will take people a while to have faith that it will really happen to their advantage. Munck realized that people's trust in the stated new philosophy would be fragile. It would be dashed, he wrote, 'if someone leaves work early one day and sees his boss glancing at her watch'.

- *Walk the talk.* By ensuring that employees saw him leave early sometimes, Munck demonstrated that it really was OK to do so, and that staying late just to show one's face wasn't necessary anymore.

- *Reward new behaviours and celebrate successes.* There's something to the old adage that you get what you reward. It's also important to say thank you. In their drive to turn Alberto-Culver Company into a group of innovators and risk-takers (see Chapter 11), Carol Lavin Bernick and her executive colleagues gave stock rewards to a group of growth development leaders and other awards to individuals and teams who made an impact by going beyond their job descriptions. They threw 'a surprise thank-you party to celebrate an exceptional fiscal year, complete with entertainment and 700 pounds of popcorn'.[9]

Finally, there is another important piece of advice for all change agents. Be patient. Even if you succeed in changing behaviours quickly, it takes longer for basic underlying assumptions to catch up. Edgar Schein warns that, approached properly, culture change can take 5–15 years. (Done any other way, it probably won't happen at all.) The only way to speed that up is to get rid of all the conveyers of the old culture and replace them with proponents of the desired culture (and that is a course of action fraught with its own dangers).

Decades ago, psychologist Kurt Lewin introduced a deceptively simple change model: unfreeze, change, refreeze. The unfreeze stage is when people are jarred out of their previous complacency and recognize the need to change. In a corporation, that's usually a result of some severe business problem. The change stage is when the organization takes all the steps to work differently. These days, many change experts fear that the refreeze stage is no longer appropriate, since any group that settles comfortably into new behaviour is likely to be jolted out of it all over again. It may be more appropriate to think of refreezing as the time when people finally internalize the values that gave rise to behaviours they've been experimenting with during the transition.

## The smartest things in this chapter

- Implementing change involves defining the desired state, assessing the current state and doing what needs to be done to get from the current to the desired.

- Good advice for beginning a change programme is to start small, but dramatically.

- It takes time for people to trust that change will be to their advantage.

- Let no success go unheralded. You get what you reward.

## Notes

1  Deal, TE & AA Kennedy (1999) *The New Corporate Cultures*. Perseus, Cambridge, MA.

2  Lewis, CS (1943) *Mere Christianity*. Simon & Schuster, New York.

3  Beckhard, R & RT Harris (1987) *Organizational Transitions: Managing Complex Change* (2e). Addison-Wesley, Reading, MA.

4  Schein, EH (1999) *The Corporate Culture Survival Guide*. Jossey-Bass, San Francisco.

5  Kanter, RM (2001) *eVolve!* Harvard Business School Press, Boston.

6 This quote from Bill Munck and those that follow are from Munck, B 'Changing a Culture of Face Time' in *Harvard Business Review*, November 2001.

7 Ibid.

8 Hamel, G 'Waking up IBM' in *Harvard Business Review*, July–August 2000.

9 Bernick, CL 'When your Culture Needs a Makeover' in *Harvard Business Review*, June 2001.

10 Hultman, K (1998) *Making Change Irresistible.* Davies-Black, Palo Alto, CA.

# 16
# You as a
# Change Agent

It wasn't chairman Lou Gerstner who first caught the Internet wave at IBM (although without his leadership the big blue dinosaur would probably never have become an e-business powerhouse). According to Gary Hamel, who described the IBM makeover in the *Harvard Business Review*, it was 'a typical self-absorbed programmer', David Grossman, 'a midlevel IBMer stationed at Cornell University's Theory Center'.[1]

In 1994, IBM was the official technology sponsor of the Lillehammer Winter Olympics, responsible for collecting and displaying the results. While the rest of the world was watching the Olympics on television that year, Grossman surfed the nascent Internet and found a rogue Olympics site where all the IBM data was displayed under a Sun Microsystems banner. Thanks to Grossman's persistence, IBM's legal department got Sun to shut down the site.

KILLER QUESTIONS

I'm not a CEO or a powerful executive. What can I do to shake up the values and norms that are holding back my organization?

But Grossman wanted more. He wanted IBM, where the word Internet was barely in the vocabulary, to wake up to the Internet's potential. So, taking a UNIX workstation with him, he travelled to the company's Armonk, New York headquarters and set up a demo in a storage closet on the executive floor. Among those who got hooked was marketing master and strategist John Patrick, who hired Grossman to work for him. They became, wrote Hamel, 'IBM's Internet tag team' and started the ball rolling toward e-business mastery at IBM.

## Leading from the middle, the bottom or the side

If organizational values and norms are keeping the company you work for from reaching its full potential, you can make a difference even if you aren't one of the top dogs. You can spearhead a change in your own work unit or even, like Grossman, influence the attitudes and purpose of the whole organization.

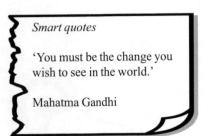

Smart quotes

'You must be the change you wish to see in the world.'

Mahatma Gandhi

Admittedly, if you're a new manager or a non-management professional, setting out to change the ways of an entire, giant corporation would be a long, daunting task. It makes more sense to start by pursuing more limited changes that will help you do your own job better and make your business unit a more effective and a more gratifying place to work.

## Where to begin

*Start with clarity and purpose.* What you need before you can spark successful change – whether you are in the middle of the organizational hierarchy, at the bottom, over at the side as an independent contributor or right up on top – is a very clear picture of what you want to achieve and a well-conceived business reason for making the change. As a change agent, you'll have the dual role of salesperson and motivator. A large part of your job will be to convince others that the change you are advocating is vital to the well-being of the organization (or your part of it) and that it is to their benefit to join the change adventure. If your thoughts are still vague, you won't be able to convey them persuasively to others.

*Relate your purpose to company goals.* Your business reason may be good but does it fit organizational strategy? Your work unit has a contribution to make to the goals of the organization. You'll gain support for your position both inside your unit and among influential outsiders if you can show that your proposed changes will help your unit make its contribution.

If there's something familiar about the last two paragraphs, there should be. They correspond to the first step – 'Determine: why change?' – in the model in Chapter 15. Make that model your guidebook. Edgar Schein, who formulated it, says it works just as well in a single work unit as at the corporate level. He uses it with the students in his change class, who work at all levels in their organizations. Whatever their position: '"The culture" then becomes the culture of that unit. It can be applied to as small a unit as a family.'[2]

## Overcoming obstacles

There will be times, as you press through the steps to change within your unit, that you'll feel the whole organization is conspiring to hold you back. For a would-be change agent who feels helpless in the face of the organizational power structure, Schein puts that plight into context: 'These obstacles will occur in some form at every level; i.e. the CEO has a board, an industry culture, shareholders, etc.' He adds, 'No one said that change is easy or fast, but the process works if you take time to work it through.'

If you're encountering massive resistance, scale back your plans to get out of the way of your opponents. You're better off starting small anyway. Small wins lead to more small wins, and they all add up to something significant.

The best way to deal with people who resist your efforts is to co-opt them. His students, Schein says, 'can always figure out something that those groups need that provides a change lever. The trick is to convert change targets into clients, to work with what they need rather than what you want and to align your goals with theirs.'

Rather than battling those who oppose you, find out what needs they have that are not being met. Figure out how the changes you propose would help them meet their needs. You'll have to be flexible, too. What changes can you make in your plan that would solve some of their problems without undermining your ultimate goal? Remember, converts make the strongest advocates. If you can win over some of your opponents you'll have formidable allies.

## Expanding your influence

If the change you spearhead turns into a groundswell and your business unit's performance improves notably, it may well spark similar changes throughout the organization. Aiming for a result like that will still be a long, daunting task, but your chances are better with some successes under your belt and a cohort of fellow travellers. To take on a challenge of that magnitude will require:

The following tips for managing change when your authority is limited are adapted from advice by Bob Knowling, who has spearheaded change in several telecommunications organizations, including Ameritech and Covad Communications.

1  Start within your existing boundaries.
2  Don't ask permission. Take some risks.
3  Pick your battles. They aren't all worth fighting.
4  Develop a change model that works for you.
5  Deal with the politics. It's always there. You can't avoid it.
6  Understand the financial side as well as the people side.
7  Walk the talk.
8  Get past the notion of change as a programme. Make it part of how you do business.

From Noel Tichy, 'Bob Knowling's Change Manual', in *Fast Company*, April–May 1997

- *Patience.* This is a change effort that may take decades.

- *Superb skills and expertise.* It increases your credibility if you are the best in some crucial function and you align yourself with other people who have the skills you don't.

- *Networking skills.* To make a difference you'll need good business relationships with the in-group, whatever you think of their values, and a network of people who share your own values.

- *Will* – to model the behaviour you want to see in others. As you climb the ladder yourself (or support the climb of someone else who shares your values), you can build a growing subculture based on the values that are missing elsewhere in the organization.

- *Up-to-date knowledge* – of the direction and performance of your company, your industry, and your competitors. And the ability to relate your decisions and recommendations to this knowledge.

- *Alertness* – to cracks in the organization's strength that your new way of working could mend. That's when the subculture you've created will start to look very good to the people in charge.

## Keeping the faith

Rome wasn't built in a day, and it wasn't built by an individual. You can't remodel it alone either. Even if you feel alone right now, when you start looking for them you'll find others who think as you do throughout the organization – in positions of higher authority, and among your peers, your internal and external suppliers and customers, and the people who report to you. Such people may be incognito right now, but they do exist. When you find them, follow the advice of Bolman and Deal and 'create a conspiracy... Converting impotent moaning into a local conspiracy opens up the potential for a more exciting and engaging game.'[3] At IBM, Grossman started out as a lone Internet aficionado off in an IBM outpost. Before long he had hundreds of co-conspirators in IBM's network of outposts, most of whom had also been secret Internet devotees with no one to share their passion.[4]

You'll need patience again. If you are in an organization where people have been punished for taking initiative in the past, they may be hesitant to join an insurgency. To quote Bolman and Deal again: 'To overcome their fears, they need time to adapt, support during transition and opportunities to learn new knowledge and skills.'[5] Your job is cut out for you, but it's worth it.

## The smartest things in this chapter

- You don't have to be a CEO to make a difference in your organization's culture.

- You do need a clear vision and a purpose that contributes to company goals.

- The best way to overcome resistance in others is to co-opt them by solving their problems in your plan for change.

- You can't do it alone. Gather a cohort of like-minded people.

- Have patience. The road is long.

## Notes

1   Hamel, G 'Waking up IBM' in *Harvard Business Review*, July–August 2000. The description of the IBM events that follow is also based on this article.

2   The quotes from Edgar Schein in this chapter are from personal correspondence.

3   Bolman, LE & TE Deal (2000) *Escape from Cluelessness*. AMACOM, New York.

4   See note 1.

5   See note 3.

# Index

Abrahamson, Eric 196
Agilent 114–15
Alberto-Culver North America 147
anthropology/archaeology 31–2
    architecture/use of space 35–8
    celebrations, ceremonies, rituals 32–4
    stories, myths, legends 34–5
AT&T 119
attitudes/emotions 38–9
AXA Financial Inc. 34

Barrett, Colleen 169
Beckhard, R 200
behavioural norms 24
    express individuality 27
    innovating 25–6
    socializing 26–7
beliefs *see* values/beliefs
Belkin, Lisa 36
BellSouth 110

Bernick, Carol Lavin 65, 147–8
Bezos, Jeff 129
Boeing 110
Bolman, Lee 1, 214
Borman, Frank 147
Brady Corporation 29
British Airways (BA) 110

Challenger, Gray & Christmas 110
change agents
    expand influence 212
        be alert 214
        be patient 213
        build subculture 213
        have skills/expertise 213
        have up-to-date knowledge 214
    keep the faith 214
    leading from middle, bottom, side 210
    overcome obstacles 211–12
    relate purpose to company goals 211

start with clarity/purpose 210–11
CNNmoney 110
Collins, James 64
communication
    broken/disrupted 112–13
    channels 28–9, 30
    continuous 114
    language 28, 29
    media 30–31
    networked 139
    routes 29–30
cultural change 199–200
    advice
        be patient 205
        develop trust 204
        enlist others 204
        reward new behaviours/celebrate
            successes 205
        stage dramatic event 204
        start small 203–4
        unfreeze, change, refreeze 205–6
        walk the talk 204
    age of organization 72
    case study 74–7
    goal orientation 72
    impact 69–72
    negative response
        confidence-shattering 195
        insulting 195
        threatening 195
        waste of time, money, effort 196
    positive implementation 196–7
    in practice 73–4
    reasons
        business is rotten 194
        competition 194
        could do better 194
        customers are screaming mad 194
        growing too fast 194
        not meeting goals 194

we need a new one 194–5
size of organization 72
strategy 201–2
    current state 200–201, 202
    desired future state 200, 202
    determine reasons for 200, 202
    outcome 203
    transition 201, 203
    work to be done 201, 202–3
cultural dimensions
    achievement/ascription 123
    individualism/collectivism 121, 123
    internal/external 123
    long-term/short-term orientation 122
    masculinity/femininity 121
    meaning of time 122
    neutral/emotional 123
    power distance 120–21
    sequential/synchronic 123
    specific/diffuse 123
    uncertainty avoidance 121
    universalism/particularism 123
cultural norms 1–2
    changing 2–3
    effect on career 3–4
culture
    characteristics 41–2
    definitions 7–11
    identification of 48–9
    importance of 61, 63, 71–2
    models 42–8
    survival 122
Cusumano, Michael 163
cyberculture
    business casual 137, 139
    dot-com legacy 136, 139–40
    examples 131–6
    faster decision making 139
    flexible/longer working hours 139–40
    networked communication 139

new responses to employee
    expectations/impatience 140
new view of conflict 139
playful perks 140–42
rise/development 127–30
team problem solving 140

Davis, Stanley M 53
De Geus, Arie 156
Deal, Terence E 1, 43, 49, 53, 64, 82,
    183–5, 214
Deighton, John 78
DePree, Max 151, 158, 195
destabilizing forces
    downsizing, restructuring, layoffs
        109–13, 114
    globalization 118–22
    loyalty 113, 115–16
    teleworkers 116–18
dot-coms *see* cyberculture
downsizing 109, 124
    awaiting the next shoe's drop 113
    broken communication channels
        112–13
    effect on culture 114–15
    goal confusion 111–12
    loyalty 113, 115–16
    role confusion 111
Drucker, Peter 147, 148
Dunham, Alison Blackman 83
dysfunctional culture 191

Eastern Airlines 147
eBay 134–6
Eckart, Robert 148
Egon Zehnder International (EZI) 70–71,
    100
Enron
    failure 175–6
    organizational practice 174

performance reviews 175
perks 174–5
Equitable Life 34

family organization 105–6
Federal Express (FedEx) 149
Feuerstein, Aaron 65–6
Fiorina, Carleton (Carly) S 35–6
Freiberg, Kevin and Jackie 169

Gandhi, Mahatma 210
Gates, Bill 31, 163
Gebler, Dan 129
General Electric (GE) 3
Gerstner, Lou 196, 209
globalization 118–20
    attitudes/beliefs 120–22
Goetz, Lewis J 127
Goffee, Rob 10, 44, 45, 68, 82
Gore, Bill 170–73
Grossman, David 209–10

Hamel, Gary 196
Harris, Jim 101
Harris, RT 200
Heskett, James 71, 88
Hewlett, Bill 18
Hewlett-Packard (HP) 35–6
Hitachi 100
Hofstede, Geert 42, 57, 120
*HP Way* 18, 35
Hudson, Katherine M 29
Hultman, Ken 205

IBM 156, 196, 209–10, 214
ideal practices 146
    continuous learning 156–7
    customer focus 157–8
    diverse workforce 157
    empowered employees 149–50

flattened organizational structure
    151–2
involved employees 147–9
risk-taking 155–6
shared sense of ownership 150–51
teams 152–5
individuality
    back socialization codes 27
    dress differently 27
    try out different lifestyles 27
innovating
    act on new idea 26
    react to change in processes/structures
    26
    react to new technology 26
    respond to new idea 26
Institute for Research on Intercultural
    Cooperation 120
International Telework Association and
    Council 116
Internet start-ups 129–30, 131–6

job security 99–102, 185
Johnson & Johnson 14, 15, 44
Jones, Gareth 10, 43, 45, 68, 82
Jones, Joe 16

Kanjer, Hanif 84
Kanter, Rosabeth Moss 128, 138–9, 201
Katzenbach, Jon 154
Kelleher, Herb 166, 167, 169
Kennedy, Allan 43, 49, 53, 64, 183
Kerr, Steve 120
Kess, Marlene 188
KittyKind 188
Kotter, John 71, 88

layoffs 110
Lewin, Kurt 205
Lewis, CS 200

Ligos, Melinda 115
Lucent 110

McGregor, Douglas 23
McNulty, Sheila 168
Malden Mills 65–7, 68
management practices 21–2
    attitudes/emotions 38–9
    behavioural norms 24–8
    ceremonies/rituals 31–6, 38
    communication 28–31
    expectations 22–4
Marriott International 69, 201–4
Maslow, Abraham 137
Matthew, David 186
Maurice Villency 100, 115
mergers/acquisitions 57, 77–8
Metricom 68, 69
Microsoft 31
    bottom-up decision making 163
    face-to-face/e-mail 163–4
    interpersonal relations 165
    perspectives on 162–6
    shared ownership 165–6
    workaholic/slow pace 164–5
models
    equality vs hierarchy/people vs tasks 46
        Eiffel tower 47
        family 46–7
        guided missile 48
        incubator 48
    risk/feedback 42
        bet-your-company culture 43
        process culture 43
        tough-guy/macho culture 42
        work hard/play hard 42–3
    sociability/solidarity 43–4
        communal 44–5
        defined 44
        fragmented 46

mercenary 45
networked 45
Munck, Bill 202–4

Omidyar, Pierre 134–6

Packard, David 18
paternal organization 103
    don't question us 104
    just do what we say 105
    trust us: we know what's best 104
    we'll take care of you 103–4
performance 64–8
personal aspects 81
    case study 90–94
    co-operation/competition 86
    coping with bad fit 88–9
    creative opportunities 87
    decision-making 87
    employee interaction 86–7
    family/work balance 86
    first impressions 82
    getting to know the company
        84–6
    knowing yourself 82–4
    living within the culture 86–7
    making choices 94
    supervision 87
personal culture
    company loyalty 184
    creating 182–3
    defined 181–2
    job security 185
    platitudes/possibilities 183, 186
    winning ground 186
        assess own values 187
        build power base 188–9
        build relationships 189
        express own values 188
Peters, Tom 145, 147, 149, 152

Porras, Jerry 64
Procter & Gamble 154, 155

Quaker Oats 78

Research Board Inc 186
restructuring 109
Ricks, Ron 169
Royal Dutch/Shell Group 16, 122, 156

Sachs, Randi 149
Samuels, Mark 37
Sawhney, Mohanbir 56
Schein, Edgar 2, 10, 11, 14–15, 109, 200,
        211
Schultz, Howard 64
SEI Investments 31, 36–7
Selby, Richard 163
Senge, Peter 156, 188
Simmons, Vicki 168
Skilling, Jeffrey 176
Smith, Douglas 154
Snapple 78
socializing
    bond with team members 27
    exclude people based on personal
        friendships 27
    go out together after work 27
    informal chats 26
    work unit/peer groups 27
Southwest Airlines 100
    company based on love 166–8
    culture by committee 169
    having fun 168
    loyalty 169
    right attitude 170
Stone, Florence 149
strategy 68–9, 201–3
strong culture
    appropriate 68–9

defined 64
impact 65
loyalty 65–7
security of employees 111
subcultures
    cloning 55
    development 51–3
    diversity/breadth of outlook 57–8
    emergence 53–5
    family tree 55–6
    generational 56–7
    mergers/acquisitions 57
Suresh, Venkat 68

task performance 24–5
    deal with failure 25
    deal with time/schedules 25
    express feelings about task success
        25
    handle conflict 25
    handle problems 24
    react to deadlines/budgets 24
    respond when someone else needs help
        24–5
    share information 25
telecommuting 116–18
Terkel, Studs 81
Theory X and Y 23
Tichy, Noel 213
TIMEeurope 110

Titeflex Corporation 154
Triarc Bevereidges 78
Trompenaars, F. 46

UNIX 210

values/beliefs 13
    artifacts 15
    basic underlying assumptions 15
    espoused 14, 15
    honesty 16
    integrity 16
    operating 17–19
    respect for people 16
    statements 16–17
Varney, David 104, 105
Villency, Eric 100
virtual companies 116–18
VisiCalc 186

Watson, Thomas J 156
WebHouse Club 131–4
Welch, Jack 3
WL Gore & Associates 137
    associates 172
    empowerment 173
    lattice organization 170–71
    leadership 173
    performance assessment 173
    principles/guidelines 171–2